Grif Stockley

Summit Books
New York London Toronto Sydney Tokyo Singapore

STOCKLEY, G.
copy 1

Summit Books
Simon & Schuster Building
Rockefeller Center
1230 Avenue of the Americas
New York, New York 10020

This book is a work of fiction. Names, characters, places and incidents are either the product of the author's imagination or are used fictitiously. Any resemblance to actual events or locales or persons, living or dead, is entirely coincidental. Although there are references to the Arkansas State Hospital, this story is not based on any real characters or events associated with the hospital. The Arkansas rules of criminal procedure and state statues have not been followed in every detail.

Designed by Deirdre C. Amthor

Manufactured in the United States of America

1 3 5 7 9 10 8 6 4 2

Library of Congress Cataloging in Publication Data
Stockley, Grif.
Expert testimony / Grif Stockley.
p. cm.
I. Title.
PS3569.T612E95 1991
813'.54—dc20 90-20346
CIP

ISBN 0-671-70920-8

To My Parents, Griffin Jasper Stockley
and Temple Wall Stockley

I

"There's nothing like death to make a man feel alive," Brent Hoover says, his normally deep voice practically chirping with excitement.

I nod in agreement. Especially if the dead person is one of the state's most powerful politicians and lawyers. I stare over Brent's right shoulder at the headline in the *Arkansas Gazette.* One would conclude we had declared war on Japan by the size of it: STATE SENATOR HART ANDERSON SLAIN AT HOME. The way Brent lisps, I'm glad he didn't read it aloud.

Brent folds the newspaper and rests it on his knees. His shirttail, as usual, is coming out and he hasn't been here ten minutes. Like me, he is wearing what Chick Brady, our only male fashion plate in the office, calls the Blackwell County Public Defender uniform: khaki pants, red tie, and blue jacket. His voice wistful, even reverential, Brent adds, "Anderson had the nicest Mercedes I've ever seen, a deep purple, like a king would own."

I smile at Brent. He is brand new in our office and follows me around like a puppy. Though I hardly have the most experience in the office, at forty-three I am definitely the oldest. I probably remind him of his father. "Maybe you could pick it up cheap at the estate sale," I tell him, looking at my watch. Everyone but me has to be over at the courthouse in half an hour (I am covering the civil commitments at the state hospital this quarter). If I had my way, I would already be at the state hospital reviewing files for the morning's hearings, but this meeting in my boss's office has become a sacred ritual. We are all seated around Greta Darby's desk in a semicircle like schoolchildren listening to a story. Chick, Greta's heir apparent, is seated on her right, in easy stroking distance. He is staring at her as if he expects she will begin to strip in front of us. He hasn't blinked in a minute.

If Chick has missed an opportunity to kiss Greta's ass, I've never seen it. The odd thing is that he doesn't have to—they both look, as they say down here, like spit from the same mouth—both have naturally curly ash-blond hair and blue eyes and an identical willowy build. At lunch in the office they have been known to pore over a Lands' End Christmas catalogue together like a couple of adolescent boys panting over *Penthouse*. Today, Chick is modeling a camel-hair blazer that would keep me and my daughter in groceries for a month. Not to be outdone, Greta, who is beginning to fidget behind her desk as we wait on Ken Averitt to finish a phone call, is wearing a charcoal herringbone jacket that has to run a couple of hundred. How do they do it, I wonder. No kids, for a start. None of us are getting rich at the county trough.

"Giddy, can you imagine the money some probate lawyer is gonna make off Anderson's estate?" Leona Maxwell, our one black attorney, asks me theoretically. Leona is originally from New Orleans. Good restaurants in New Orleans. Judging from Leona's waist, which is as big as mine, she didn't miss too many of them. Louisiana to Arkansas. A lateral move (if you throw out New Orleans) after the price of oil slides below the quart level on the dipstick.

I like Leona, but I hate to be called "Giddy." Gideon is bad enough. With these kids I feel straight out of the Old Testament as it is. Like me, Leona has done it the hard way, going back to school at night. She has three kids, an ex-husband who is safely in Spain, and a mother dying of cancer. Leona has no money for clothes, and I can imagine her getting up at the crack of dawn to wash and iron the plain white blouse and straight navy-blue skirt she seems to wear every other day. The truth is, I can't imagine the probate fees, having snoozed through the Wills and Trusts course in law school. Anyone who could stay awake through that course deserves to get rich.

"No," I say truthfully, "I'm out of my depth with any number that has more than three digits."

Greta, pretending to ignore our conversation, has swung her chair around to look out her windows, which are on the sixth floor of the Thompson Building. Her office is the only one that has even a partial view of the Arkansas River. Because of the usual crowd in her office, two potted plants hang from the ceiling near the windows. Her usual demeanor, a grimace that borders on a sneer, conveys the feeling that she prefers more plants and fewer people. To my right is a cloth wall hanging that Greta claims a friend got for her in Japan. It is classy-looking, a distinctly Oriental design that suggests a pink sun glowing softly beside green trees against a beige background. Visitors typically comment on it, but I have seen one almost identical at Sears. Gone is the Persian rug in front of her desk. Too many people (me included) were spilling coffee on it. Greta will have to wait until she moves to a more sophisticated environment to decorate in style. Unless I miss my guess, that won't be too long. Blackwell County's public defender (the rest of us are deputy PDs) has the look of a woman who is having a ticket punched for a different career track. The rumor is Greta has her resumé in at the U.S. Attorney's Office. This child is bound for a different kind of glory. I can see Greta in fifteen years at the Justice Department in Washington. A Republican administration, of course, culling applicants for federal district judgeships and finding very few right wing enough to meet her standards. For the moment, however, she has to ride herd over lawyers who defend ordinary rapists, murderers, car thieves, and people with mental illness. The door to her office swings open, and Ken slides in and takes the vacant seat between Brent and Chick. Our undertaker, Chick calls Ken behind his back (he almost always wears black unless he is feeling unusually optimistic, in which case he wears brown—today it's midnight black). He says, "Sorry," to Greta's profile and nods to the rest of us.

"Has anybody heard of Perry Sarver?" Greta asks, turning to face us. "We'll be defending him if he's indigent."

The room is silent as a tomb. The thought of having to represent the killer of a man as famous as Anderson is not a happy one. Plainly, no one in our office wants to touch it. After all, it is a fellow lawyer who is dead and a popular one at that. If Sarver is competent to stand trial, it would be the kind of case that you pat yourself on the back about if you can plead him out to twenty-five years or so. While we watch, Greta cups the phone to her left earring and calls the prosecuting attorney's office to see if charges have been filed and whether a lawyer has called in to say he is representing Sarver.

I glance at Brent, my best friend in the office. He is polishing his glasses with his shirttail, deliberately trying to provoke Greta, I suspect. Beside him, Ken yawns, showing a mouthful of crooked yellow teeth. We are a motley-looking crew despite our Barbie and Ken dolls. Fortunately, our counterparts in the PA's office, except for a couple of the women and the prosecutor himself, Phil Harper, are usually just as scruffy. With the exception of a few insurance defense attorneys and a couple of personal-injury hot-shots, the lawyers who wear five-hundred-dollar suits in Blackwell County, deal makers like Hart Anderson, rarely appear in court.

Greta lays the phone down gently, as if she is about to deliver some bad news. "It's in Jamison's court," she says to us. "Plea and arraignment will be in half an hour. Nobody has shown up for Sarver yet."

Brent, who is often the butt of Chick's barbs for the way he dresses (or looks after having tried to dress), cannot suppress a smirk, because his nemesis is covering Judge Jamison's division this quarter. His cheeks, already fat as a baby's, puff out like a successful cake.

"Tough luck, Chickie," consoles Ken, our most experienced attorney. He reaches over and pats Chick on the thigh. "Maybe Perry Sarver was out there to repossess some furniture, and things got out of hand."

This gets a laugh from everyone except Chick. According to the account in the paper, Sarver showed up at Anderson's front door and shot him inside the house. Anderson's wife, a psychiatrist, talked him into letting her call the police. Sarver was one of her patients and was waiting more or less quietly in the living room with her when the police arrived. Chick looks helplessly at Greta and pleads, "I'm loaded to the gills."

If I liked Chick, I would be sympathetic. He has several major trials in a row coming up, but he will live through them. The problem is that Sarver may not. Chick will walk through this case as if he were asleep. Anderson was too much a local hero for Chick to dig in on this one. "I'll take it if Jamison appoints us," I say quietly. "I've got the time."

Chick, mouth open and a smile beginning in his eyes, looks as though a doctor has told him he won't need a prostate operation. "It would really be a help," he appeals to Greta.

Greta gives me a quizzical look. I am not known for helping out Chick. "It's fine with me."

Brent's thick right hand stings my back. "Who said there wasn't one born every minute!"

I laugh along with everyone else. No one in the office knows about my father, who hanged himself at the Benton Unit of the state hospital over thirty years ago. If he'd had a lawyer to fight for him, I'm convinced he would have lived to see the advent of the wonder drugs that let many persons with mental illness live relatively normal lives. The attorneys in the office know I'm the only one who doesn't mind the civil-commitment rotation, but I've never told them why.

I tell Greta, "I need to go call Hugh and tell him I'll be a little late." Hugh Bixby is the magistrate who hears civil-commitment cases at the state hospital. The position seems like a juicy plum for a young attorney like Hugh until he realizes what a dead-end job it is. He does the work of a judge and receives the salary of a law clerk.

Leona, relieved that Greta won't be dumping another case on her, says cheerfully, "Giddy, the guy's probably nuttier than an almond Hershey. You can drop him off at Rogers Hall."

Rogers Hall, located on the grounds of the state hospital, is the fortress built to house the criminally insane. I glance around the room and see that all my colleagues are breathing easier. Everyone likes a chump.

"I'll see you at the courthouse, Giddy," Chick says amiably as we leave Greta's office. He slaps me on the back as though we've been buddies since junior high. "Appreciate it."

I resist the temptation to tell Chick that I think he would lie down on this one. "No problem," I mutter, unable to return his fake smile. I proceed to my office to call the state hospital. I wouldn't put it past Greta to know already that Perry Sarver hasn't got the price of a bottle of Ripple in his pocket. Like every professional manipulator, she has her sources. I wonder if Chick is banging her. She has never liked me and wouldn't have hired me if old Judge Hodges hadn't called in a favor from the other judges and put the squeeze on her. A lawyer, no matter how skilled, won't serve as an effective public defender for any length of time if he or she can't make the judges happy, and Greta probably didn't have much choice. Why Judge Hodges, thank the Lord, took a shine to me, I'll never know. I interviewed for a clerkship with him, and when his clerk changed his mind and decided to stay, Judge Hodges found the job for me. Greta can't punish the judge, who is now retired, but she can take it out on me. It would have been just like her to assign the case to me, but since I volunteered, she can let me punish myself. I really don't give a damn what she thinks. I phone and get Hugh Bixby's secretary, who puts me on hold, so from the left corner of my desk I pick up a framed snapshot of my wife and daughter. It was taken in the backyard about a year before Rosa died from breast cancer. They are dressed in shorts and tank tops and have big grins on their faces: each is holding a tomato the size of a baseball in her hands. I realize I haven't seen a smile that big on my daughter's face since I snapped that picture.

What am I trying to prove by offering to take this case? I can't bring my father back. Barbara, Hugh's secretary, says for me not to worry about being late, and as I am getting off the phone, Brent pops into my office, as usual stuffing his shirt into his pants, and asks, "How come you're willing to take this wienie?"

Though I would trust Brent to keep his mouth shut, this isn't the time or place for true confessions. I pick up my briefcase and walk out to the elevators with him. "I've got nothing to lose. If I get a verdict of not guilty by reason of insanity, I'll be a star," I tell him.

As we walk out into brilliant sunshine I ask, "You want to be my agent? Negotiate the TV and book contract if we get the Sarver case?"

Brent, God bless him, asks, "You really think it could be that big?"

I smile as we cross the street. Brent is so naive sometimes that I want to burp him. The boy is as good as gold, too good to be stuck in our profession. He is forever badgering me to chip in and help buy groceries or pay the utilities of the families of our pitiful clients. With experience, he will be a smart lawyer, too, but I hope he doesn't get too smart, or he will probably forget what makes him a decent human being.

At the courthouse there are all kinds of rumors flying around about Anderson, and the guy hasn't been dead for twenty-four hours. Judge Jamison's courtroom deputy pours me a cup of coffee in his office and tells an old story I had heard in law school that Anderson's wife had caught him screwing a girlfriend in his law office and had personally kicked her out. Before I can escape, I hear stories about Anderson's legendary temper and capacity to put away booze. No telling what will come out after they get the guy buried.

In the hall TV cameras from channels 4 and 11 are outside Jamison's courtroom and the press is out in full force. I enter the courtroom through a side entrance and take a seat by Chick at the defense-counsel table. Temporarily friendly, he chatters merrily about the press coverage and the gossip surrounding Anderson as we wait for plea and arraignment to begin. Amy Gilchrist, the assistant prosecutor who covers Jamison's court, strolls across to the defense side and sits down across from us.

"What are you doing here, Gideon?" she asks, a broad smile on her elfin face. "I haven't seen you for months."

Chick leers at Amy and snickers, "We've brought in our top nut specialist in case Jamison appoints us."

Amy's face is all sympathy. "State hospital beat, huh?"

I nod and grin like a schoolboy. Amy is a speck of a woman with blue saucer-size eyes that are warm and friendly. She is cute and perky, and all the men in our office admit they are all a little in love with her except me and I'm too old to say so. Women lawyers. They are not so different from us despite all the efforts to appear otherwise. Their styles are usually different, but men can get used to anything. Who ever would have thought twenty-five years ago we would have black judges in Arkansas? Not me.

"Civil-commitment proceedings are good for one's sense of humility," I say, unable to pull my eyes from her. Amy is a perpetual-motion machine, her eyes darting from me to Chick and then over our heads to see who is entering the courtroom.

"Tell me about it," she says. She perches on the edge of her chair and leans forward as if she is about to reveal a dark secret. "We've all done our duty out there."

Even Chick the Prick nods. If the state psychiatrist said something in Arabic, we would all nod solemnly and say: "Yes, Doctor." There is no money to hire a private expert witness for all these cases, so whatever the state hospital doctor wants, the doctor gets, within the limits of the statute. The hearing is designed for efficiency. Why else have they moved it to a vacant ward of the state hospital? Obviously so the almighty shrinks won't even have to get wet. The defendants are poor and crazy, not a combination to attract much judicial respect, so a magistrate is appointed by the judges to hear the so-called facts—translate that "opinion of the doctor." It's nothing to me, but I shake my head when I hear people blaming lawyers for the revolving door at the state hospital. If I had my way, nobody would stay locked up, but, in truth, it is the psychiatrists who run the show in and out of court.

"What do you have on this guy Sarver?" I whisper. "There wasn't much in the *Gazette*."

Amy studies a tiny spot on the sleeve of what Greta maliciously calls her imitation houndstooth, then looks down at the file in front of her. "There never is."

This isn't fair. For a while after the Gannett chain (USA) bought out the *Gazette*, the news hole began to vanish like the Brazilian rain forest, but it has gotten better. Amy, about to fall off her chair, leans back and crosses her legs. "We know just enough to charge him with a capital offense."

The death penalty for this? My blood begins to boil and I don't even represent the guy yet. "If the paper is anywhere close," I snort, "it wasn't even close to being premeditated."

"Anderson was an elected official," Amy says primly. "That's enough." She licks her lips involuntarily as though something is making them burn.

"You've got to be kidding," I say, jiggling my keys irritably. Once I did that during a trial and was reprimanded. I decide to back off. I have nothing to gain by making her mad. I ask, "Apparently they couldn't get much out of Anderson's wife. Did you know him?"

Amy gives us her grin. "Oh sure. With all my contacts with politicians, he'd been begging me to join his firm. Are you kidding?" she throws back at me.

Anderson's firm has the biggest bond practice in the state, and in Arkansas, at least, politics and bonds have a way of going together. I can never tell whether Amy is a flirt or simply mischievous. She and I will forever be competing for the same jobs. If a student doesn't make *Law Review*, he doesn't get in the front door at the big firms.

Chick feels left out if the conversation goes for a minute and isn't about him or doesn't include him. "Have you heard the rumors about Anderson?" he asks Amy.

Amy studies her watch, whose old-fashioned numbers I can read across the table. "About running for governor?" She frowns. "That's old stuff."

We tell her the recycled stories, which she probably has heard three times already. Lawyers love to gossip as much as preachers. She is not impressed, which is fine with me. Considering the sources, I'm not either.

"Do you know anything about Sarver?" I ask, keeping my voice low. Actually, there is no need. Until the judge comes in, the courtroom will sound as noisy as a livestock auction.

She rummages through an almost empty file, rings on both hands. "Hmmm. It's funny on this guy. Usually, somebody crazy who'll break in and shoot a victim he doesn't know will have a string of priors or civil commitments, but he's been hospitalized once at St. Thomas and that was a voluntary."

I trot out a theory that has been cooking in my brain since I picked up my newspaper this morning. "You know Anderson's wife was his psychiatrist?"

"Yeah," she murmurs, not looking up. "Why?"

I talk to the red highlights in her hair. "Sarver, a real fruitcake, thinks he's fallen in love with her and decides on some direct action. Transference. It happens all the time, according to the shrinks." Actually, a therapist I saw after Rosa's death told me this.

Amy crinkles her unwrinkled brow, obviously impressed with my guess. "Maybe so. Maybe so. We'll see. She was too hysterical to say much more than Sarver shot her husband right in front of her."

"What did Mr. Sarver say about all this?"

Amy looks up at me and strums her lip with her forefinger. "Bubububu . . ."

I laugh, despite myself. Why do we laugh at signs of mental

illness? It must be a release of tension that we don't know how to deal with otherwise. "How's he doing?"

Amy seems nonplussed. "The deputy said he's not bouncing off walls or anything. He just doesn't make much sense. You know the type. Extremely labile. Can't connect one thought with another."

"Just real goofy, huh?" Chick says, practically slapping his leg as he tries for a laugh.

Amy giggles obligingly. "God only knows what they did until the police arrived. He apparently didn't want to hurt her, and just hung around while she called the police. They're going to try to talk to her some more today. They got her sedated pretty quickly."

She taps the file in her lap with the index finger of her right hand. "I've got to look over some stuff," she says and walks back to the prosecutor's table. This is one woman I'm not ashamed to be seen with. Amy will never see five feet two despite wearing what Chick calls "fuck me quick" four-inch spikes, but her liveliness and basic good humor make me concentrate on her face, which always has a fresh, clean look. Greta, on the other hand, looks as though she has been up since 3:00 A.M. plucking her eyebrows.

I look around the courtroom, which is filling up rapidly with lawyers, and I begin to feel a little self-conscious. Aside from the merely curious, some of these appear to be Anderson's friends, for they act as if they are sitting down for a funeral service. Their faces are grave, troubled, uncharacteristically quiet.

There are some big-name attorneys I don't ordinarily see. Walking in together are Steve Hicks, an insurance defense lawyer from the McCallister firm, Martin Purvis, a medical malpractice specialist, who is also talking about running for governor (perhaps he is merely confirming the death of a potential rival), and Charlie Blanks, who, I read last week in the *Gazette,* is acquiring a national reputation as a divorce lawyer. I look over at Amy, who seems as impressed as I am. Behind them come some members from Anderson's firm, including Jerald Olson and Mathew Beavers, who was almost as prominent as Hart. I expected a crowd but not the whole courtroom to fill up just for plea and arraignment. If this goes to trial, I wonder how they will fit everyone in. When it was completed in 1885, the Blackwell County Courthouse, hewn from Fourche Mountain granite at an original cost of $60,000 and added onto in 1920, was Southern Gothic at its best. Today, though it was renovated in 1975, the building seems like a high-density housing project, its daily residents packed together like the intestines of a pregnant rat.

I check my watch. Eight fifty-five and they're still coming. It looks more and more as if we are getting this case. It would be a nice irony now though if Chet Bracken, the premier criminal-defense attorney in the state, suddenly walked in, but there is no sign of a lawyer for Sarver.

Nine o'clock on the nose, and there is an air of expectancy in the room. There must be a hundred people. It dawns on me that there is a dynamic at work here I hadn't picked up. Anderson wasn't just prominent, he was a lawyer, and consciously or unconsciously, the pack is drawing together in the face of a common threat.

The doors swing open and Jamison steps inside the courtroom as his clerk goes through the time-honored ritual of announcing him. As I stand, I think that everyone must know this is much ado about nothing, but this is the one chance to see the killer of one of our own. As he sits, Jamison bellows: "Be seated!" and somehow the tension is broken now that we are back on familiar ground. Jamison is old, deaf, and ready for retirement. He calls: "State of Arkansas versus Perry Sarver, Blackwell County Circuit Court number 48736."

While we wait for Sarver to be brought in, I study Jamison's face. The furrows on his forehead are so deep that when it rains, Brent has cracked, Jamison is in danger of a flash flood. A dark, angry "V" forms today on his brow, and I wonder how well he and Anderson knew each other. State court judges in Arkansas are elected, and for all I know, Anderson may have been a big contributor. Jamison is playing with his gavel like a toy, passing it from one hand to the other. Is he reverting to second childhood in front of us? Surely he doesn't know how childish he looks, but maybe since he isn't running for reelection he just doesn't give a damn. Certainly no one in this audience will tell him. Bob Oatie, a three-hundred-pound deputy sheriff, opens the door to the room where the prisoners are kept for trial and we see the defendant for the first time. He is led by Bob, who pulls him gently by the arm toward the podium. Sarver stops, giggles, shoots his right arm into the air, and then mumbles something. The bailiff tugs at his arm, and Sarver frowns, then giggles again.

Amy stands and is about to speak, when Jamison yells: "Mr. Sarver, do you understand what I'm saying?"

Sarver, who is a slightly built man of about thirty, not bad-looking really, half turns to the spectators, and makes a snorting sound as if he is drunk. His balance seems to be off, and he looks as if he might fall despite the grip of the deputy. His movements are spastic, but it is the goofy grin that transfixes his audience. His features change so rapidly I can't get a fix on what he looks like. The man is so obviously insane he hasn't got the slightest idea where he is. A chill runs down my back, and I suddenly feel sorry for Carolyn Anderson. She'll never be the same after last night. He is saying something like: "Round her waist . . . round her face . . . hee . . . hee . . . Ralph Waldo, Fatso . . . had a wife and couldn't keep her . . . uh . . . sleep her . . . Humpty . . . fucky . . . hee . . . hee . . . hee . . ." He looks at Amy and smiles. Amy shrinks back visibly, and some of the spectators in the audience actually gasp.

Jamison's "V" is an inch long, but he takes control. "Deputy, return this man to the jail." He looks at Chick and me, confused that we are both here. "Who's representing the public defender's office today?" he barks, pointing his gavel at Chick.

I stand. "I am, Your Honor, if we're appointed on this case."

Jamison frowns. He is used to the same person showing up every day. "Mr. Page, I'm appointing you to represent Mr. Sarver. If you come into any evidence that Mr. Sarver is not indigent, you shall report this immediately to the court. I am ordering Mr. Sarver to be transported to the Arkansas State Hospital for observation to determine his competency to stand trial and his mental status at the time of the alleged criminal act of capital felony murder." He looks out over his courtroom. "I'm going to take a five-minute recess so as to let our friends in the press and others go about their business if they wish." He stands and walks briskly back into his chambers, flipping the gavel in his hand like a baton.

I have a strange feeling of incompleteness. Maybe it is because I wanted to at least say good morning in front of the biggest crowd I've had watch me in a courtroom. I look at Amy, who shakes her head at me, her eyes now the size of dinner plates.

"Jesus Christ," she whispers, "I'm glad he's your client."

I mouth the made-up word, "fucky-fucky" at her, and she rolls her eyes back in her head.

What is there to say? Jamison has the power to do exactly what he did. On his own motion he has the authority to commit a defendant for observation. The prosecutor and the defense attorney can take a nap if we want. It's the judge's ball game. Of course, if he hadn't, we would have, and maybe that's why my nose is a little out of joint. If I've got to do this case, I want to represent my client. Bullshit. I like to see my name in the paper as much as anybody.

Chick slaps me on the back, "Nice work, Giddy."

I pick up my briefcase. "I suspect you could have managed this, Chick." This doesn't make me feel better, but I'm glad I said it.

The corners of Chick's mouth turn up in a sour smile that acknowledges I got him pretty good. I speak to a couple of reporters from the TV stations who want to know when Sarver will be taken out to Rogers Hall. That's not my job, and I tell them to ask the deputies. That's what the media wants: pictures of Sarver on TV doing his thing. Amy comes back to the table as I'm about to leave. "The judge wants to see us." I frown, but she shrugs. "Who knows?"

We go back in chambers and close the door.

"Gid-yun," Judge Jamison says, pronouncing my name without the middle syllable, "I didn't want it to get to be a circus out there. I don't like to take over for the lawyers," he drawls, looking at Amy, "but I didn't want things to get out of hand, if you know what I mean."

Still standing at the door with Amy, I find myself agreeing a little too unctuously, "I understand, Judge. I understand." But Jamison is from the old school and he loves it. A Southern gentleman. When he heard the "F" word it was all over. He did it for love. I can't wait to razz Amy when we get out of here.

"Miz Gilchrist?" he asks, laying his scepter aside on his cluttered desk now that he has no crowd to entertain.

"Yes, sir?" Amy preens. Is he going to ask her for a date?

His snow-white eyebrows rising as if to add emphasis to his words, the judge orders, "You make sure he gets in the state hospital today, okay?"

Amy is all Southern womanhood. "I'll try my best, Your Honor."

The eyebrows go up again. "That man needs treatment."

There is a slight tremor of doubt in her voice. "Yes, sir."

"I know there's a waiting list, but you tell 'em that I want him in today, okay?"

Amy nods vigorously, having received the imprimatur of authority she wanted. "I will."

"If you have any problems," Jamison purrs, "you let me know."

They are two pussycats now. "I certainly will, sir."

We finally escape his office, and I nudge her with my elbow as we walk back toward her office which is only three doors down the hall. "He didn't want little Miss Amy to be offended by that nasty crazy man."

Touching her forehead with a knuckle, like a heroine in an old silent movie, she says with mock dismay, "And just when it was starting to get interesting!"

Having left by the south entrance to Judge Jamison's chambers, we have missed the photographers and TV people. They are still waiting outside the courtroom. I am not even going to be interviewed. "Aren't you going to tell the media what's going on?"

"I'll go back and tell them after I call." We are at the door of the prosecutor's office. There isn't anything for me to do now but leave.

I look down at her and preach: "I still can't believe Phil would go for capital felony murder."

Amy adjusts a shoulder pad. "He wouldn't be the first defendant to fake mental illness."

I tower above her, shaking my head. "You prosecutors are all alike. Did he look like he was faking to you?"

She rubs her chin, pretending to give my question some thought. "No." She smiles. "You did a good job."

I feel myself getting red, realizing she had overheard us. "Chick's an asshole."

She hunches her shoulders, not impressed. "Tell me about it. I'm against him every day now."

I think of Chick and pretend to shudder. "He's so far up Darby's butt you can't tell whether it's her tongue or his."

Amy laughs loudly. "Gideon!"

"Well, he's shameless." I regret instantly having spoken. It will be all over the prosecutor's office in five minutes and undoubtedly will get back to Darby. I don't care if it gets back to Chick. I do, too. I say meekly, "Will you keep that last remark off the record, please?"

She giggles, thinking about it. "Sure."

I'll bet half my salary she won't. People can't keep their mouths shut, me included. "Thanks."

I look at my watch: nine-fifteen. Suddenly, it's just another normal workday, and I feel depressed. What was I expecting to happen? The human ego is a pathetic toy. In the middle of all this horror, I wanted some attention. Look at me! Interview me. Put me on TV. Now I get to go out to the state hospital and do civil commitments all day. Whoopee.

2

I remember two occasions from my social-worker days when I had to visit people who were confined at the Arkansas State Hospital. I remember being frightened and not so secretly checking my watch for a decent interval to pass before I made an excuse to leave. Mental illness always has a horror about it even when I can dissociate it from my father's death.

Now, before a mental-health advocate can say the word "deinstitutionalization," involuntarily committed patients are released from the state hospital. It has fewer patients every time I come out here. I drive behind John A. McClellan VA Hospital so I can get a glimpse of Rogers Hall, the maximum-security unit for the criminally insane. For all I know, Perry Sarver may already have been whisked out here.

Rogers Hall was recently found unconstitutional by a federal judge because it doesn't provide a therapeutic environment, and the state of Arkansas is being forced to spend millions of dollars to create a minimally acceptable treatment center for those men and women it finds criminally insane. In court the state didn't even try to defend Rogers Hall. From the outside the building resembles a large police station in an unfriendly neighborhood—all brick and barred windows. Inside, it is even more grim, with so little space for patients and staff that no wonder its occupants are crazy. I find myself wondering about Perry Sarver and how he will manage there. If his doctors don't have him controlled on medication, somebody will knock his teeth down his throat. Fights are not rare between inmates, and more than one psychiatrist has suggested to me that employees ought to get hazardous-duty pay for working in Rogers Hall. I do not usually agree with state-hospital psychiatrists, but I have no trouble with that proposal.

Yet, on the open units, the "Hill," as the rest of the hospital is known, is considered by some a model system. Patients stroll the grounds, play volleyball, listen to ghetto blasters. Occasionally a few patients pair off, and not always members of the opposite sex, though of course that is discouraged. The legislature would not like to hear that it is providing beds for homosexual crazy people. But now it is even rare to be committed to the state hospital; individuals are committed to the Arkansas Division of Mental Health and diverted to a community mental-health center. We are quite progressive, having modeled our system after Wisconsin's, I am told, but unfortunately we haven't provided the money to run a community-based treatment system. As a consequence, the mentally ill of the state are our newest eyesores. The mentally ill are like hazardous wastes; we haven't figured out how to dispose of them.

Parking space is at a premium at the state hospital, which is next to the University of Arkansas for Medical Sciences, the state teaching hospital and medical school. As I get out to feed the meter (the best bargain in the country at a nickel an hour), I look across the street at two gleaming high-rise towers of education. The state legislature has, in effect, told the medical indigents of the state they can go to hell and put its money into research and training doctors who have to be bribed to practice medicine in the small towns that mostly constitute Arkansas.

As I pick up a visitor's pass in the administration building, I contemplate the plaque on the wall commemorating the construction of the architecturally heralded main units of the state hospital:

the man responsible is the archvillain former governor Orval Faubus, the politician who forced President Eisenhower to send troops of the 101st Airborne Division into Little Rock to escort nine black children into Central High. I glance at his portrait, a flattering likeness, and feel a strange kinship: if I get Perry Sarver off, I, too, will be remembered in an unflattering light regardless of what else I do.

Armed with a pass nobody ever checks (my face is now familiar to even the most doped-up patients), I pass through the glass doors onto the covered walkway that leads to the hospital wings. What makes this area attractive is its openness: the six separate treatment units open onto small though pleasant courtyards that patients use to sun themselves. In rainy weather the roof covering the walkway leaks, making me wish the architects had devoted as much care to construction as they did to design.

I enter the main area on Unit Four, which, as the hospital census has dipped, has been made into a patient recreation area. Four patients, all men in their own clothes, are standing around a pool table and ignore me as I pass by on my way back to the area that serves as the venue for civil-commitment proceedings.

Waiting patiently for me outside my office, which opens onto the room where the hearings take place, is my first client, an old, entirely harmless black woman who at first seems so despondent that I can't understand how she has been evaluated.

"Mrs. Williams, how are you doing?" I ask, leading her inside my office and closing the door. This is her forty-five-day hearing. She has already had her probable-cause hearing, which allowed the state to detain her in the state hospital for a seven-day observation period.

She sits down heavily across from me and holds her head in her hands. After what seems like an eternity, Mrs. Williams sighs. "When kin Ah go home?"

Despite her age, eighty, she is not unattractive. Her fine white hair is done up in a tight cotton bun. Gold spectacles rest on the end of a strong but not too broad nose, and her eyes are clear and bright. Her dress, an old woman's Sunday best, is clean and unwrinkled, a good sign. She is hardly a candidate to elope, but her chances for release are vastly improved by her being allowed to wear her own clothes. I have learned the hard way to avoid answering her question. Her son has already testified at the probable-cause hearing that he had found his mother talking to herself and he couldn't get any sense out of her. There was no food in the house, and she appeared to him to have lost about twenty pounds. He had filed a petition alleging she was "gravely disabled," meaning she was unable to provide for her own food, clothing, or shelter as a result of mental illness. Based on what I have seen this morning, Perry Sarver meets this definition in addition to being "homicidal."

I lean across my narrow desk and pat her right hand which is anxiously working the buttons on her blue gingham dress. "That's what the judge is going to decide."

"Jedge?" She peers at me over the half-moons of her dollar-store magnifying glasses.

"Yes, ma'am," I answer, guessing this woman may be headed for a nursing home. As much as I hate mental institutions, I've often thought that I would rather be crazy than old in America. The attorney general of the state is going to run for governor on the strength of his nursing-home investigations. "Remember the judge in your hearing last week? We are going in a few minutes to another hearing where the judge is going to decide whether the Division of Mental Health can make you take medicine and decide where you live for forty-five days."

Mrs. Williams blinks at the indignity of it all. "Ah got me a place, an' Ah don't need no medicine."

It is my turn to sigh. I have no chance of winning this case. "But your son says you have lost a lot of weight lately."

"Ah's too fat," she says nervously. "Is you my lawyer?"

Touché. "Yes, ma'am." Irritably, I worry at a hangnail on my right thumb. I feel about as useless in her case as I do in Perry Sarver's. There is no way in hell the magistrate is not going to find her "gravely disabled" after the psychiatrist gets through testifying. "Are you sad about something, Mrs. Williams?"

She looks at me as if I'm the one who is crazy. "Ah's sad 'cause Ah cain't go home."

She does not add, perhaps out of courtesy, "Wouldn't you be?" This woman may be ignorant, but she isn't stupid. I suspect a week of balanced eating and some sedatives have done wonders for her mental state, but it will be too late, if this case goes according to form.

I pry a little further. "Who is it you used to live with?"

"My husband," she says, her tired brown eyes mournful.

I ask, "How long has he been gone?"

Suddenly, she starts to cry, tears falling behind her glasses so rapidly I feel foolish for not having tried to phrase the question more delicately. "He passed last year," she wails.

I search in vain for a tissue from my desk drawer. "I'm sorry, Mrs. Williams."

"We was married fifty-two years!"

This seems like a case of simple depression. Simple? I have fallen into the habits of the professional. This woman is dying of a broken heart. "Do you have any family you could stay with?"

She shakes her head sorrowfully. "Nobody but my son, an' his wife don't want me."

She needs an aggressive social worker, not a lawyer. What community services do they have for an old, worn-out black woman whose family has died or doesn't want her? This isn't a legal problem, but we are used to legal solutions in this country, so a son throws up his hands and tries to commit his mother to buy himself a little time. I tell Mrs. Williams I'll be back and go look for Danny Goetz, the assistant prosecuting attorney assigned to the state hospital. Danny is nearly half my age and so is the magistrate. What am I doing here? I should be in a firm, practicing real law, not trying to play nursemaid to a woman whose only problem is that she is old and nobody wants her. But I do not want to see her committed.

I find Danny in the break room flirting with one of the student nurses, a girl whose figure has Danny staring like a blind man. He is outrageous, but the girl, a size-five redhead, doesn't seem to mind. "I know how busy you are, Danny, but could I see you for a second?"

Danny, who has somehow managed to grow a beard on a non-existent chin, turns and smirks at me. "Hi, Gideon."

I find myself staring a bit, too. "Can we go to your office?"

"Sure," he says, not looking at me now. "Come see me, Heidi."

Awwuu, you're leaving, Heidi's look says, but she does not speak. Can she speak? Maybe Danny likes them mute. Less trouble that way. No awkward phone calls later.

We walk down the hall side by side to his office. "Isn't she a little young for you?" I ask as we turn into his cubicle, identical in size to my own.

Sassy as only sex can make humans, Danny, hands jammed in his pockets, leans against the wall behind his desk. "A little young for you, maybe, you mean, Grandfather."

"Heidi—is that really her name?" I ask. "Is she trying to get in *Playboy* or what?" Her middle name is probably Bambi.

"It'd be okay with me," Danny says, fingering his surprisingly luxuriant beard. Before affecting this copper-colored camouflage, he looked like an unhappy choirboy. Pimples were all that bony structure supported two weeks ago.

I try to explain to him the futility of a civil commitment for Mrs. Williams. Despite his thirteen-year-old mentality, Danny has a good heart and hears me out.

"I don't mind dismissing it," Danny says, picking her file from his desk yet not bothering to open it, "but what do you suggest?"

I have a plan, but it will take more paperwork than anyone wants to do. "Why not call Adult Protective Services and get them to file a petition on her? They can hook her up with the Visiting

Nurses Association and arrange for them to look in on her and get her some Meals on Wheels. Between Medicaid and Medicare and Social Security they ought to be able to keep her in an apartment for a while longer. You don't want to try to dump her in a nursing home."

"Not really," he admits, examining an unruly whisker he has plucked. "You want to get this passed?"

We go to Hugh Bixby's office and have the case postponed until we see if we can get it worked out. While we are sitting in his office waiting for some calls to be returned, Danny asks, "Did you know Hart Anderson?"

I sip at a cup of some of the most abysmal coffee I've ever drunk. "I'm afraid we didn't run in the same circles."

"Want to hear some gossip?" Danny asks, putting booted feet up on his desk as if he is through for the day instead of just beginning.

I try not to smile. "If you insist."

"There's a rumor going around that Anderson used to hang out at The Darkroom."

The Darkroom is a bar on Delphi Street for gays. "So what?" I say irritably. "I've been to The Darkroom with a friend myself."

"So nothing," Danny whines, lighting a cigarette and taking a long drag.

I watch Danny's cigarette ash to see if he will set his beard on fire. Despite myself, I begin to feel a little sorry for Anderson. So what if he could have been gay? I play racquetball at the Y regularly with an old friend who has recently confessed to me what I have suspected for years.

"I told you it was just a rumor," Danny says, miffed that I sound so high and mighty.

Danny disappoints me by flicking the ash into a coffee cup. Trying unsuccessfully to sound casual, I say, "I'm representing the guy who shot him."

"No kidding!" Danny responds, now understanding the edge in my voice. "What's Sarver like?"

Instantly I have acquired an importance I didn't have before. Danny doesn't rotate through at the prosecutor's office, so it is easy to impress him. He will stay out here until someone new is hired or maybe indefinitely if he doesn't get the hang of the politics in the prosecutor's office. I look down at my teeth marks in the Styrofoam. Have I already begun to get nervous just thinking about this case? "I'd say he's got a definite edge on Mrs. Williams as far as mental illness goes."

Danny grins. "Jeez! I don't care how nutty he is. You've got a tough case. Anderson had a hell of a lot of friends."

I nod, embarrassed. Danny is looking at my cup. "That's what I hear."

Danny leans back in his chair. "Look at it this way. This case can make you famous."

"Sure." Infamous is more like it. The deck on this case is too stacked for me to get really revved up over it, but the more I think about it the more irritated I become. Assuming he becomes competent to stand trial, Sarver is supposed to help win a judgeship for the prosecuting attorney. Talk about shooting ducks in a barrel! But that's how politics works. If he can't get a jury to burn Sarver, first-degree murder will take him off the streets, and Phil Harper can wrap himself in Hart Anderson's shroud. I can hear Phil preaching to the jury, "Perry Sarver wasn't too crazy to pick out for execution one of the finest public servants this state has ever produced." Well, I'm not going to roll over just because Hart Anderson was supposed to be the next Dale Bumpers, Arkansas' senior United States senator. I realize I am making more teeth marks and throw my cup into the trash.

The phone rings, and we get the details worked out on Mrs. Williams. I have a friend at Adult Protective Services who promises to work Mrs. Williams' case as though she were George Bush's mother and keep her out of both a nursing home and the state hospital. I hang up, feeling I have beaten the system at least once.

The rest of my day is not so successful (if this is a success—it is only a matter of time before the system gobbles up Mrs. Williams), since judges inevitably want doctors to tell them what to do in these cases. The fact is (not that it bothers most judges), psychiatrists can't predict dangerousness, can't even agree on diagnosis. Since I have been doing civil commitments I have learned that study after study proves the impreciseness of psychiatry generally and forensics in particular. Hugh can barely keep his eyes open as I pound away during cross-examination: "Dr. Bayless, if you admit that psychiatry can't predict future behavior with any accuracy, then what do you base your opinion on?"

"My clinical judgment," comes the insufferably smug and asinine reply.

"Doctor, have you kept records on the behavior of your patients after you released them?" I ask, seated at the tiny desk provided for counsel. The furnishings for the judicial system at the state hospital look as if they were on loan from the warehouse of a movie studio that produces B-movies with trial scenes in the poorest of third-world countries. Danny and I could carry out defense and prosecution tables on our backs. Hugh's "bench" is a flimsy table that looks as if it could not bear the weight of his elbows. It does not take a great deal of savvy to figure out that the medical profession's respect for the trappings of due process is on the thin side.

In his reply, the hospital psychiatrist is ever so bored. "I'm a clinician," Dr. Bayless says just audibly, not deigning to waste more energy than he has to, "not a professor."

So what if there is no meaningful evidence that someone is dangerous? It's a cattle call, and I function as a coyote, occasionally picking off the weakest member or even occasionally thrown a bone by Hugh in the name of due process of law.

Before noon I take the bold step of inviting to lunch a social worker by the name of Rainey McCorkle. Since no one I know at the state hospital is willing to admit he has information about Rainey's status as a free woman, I have seized the bull by the horns, and over two salads at Wendy's, she tells me in a roundabout way that she hasn't left her house in a month except to come to work. I silently curse myself for not having had the courage to call her before. We have worked together a couple of times before and have hit it off pretty well. She is probably just barely on the good side of forty, not bad-looking, and has seemed vaguely interested, possibly because I didn't breathe fire at her. "I heard that you were involved," I say once we sit down with our food.

"The most intimate relationship I've had lately," Rainey says blandly, staring into a cup of ice water, "has been with my gynecologist."

Is she joking or what? "I suppose that could get a little intense," I say carefully. Surely she isn't serious.

A droll smile crosses her face. "My doctor is a seventy-year-old great-grandmother."

For some reason I feel relieved. I bend down to rescue my napkin, which has slipped from my lap, and notice that one of her shoes has a hole in it. Somehow it is consoling to know she is poorer than I am. "You can't be too safe these days," I say when I am back at eye level with her.

"Trust me on this one," she says solemnly. "Actually, I've had one guy in my life, but that's over."

"Did you know you have a hole in your shoe?" I ask, not entirely innocently. I remember now. I've seen her with a psychologist from the state hospital. A giant, hairy guy.

Rainey threads a straw into her ice water. "So that's what you were doing under the table. I thought you had gotten excited and were trying to look up my dress."

I try to keep from smiling. "It usually takes a little more to get me going than a story about an elderly gynecologist."

"Good," she says, putting her water down and laying her hands, palms down, flat on the table. "You look a little eager to me."

What a mouth on this woman! "I do not."

"Do too," she says, her lips barely moving. "Which one?"

I look at her, puzzled. "Right, I think," I say, catching on and trying to keep from being confused. Her legs are crossed.

Still deadpan, she says, sucking through her straw, "You should see the left."

I confess, "I'd like to sometime."

She grimaces and I see teeth as white as my daughter's.

"Actually, I hate all this cute talk," she says, her thin, unpainted lips beginning to pout. "You lawyers like to get into these verbal jousts. I thought I'd try to make you happy, but it's not worth it."

I swell up my chest and then let the air out in mock relief. "I'm glad. You're pretty good at it."

Rainey turns and waves to a secretary on Unit Two. "I'm pretty good at a lot of things," she says seriously.

Is she for real? Most forty-year-old women aren't like this. She reminds me of a precocious twelve-year-old, but I am intrigued. "Like what?"

"Ping-Pong, chess, cooking, auto mechanics, poker, bridge, running. I came in third in my age group in the Pepsi 10K last year." She picks up her fork and starts on her salad. "Are you good at anything?"

I plunge into my chili, wishing I had started sooner. So far I haven't had time even to taste it. "Racquetball," I answer. "I'm okay at racquetball."

She opens her crackers. "Not much of a Renaissance man, are you?"

"I suspect I could beat you at Ping-Pong," I say. She looks in pretty good shape.

We spend the rest of our noon hour gossiping about the state hospital, which, as usual, is in a turmoil, with the legislature, the legal system, and everybody else (including myself) wanting a free potshot at a beleaguered public institution. Rainey, I notice gratefully, is still as petite as the last time I saw her, which was a couple of days ago. If she has breasts, they are not particularly conspicuous, so I will not be lectured on that score by my daughter, assuming the two meet. And they will meet, if history is any guide. Women are invariably intrigued by a widower (a possibility of undamaged goods), and since Sarah is such a neat kid, I have no qualms about inviting them over to the house. Part of me wonders sometimes if this is not a not so subtle attempt at garnering sympathy for myself. Look at this nice, harmless man with his sweet little daughter. How sweet they are, and what a nice little house, if it were in a decent part of town. When and if we do it, it's gonna be at my place. It would be nice to believe that I am not capable of such guile. At the age of forty-three, I find, however, that regardless of my motivation or whatever rationalizations I offer, I do what works best for me.

I notice approvingly that Rainey has the daintiest of table manners. One hand stays in her lap on top of her napkin, which appears only to dab at her lips which somehow remain closed while she chews. Most women I've gone out with since Rosa's death eat as though they're afraid someone is going to steal their food.

"Have you heard about Hart Anderson?" I ask. I am not sure why I am doing this. Do I think it will impress her that I am going to be his killer's lawyer, or what?

She hunches her shoulders. "Gross! His poor wife. She's really a nice lady and a good psychiatrist."

I find myself slowing down, too. If you chew food, you can actually taste it. However, I have waited too long with this cold brown sludge pond. I put down my spoon. "I didn't think there was such a thing."

She smiles. "You lawyers are just jealous. They make more money."

"You couldn't pay me to be a shrink," I say honestly. "How come you know Anderson's wife, uh, widow? I've never seen her at the state hospital."

"Mental-health conferences, things like that. She's in private practice," Rainey mumbles, still chewing away.

She would sooner let me see her naked (I hope) than open her mouth while she's eating. Fine with me. I tell Rainey my transference theory. I'm beginning to sound like the Ancient Mariner.

She holds up a finger to signal she intends to chew in peace, then finally says, "God, there could be a million reasons, don't you think? Maybe it was a drug deal and Anderson owed him money."

Disappointed she isn't impressed, I say, "Sarver's nuts: he just stood there babbling. Besides, Anderson wasn't on drugs."

She wipes her mouth primly. "How do you know? Maybe the guy is faking. Maybe *he's* on drugs."

I amend my statement. "Well, I hadn't heard Anderson was on drugs."

She folds her napkin neatly and places it on the table. The corners of her mouth turn up in a little smile. "That's impressive legal work," she says, apparently wanting to see how long I can be teased.

A long time, if it's by someone I like. She's right, too. I don't know a damn thing about this case, and I think I've already got it figured out. Assumptions are my worst enemy, since mine are invariably wrong. "Who knows? Maybe they were all stoned out of their minds. Sarver sure acts crazy. I know that."

She relents. "He probably is."

I can't restrain myself any longer. "Guess who his lawyer is."

"Well, congratulations," she says, stacking our mess into a neat pile. "Should I be impressed?"

"No," I lie. She shouldn't be, but that's what I want.

"He'll probably be over on the Hill before you know it and then out of here the week after that," Rainey says.

"Whatever happens, it won't be that quick," I answer. But she has a point. A 1981 Arkansas Supreme Court decision giving a literal interpretation to the state constitution requires criminal defendants to be committed civilly after a finding of not guilty by reason of insanity. That gets them out from under the thumb of the criminal-court judge a lot sooner. Given my feelings about locking away the mentally ill, I have no problems with that decision.

I wait for her to take out a cigarette, more and more a real turnoff. She offers me a breath mint instead. I finally ask, "Would you like to go out to dinner tonight? I promise we'll do better than Wendy's."

"Just a second," she says and, looking through her purse, pulls out a small calendar. Flipping through it, she says, "Nothing on it until the year 2025. I guess I can work you in."

I laugh. I think I'm going to like this woman. "Are you sure?"

"I don't know," she says, smiling. "If it's on the news tonight that you're representing the killer of Hart Anderson, we might not get served."

I'm not quite ready to tell her my life history. "Somebody has to do it," I mutter.

She studies me for a moment. "Don't give me that crap. Down deep, you're probably tickled to death. All that publicity. The White Knight standing alone against the establishment. If you win, you'll probably be able to get out of the public defender's office and make some money."

It is all I can do to keep my jaw from dropping to my ankles. Is she clairvoyant, or is this all so obvious I can be mistaken for a neon sign? "You're not too old to get into law school," I manage.

"Thanks." She grins. "I'm a glutton for punishment, but I'm not crazy, not yet anyway. Come on, am I right? You're not at all depressed about this case, are you?"

"No," I admit. But I have not understood until now that I am getting pumped up about it. This woman, whatever else, is interesting.

After arranging a time, we walk back across the street to work, both of us probably wondering what we are getting into. I think I like her, but she seems like a lot of work. Anyway, it is Friday. We deserve to get out of the house. Hope springs eternal in the human genitals.

At the end of the day I find myself worrying about Mrs. Williams. Maybe she would not be so lonely in a nursing home, but there are too many horror stories in the media, thanks to the attorney general's preelection efforts to stake out this issue. As usual we are through before five (a judge not hung up on due process can cover a lot of territory), and I call Amy to see what the poop is on Anderson.

"Pretty gruesome," she says, her voice husky with fatigue, "according to the cops. The wife said this morning that your client came to the door, pushed his way past her, and shot Anderson as he was coming to the door to see who it was. She was so shaken she can't remember much about what he said. Besides, he was babbling anyway. She got him to sit down in the living room and she called the police."

I put my feet up on my desk and complain, "So far you haven't told me anything we didn't already know from the papers."

"I know," she admits. "Here's something else you already knew: he was a patient of hers and she arranged for him to go in on a voluntary a few weeks ago."

"What was his diagnosis?"

"Just one little second," Amy says. "It's on here somewhere . . . schizophrenic. She said he had acted sexually inappropriate a couple of times. . . ."

I interrupt. "You don't need to be quite so delicate, Gilchrist. What did she say?"

"Those were her words . . . wait . . . you know how these cops write. Okay. 'He had told me earlier he wanted to have sex with me. I replied that I was a married woman.' "

Bingo. If she had told him she couldn't because she was his doctor or that she didn't find him sexually attractive, her husband might still be alive. But maybe not. I make some notes. "I suspect he took that as some kind of a challenge."

Amy's voice is running down like a dying tape recorder. "Oh yeah, you better believe it. That comes through loud and clear. Look, you want to pick up a copy of this on Monday? I'm beat, and I've got to go home and get ready for a date."

"When're you going to settle down, Gilchrist?" I tease her.

"Oh, I'm really a wild woman, all right," she says, without much humor in her voice.

Perhaps Freud was right. All any of us really think about is sex.

I can't worry about Amy's love life now that I might have one of my own.

"I'll let you go, Amy. Thanks." I hang up, wishing I had asked her what Carolyn Anderson and Sarver did until the police came, but it will keep. Since I'm already out here, I decide to go by and have another look at Sarver.

Rogers Hall is less than a football field from the Hill, but I am too spoiled to walk, and since I am going on home afterward, I drive over. As I get in my car, I realize I am rushing things. It could take a month for him to get examined, and he might be found incompetent to stand trial. Rainey's words make me question my motivation. Am I genuinely concerned, or am I merely wanting to play at being Sarver's lawyer right now? I'm not so sure. He could be found incompetent to stand trial without even going back to court. All the psychiatrist has to do is write a letter to Judge Jamison, who can find him insane based on his report. Given the individual Sarver killed, though, it won't happen that way. Judge Jamison may not be running for office again, but the prosecuting attorney is.

I barely know the three-to-eleven shift, but the woman at the front desk presses a button to open the sliding doors after I tell her I'm Sarver's attorney and show her my Blackwell County Bar Association ID card. She presses another button, and the sound of metal against metal explodes in my ears as the door unlocks. Nobody is too worried about Sarver's busting out. What is obscene about Rogers Hall is that it was built as a prison for the criminally insane, not as a treatment facility for persons with mental illness, reflecting the unspoken belief that mental illness isn't much of an excuse for criminal behavior. As I wait for a technician to bring Sarver from the cell block where all defendants held for observation are detained no matter how sick they are, I watch as perhaps twenty men shuffle into the dining hall. Several look like zombies, made docile by massive doses of antipsychotic drugs such as Prolixin, Mellaril, Thorazine, Haldol, and Stelazine. At least two of the group seem to be experiencing tardive dyskinesia, a side effect that causes involuntary facial movements. One man's tongue goes in and out of his mouth like clockwork. My theory is that the shrinks attempt to minimize this problem out of fear of malpractice suits.

Since it is after four-thirty, I can interview him in any office I want that I can find unlocked (usually there isn't one, as space is so limited). I ask the tech to wait outside the door and pick the break room to observe my client. Sarver is still going through his goofball act, grinning, muttering, glaring, rhyming. Now that I have him, I'm not sure what to do with him. Since the secretaries have gone, there is no one to give me what few records they have on him. So I watch. Usually, in this situation, I am at least a little nervous, but this guy doesn't seem dangerous at all.

"Mr. Sarver, I am your court-appointed lawyer. Do you know what day it is?" No response to that one, so I ask: "Why did you kill Hart Anderson?" For a split second I think he knows exactly what I am talking about. His eyes seem to take on a guarded look, but I realize I have no way of knowing what he is thinking. He knows what he did. What he apparently cannot do now is assist his attorney in preparing his case, and that threshold question must be answered in the affirmative, or the court will never get to the issue of why he murdered Anderson.

Certainly he can't answer that question now. When they get him on the medication Carolyn Anderson surely had prescribed for him, he will begin making some sense. Now he is even less comprehensible than he was in court this morning. It sounds as if he is saying something like "Lexis, mexis . . . sexis . . ." Where this morning he made words, now he is making sounds. They will watch him for a suicide attempt, but in here it will be next to impossible. His face is absorbing to watch. He is responding to some inner world, his head bobbing as if in response to some command.

"Can you hear a voice telling you something?"

Again I have a sense that he has heard me. His mild blue eyes scan me quickly, then are out of focus again. I have had lots of clients who are oblivious to their surroundings. My last case today was a seven-day observation hearing, and the guy was somewhat like Sarver, though more aggressive. He was more obviously hearing voices. Despite their side effects, the antipsychotic drugs do wonders for some patients and in an amazingly short time. Often, I have had clients who have been released at their forty-five-day hearing on an outpatient status, yet who had been wild when they were brought in less than a week earlier for their probable-cause hearing. This is the theory that the division is trying to push-manage people in their own community mental-health centers if it is possible. I am all for it.

I take one last crack at Sarver: "Do you want Dr. Anderson to come visit you?"

Though his face seems frozen in a manic sneer, I think I can see a change in his body language. His movements seem quicker. Sure enough, he giggles, but does not say a word I can understand. "Sh . . . sh . . . fee . . . fee . . . he . . . he . . ."

This is futile. Doubtless, I am seeing what I want to see. I knock on the door, and the tech leads Sarver away. What am I trying to find out? Nothing really right now, just enough to satisfy my curiosity or more probably to give me something to talk about. After all, I have, in theory, a big case. But if he isn't competent to stand trial, he'll never be brought to trial. Something in his eyes, though, tells me he will be brought around soon. He is not that far out of it. I drive home wondering about Perry Sarver, when I ought to be thinking about Rainey McCorkle. I am safe from Sarver and the memories he will evoke at the moment; something tells me I may not be from Rainey.

I turn into my driveway, trying to remember what my daughter told me she was going to do tonight. Sarah, a carbon copy of her mother, who was a native of the northern coast of Colombia, is fifteen and doubtless will remind me. Some Peace Corps volunteers in the sixties brought back emeralds, parrots, monkeys, and gonorrhea from Colombia; I brought back a woman who made me happy every day for twenty years until the day she died from breast cancer.

As I reach for my keys, I can hear through the door Woogie barking furiously and Sarah yelling at him to shut up. Woogie, half beagle and half God knows what else, has never barked at a stranger; he only yelps at me and Sarah. Should we be attacked by a burglar, I would fully expect him to join in. As Sarah says, Woogie, now five, is still a little unclear about his role.

I open the door and, snarling, Woogie comes for me as usual, which never fails to convulse Sarah. She is sitting in the recliner with a bag of potato chips in her lap, giggling at me. Only at the last moment does my dog collapse at my feet and slavishly begin to lick my shoes. I shake my head and take off my coat, knowing that my shoelaces will be slimy the rest of the night.

"How was your day, Dad?" my daughter asks, as soon as she can keep a straight face.

"Hi, babe," I say, shaking Woogie off my shoes. I hang up my coat in the hall closet beside Sarah's. "You actually put your coat on a hanger," I marvel. "It must be allowance night."

Sarah rolls her beautiful brown eyes at me and calls Woogie over to hand him a potato chip. He almost takes her hand off. "You're a terrific motivator, Dad," she says cheerfully, teasing Woogie with another chip. "The adoring daughter making the home neat as a pin as she waits patiently for her tyrant father, and as usual the first thing out of his mouth is scathing sarcasm."

I grin and go into the kitchen for a beer. If this kid isn't headed for the stage, she's missing a sure bet. One thing is certain: she is going to be pretty enough. There is something about women on the northern coast of Colombia. Indian, Negro, and Spanish come together to produce a rich caramel blend. I have no pictures of Rosa when she was a teenager, but I have made certain I have plenty of her legacy to me. I open the refrigerator and call back over my shoulder, "Are you going out tonight? I can't remember."

Sarah waits for me to come into the living room before she

answers. I sit on the sofa across from her and reach for the bag of chips on the table between us. Woogie, now in Sarah's lap, eyes me hopefully. "You wouldn't remember if I was getting married tonight," she says with mock self-pity in her voice. "I'm spending the night with Donna."

I put my feet up on the table. I don't pick Rainey up until seven. It wouldn't kill me to go take a shower. "It looks like I've got a date tonight," I try to say offhandedly.

Sarah puts her left hand under her chin and supports her elbow with her right. She has the same twinkle in her eye that her mother had when she was amused. "Looks like, huh? Have you been to a fortune-teller or what? What's her name?"

I sip at the Miller Lite and shiver. The house needs a new furnace, but I can't afford it now. I was more than two-thirds through a successful attempt at a career change (social worker for Blackwell County during the day and law school at night) when Rosa, a nurse, was diagnosed with cancer. I'm still repaying the loan and the bills. A public defender's salary isn't enough to let me pay all my debts and send Sarah to college, too, but it's a start. I get up and check the thermostat on the wall nearest the front door. I'm not sure what a hot buttered rum is, but I wish I had one. "Rainey McCorkle," I say carefully. This is a subject that is a little sore. My track record with women since Rosa's death isn't so hot. According to Sarah, my typical date's bra size has been larger than her IQ. And those are the ones I've brought home. I haven't felt like too many intellectual discussions in the last year or so. "She's a social worker at the state hospital."

Sarah picks up a Coke Classic tab ring from the table and puts it on her ring finger. "What does she look like?"

"Nice," I say evenly, trying not to mock my daughter's prudishness. "She probably doesn't weigh more than a hundred pounds."

Sarah tries unsuccessfully to spin the metal on her finger. "Just your type if fifty of that is on her chest," Sarah says maliciously.

Has it been that bad? I try to think of the last woman I brought home, but they all start to run together after a while. "That's not a very nice thing to say," I sniff, letting Woogie jump up on the sofa beside me.

"My God, Dad!" Sarah says fiercely. "The last one looked like she had bowling balls implanted in her chest."

And they were just as hard too, I don't add. "Well, you'll approve of Rainey McCorkle if she ever makes it over here for your divine judgment," I say, plunging my right hand into the chips. "You have the same sweet, nonjudgmental nature in common."

"I'm not being judgmental!" Sarah protests. "I'm just being honest, and you know it."

"All kids your age are judgmental," I say benignly, knowing I am infuriating her. I am not fighting fair, but it is past time to change the subject.

In the shower I realize I have not told Sarah that I am representing Hart Anderson's killer. I will tell her, but not just yet. Why not? I know it is an illusion that I can protect her from the world, but I like to think it is possible. As I dry off in my bedroom, the expression on Rosa's face in the picture by my bed seems to be one of disapproval. My wife was a realist: she didn't believe in pretending the world isn't a scary place.

3

"Sarah, you up?"

"Yeah, Dad," my daughter calls from her room as if she has never considered being late for school. Actually, she is as compulsive as the first-year psychiatric residents who play at being baby shrinks at the state hospital. Nevertheless, I like to check on her. Occasionally, I'll call her name just to hear her voice. As it grows deeper, she's beginning to sound like her mother.

With Woogie at my heels I walk from the hall back into the kitchen to finish the paper at the kitchen table. For almost the first time in two weeks there is nothing in the *Gazette* about the Anderson murder. Because of all the media coverage, Hart Anderson has become a state hero. His funeral was the biggest thing in the state since the Razorbacks went to the Cotton Bowl. Besides live coverage by the three TV stations, the *Gazette,* in its battle to outdo the *Arkansas Democrat,* made up a special section lacking only a black border. If they had stuffed him and stuck him under glass in the rotunda of the state capitol, no one would have batted an eye. Overnight, Hart Anderson became for about a week the greatest legislator in the history of Arkansas. There is nothing like death for a ratings boost. The Senate was in recess an entire day. Praising a popular rogue like Anderson diverted attention from the sorry legislative session, and everyone from the governor on down made

Anderson's death sound like a national tragedy. A friend of education! A friend of children! A friend of the elderly! What were we going to do without that great man to lead us? Who would get all that bond business from the state? I was tempted to attend the funeral simply out of curiosity, but it would have been stretching things for one of the mourners to be the lawyer for the dead man's killer.

In the two weeks since the murder, I have been to see Perry Sarver twice. On the last visit I was convinced he had improved enough to know he was going to be able to stand trial. Though he is still acting bizarrely, he has admitted he remembers killing Anderson. No one, including me, has been able to get any more than this.

I get up to pour myself a second cup of coffee, and look out the window and see old Mr. Cutter standing on his steaming dead-brown grass in the back of his yellow-bricked duplex, almost visibly wishing for spring. Rosa and he used to consult every day across the silver diamond-shaped five-foot wire fence separating our backyards about tomatoes, squash, cucumbers, their brown skins burnished in the torrid and humid heat of a central Arkansas summer, an "African-American" man, as I am told to say now, and a Colombian woman, my prize from the Peace Corps in what now seem my radical days. They could have passed for father and daughter if anybody had ever seen them together, but nobody did, because Mr. Cutter, despite Rosa's entreaties, never darkened our door until the blazing day in July she died, and then he brought over a grocery sack of tomatoes and left without saying a word. Since Sarah and I rarely use the backyard, we have little to say to Mr. Cutter or he to us. So much for social integration in Blackwell County.

I sip my coffee and think about Rosa. The kitchen especially has Rosa's ghost in it. Though it has been eighteen months, it still seems like yesterday that she was sitting across from me at this mahogany table she cherished with a pride that went beyond all normal joys of ownership. We had gotten it one rainy weekend at an antique sale in Hot Springs, and had spent far more for it than either of us had intended.

"You keep it polished for me!" she said fiercely two weeks before she died. We were looking out the window at her garden I had vainly tried to keep going for her. I promised I would, and while I wait for Sarah I wipe off the surface and then get up and go look under the sink for the bottle of furniture polish and a rag.

"Come on, Dad," Sarah says as she comes into the kitchen, her arms full of books. "We're going to be late if we don't hurry."

"How's your room?" I ask, feeling a middle-aged muscle creak in protest at the base of my neck as I stretch. A closed door is a sign that housecleaning isn't one of my daughter's priorities this morning. So what else is new?

Sarah hugs her books to her chest and gives me a stare that warns me not to get started on one of my favorite subjects. "I read this week that Sandra Day O'Connor's room was a mess when she was my age."

Sitting at the table, I pour liquid onto an old torn undershirt and grin at her. "Sure."

This kid makes me smile. She barely tolerates me now, but it'll get better. I bug her to death, but she could do a lot worse. I worship the ground she walks on, and she knows it. I don't know a thing that's going on in her head, but maybe I don't want to know. What is going on? Boys, for sure, the way she's built. I'm embarrassed to look above my own child's knees.

"Are you polishing the table again?" she asks. "You do that a lot, you know?" she accuses me.

"Yep," I say and begin to coat the table. There is something deeply satisfying about honest-to-goodness wood furniture. Like a person, it acquires a history all its own.

"Dad!"

I will do the chairs tonight. Afterward, I put the rag and polish back under the sink, hearing my knee joints snap as I bend. If I am this stiff now, what will old age be like? Under the sink is an arsenal of household cleaning products: Comet, Resolve, Spic and

Span, Liquid Wrench, Lysol, Glass Plus, Brasso, Formula 409. Foreign names to my daughter. If cleanliness is next to godliness (so said my scoutmaster when I was thirteen), this may be my only chance for sainthood.

Knowing she can't hurry me, Sarah puts her books on the counter and waits, her arms folded under her breasts. It is all she can do to keep from tapping her foot. "Got a date with Rainey this weekend?" she asks, not altogether innocently.

"Friday night," I say, turning to face her. When she is impatient, as she is now, Sarah's eyes somehow take on a lighter color—cinnamon perhaps. Whatever, they are gorgeous. "She's an interesting woman."

"Interesting?" Sarah practically snorts, slapping her flat stomach with her arms for emphasis. "I've never heard you call a woman interesting before."

I go into the den and turn down the thermostat to fifty-five. I could say more but don't. We've had two dates. Last Saturday night Rainey came over for dinner, and she and Sarah really hit it off. Before the night was over, they were ganging up on me as if they had been doing it all their lives. Rainey is funny, quirky, sexy, and honest. She slices through my bullshit the way nobody has since Rosa. I'm more attracted to her than I'm willing to admit, but it's too early to get excited. For starters, she hasn't exactly worked herself up in a lather over me, but neither has she refused an offer of a meal. "You've never heard a lot of things."

Sarah bends down to pet Woogie, who has jumped up against her legs. "If you can't beat 'em," she says to Woogie, "be condescending."

I go back into the kitchen to see if I have turned off the stove. A quarter of my day seems to be spent wondering if the house is on fire or flooded. It is off. Standing by his ally, Woogie looks at me disapprovingly. Water. He might enjoy his day a little more if I put some in his bowl. I transfer water from the yellow teakettle on the burner into his water dish. "Sorry, Woogs, you're not a priority item today."

"Why not?" Sarah says, absently twisting a strand of her glossy, naturally curly hair. The Negro in her blood must have won this battle. Yet her nose is almost as narrow as the fingernail file she rummages out of her purse. "We usually spend a good part of the day talking about Woogie."

True. A safe subject if there ever was one. When I finally told Sarah I am representing the killer of Hart Anderson, she had visibly winced. Death isn't just an academic subject between us, and I like to avoid it when I can. "You want to stop and get a doughnut?"

"Good, Dad," she says, her eyes downcast, as she works on a cuticle. Her nails are red as a Christmas ribbon. Women in northern Colombia are big into color, and Rosa passed this tradition on to her daughter. "Trying to buy me off with a sugar fix. That's really superb parenting. We haven't got time."

What a mouth on this kid! I'm afraid I know where she got it.

"Has Woogie gone out?" she asks. "He looks pissed."

I cringe at the word "pissed," but I let it pass. If I had even thought it in front of her grandparents, they would have had me put to sleep. "He was about to go on a fast and didn't particularly like the idea."

"Dad!"

I know it is my week to take care of him, but I can't avoid martyrdom. It's in the Page blood. "I'm not the only person who's got two hands in this house," I complain.

Sarah crams her nail file back into her purse. "I've forgotten to make my lunch. Will you give me some money?"

"We've got time," I say, stooping to wipe up water I have splashed on the floor by Woogie's bowl. The linoleum at this distance is not a pretty sight, but it will have to wait.

Sarah sighs and puts down her books and goes to the refrigerator and gets out whole wheat bread, mayo, and turkey slices. "We need a wife," she says, hastily putting together her sandwich.

I throw into the trash a soaked and dirty paper towel. This is interesting. Sarah has never mentioned the possibility of my remarrying before. "Are you nominating Rainey McCorkle?"

"You could do worse; you've dated some real weirdos," Sarah says, going through the drawers twice before she finds the plastic bags. She sighs melodramatically as if she had spent a year of her life looking for them. "We need to get better organized, Dad."

Why, I wonder. We are doing all right. Ever since Rosa died, I have realized how precious these moments with Sarah are. I worry that she will become fatalistic and won't do things like check her breasts for lumps. Marty, my sister, has pledged in blood that she will continue to talk to Sarah about things like that. Despite all our chatter, there are certain subjects that we don't mention.

"We're pretty organized," I say, putting on my coat, finally ready. "Aren't you going to wear a jacket?"

Sarah shrugs. "It's not that cold."

We go out the door. It must be forty degrees. Sarah is wearing a close-fitting lavender sweater that will have every boy at her school running into walls. Her mother had the same perfect body when I met her in a hospital in Barranquilla, where I was recovering from a grenade disguised as a kidney stone. Rosa, my day-shift nurse, giggling hysterically at my atrociously accented eastern Arkansas Spanish, invited me to a New Year's Eve party, and three months later I was writing my mother I had a surprise for her. My mother, who told Marty the day before we got home that her worst nightmare had been realized, found herself loving Rosa almost as much as I did. The fact that Rosa was gorgeous didn't hurt. I could always imagine her thinking, If she were just a little lighter . . .

I grumble, "An IQ of 130, and you won't wear a jacket."

"You don't know what my IQ is," Sarah points out, skipping down the concrete steps like a five-year-old. "Besides, nobody wears a coat in this kind of weather unless it's denim, and mine's in the dirty clothes."

"Except normal human beings," I say and go back and check the door to make sure it is locked.

"You mean adults," she says, opening the door on the driver's side of the Blazer. It sounds like a parrot being strangled, and I make a mental note to walk over to Freeman's Hardware and get a can of 3-in-1 oil. I have forgotten two days running now.

"Precisely." I look up the gutter and notice the paint peeling over my bedroom window that I usually manage to avoid seeing this time of day. Fix it up or quit worrying about it? Our neighborhood tipped long ago. As the unending battle over school desegregation in Blackwell County continues to rage, realtors and developers rub their hands with glee. The western edge of Blackwell County used to be considered an uninhabitable wilderness. Now it is being touted as the only civilized place to live. Married to a woman who was as dark as some of my neighbors, I don't have the same thoughts about race that many of the people I grew up with do.

"Cute, Dad!" my daughter yells, strapping herself in. "Will you come on?"

I hand her the keys to the Blazer, now four years old, and as usual we argue about the radio. She wants rock, and I want National Public Radio, so we compromise by turning it off. Sarah concentrates on her driving, which has won no awards. She seems to think too much about it, the way her mother used to. I miss Rosa most in the mornings. When she worked the day shift, I would get up and make breakfast for her. She thought I was a saint for doing that, but it was always a good time of day for us—no bills, no rushing to school for night classes. She would be so proud of the way Sarah is turning out.

"It looks like a C again in geometry, Dad," Sarah says, adjusting an earring, a silver elephant, with her right hand.

On Stinson Street heading east toward her school, we seem to be intent on creeping up the rear end of a Buick. I realize my legs are stiff against the floorboard. We don't have to sodomize this car. I try to concentrate on the scenery. To my right is Pinewood Courts, a housing project that when we first bought out here was mostly all white. Now it is almost all black and a haven for drug dealers. Late at night we think we can hear gunshots. Many of the blacks who can afford it have moved out west, too.

I turn my head to the front and try not to shudder. "Think you're a little close, babe?" I ask, making my voice light. Criticism only makes her drive worse. The harder she tries, the more erratic it gets. There is a ringing noise that sounds as if it is coming from the right wheel. The bearings going? I pretend it is my imagination. I can't afford another repair bill. Last month it was the clutch. The way Sarah rides it, no wonder.

She eases off the accelerator and her face becomes solemn. "I could spend the rest of my life studying and never make an A in geometry."

I sympathize. "You've got my math brains, unfortunately. I had it first period and was constipated the rest of the day."

She giggles, shaking the elephant I can see peeking out from her thick hair. "Are you serious?"

Here we go again. Maybe we ought to hook onto their bumper. Does she know these people? "Not really." Maybe I only imagined it. Thank God her school is in sight. And I worry about a disgruntled or crazy client shooting me.

"Have you thought any more about a new car?" Sarah asks.

Lots of times. "What's wrong with this one?"

She wrinkles her nose as if the Blazer, whose body is chartreuse, were putrefying before our eyes. "It's old." She cuts her eyes to me. "Can you hear a ringing noise?"

"A little," I admit. I grip the door handle as she waves at a black girl whose jeans are so tight her hips seem dipped in denim. "Four years old—the prime of life."

"Oh, Dad!" She pats my knee. No physical contact that can be seen now that we're near school. I've offered to wear a paper bag over my head. She loves me, but I'm an embarrassment. I'm told this is normal. What she doesn't realize is that when we're together, nobody sees the slightly balding, almost six foot, 180-pound, forty-three-year-old hunk beside her. What they are gaping at is a five-foot-four-inch piece of Colombian-American teenage heaven, and you could drive a truck down the throats of some of the boys who see her for the first time. I hold out my hand formally as she grinds to a stop a good half block from her school. "Nice to see you, Sarah."

She can't resist a grin as she takes my hand. Her teeth, thank God—my one genetic gift to her—are perfectly even and straight. "Nice to see you, Dad."

I rub her soft, small palm with my middle finger, knowing it will make her laugh. "You're not a bad kid." I can't remember what that meant growing up. It was supposed to be dirty, and that was all that mattered. Fuck you, or something clever like that.

She snorts, pursing her lips, which match her nails. "Dad!"

I lean back against the door and snicker delightedly. "Got you again."

She shakes her head in mock despair, her shoulder-length hair too thick to follow the motion of her neck. "You act like a ten-year-old."

I study my daughter's face, wishing I had a snapshot of her in this pose. She looks so innocent and alive. "What do you have against ten-year-olds?"

"They're pests!" she says, doing a quick study in the mirror.

There are worse things in life, but I bow my head contritely. "I'll do better."

"Remember that Friday I'm going to a movie with Donna."

"Can I go?"

"No, Daddy," she groans, patting a curl on the side of her face. "I've got to go."

"Bye."

Her eyes crinkle with pleasure at me. "I love you."

"I love you, too."

"Will you let go of my hand?"

I pretend to have forgotten. "Oh."

She shakes her head again and gets out. I watch her until she turns around and glares. Why do I act so silly around her? I can't say. I know it makes me feel good.

. . .

As I approach the downtown area, the traffic thickens. The traffic engineers in Blackwell County seem to have been paid off by the oil companies. The idea that traffic signals could be timed so as to permit a relatively decent flow of traffic hasn't made a dent here. Blackwell County is no longer growing as everyone hoped. The school situation is a mess, and businesses don't want to locate here. Nobody knows where Arkansas is, anyway. The governor used state industrial development funds to run an ad in *The Wall Street Journal* just to tell industrialists where we are. Our license plates used to say, "The Land of Opportunity," but now they read "The Natural State" as if we've given up on development. My friend Brent at the office says they ought to read "The Nowhere State." No wonder we have an inferiority complex. We are not truly Southern (only the eastern part of the state, which is pure Mississippi River delta land and is so poor it is increasingly referred to as a part of the third world, should be called Dixie); not truly hillbilly (though the Ozarks have their share of real mountain people). Arkansas probably takes its identity from its many neighbors: Oklahoma to the west, Texas to the southwest, Louisiana to the south, Mississippi and Tennessee to the east, and Missouri to the north. In the center, confusion and resentment reign supreme as the politics of race and class promises to accompany us through the year 2000.

As I wait at the corner of Kline and Brewer, I see a street person staring blankly into Olmstead's, an office-supply store, his grocery cart crammed with cans, clothes, and what appears to be an Airedale as filthy as he is. If my father had lived in an era when people like himself were allowed to roam the streets, he would have possibly become a street person. The old man turns toward me and glares, and I edge forward, anxious for the light to turn. It has only been since Rosa died that I have been able to admit how ashamed I was of my father. My therapist said it couldn't have been otherwise for a child of fourteen. But I could have demanded to go see him. Marty did, and she was only a year older. Did I join the Peace Corps to get as far away from my father's memory as possible? Perhaps. But why did I come back to Arkansas, The Nowhere State? I still don't know the answer to those questions. As I roar off, I turn my head and still see the old man glaring at me.

At three in the afternoon I am sitting in the office reserved for the public defender at the state hospital, reading a file for a hearing tomorrow when Brent calls me from the courthouse.

"You won't believe this," he says, his baritone voice booming over the phone. "Jerry Kerner has just been charged with hiring Perry Sarver to kill Hart Anderson."

I am utterly dumbfounded by this news. Jerry Kerner is a Ph.D psychologist, known around Blackwell County for being a hired gun who will testify to just about anything a lawyer wants. But so far as I know, he has never been even remotely involved in anything illegal—just unethical.

I stand up, almost knocking my chair over. "I'll be at the prosecutor's office, Brent. Thanks."

It is to the office of Amy Gilchrist that I go, after searching for a parking place. The public defender's office is five blocks from the Blackwell County Courthouse. Space and politics make strange bed partners. Politics is not my game, so I don't pretend to understand why we do not have office space in the building where we spend seventy-five percent of our time. I understand this much: the public defender's office does not have a great deal of clout. It is the prosecutor who goes on to run for attorney general and governor. Obviously, it is more appealing to be able to claim that you got a thousand criminals off the street than to run on a record of having put rapists, car thieves, and murderers back out there.

Nelda Carson, the secretary at the front desk, waves me on back, and I find Amy on the phone. She motions me to come in and hangs up as soon as I sit down. She looks great, as usual, dressed in a yellow lamb's-wool cardigan over a blue pinstripe shirt. Her eyes flash merrily at me. "Surprise!" she laughs.

I see my insanity defense crumbling before my eyes. "What the hell is going on?" I ask irritably, taking off my overcoat. It is burning up in her office.

She shoves a manila file across her desk at me. "I told you your guy was a fraud, didn't I?"

I flip through the file. It is filled with pleadings from the case. I know I'll be spending plenty of time with it later. "What conceivable reason would Jerry Kerner have to want Hart Anderson killed?"

Amy leans back in her chair and rests her chin on her knuckles. "Revenge," she says simply. "Hart represented Jerry's wife in their divorce about a year ago and took an awfully big chunk of Jerry's change. The story we've got is that it was almost blackmail. Jerry was screwing everything that wasn't nailed down, including his own female patients, and Hart had the pictures to prove it. Jerry's license could have been revoked, so he gave Hart an extra hunk of cash in exchange for the negatives."

I loosen the knot on my tie. Kerner has that kind of reputation. A real ladies' man. According to some trial lawyers I know, women practically swoon as soon as this short, sandy-haired man in his thirties opens his mouth. Supposedly, he can talk about psychological pain in a way that female jurors relate to and they respond accordingly with big damages. "So how does this connect up to Sarver?"

Amy has a way of teasing me and does so now. "Relax, I'm getting to it. The way we knew Kerner was a suspect is interesting," she says, inspecting a fingernail and then smiling at me. "You remember Dickie Rossiter, who was an assistant prosecutor until last year? After Anderson's funeral he came by the office and told us that after Kerner's divorce went through, Hart had called and told him he wanted our office to file a terroristic threatening charge against Kerner. According to Hart, Kerner threatened to kill him. Dickie, who was a good friend of Hart's, talked him out of it, because he figured it would simply escalate, and there were some skeletons in Hart's own closet. He talked to Kerner, got him to promise to calm down, and that was about it." She grins tantalizingly and clears her throat.

"Okay," I say, "get to the good part."

"You men are so impatient," Amy says comfortably, giving me the merest brush of a wink. "So we start to investigate Kerner and, sure enough, your client's name turns up. Now, isn't that interesting?"

Despite my irritation, this woman makes me smile. "That's a fantastic case you've built," I say sarcastically. But the reality is I'm not feeling optimistic about this case any longer. Kerner could have easily taught Sarver how to fake mental illness.

"I'm not quite finished," Amy says, rocking slightly in her swivel chair. "We have a witness who told us that in the last six months Kerner had told her he'd pay good money to see Anderson dead."

I cannot help but let out a sigh. I know the worst is yet to come. I have had a horrible day already (each client has been crazier than the last) and I slump in the chair, trying to get comfortable. "I suppose, not long after that," I say, surprising myself with a yawn, "Sarver became one of Kerner's patients."

Amy nods, her cute face bobbing like a piece of wood tossed in the ocean. "You're a quick study, Gideon."

I prop my knee against her desk. "You don't have shit," I say bluntly, "unless my client testifies against Kerner."

Amy scratches the back of her left arm, which is as small as a child's, but I am told she can hit a tennis ball harder than most men who are willing to play her. It is all in the timing. "Like I say," she repeats, "you're a quick study."

I am being led somewhere, and finally it clicks into place. Of course. They want my client to agree to testify against Kerner, and, in exchange, they'll give him some kind of a deal. It is too early to talk about it, since Sarver's competency hasn't been resolved, but as soon as the state hospital psychiatrists read the newspapers tomorrow, I have no doubt what their report will be, regardless of how fooled they were.

"Well," I say, tapping my knee with the manila envelope that contains the file Amy has had copied for me, "he certainly fooled me, didn't he?" The truth is that I am still fooled. I have seen a lot of mentally ill people, and I'm not convinced, by a long shot, that Perry Sarver is faking.

Amy's lips stretch tightly against her teeth, making her face somber for the first time. "To be honest," she says, "I would have bet you my next month's paycheck that Sarver was crazy as a loon."

Amy is staring at me, and I look away, feeling self-conscious, because this morning I missed a place under my nose while shaving, and I have been unable to resist touching my face all day. I do so again. Could Kerner have somehow hypnotized Sarver into killing a man? Everything I have heard is that you can't make somebody do something they don't want to do, but that is lay knowledge talking. A mentally ill person would surely be more susceptible. I sit there wondering what Carolyn Anderson thinks about Sarver. I'm going to talk to her as soon as I can. I break what has become a long silence by asking, "How did you find out Sarver was seeing Kerner?" Sarver and Kerner—they sound like a piano duo.

"Jerry Kerner has made a lot of people unhappy," Amy says, her mouth now firm, apparently not willing to speculate further on the possibility that Sarver may really be mentally ill. "One of them is his former secretary. She spilled the beans on him."

I need to get out of here. My stomach is telling me I am sitting on a volcano of gas, and Amy isn't the type to ignore an unfortunate odor. I can imagine her saying, "As soon as I told him about Kerner knowing his client, he cut one that nearly cleared the office." I ask, "Was he screwing her, too?"

Amy laughs, releasing the tension that has been building between us. "He wouldn't screw her."

Damn. What does Kerner have that the rest of us don't? A murder charge, fortunately. I think of what she said about Kerner's not making people happy, and I remember now that about a year ago Kerner's testimony convinced a jury to find not guilty a defendant charged with sex abuse. Amy had tried the case with her boss, Phil Harper, the prosecuting attorney. Kerner had told the jury he was certain that the six-year-old-girl the state claimed had been raped was lying. Supposedly Phil was so mad that half his staff called in sick the next day. I say casually, "I guess Phil isn't terribly upset about having to charge a fine, upstanding professional like Jerry Kerner, is he?"

A hundred-watt smile spreads rapidly on Amy's face. "I think he'll get over it."

I nod, now remembering. Amy had reportedly done a beautiful job on direct with the little girl's testimony. The case was a winner until Kerner prostituted himself and planted a reasonable doubt in the jury's mind. "You're not going to lose any sleep either, I suspect."

She shrugs, not wanting to seem too bloodthirsty, although she didn't mind making her boss seem a little eager.

I stand up. "Who's representing Kerner?"

For the first time Amy frowns. "Chet Bracken."

Bracken, the best criminal-defense attorney I've ever seen, is hard as a diamond and just as expensive. "I guess Jerry Kerner is taking this charge seriously."

Amy stands and stretches. "I would think so." Chet Bracken is good, but if Perry Sarver admits to faking and testifies against Kerner, Chet will be swimming upstream in this one.

I ease over to the door, just in case my sphincter gets the better of me. "If Anderson cleaned him out, how can Kerner afford Chet? I hear he doesn't come cheap."

Amy picks up the suit coat that is on the back of her chair. "You can always count on the Jerry Kerners of this world to hide something away for a rainy day. Hart was lucky to find what he did."

I stuff the file into my briefcase. "I guess you and Phil would like to keep in touch," I say, unable to control the sarcasm in my voice.

Amy comes around her desk and says sweetly, "We always like to keep in touch with you, Gideon, but I suspect especially in this case we'll have more to talk about than you and Chet Bracken."

She is undoubtedly right, but I manage to sound cavalier: "Who knows?" I am not fooling her, I can tell by the smug expression on her face. "By the way," I ask, "is Kerner out on bond?"

The satisfied look on Amy's face disappears immediately. "Shit, yes!" she exclaims. "Jamison said he doesn't believe Kerner is a threat to go anywhere. Fifty-thousand-dollar bond. Two phone calls later, and Kerner goes back home."

If Jamison were running for reelection, the bond would be a million, and we all know it. "The power of Chet Bracken," I say simply. The man's reputation affects judges. Even decent ones like Jamison. I've never worked with Bracken, but I've watched him. He deserves his reputation.

Damn this job, I think, as I walk briskly to my car. I send a loud fart, my only weapon in this case, it seems to me, into the winter air.

In our office nobody is talking about anything except Jerry Kerner. Before I can get my coat off, Brent comes into my office. Standing in the doorway, like Amy the day of Sarver's arraignment, he strums his lip like a banjo, "Bububu."

Bububu, yourself, I think, throwing the file onto my desk. "What if my guy's really nuts?" I ask rhetorically, no longer believing he is. "Phil hates Jerry Kerner. He'd love nothing better than to ruin him even if he can't convict him."

Brent jams his hands into his pockets. "He wouldn't go that far."

Through my doorway for the story come Leona and Greta, who, along with Brent and myself, are the only ones left in the office. I run through what Amy has told me.

Greta, who has seated herself in my best chair, waits until I am finished before pronouncing, "Jerry Kerner cooked his goose when he threatened to kill Anderson. You better get out to Rogers Hall and start your boy singing."

Before I can respond, Brent, who normally won't agree with Greta on what day it is, chimes in, "Did Amy offer you a deal?"

I profess amazement at their haste, but it seems like a one-way street to a plea bargain at this point. It is five o'clock, and Greta and Leona head back to their offices to get ready to leave. As he usually does, Brent sticks around to talk. He puts his feet against my desk and pushes his chair back at an angle. "And I thought you were going to get your guy off," he says, genuinely sad, I think.

From my desk I pick up a picture frame that holds a snapshot of Sarah leaning back against the side of our house. I took it last year. She was pretending to smile, but she was sad because her best friend had just told her she was going to be gone all summer. I ask Brent, who was at the arraignment, "Didn't Sarver fool you, too?"

Brent rubs a thumbnail at a spot on his jacket that has been there since he started work. "Sure," he says, "but I don't know anything about wackos. Maybe it's easier than you think."

I wince at the word "wacko," even though I use it all the time. My father was a wacko, a small-town pharmacist who endlessly walked the streets of the eastern Arkansas town where we lived and harangued anybody who would listen about the threat of the international Communist conspiracy. Politicians made a career out of this obsession; ordinary citizens were supposed to know better. If he hadn't begun to drink, too, he might still be there, but it got to be too much of an embarrassment and a nuisance, and they carted him off one day. Maybe Brent is right. Maybe it is easy to fake, but I've seen too many people who obviously weren't faking to feel comfortable with the idea yet.

After Brent leaves, I phone Carolyn Anderson's office, explain who I am, and say that I'd like to make an appointment to see her as soon as possible. She may not want to talk to me, but it is worth a shot. Sarver was her patient. If I'm going to be blown out of the water, she can do it quicker than anybody else. Her secretary tells me in a cool voice she will check, but it will take a moment.

As I am waiting, Leona comes to my door and tells me that Chet Bracken is waiting to see me. I tell her I'll be off the phone in a second. I try to act as though it is an everyday occurrence that the best criminal lawyer in the state is waiting to see me, but there is no one to kid, since Leona, with her coat on, leaves. I look at my watch. It is after five. Time flies when things start going to hell. I switch on the speakerphone so I can free both hands and try to straighten my desk. I tell myself it is no big deal, but I have never cleaned off my desk any faster. I've been aware of Bracken's reputation as long as I've been living in Blackwell County, and since I've been at the public defender's office I've tried to watch him every chance I get. He dominates a courtroom in a way that is almost chilling. I'm not bad and getting better all the time, but I'll never be as good as Bracken. I console myself that nobody else I know will be as good either. The secretary at Carolyn Anderson's office tells me that Dr. Anderson can see me tomorrow at five. I thank her and go out to the reception area to get Chet Bracken.

From the moment I see him I get bad vibes. In the courtroom his energy is harnessed; outside of it, nothing about him looks under control. Instead of sitting, he is pacing around in our reception area, his eyes darting everywhere, though there is absolutely nothing to see, since the office is now deserted. Though it is freezing outside, he has no overcoat.

"Chet," I say, using his first name, since we have met at least twice before in the clerk's office, "I'm Gideon Page."

"Isn't this the most vindictive crap you've ever seen?" he says, his hand barely touching mine, as if he doesn't have a moment to lose. He doesn't even look me in the face. He is plainly angry, but I would have expected him to go through the motions of civility. Surely he expects us to try to work together.

"You want to come back to my office?" I ask.

"Sure," he says, his voice curt.

I indicate the way, and he leads me back to my own office. I notice with some satisfaction that I am taller than Bracken. He is not even medium height. In the courtroom he makes you forget that he is a short, ugly man with jug-handle ears, thick lips, and red eyes that are decorated underneath with purple pouches.

Throw in a considerable paunch, though he is only in his mid-thirties, and you have outside the courtroom a remarkably unattractive man. Inside it, the only thing you notice is his voice, which has the range and depth of those organs they used to have in movie theaters. "First right," I say, and as I follow him in, I almost expect him to take my chair. He doesn't, but instead of sitting, he slouches against my filing cabinets, oblivious to the drawer handles cutting into his back.

"That son of a bitch we have for a prosecutor," Bracken hisses as I sit down in my chair, "ought to be removed from office for what he's done. He knows he doesn't have a shred of evidence." Bracken looks at me directly for the first time, daring me to disagree. I notice he didn't say that his client was innocent. I try to relax, tipping my chair back and pleading mostly honest ignorance. "All I know is that Kerner has been charged. I haven't seen a thing yet."

Bracken recites the story Amy told me about the sex-abuse case that Kerner testified in, and I soon learn why he is carrying on so. He was the lawyer for the man who got off and thus was the one who hired Kerner. He sees the charge as a personal attack on himself. "Phil Harper thinks he can smear me, too," he says, his voice practically shaking with rage, "but I can promise you this—it's gonna backfire on him. Your client hasn't breathed a word of any kind of a deal between him and Jerry, has he?"

I realize my own pulse has quickened in the few minutes Bracken has been in my office. It occurs to me that, as good as he is, Chet Bracken is not the best lawyer to represent Jerry Kerner on this charge. He is too involved, too angry. "My client," I say, hoping he will pick up on the irony in my voice, "isn't in good enough shape to tell me much of anything."

"I want to see him tomorrow," Bracken demands, beginning to pace back and forth. "You don't have any problems with that, do you?"

If I let him, Bracken will steamroller me. "The state hospital isn't going to let Sarver talk to anybody but me," I say firmly, "until they finish evaluating him." I see no point in pissing him off, but I'll have no choice if he pushes too hard.

Bracken picks up a statute book from my shelf and flips through it. "What exactly has Sarver told you?"

"Nothing yet," I say. "All he's said is that he remembers shooting Anderson."

Bracken slams the book down on my desk. "You go out there and tell him that Jerry Kerner has been charged with murder, and see what he says," he orders. "You know that Harper's charged Jerry Kerner hoping your client'll talk in exchange for a deal."

I am tired of being bullied by this man, hotshot or not. Yet I know he has information that can help Sarver. "Assuming it's true, I'd kind of like to know myself what Kerner told my client," I say, not caring if he thinks I'm beginning to sound as snotty as he does.

Bracken finally sits down in a chair, his shoulders slamming back against wood and making it squeak. "That's about the only fact Phil Harper has in this case."

That and an unfiled charge of terroristic threatening, but I do not want to give Bracken an opportunity to go off on another tangent. Is this guy always on such a tear? I do not have the energy to act like this for longer than five minutes. "I take it Sarver saw your client in a professional capacity."

Bracken leans forward, his ample belly straining against his shirt. I realize now that what he does in court is not an act, not consciously anyway. He is really this aggressive. He takes a stapler from my desk and, pressing the lever, empties a staple into his hand. He straightens it and begins to pick his teeth, obviously thinking about how much to tell me. Finally he says, his voice dropping to a whisper, "If this case goes to trial—and I can't believe it ever will against Kerner—it'll come out that Jerry Kerner is a cocaine addict who can barely remember even seeing Perry Sarver."

I could have believed a lot of bull, but this I can't swallow. I try not to squirm in my seat, but it is impossible. I saw Kerner on TV two weeks ago (he was being interviewed on Channel 7 about the possible motive for a double murder in Blackwell County), and he looked as if he was announcing to run for public office. I have defended too many addicts to think I can't spot them, but then, so has Chet Bracken. I say politely, straining the limits of my patience, "Maybe he took some notes."

"Page," Bracken says, calling me by my name for the first time, "I know your shit detector is working overtime, but I believe the guy. The air base out at Jacksonville had Jerry on contract to see some of its airmen when their therapists got overloaded, and they sent Sarver to see him, but Jerry didn't take a note; he doesn't remember hardly a thing. Jerry saw him twice and admits he was stoned as a monkey."

I look at Bracken, who for once is still in his chair, staring me directly in the face. What crap! If he has to sell this load of horseshit to a jury, even he is in trouble. I look down between my legs, wondering if I should be getting mad. Does Bracken think so little of our office that he can come over and peddle the first thing out of his mouth? I look up and see a hint of a smile on his brutal face. What is he telling me? I don't know how to read this guy. I blink, wondering if this is all a bad dream. Is this really how we have to make a living?

Moments later, he is gone, having secured my promise to keep quiet about what he has told me. I have also promised to call him as soon as I have talked to Perry Sarver again and can get anything out of him. I pick up the file Amy has given me and put it in my briefcase. I will call Bracken. But I am glad that first I have an appointment with the wife of the man Perry Sarver killed. I have no doubt she will not be, as the best criminal lawyer in the state so eloquently puts it, "as stoned as a monkey."

4

I wonder if I look like one of Dr. Anderson's patients. I tighten my tie and sit up straight, even though there is no one with me in her waiting room. I could do a lot worse. Her office on the ninth floor of the Wiley Building has a lush royal-blue carpet I wouldn't mind sleeping on, but then, I am used to walking on the hard but easy-to-clean surfaces at the state hospital. I suppose I expected to find her office draped in black. The *Gazette* ran a picture of Carolyn Anderson a couple of days after the murder, and I was surprised at how young and good-looking she was, until Brent pointed out it was Anderson's second marriage. No graceful passage into late middle age for him. He wanted it all.

I think of the tabloid-sized headlines in the papers this morning, trumpeting the arrest of Jerry Kerner. Chet Bracken's picture and words have been everywhere: on the front page of both papers and on the ten o'clock news last night, on my car radio this morning. He is receiving as much coverage as Jerry Kerner. There is no mistaking the feeling I have: envy. When Perry Sarver was arrested, the only thing the media reported was that he was being represented by the Blackwell County Public Defender's Office. My name hasn't been mentioned once. Maybe Dr. Anderson can give me a pill for it. I need something to recover from Chet Bracken. He treated me as though I were nine years old. My colleagues are for once equally skeptical of his claim that Jerry Kerner can't remember his conversations with Perry Sarver. If this case goes to trial and Perry implicates him, I suspect Kerner's memory will begin to improve dramatically. It is amazing what people begin to remember when they are in trouble.

At five o'clock the secretary, a girl whose bubble gum I want to snatch out of her mouth, leaves, telling me Dr. Anderson will be out in a moment. I see a door open down the hall and a woman walks out and turns toward the elevators. For a moment I think Dr. Anderson is taking a powder on me, but then I realize it is another exit to allow patients to leave without being identified. A nice touch, I think. I hated going to therapy and running into people I knew as I went in and they were leaving or vice versa.

The door opens, and a stunning blonde comes out in a hot-pink sweater and skirt that a professional model would be proud to be caught dead in. A strand of real pearls leads these tired old eyes to her chest, which under her sweater needs no diversionary action. Silver bracelets adorn both arms, which end in pink-enameled nails. This takes so long that, embarrassed, I return my eyes to her face and see that, at the end of the workday, her makeup is perfect. She is better-looking than her picture, and the picture was good enough. I remind myself that people do handle death in different ways. After Rosa died, I got a little seedy until Sarah started complaining.

"Mr. Page," she says, her voice low and throaty, "I'm Carolyn Anderson. Would you like to come in?"

"I appreciate you seeing me," I say, walking in past her. "I'm sorry it's under these circumstances. I didn't know your husband personally, but I know he had many admirers." I had debated what to say, hoping I wouldn't sound too hypocritical. All day I waited for a phone call from her office. I had been afraid that today's headlines would traumatize her and she would cancel our visit. I look around the walls and wonder if she is for real, for they are covered with Cubist reproductions and other modern art. Weird stuff like an eye in the middle of a forehead and a disembodied hand. If her patients aren't crazy before they walk in, they will be soon.

"Thank you," she says, ignoring my continual staring, her voice almost a whisper. She motions me to an expensive cream-colored couch that I wouldn't let Woogie near in a hundred years. "Would you like to sit down there? You'll have to excuse my voice. I've had a cold."

She draws up a comfortable-looking rocking chair close to the couch until we are just a foot apart. No wonder Perry Sarver hit on her. I wonder if everybody gets this treatment. I notice the lights are dim. A small desk over in a corner is mostly glass and seems to have blended into the background. I am beginning to wonder if at five o'clock this place changes into a massage parlor.

She says, "Forgive me for invading your space, but I can't raise my voice above a certain level or I lose it entirely."

I can live with this. She smells wonderful. I don't know what it is, but I recommend it. I tell myself I need to calm down: this woman just lost her husband and woke up this morning to another unpleasant reminder of it. I think about but reject the idea of offering to come back another time. She probably wants to get this interview behind her. I would. Her day can't get much worse.

"That's all right," I reply softly. "I won't take up much of your time. I just need to ask you a few questions, okay?" I can see the headline: ATTORNEY FOR INSANE KILLER GOES NUTS AND RAPES WIDOW!

"Of course," she says, returning my stare.

I look down at a copy of the report containing her brief statement to the police. "In light of yesterday's allegations that a psychologist by the name of Jerry Kerner hired Perry Sarver to kill your husband," I ask, "do you stand by your statement to the police that at least when he was under your care you thought Sarver was mentally ill?"

For a moment she closes her eyes, whose lids are tinted with blue eye shadow, then says hesitantly, "The woman at the prosecuting attorney's office said it was permissible for me to talk to you."

I assume she means Amy. "Of course." For all her glamour, I notice how tentative she is. She is probably, I remind myself, in shock. I'm sick, I think. All I can think about is how good she looks.

She holds her hands in prayerlike fashion up to her face and asks, "Is it okay if I start at the beginning?"

"Please do." Leave it to me and I'll ask what color your underwear is.

"Well, he was my patient," she says, turning to pick up a file on her desk. "He first began coming to see me in July of last year. He was in such bad shape I recommended he go into St. Thomas as a voluntary patient for two weeks, which he did."

I try not to stare at this gorgeous creature and look over her shoulder at what appears to be a woman's breast attached to an elbow. What is she trying to prove by this stuff? "What was his problem?"

She turns her mouth to cough gently into her hand. "I was extremely worried he was dangerous."

She turns back to her desk and takes a glass half filled with water and sips at it, and I get another whiff of whatever she is wearing. Wow! I should be locked up with Perry Sarver.

"Excuse me," she says demurely, "this is for my throat. Can I get you anything to drink?"

I wouldn't mind a beer, but despite the ambience I doubt that she has a liquor cabinet. "I'm fine. Take all the time you want," I say sincerely. "Can you tell me his diagnosis?"

She nods eagerly, as if she were about to volunteer this information. "Are you familiar with the classifications in *DSM III?*"

"A little," I admit. Through my defense of civil-commitment cases, I have learned that *DSM III* is the psychiatric Bible. *DSM* is short for *Diagnostic and Statistical Manual,* which contains all the labels and definitions of mental illness.

She looks again at the file in her lap. "My diagnosis was that he was schizophrenic, paranoid type."

I'd be paranoid myself if I spent too much time in this room. I ask, "After what has been in the papers and on TV for the last twenty-four hours, do you think Perry Sarver was faking?"

Carolyn Anderson lowers her eyes to the paper in front of her. Psychiatrists are loath to admit they have been fooled. Obviously, it casts doubt on not only their ability, but the profession as a whole. Yet, in view of the bitterness that she must feel and the possibility that Jerry Kerner could have easily taught Sarver what to say, I am prepared to see my case begin to disappear. She is motionless for a long instant, and I wonder if she is okay, but she blinks and raises her eyes to me.

"It's possible, of course," she murmurs, "but I saw him too many times. I think I would have suspected something at some point, and frankly, I never did."

I find myself sighing at these words. I want to sink to my knees on her carpet in gratitude. And take her with me. Until this moment I couldn't imagine Bracken's story yesterday to be true. Now, for the first time, I can. I notice I am doodling on my pad and stop. Doubtless, my drawings of a spaceship could be interpreted as some kind of erect phallus. Now that I've gone this far, I might as well ask the sixty-four-dollar question. "Do you think he was having some kind of schizophrenic episode when he shot your husband?"

She is silent again for a moment, and then her eyes fill with tears. I feel I've blown it by the abrupt way I've charged into this. It dawns on me that this woman must feel guilt for her husband's death, and I'm taking advantage of it. She turns again and takes a tissue from the top of her desk and wipes her eyes. "I'm sorry."

I try to keep from falling all over myself. "I'm the one who's sorry," I say, feeling as helpless as she looks. "I'm not trying to upset you."

She sniffs, and her mascara begins to run. She does not look so perfect now, and I feel a growing shame at what I've been thinking.

"I know you're not," she says, dabbing at her eyes. "I don't know for sure, of course, but, yes, I think he was definitely mentally ill when he shot Hart."

Elated, I write her exact words as fast as I can. "Can you tell me a little about what caused his problem, if you know?"

She sighs, and her eyes go back to the folder in her lap. "He wasn't the most articulate or forthcoming patient I've ever had, but I think about a month before he came in he may have come close to a breakdown. He never told me much that I could pin down, but I suspect it had to do with his being jilted by a woman he was deeply in love with. I can't swear to what I'm saying, though. Many times we never know the cause; we only treat the symptoms." Despite the symptoms of a cold, her speech is rapid, full of life, like that of a teacher who is enthusiastic about her subject. Sarah complains that at the end of the day my voice is flattened out by fatigue.

I nod sympathetically. Not only is this woman gorgeous, she is honest. While I'm in this far, I might as well keep going, though I know this is hard on her. "How many times did you see him?"

Dr. Anderson nibbles at a hot-pink nail that matches her lipstick and sweater and skirt as she flips through Sarver's file, but then catches herself. She is obviously trying to hold herself together, and I'm not helping. "Every day while he was in the hospital, and then every two weeks until it happened," she says, her voice trembling. "Can I ask you a question?"

I put down the pen, knowing she wants to ask me how much I know about the arrest of Jerry Kerner. "You'd like to know why they charged Kerner, wouldn't you?"

She nods emphatically, her golden earrings swaying. "I could be wrong, but I just don't think anyone else was involved."

This woman is practically an ally, and I decide to treat her like one. She listens carefully, and I am impressed by her self-control. It is easy for me to talk about murder; in fact, I realize I am enjoying myself. It is like her perfume, intoxicating. I tell myself not to sound so happy. All of this must sound sordid to her, and it is. After I'm finished, I ask, "Did Perry mention that he had been to see another therapist or doctor?"

She looks down at her file. "I don't see that he did."

I am disappointed. Yet there are several reasons why he wouldn't have mentioned it. As crazy as he is, he may have forgotten that he saw Kerner, and, too, as messed up as Kerner is, Sarver may not have counted that as a doctor's visit. I can see Amy and Phil seizing on this omission in Carolyn Anderson's records as proof of a plot, but I don't think it will fly. "Do you know Jerry Kerner or anything about him? Did your husband mention him?"

"Hart never talked about his cases," she says somberly. "There's lots of psychologists I don't know."

I can't resist a small smile here. "Psychiatrists and psychologists haven't formed a mutual-admiration society, have they?" It is a turf battle—money, to be precise.

For the first time she grins, revealing beautiful teeth. I try looking at her high heels, which also cause me emotional turmoil. Naturally, they match her skirt, which is creeping up her thighs, the lower parts of which are firm and tan even in January. Has she got a modeling job after work? I want to direct the conversation back to Sarver, and ask, "What was Perry like when you first saw him?"

Her smile disappears, and she holds Sarver's file with both hands. "He was sick," she says earnestly. "He admitted that he had begun to hear voices telling him his girlfriend was having all kinds of affairs."

I blink and look straight at her. I do not want to be the devil's advocate in this interview, but I ask the obvious question: "Is it possible she was?"

Her tone becomes slightly dry, and she raises her eyes to meet mine. "Anything's possible, I suppose, but he said the voices told him she was sleeping with her best friend's husband, her boss, and a male friend of hers. I doubt that she had that much time. Actually, it was his boss who encouraged him to get some help. This was after Perry was discharged from the Air Force. He said Perry had been a good worker but that he was going to have to fire him and he didn't want to."

Everything she has said has been dynamite. I can see putting this case together after all. As he got sicker, Sarver transferred his love to this woman and was insanely jealous of Anderson and killed him. "Who was his employer," I ask, "after he got out of the Air Force?"

She flips through the file. "At Your Service—it's a food-catering place on Darnell Road."

I have never heard of it, but then my parties don't require the services of a caterer. "I suppose he was on medication."

This statement brings a grimace to her lips. Her back stiffens and her voice takes on a defensive quality for the first time. "He was supposed to be. I had him on Prolixin four times a day when he was in the hospital, but reduced it as his symptoms resolved. I'm afraid he may not have been taking it at the time this happened."

She seems hostile for the first time since I've been talking to her, and it occurs to me that possibly she had him on too low a dosage when he went off. If that's true, no wonder she feels guilty. This is not the time to suggest it. "Why do you think that?" I ask innocently.

She takes a deep breath. "He missed his last appointment the week before."

She must feel horrible, but this has been extremely helpful. She doesn't blame Sarver; she blames herself! "He obviously was doing better if you had him down to a real low dosage," I say sympathetically, hoping I'll get some kind of admission out of her that she may have screwed up. I feel like a bastard, but I think I'm close to getting her to really help me.

She nods. "He was doing much better, much better. I may have . . ." Her voice trails off. "I don't know."

I hold my breath, but she doesn't continue. I don't blame her. I represent Sarver, after all. She is probably thinking I may advise Sarver to sue her for malpractice once he is well. The irony of our legal system is too much! Her patient kills her husband and then could sue her for it! I don't really need her to admit she may have underestimated a proper maintenance dosage. It's not essential, but it would be a tasty nugget for the jury. I can see myself before the jury: a horrible tragedy, yes, but when mistakes are made, someone usually pays. God, lawyers!

I say quietly, "Why do you think Sarver killed your husband? You think he kind of got confused or something?" I do not want to put words in her mouth. Of course I do.

She is crying again, tears making tracks down her makeup even while she speaks. "I'm sure you've heard of the concept of transference."

I look down at my notes and pretend not to have thought of it. "Is that what you think happened?"

She nods, and turns and reaches for another tissue. "Patients often think they're in love with their doctors."

I lean forward and prompt her. "And he got that idea, too, you think?"

She nods, again dabbing at her face. It is as if we now both accept her tears as a normal part of this interview. "I told him I was happily married and explained about transference as best I could. I don't know how much he really understood." Working the tissue in her hands, she shakes her head vigorously. "Ever since I heard the news last night, I've thought about the possibility that this man Kerner could have coached him. Maybe if I had seen him once, but not as often as I saw him. He was just too consistent, so I can't believe he was following a script. I've seen hundreds of patients with mental illness. He was sick. He still is."

I realize I am nodding as she tells me this. I believe her and I think a jury will believe her, too, but if she is too rigid, she can be made to look bad on cross-examination by Phil Harper, who has a well-deserved reputation for being hard on the medical profession.

As if she is reading my thoughts, she says, a bitter smile coming to her face, "As I'm sure you know, we doctors are even more arrogant than you lawyers. Of course he could have fooled me. Show me some evidence, and I'll be more than happy to say so."

I am sure she would, and who could blame her? I lean back on her couch, realizing I feel more comfortable with this woman.

"What I know about this case so far," I tell her, "is that there's little real evidence to suggest there was a conspiracy between Perry Sarver and Dr. Kerner."

She shakes her head. "I can't understand why they have charged him. Did Perry tell anybody Dr. Kerner had anything to do with it?"

I uncross my legs and put both feet on the floor. The feeling that Carolyn Anderson was coming on to me has vanished entirely. What an ego I have. Leftover machismo from Colombia is how Rosa would have explained my delusion. "Not that I know of," I say and then tell her as much gossip about the prosecutor as I know, including the story that Phil Harper could be trying to punish Kerner for his testimony in the sex-abuse case. I notice that she is showing signs of fatigue and wrap up quickly. She must hate lawyers. I feel genuinely sorry for her, because it will be a while before she is through dealing with us. "Dr. Anderson," I say, and she pushes her chair back as I rise from the couch, "thank you for seeing me. It would be ridiculous for me to say I know what you're going through, but I am sorry."

More tears come to her eyes as she attempts a smile. "This hasn't been as bad as I thought it was going to be." She escorts me to the main entrance. With high heels she is a tall woman, only an inch or two shorter than I am. She has it all—beauty, wealth, intelligence—living proof that happiness had better be a state of mind or a lot of us are in trouble.

"Good," I say sincerely and resist an urge to pat her arm.

She wipes her eyes and says, "I just remembered that I wanted to suggest something to you, if I may."

"Certainly," I say, wondering if she is going to ask me to take a cold shower before I talk to her again.

"If you're going to hire a psychiatrist to examine Perry," she says, clearing her throat, "I'd recommend a woman by the name of Margaret Howard. She's young, but she's very good."

I nod. "I haven't gotten that far yet, but thanks."

She manages a smile that is dazzling. "You're welcome."

I leave her office wondering how in the world a man like Anderson got this woman. Money and power make up for a lot of bad qualities, but she doesn't seem the type to gravitate to a politician like Anderson. Maybe he wasn't such a son of a bitch after all. I review my own performance with her and realize he may not have been much different from me. It occurs to me now that Carolyn Anderson wasn't coming on to me; I was coming on to her! I look at my watch. Though it is after six, I can't resist the temptation to swing by Rogers Hall and see if I can get anything out of Perry Sarver.

It is an odd hour for visiting, but Perry is brought to me in the room usually shared by two secretaries next to the office of the director of the Forensic Unit. It is empty at this time of day, and Perry, dressed in his usual jeans and a T-shirt, sits down quietly behind a computer. The amiable female technician who has brought Perry to me instructs me to take him to the security office when we are through.

For her to be that casual leads me to conclude that Perry has begun to improve, but I have my usual trouble getting much from him. When I ask him if he has heard the news that Dr. Kerner has been charged with Hart Anderson's murder, Perry looks genuinely puzzled, though he admits that several patients have mentioned to him that they have heard his name on TV.

"Do you remember seeing Dr. Kerner?" I ask, louder than I intend. I try to remember that Perry is crazy, not deaf, but it is not the first time I have shouted at a schizophrenic I was representing.

Perry looks down at his jeans and rhythmically begins to rub his knees. When I was a kid, we used to do this to make them soft and worn-looking. I do not know what Perry's motive is. Finally, he looks at me and says slowly, "I might have. Is he in the Air Force?"

No, but this is close enough for right now. I take my pad from my briefcase and begin to make some notes. "I think the Air Force arranged for you to talk to him," I say. "He's the kind of doctor you see when you're upset about something. Did you have some problems in the Air Force, Perry?"

Sarver shakes his head vehemently. "No!"

From my own representation of clients with mental illness, I am not surprised by this answer. The sickest clients are the ones who deny their illnesses the most fervently. I try to probe his relationship with Kerner but get nothing. He either says he doesn't remember or simply stares until I ask another question. He gets up to pace, and I realize I am not going to get anything further from him and leave.

On the freeway home I try to assess what I have learned: Sarver's initial answer was reassuring. If he is faking, he'd almost surely say that he had never heard of Jerry Kerner, because there is no way for him to know about Kerner's ex-secretary, who said she had seen him. The crunch will come when the prosecutor offers him a deal to talk, but it is too early to discuss this, since nothing has been made explicit.

I notice a brown Mercedes in the lane next to me, and my thoughts turn to Hart Anderson. I realize that a lot of the stories about him may be the result of simple envy. How many men or women are as successful as he was? The answer is damn few. There are ugly rumors about almost every big shot in Arkansas, and if there aren't, it may mean they aren't big shots yet. People will say anything out of malice. Anderson was guilty of nothing that politicians don't do every day of the week—he used his position to enrich himself, but why should he alone take a vow of poverty? He broke no laws. Was he supposed to say his firm didn't want the state's bond business? Let it go to a rival firm? He was smart, hardworking, superb at what he did, and he knew exactly which buttons to push, and when, to obtain what he wanted. Everything else is sour grapes. What if he did have an affair and his first wife caught him at it? I suspect that has happened before in the history of the world. I wonder if the woman was Carolyn.

The usual westbound traffic on the freeway doesn't upset me as it usually does. Rain that looks as though it is changing to sleet begins to fall in the darkness of late January. We are stopped completely. The radio is on the blink, and normally under these circumstances I am irritable and impatient, but because of my interview with Carolyn Anderson I am feeling better and hope like hell I get to try this case. How can I judge anybody when I feel like that? If I wanted the best for my client, I'd be hoping this would go off on the state shrink's report. It wouldn't be the first time they had recommended acquittal. The public isn't aware how often that occurs, because these cases rarely make the papers. Who cares if a burglar is found not guilty by reason of insanity? It's the murderer who gets the attention of the media. And consciously or unconsciously, there will be pressure on a state psychiatrist to come back in a case like this with a report in which there is a finding that the accused is sane. A finding of nonresponsibility could happen, but I'm betting it won't in this case. Anderson was too big, too important. With today's newspaper headlines, there is no way, no matter what Carolyn Anderson says.

As we begin to crawl, I think how precarious things are. Anderson was on top of the world, and one night he goes to the door and is blown away by a man his wife was trying to help. How strange that my career may benefit from this tragedy. I realize again that I may not be too different from Hart Anderson. But I didn't make the rules of the game. I didn't beg or bribe anyone for this case, but now that I have it I'm going to make the most of it. That is all he did.

We creep past a bad wreck, and I see that both cars are demolished. It seems unlikely everyone walked away from that. It could have been Sarah, but she should have been home two hours ago. It gives me a chill just thinking about it. Though I pretend to myself that I have gotten over Rosa's death, at moments like these I know I have not.

5

The last hour has made me anxious, and by the time I come through the front door, my voice is shrill. "Sarah!"

She comes out of her room, dressed in a white terry-cloth robe. "I was about to get in the shower," she says, her hair hidden under a yellow shower cap. "Is anything wrong?"

I want to tell her to sit down and not move out of my sight for a solid hour until I calm down. I want to ask her if she is checking herself for lumps; will she promise to remain a virgin until I die? I want to ask her why she is taking a shower at six in the evening, but even this innocent question sounds pathetically insecure. "No," I answer. "Where's Woogie?"

She hunches her shoulders. Has the old man lost it completely? What's the big deal? "Asleep on my bed."

"It's your night to cook," I say angrily and watch her nod and go back into her room. I go into the kitchen to get a beer. What I should have said but didn't, is: Sarah, I'm so glad you're alive and I've got you two more years.

I sit down at the kitchen table and force myself to relax. I will run her off if I'm not careful. I knock back half a can of Miller Lite and tell myself I feel better. Sarah comes into the kitchen wearing jeans and a T-shirt that reads: Cartagena, Colombia. It was her mother's. I haven't seen that shirt since the summer Rosa was accepted to do training on the medical charity ship *Hope*. Walking the beaches behind the hotels in Cartagena late at night after Rosa got off work had a lot to do with Sarah's being in this kitchen, but I have never told her that.

"I'm sorry I seemed mad when I came in," I apologize. "I had just seen a bad wreck on the freeway."

She smiles. "You scared me to death." She takes an envelope from the counter. "I got my report card today. Four As and a C, naturally."

"Let me see it!" I demand. I sit at the table and study it while she makes a "Geek" salad, as she calls it. A Geek salad is plain vanilla: iceberg lettuce, carrots, and out-of-season tomatoes.

I love looking at her report card, though I object to its flimsiness, a result of the computer age. Sarah is a much better student than I was. When I was a kid, I woke up in a different world every day. "It's great, babe!"

As she slices a carrot, she complains legitimately, "When you went to the store Saturday, you didn't get half the stuff on my list."

"Sorry," I say brightly, not even pretending contriteness. I would rather have eye surgery than shop.

"I'm going to put in this hideous-looking onion."

"Fine with me." Why not? I don't have a date tonight.

I go to the refrigerator and take out another beer to celebrate my daughter's grades. What am I going to do when she grows up? This probably isn't good for her. We are like a married couple, arguing over whose turn it is to take out the garbage. "Who's the lucky boy this weekend?"

She doesn't deign to answer. Instead, she takes out two hamburger patties from the refrigerator and puts them in the skillet on the stove. Hamburgers again. Since Rosa died, we've personally been responsible for the opening of two new McDonald'ses. It seems we eat them every time Sarah cooks. Our eating habits are an argument against bodily resurrection, because Rosa would be coming out of the grave if she knew how we eat.

"Remember I'm spending Friday night with Donna again," Sarah says. "I'm going to need a ride."

I perk up at this news I never heard the first time. Even though she's fifteen, I don't like to leave Sarah by herself past eleven or so at night. "I think it would be nice for you to take the bus," I say, knowing this will provoke her. Spoiled rotten, she wouldn't take the bus if it stopped in our living room. The very idea is obscene to her.

She gestures at me with our main carving knife, whose blade I can see is getting so dull she might as well use her fingernails. I should sharpen it after dinner. She says, "Why don't you take a bus, and I'll take the car?"

I am tempted to say go ahead, but she'd never do it even if she were legally of age to drive by herself. Rosa's death has left her a little insecure. Maybe that is why she doesn't date yet. If I were a boy, I'd be barking like a dog just at the sight of her, but maybe they sense she is too uptight once she gets away from the old man. They don't know what they are missing, and that is fine with me. About twenty is a good time to start going out.

Sarah opens the refrigerator door and takes out ketchup, mayonnaise (canola—lowest in saturated fats, according to Rainey) and Ranch Dressing, which is undoubtedly not. She asks, suddenly serious, "How can you try to get people like Perry Sarver off?"

I wish I had made myself a bourbon and Coke. It is too cold outside to be drinking beer. I manage to knock back a healthy swallow despite what seems like a sour taste. "Why is this coming up tonight?" I ask. Last night would have made more sense with the fresh news about Jerry Kerner all over the place.

Sarah spins the lids on the jars. "Just some kids at school were talking about it."

I put the chilled can down on the table mat in front of me, careful to keep it off the wood. It would make a ring for sure. I am tempted to be glib, but this is a fair question. I explain about the concept of *mens rea,* which is the old English common-law idea that a person, to be found guilty, must be sane enough to form the intention to commit the crime he or she is charged with perpetrating. "It wouldn't be fair," I tell her, giving the hoary law-school example, "for a man to be convicted of first-degree murder if he honestly believed that a bear was attacking him, would it?"

Sarah shrugs as she flips the hamburgers over. "But how do you really know what a person is thinking, especially in this case?"

I spin the beer can in my hand. I have wondered that myself. "It's obvious in some cases."

Sarah reaches into the cabinet by the sink for the silverware. "But not so obvious in others, is it?"

I ask, "Who have you been talking to?"

Sarah blushes and replies, "Oh, just some boy at school was talking about the case and the insanity defense."

"Who was it?" I pry. By the changed color of her face, I conclude my daughter may develop a love life, after all.

Sarah hands me the silverware to place on the table. "Just some guy in class," she says irritably.

I set out the knives and forks. "Come on, what's his name?"

She opens the refrigerator for a carton of milk. "God, Dad! Why don't you read me my *Miranda* rights?"

Cute, but I get the point. My sister Marty says the Eleventh Commandment for parents is: Thou Shalt Not Grill. "I'm sorry," I say, trying not to sound huffy. "I just thought it might be some lawyer's kid."

Sarah stands over the hamburgers and sips at her milk, deciding how much offense to take. "You don't have to be a lawyer to talk about this stuff, but, as a matter of fact, his name is Eric Brady, and his older brother is a lawyer."

I nearly choke on the beer in my mouth as it hits me who this kid is: Chick the Prick's baby brother. It took Chick's parents a long time to get up the nerve to try again, but, damned if they didn't. I want to ask if the kid sucks up to his teachers but restrain myself. What you hate, they love. Who knows? Maybe the kid hates Chick, too. "So you think," I ask, getting up to search for the pickles, "they ought to do away with the insanity defense, or what?"

Sarah pushes her dark hair back from her face, a sign she is digging in for an argument. "Maybe," she says stubbornly. "It doesn't seem right for a person to be able to murder somebody and get away with it just because her thoughts at the time didn't match up with what she did. Society should focus on your behavior, not what you think. After all, people get punished for what they do, not what they think. So why should what they think make a difference in this case, if your client really is mentally ill?"

I think about this as I look for and finally find the pickles. I hold a new jar of Kosher Crunchy Dill between my knees and twist until my fingers ache. "Am I answering Eric or you?"

"Both," she says, apparently pleased with my struggle. Her voice is uncharacteristically smug.

The lid won't budge. My fingers are as white as her milk.

This conversation is proving Sarah's point. I have no idea what is going on in her head most of the time. "I don't know what else to say except to go back to the concept of personal responsibility's being an element of the crime. Besides, a mental hospital isn't exactly a vacation."

Sarah has put down her hamburger to watch. "Eric says they get out pretty fast if they're insane."

I could get up and run some water over the lid, but suddenly the jar is like a test of my manhood. Sensation has returned to my hand and I try again. "Some do, some don't." Eric this, Eric that. "When's the wedding?" I ask glumly.

She sips at her milk. "You won't be invited if you're going to act like a baby."

The lid finally pops free. I wonder if my dignity as a father is at stake in this conversation. She has a mouth on her. Come on, Dad, lighten up. It's not like she's telling me she's six months pregnant. That may be our next conversation though. I need to invite Marty to supper and then leave the room for a while. I don't think I'm up to dispensing birth-control devices.

We get through the meal and do the dishes without any further constitutional debate. As we finish, Sarah says, "I think you work with Eric's brother, don't you? Eric says he's kind of a prick."

I feel better instantly, and we leave the kitchen reconciled, she to do her homework and me to read in the living room. Everyone thinks their kid is marvelous, and I'm no exception. What did I think about when I was her age? Sports? Sex? I don't remember. Not the insanity defense, that's for sure.

Later, I get into bed thinking about Carolyn Anderson and Perry Sarver. Even if he's insane, why should he get off? He killed a man because he loved his wife. It's hardly the most unusual crime ever committed. Assuming he wasn't hired by Jerry Kerner, why should he get off just because he didn't try to run away? Yet, what Sarver did doesn't make sense. What man would go kill somebody in those circumstances unless he was crazy or faking mental illness? Of course, "crazy" means behavior society doesn't accept as normal. Assuming this case goes to trial, my job will be to make the jury accept the notion that Perry Sarver shouldn't be punished for acting irrationally. And if the primary victim, Anderson's wife, doesn't want him punished, then why should the jury? God knows, she has suffered enough. Can I get away with saying that to a jury? It sounds pretty good in my head in my own bedroom at eleven at night, but will it sound too hokey to twelve men and women who will be told that Perry Sarver deliberately conspired to kill one of the finest men ever produced by the great state of Arkansas and that they have a duty to protect the state against people like that, regardless of whether his wife screwed up?

I can hear Sarah singing to herself in the bathroom. It will serve me right if her first boyfriend is Chick's brother. At least then she will have nowhere to go but up. Chick, as usual, made it his business to find out if there was any dirt on Carolyn Anderson. A few years ago she was involved in a messy divorce. So what?

Having met her, I wouldn't be surprised if she doesn't still feel guilty over that, too. The only thing I have against her is her bad choice of husbands.

Friday morning, from my office at the state hospital I call Chet Bracken and tell him the results of my interview with Carolyn Anderson. He brushes off her comments more lightly than I think makes sense and asks, "Did you talk to Sarver?"

I can feel my neck muscles growing tense, and I haven't been on the phone three minutes with him. I do not like this man. But then, I'm not paying the fee. I say, not entirely untruthfully, "I couldn't get anything out of him."

Bracken says quickly, "I didn't think you would."

I try to uncoil my body, but it is useless. Bracken sounds too relieved for me to be comfortable. "What I mean," I say, "is that he is still too out of it for me to talk to him."

Bracken's voice is immediately impatient. "You said the last time he remembered killing Anderson."

"Mr. Bracken," I say, looking at my watch, "I don't know how many mentally ill people you've represented, but in my experience, they don't necessarily improve exponentially from one time to another."

Bracken, for the first time, backs off a little. "Look," he says, his voice a gentle roar in my ear, "I just want to talk to the guy. When he's able, you let me know, okay?"

"Okay," I say, and hang up. Bracken needs me more than I need him. We both know what his client will do—lie his head off.

In the next hour I have a legitimate though tragic civil-commitment hearing. I am convinced that my client, Mrs. Hardin, a sick forty-year-old woman, should not be committed. It is clear to me her husband, who is perhaps fifteen years older, has another woman he wants to move into the house as soon as she is out the door. Yet this guy has been married to her for twenty years and has devotedly taken care of her as her schizophrenia has worsened. My client admittedly is a little marginal right now, mainly because the son of a bitch has probably hidden her medication from her. However, he is in love, and anxious to dump her. Love! The sins people commit in its name. If there is a hell, this is one you could burn for: On the other hand, my client loves him because he has always been so good to her.

On cross-examination I do my best to bring out the fact that he has another woman waiting in the wings. He denies hiding my client's medication. But he knows her sister is going to testify about his little honey, so he grudgingly admits that he has seen a lawyer about a divorce. This makes Hugh Bixby's ears prick up, something that is ordinarily hard to do. Lover boy has alleged as his grounds for commitment that his wife is "gravely disabled," which is defined as someone who is unable to provide for her food, clothing, or shelter, as a result of mental illness.

Danny Goetz objects perfunctorily that Mr. Hardin's love life is irrelevant to whether his wife is gravely disabled, but Hugh knows that it goes to credibility and simply shakes his head at Danny, not even bothering to deny his objection for the record. I ask for a recess, because even if I get this thing dismissed, my client has a problem. She wants to move right back with her husband, presumably until he kills her.

Hugh, who is always delighted to be taken off the hook, is only too happy to take a break, and I huddle in my office with Mrs. Hardin's sister to work out a deal: she will go get her sister's possessions and arrange for Mrs. Hardin to move in with her until she goes back on her medication. I call Legal Aid and make an appointment for Mrs. Hardin, since she is going to need a lawyer for a divorce. I then ask Mrs. Hardin to come into my office so that her sister can try to sell her on moving out of her home.

I sit behind my desk and watch my client's sister try to contain her anger at her brother-in-law and be diplomatic at the same time.

"I'm afraid Bob doesn't want you anymore," her sister, whose wrinkled face and rough hands indicate she, too, has had a hard life, tells my client. Naturally, Bob, wonderful man that he is, has told his wife he was committing her for her own good.

"He does, too," Mrs. Hardin says, but her eyes are already filled with tears. My client is not unattractive. Most of my clients are unkempt, but Mrs. Hardin is wearing a stylish red jumpsuit that accentuates a good figure. Her blond hair is clean and combed, and she is even wearing makeup. Her immediate symptoms are that she is badly confused about where she is and what she is doing here. "He's just mad because I wouldn't clean up the house yesterday."

Her sister, her green eyes flashing through a weariness that seems eternal, takes off the velvet gloves and gives it to her straight. "He's gonna move Imogene Fenton in as soon as he gets you locked up."

Mrs. Hardin lowers her head and says uncertainly, "Bob wouldn't do that."

Her sister looks pleadingly at me, and I add gently, "You heard him say he had already gone to a lawyer about divorcing you." If I didn't know she had a long history of schizophrenia, I wouldn't be convinced she was sick. Many women have been as deluded as my client.

There is a knock on the door, and Danny asks if we are ready. I go outside and tell him what I'm trying to do and ask him to go talk to Hardin about requesting a dismissal. Hardin will get his wife moved out of the house, and my client will have a chance to get out of a no-win situation. Danny is more than amenable now that he is aware of Hardin's motive.

After Danny talks to him, Hardin agrees to dismiss the petition. I should feel more contempt for Hardin, but somehow I don't. An obese, sunken-eyed farmer in his fifties (and in bad health, judging from his wheezing), he probably thinks he has done his duty by his wife and feels he ought to grab the last opportunity he will have to be loved by a presumably normal woman. I suspect he is getting a first-class bitch, but some of us have the misfortune to get what we want.

"How is the state hospital these days?" Greta Darby asks as I stand in the middle of her doorway at four. She is flipping through a copy of *Vogue*. I'm surprised Chick isn't drooling over her shoulder. Greta is asking so she can say that she was checking up on my work if something blows up in my face.

Merely to irritate her, I say eagerly, "Would you like to run down the cases this week out there?"

Dressed in clothes that would be more appropriate for a cocktail party than court (a black sheath dress that is scooped out in back), she pretends to remember something and picks up the phone. "Not right now. I've got to make a call. Maybe next week."

Before I leave for the day, the telephone rings. It is Amy Gilchrist. "I tried to reach you at the hospital. I got the report this afternoon on Sarver."

I find a pen that writes and a yellow pad, holding my breath after asking, "What does it say?"

"We're going to trial," she says. "Competent and responsible."

I rub the bridge of my nose. A headache is beginning to form over my left eye. "I'm really shocked," I answer sarcastically.

"You'll be interested to know," Amy says loudly into the phone, "that the psychiatrist who examined Sarver thinks he may be mentally ill."

I want to kiss the phone. "Who is it?"

"Raymond Berrenger," Amy says. "He's brand-new out there."

I write his name on the pad. "I guess we'll get to know him."

"I guess we will," Amy answers briskly. "I'll get us a trial date and check it out with you and Chet."

I decide to test the waters a bit and tell Amy what she and Phil Harper will be finding out for themselves from Carolyn Anderson. "She's convinced Sarver isn't faking, and this report by Berrenger just corroborates it."

"Bullshit," Amy says, sounding more confident than she has a right to at the moment. "Berrenger's report isn't a guarantee your guy's on the up-and-up, and Dr. Anderson is probably eaten up with guilt over what happened."

I reach for the aspirin bottle in my drawer. "It's two to zip, Amy. Chet Bracken's going to make Phil pay for this one before it's all over."

Amy clears her throat. It is not a ladylike sound. "Have you asked Sarver," she says, her throat raspy, "about his association with Jerry Kerner?"

With one hand I pry the lid off the aspirin bottle. We are getting to the point. "Why should I?" I say, smiling at Brent, who has come into my office. His tie looks like a noose around his bulging neck.

Amy's irritation comes across loud and clear. "It just might be in your client's interest."

My headache seems better. I put the aspirin away. If I can dangle a decent plea bargain in front of Sarver, I just might get the truth out of him. "What are we talking about, Amy?"

Her voice is sullen. Things are going faster than she wants. "I haven't fully cleared it yet," she says, "but I suspect Phil can live with ten years for Sarver if he is willing to testify against Jerry Kerner."

I raise my eyebrows at Brent. In my previous experience with Amy she has always been honest, but the way this has come across, she and Phil want to nail Kerner so badly they don't care how they do it. I wish I were recording this conversation. "What if Sarver doesn't budge?"

Amy's voice is harsh. "Your guy's in trouble, then. We may not get Kerner without his testimony, but a jury will be able to figure out why and will take it out on your client."

I put my finger to my lips and press my speakerphone button so Brent can hear. "You and Phil sound a little desperate to me, Amy."

Amy, who must have a cold, clears her throat again. "Don't get me wrong, Gideon. If you think your guy's really a fruitcake and Kerner really just saw him as a patient, then let's go to trial. But there's no point in your guy doing all the time if Kerner was in on this."

I hunch my shoulders at Brent. That sounds harmless, but I wish he had heard Amy a few seconds earlier. "I quite agree," I say. "When he's better, I'll get back to you."

I hang up and fill Brent in. He lets out a low whistle. "Damn," he says. "They want Jerry Kerner in the worst way."

I nod. Emotion can cloud anyone's judgment, but I don't think Phil is so foolish that he would want a co-defendant to lie just for the sake of revenge. He has a career to think of, and this is the kind of thing that can backfire on him. Still, Amy was awfully close to the edge.

Brent looks at me wistfully. "Do you think Greta will let me help?"

His shirt looks as though it had been wrapped around his fist. "If you will buy an iron," I deadpan, "I'll ask."

His face lights up like a kid who has never seen Nintendo.

Greta has her faults, but she won't take this case away from me and try it herself. I have to give her credit for that. The problem will be to get her to turn loose the money for a decent shrink of our own. That is going to be a problem, because probably few local psychiatrists will be willing to touch this case, and there is no way Greta is going to fly one in from out of state. Besides, that's not such a hot idea anyhow. The truth is that we don't like outsiders coming in and telling us how to run our business. Actually, nobody does, but xenophobia is particularly alive and well in Arkansas. Our defensiveness about being a poor state invariably manifests itself in situations where so-called "experts" fly in and tell us we don't know what we're doing. I can see the jury thinking, Well, Sarver may pass for crazy in Illinois, but he's just another mean son of a bitch here. If I could go out of state for an expert, I'd head south. The Civil War is dead and gone, but "Yankees" are everywhere.

On the freeway home I find myself wondering who this Berrenger is and what he's like. I hope he is from New York and sounds like it, too. It doesn't matter how long you've lived in Arkansas if you're not from here. The jury will pick up on an accent instantly. If they have to trust a shrink, they'll take a local one any day. At any rate, Berrenger is probably going to be a little weird. No doctor in his right mind wants to treat an unending stream of chronics among which are included a fair number of outright sociopaths and guys who will take you out if you blink at the wrong time. As far as I'm concerned, you'd have to be masochistic to take the job. This type of practice does not lead one to the society pages of the *Arkansas Gazette.* Actually, I know some of these people to be the most dedicated and caring people in the state, but this is no time for sympathy. For whatever reason, psychiatrists generally are thought to be strange, and I would like somehow to exploit that feeling without its contaminating my own doctors. Without a doubt the jury won't find Carolyn Anderson strange. All I have to worry about is women on the jury being jealous of her. As I hit the inevitable bottleneck, I wonder if Rainey McCorkle is the jealous type. At the rate we are going, we may not have to play those games. Maybe I'll find out tonight.

6

Be good, Dad. Sarah's words echo in my head as Rainey McCorkle invites me inside. I smile. I do not want to be good. At some point tonight I want me and Rainey to take off our clothes and jump into her bed. That would be very good. Rainey and I have hit it off the last couple of weeks as if we had known each other all our lives, and tonight has been just as comfortable. We have been out to eat and have just seen *Dangerous Liaisons,* a movie that has made me fall deeply in love with Michelle Pfeiffer.

"You don't think I look like her, huh?" Rainey says, turning on lights in her house, which is in an area of town known as Baker's Hill. Much of this section is expensive, as old as money gets in Arkansas, but Rainey lives at the bottom of the hill.

"Well, maybe a little. She looks short, and you are short," I say. Rainey, I'm discovering, has no illusions. She is no movie star, but actually she looks pretty good. She has frizzy red hair and a body that has avoided plumpness by dint of incessant Jazzercize. It is her blue eyes I like best. They flash constantly, whether she is laughing or arguing.

"I prefer Glenn Close myself," she says, taking my coat. "Want a beer?"

I nod, and tell her, "For such an amoral movie, it sure was moral. Love conquered all."

Typically, Rainey gives it her own twist. "Or jealousy," she says, disappearing into her kitchen.

I look at the furniture in her living room and sit immediately on the couch, hoping she will follow suit. She brings out a bag of Doritos Light (one-third less oil, I note on the package) and picante sauce along with two Miller Lites and sits down beside me on the couch. But she draws up her legs so that her knees jut out toward me like protective clubs. Rainey is not one for dressing up. She has on old Levi's and a canary-yellow sweater I've seen her wear at work. I loosen my tie and unbutton the collar on my nicest shirt—a buttoned-down green pinstriped Arrow Dover that I save for special occasions. It is apparently wasted on Rainey.

"Has my little lawyer man got his feelings hurt?" she teases me. "Did you expect me to come out from the kitchen in a sexy negligee?"

"No," I say, pouting. I feel as if I were at one of Sarah's slumber parties.

She reaches over and pats my hand. "Look, little lawyer man, we're having a real nice time together. But I'm not ready to go to bed with you, and I'm not going to argue about it."

"That's a switch," I grumble. "You usually want to argue about everything else."

"Have a Dorito Light," she says, thrusting one in my mouth, "and tell me some more about the Sarver case. That's all you talk about anyway."

Eager to defend myself, I practically swallow the chip whole. "It is not."

Rainey yawns and stretches. "When you're not bragging or wringing your hands over Sarah."

"Why are you punishing yourself with me?" I ask pathetically.

Her eyes flash merrily. "I'm a female gigolo. Your office and daughter were worried about the quality of women you had been going out with and took up a collection."

I feel my whole body stiffen. "Did Sarah say something to you?" I demand.

"Not in so many words," she says, studying her nails, which could use some work. "It was more like a prayer of thanksgiving."

I feel my face beginning to radiate. "What did she say?"

"None of your business," she says, opening my beer, "and don't you dare say a word to her either."

"Thank you," I say, taking the freezing can and wanting to place it against my cheek.

Rainey snaps open her can. "If you had any fingernails I wouldn't do this for you, but by the time you get it open the beer has practically evaporated."

I chomp on a handful of chips and sip the beer. "What would I do without you?"

A smile comes to her eyes. "Please don't tell me."

I don't. We do talk about Perry Sarver, but we also talk about her. She has an eighteen-year-old daughter, the product of a disastrous early marriage that went on for ten years. Her ex-husband has remarried and lives in Louisiana and finally pays her child support, thanks to the beefing up of the child-support enforcement laws, but I get the impression that it isn't men she distrusts but me. I try to convince her that I'm not so bad, but she is wary, and why not? Since Rosa died, I have not dated a woman more than a month, usually long enough to hurt her feelings and make her feel guilty and bad because we ended up going to bed. Rainey, I'm learning fast, is not interested in the short haul. Despite her teasing, she is as serious a person as I have run across in a long time.

On the subject of the Anderson murder, she doesn't approve of the possibility of Perry Sarver's not being punished even if he is mentally ill, an attitude that surprises me.

"Do you honestly think he ought not pay for what he did?" she asks, staring at me as if I were Sarver himself.

"If he's really crazy, yeah," I answer, returning her stare.

"Do you think he is?" she asks, her voice husky with a week's fatigue.

I have not told her everything. If I did, surely she would soften her attitude, but there are too many questions about this case that bother me. I don't want to start a rumor about the prosecutor's being out to get Jerry Kerner, and if I don't begin to keep my mouth shut, that is exactly what will happen. I give her the answer that is so infuriating to the public. "It doesn't matter what I think."

"Bastards," Rainey says quietly and surprises me by reaching over and kissing me flush on the mouth. "A profession of bastards!"

She grabs me by the hand and pulls me from the couch. I don't need any encouragement. Without a word she leads me from her living room. I have learned that single women have a habit of changing their minds about not having sex. Maybe, she thinks, once we get this out of the way, we will communicate better. Maybe we will.

She pulls me into a dimly lit hall and opens the door next to a bathroom and turns on the light. A Ping-Pong table stands in the middle of a bare room. "Which end?" she demands, handing me a paddle. My expression probably tells her this isn't what I had in mind, but I will be damned if I am going to admit it.

"Doesn't matter," I say, as offhand as I can make it. "I'll beat your brains out at either end." I'm better at racquetball, but I played my share of Ping-Pong in high school and college.

"I told you I'm good," she warns me, popping her knuckles by interlocking her hands and pressing outward.

"Talk is cheap," I say, picking up the ball and hitting it to her, "but I'm not bad myself."

We warm up, but after five seconds I know I'm in for a rough night. It doesn't seem possible that a game of Ping-Pong could wind you, but Rainey runs me around my half of the table until I'm panting. I can reach each ball she hits, but just barely. As she hits the ball from side to side, it is as if she were toying with me. I look up during one of these futile chases and see she is grinning. "Sadist," I mutter and smash the ball, missing the table by six inches.

"Men have no patience," she says, putting a spin on the ball that makes me return it to her forehand every time. "I think that's why you die sooner." Her return of my return ticks the top of the net and dribbles over to my side. She smiles and says, "You're better than I figured."

The game is over. I have scored eight points to her twenty-one. "Thanks," I say dryly, tapping the ball back to her.

She catches it with her hand and throws it back, saying, "Sucker's serve."

Okay, now it's down to business. "Ready?" She nods. I serve into the net.

"Zero, one," she says sweetly.

Thirty minutes later I have scored twenty-one points. But my total has been accumulated over three games. "Can we quit?" I beg and begin to laugh.

She puts her paddle down on the table and comes around to my side. "I've been thinking you are awfully masochistic."

She turns off the light and leads me back into the living room. I collapse on the couch while she gets me another beer and I have time to look around her living room. Now that I take the time to notice, I see that one wall is nothing but a bookshelf. I am surprised, because she doesn't act like someone who spends much time with her nose in a book. I get up and take a look. She has everything from *The Joy of Sex* to *Zen and the Art of Motorcycle Maintenance.*

I turn and she hands me a beer.

"You got a bunch of books."

She stands beside me, barely coming up to my shoulder. "Of all my books, you were looking at *The Joy of Sex,* weren't you?"

I notice she has already opened the can for me and consider this a victory. "It's not against the law to think about it, is it?"

"No," she concedes. "Even I think about it."

"That's a relief," I say as we go back to the couch. We sit. "I don't know of many single women who have a Ping-Pong table."

Rainey reaches across a magic line she has drawn and pats my knee. "There are lots of things you don't know about single women."

I wouldn't be too sure about that, I think. I reach for a chip.

"For example," she says, putting her head against her hand on the back of the couch, "you were thinking I had changed my mind when I took you back and beat your brains out."

I am embarrassed. "Well, it was a logical thought."

Her hair, dampened slightly by our exertions at Ping-Pong, stays tight against her head as her face turns back and forth as rigid as a metronome. "No, it was a cynical thought. You lawyers—bastards, I'm afraid," she says gravely, her face soft in the shadows of the room. This time she does not kiss me.

I go on the attack. "Talk about a generalization," I say, pretending indignation as if I were before a jury professing horror at the tactics of the police.

"Okay." She smiles to take the sting out. "You, then."

I want to justify myself to this woman, but I don't know how. She has a way of reading me that is uncanny. I open and close my mouth like a fish, trying to think of something to say that will not sound defensive. I put my can of beer down on the napkin she has given me. "Well, what was I supposed to think?"

Rainey picks a quark-sized piece of lint from her jeans. "Telling you what you're supposed to think is the last thing you want me to do. Neither of us has that kind of time. Besides, this is a date, not a lecture on what makes a person a decent human being. When I get that down pat myself, maybe I'll give it to you, but until then, I'll confine myself to reading the parts of your mind you're not likely to advertise."

I try unsuccessfully to read the expression on her face, but she is inspecting her jeans. I can tell she isn't smiling. "The dirty part, huh?" I say glumly, resigned to hearing the truth from this woman whether I want to or not.

She looks up at me, her eyes less guarded than I've seen them at any time since I've known her. "I'm not saying you're a jerk, okay? But at the age of thirty-eight, I'm not exactly Orphan Annie, wondering when Daddy Warbucks is going to come rescue me. The McCorkle theory of human personality says that the same forces that make a person, for example, courageous, assertive, and willing to take risks, are the same ones that make that person aggressive, manipulative, and arrogant. It's just the other side of the same coin that we all carry." She crosses the imaginary line and pats my knee again. "I think you're a neat man, otherwise you wouldn't be here, but I don't happen to believe you're a saint."

A mixed review, but I'll take it. I see no point in adding an "Amen!" When I do not respond, she gets up and says, "I believe I deserve another beer for all of that." Without waiting for me to reply, she disappears into the kitchen.

I look around at her walls, realizing there is more to this woman than what she has learned from her bookshelves. By this time the other women I've been out with since Rosa died have told me their life story and have rewarded me for being such a good listener. A good Catholic, Rosa, come to think of it, didn't reward me either.

I go home at one, exhausted, sexually frustrated, irritated, and wondering if I am falling in love.

7

Saturdays are workdays at our office only if an attorney has a heavy trial schedule. Since I have been on the civil-commitment rotation I haven't been down to the office on the weekend in months, but Saturday morning I go in to start familiarizing myself with the insanity defense. In our office no one considers the civil-commitment process at the state hospital a trial. It is merely thought of as a hearing, over in an hour, sometimes less. Despite all the due-process requirements that now attach to the involuntary commitment of someone to a hospital and treating the person with major mind-altering drugs, there is a pervasive feeling that since it is for the person's own good, the less trouble the better. On the other hand, an insanity trial in criminal court is treated by the system as a major case that will run a day or longer, depending on the resources pumped into it. Sarver's trial is going to be at least a couple of months away, but it is moving so quickly I have begun to feel anxious, and the only way to deal with it is for me to go down to our library and see what I can find on the subject of the insanity defense.

I don't see Sarver implicating Jerry Kerner. He may, but at this point I don't think it was a conspiracy. I think Phil and Amy are way off base on this one, but I've been wrong before. If we go to trial, it won't be easy convincing a jury that Sarver shouldn't be held responsible. The Letters to the Editor sections in both papers have been crammed with suggestions for dealing with the mentally ill since Hart was shot: abolish the insanity defense, pass a guilty-but-mentally-ill statute, impose mandatory sentencing for crimes committed during mental illness. The state penitentiary is flooded with mentally ill prisoners, who, doped up on the wonder drugs, are perfect targets for the rest of the prison population, and Sarver will be no different.

On my way in I see a street person going through a dumpster behind the Holiday Inn downtown a block from the office, and I realize I dreamed about my father last night for the first time in years. In the dream he was as I remember him just before he died: a tall, vigorous man in early middle age with thick prematurely gray hair; he was in the state hospital sitting on a bed. That's all I remember. My father didn't have an advocate, a lawyer. I have known this intellectually, but for some reason it hits me for the first time that a competent attorney maybe could have gotten him out, could at least have done something for him. Maybe he wouldn't have been cured, but he wouldn't have died like a caged animal.

Inside our office I see a light in the reception area. I unlock the glass door and step inside and relock it. The only sound comes from the cheap, noisy wall clock behind our receptionist's desk, but on the way to my office I see Chick and Ken Averitt behind their desks. After saying hello to Chick but resisting the urge to tell him I don't want him for an in-law, I go get a cup of coffee in the break room and stop by Ken's office. Unless he is going to a wedding or funeral I don't know about, the most formal place he will be going today is a McDonald's, and yet he is wearing a dark blue blazer, gray wool slacks, and a maroon tie. Unless he has no choice, what makes a man get out of bed on a Saturday morning and put on a starched white shirt buttoned to his throat when all he is going to do is a little paperwork? Shades of Richard Nixon. Obviously, he feels more comfortable that way, but why? After two years, I don't know the man well enough to ask him.

Unlike Chick, his next-door neighbor at the office, Ken isn't an asshole. He just doesn't like to talk, which is strange for a trial lawyer: running our mouths is our stock-in-trade. I almost turn around and go to my office, but after eight years, surely he has some experience with the insanity defense. Though I have handled over a hundred civil-commitment cases in the last two years, not once have I had an insanity defense in criminal court that went to trial.

Ken's cubicle looks the way I imagine a junior civil engineer's office. Not a single piece of paper shows from the one file that is perfectly centered in front of him on his desk; his filing cabinets are evenly lined up and every drawer is shut; even his plants seem the same height. His law school diploma from the University of Arkansas at Fayetteville, his license to practice law, and an undergraduate diploma from Arkansas College at Batesville look as if they have been hung twenty times, judging from the nail marks on the wall. He is the most well-organized person in the office. The other side of this is that he is the least aggressive. Good trial lawyers are both organized and aggressive. Even Greta, who can keep her mouth shut most of the time about her staff, let slip a comment that Ken would have made a wonderful law librarian.

"How many of these insanity defenses have you taken to trial?" I ask, standing in his doorway, not wanting him to think I am trying to dump this case on him.

Ken leans back in his chair and stares over my head. Not only is he quiet, he has the reputation of being a loner. For all I know, this information may be too difficult to share with me.

"No more than two," he says finally. "You know the public has this misconception about the insanity defense. They think criminals are getting off right and left by pleading it, and the truth is that it's rarely raised as a defense, and when it's contested, the defendant usually loses. What almost always happens is that when a defendant pleads successfully that he's not guilty by reason of insanity, it's because the state hospital thinks the defendant isn't responsible either. It's awfully rare that the prosecutor will do battle with a state-hospital shrink who is willing to testify that a defendant is too crazy to be held responsible."

I lean against his doorsill, since I'm not invited to sit. I don't want to press my luck. This is the longest conversation I've had with him since the office Christmas party, when he surprised everyone by getting shitfaced on a rum punch that knocked all of us silly. "I've had a few myself that didn't get past the psychiatrist's report that my client was either incompetent to stand trial or too crazy to be held responsible," I say, remembering at least three in that category. Paperwork is all those cases have been. The couple that could have gone to trial were pleaded out before I did any real work on them. My clients were offered reduced charges because the prosecution had real doubts about proving its case. I ask, "Who'd you get as an expert?"

Ken shrugs. "Nobody with the kind of reputation you'd like to have on your side wants to get involved." He gets up from his desk and goes to a filing cabinet and immediately pulls a fat transcript and hands it to me. "This case will help you get started. I can talk to you as much as you want after next Thursday."

"Thanks," I say, taking the transcript back to my office, thinking he must have lost both cases. We usually do. No prosecutor who cares about reelection is going to let his assistants take many cases to trial they are going to lose. Those are plea-bargained. I slip on my dollar-store magnifying glasses and look at the tan cover. *State of Arkansas* v. *Lloyd Bowker.* A tiny bell rings. I remember Ken's saying he thought he had a shot at getting a reversal on this case, but he didn't even get a dissent. The trial judge was my old buddy Judge Hodges. Too bad he's retired. If my case goes like *State* v. *Bowker,* I'm in trouble. Bowker had a long history of schizophrenia and while off his medication held up a 7-Eleven store. The first report from the state hospital came back parroting the legal standard: in the opinion of the shrink, Bowker was schizophrenic at the time he committed the alleged act and "lacked the capacity to appreciate the criminality of his conduct or to conform his conduct to the requirements of the law."

I sip at my coffee. No wonder Ken almost got excited for once. He thought he was going to win one. But as I read on, I discover the psychiatrist changed his mind and got away with it. I learn that a person can be schizophrenic and have an antisocial character disorder at the same time. The shrink at the trial said the first diagnosis was mistakenly made before the state hospital had all the details on the crime. The shrink claimed he hadn't known that Bowker had fled after committing a robbery. This behavior wasn't consistent with schizophrenia, which is typified by disorganized and impulsive actions. Bowker knew he was involved in criminal activity because he had tried to get away; Sarver stood around until the cops came. I pull off my glasses for a moment and rub my eyes. Unless Berrenger thinks Sarver is faking, and there is no mention of it in his report, how is he going to explain Sarver's failure to run?

The doctor who testified for Ken was a joke. Elderly, retired, he could barely remember his own name. He said it was his opinion Bowker wasn't responsible, but on cross, the prosecutor (Amy, it turns out) beat his brains to a pulp (what little remained). Amy may be tiny, but she has no mercy. By the time she got through with him all he had left was his unsupported opinion, and, of course, he had been paid for that. Not much, given our sorry budget, but Amy was too shrewd to ask how much we gave him.

One thing the state hospital shrink said at the trial in the Bowker case is helpful: at one point he testified that schizophrenics who commit criminal acts as a result of their disease usually are charged with crimes like assault or murder, acts that may occur on impulse. Sarver's murder fits that pattern, I assume. Showing up at somebody's house at eight at night and pulling the trigger when he comes to the door isn't the most elaborately planned murder I've ever read about—unless, and it is a big word here—it was one of the most elaborately planned murders I've ever heard about. I think about the type of mind Jerry Kerner would have to possess to hire a killer, teach him to fake mental illness, and then wait for months.

He'd have to be organized and painstaking as hell and incredibly patient. He'd have to be somebody like . . . Ken.

I pull the statutes on criminal responsibility and find out that in an insanity plea the defendant has the burden of proof. The defense has to prove insanity by a preponderance of the evidence. Great. But thinking about it, I realize it makes more sense than the state's having to prove the defendant is sane. Few people in today's society, myself included, would ever be convicted if that were still the law.

At eleven sharp Ken stands at my door with a book in his hand. His voice is flat, "without affect" as the shrinks say sometimes about their schizophrenic patients and my clients in civil-commitment hearings. "A few years ago I got all excited about saving the world with the insanity defense and went out and bought a book about the Hinckley case. You might find it interesting."

His excitement has apparently worn off. I shove the Bowker transcript aside. "Thanks. What is it?"

Without further elaboration he places the book carefully on the corner of my desk that isn't covered up with a file, book, legal pad, calendar, coffee cup, or transcript, and he is gone. He must be serious about not talking until Thursday. What a weirdo. I call Sarah at Donna's house and arrange to pick her up at noon and settle back to read a few pages from *The Insanity Defense and the Trial of John W. Hinckley, Jr.*, by a guy who turned an article in *The New Yorker* into a book. All I can remember about Reagan's getting shot in 1981 is the story about his joking with his doctors about whether they were Democrats and Hinckley's liking Jodie Foster. The book makes for depressing reading. Sure, they got him off, but the author estimated that if his lawyers had billed even half the hours they spent working on the case, their fees alone would have been easily over half a million dollars. My salary is somewhat less than that. As I flip through the book, the most discouraging figure jumps out at me: in 1978, the number of criminal defendants who successfully invoked the insanity defense was less than a tenth of one percent of those who were charged with a crime and went to trial. So far as I know, today things aren't that much different.

On my way out before noon I hear Greta's voice and stop by her office. She is wearing jeans and a blue flannel shirt, the same as Chick, who, naturally, is in her office. I wonder if they, like girls in grade school, check to see what each other is wearing.

"Look who's here," Chick says to Greta, who nods at me. "Giddy doesn't even have a trial date, and he's hard at it. If he works as hard at walking Sarver as he does on his civil commitments, Sarver can count on a vacation in Florida this summer."

The S.O.B. can't keep his mouth shut. Chick is our resident wimp on civil commitments. Like many private attorneys in this area, he substitutes his judgment for his client's. Doctors love him because he does exactly what they tell him to. If a psychiatrist wanted to keep Chick's client in a straitjacket for the next ten years, Chick would smile and say, "He's all yours, Doc!" I respond, "Greta's not complaining, Chick. Why should you?"

"Boys, boys, let's not start this again, okay?" Greta says, forcing a smile. "Everybody has their own style."

This is a copout, but since she is the boss she can get away with it. Chick and I have argued ad nauseam over the attorney's role in civil commitments. I argue that the attorney violates his ethical duty to his client unless he takes a completely adversarial position in the proceedings. He claims that you have an obligation to substitute your own judgment and act in your client's best interest when it is obvious he is mentally ill.

My eyes dart from Chick to Greta, again checking their matching clothes. Incredible. The same powder-blue flannel. "I'm going on," I say. "I'll see you Monday."

"Bye," Greta says pleasantly, relieved that I am going. Maybe after I leave, they will try on each other's clothes. Chick barely nods.

Outside, the wind is coming directly from the north, and I zip my jacket, Japan-made, naturally, and as much rayon as cotton.

It has been a mild winter, but February has turned on us. By the time Sarver comes to trial the weather should be changing for the better. The Blazer starts reluctantly, no happier with a cold wind than I am. On the way to pick up Sarah, I realize I haven't told Greta the lastest developments in the case. I don't trust her. If she can see a way to make this case go down quietly, she may do it. Our budget is due for its first increase in years in July, when the next fiscal year starts. This litigation is getting awfully messy, and Greta always has one eye on the powers in the county who control our budget. They have the power to punish us, and Greta is far more aware of this than I am. I will have to watch her to see what kind of pressure she puts on me. Screw her.

I pull up at 1818 Riverview, the address that Sarah has given me (I forget it every time). The homes here, overlooking the Arkansas River, are in the half-million-dollar range. This address has a couple of short, fat columns, but is spread out as if the architect couldn't decide between the Old South and a Texas-style ranch. If Sarah were half black instead of half Colombian, she would be coming out of this palace in a maid's uniform instead of the yellow warmups she is wearing.

"What's wrong, Dad?" Sarah asks, as she gets in the car.

"Nothing," I say, forcing the kind of smile that Greta just gave me in her office. I am still hacked at Chick and worried that Greta will try to pull a fast one in this case.

"You look mad," she says, as she throws a bag in the backseat.

I look in the mirror and see a scowl. "I'm fine," I say. "Did you have fun?"

She collapses in the front seat. Her voice is hoarse, the way it becomes when she has a cold. "Yeah. We stayed up until two watching movies."

"Call any boys?"

"Sure," Sarah says, yawning. "A couple came over and spent the night. Donna's parents were gone, and we thought we'd have some fun."

"They weren't there?" I yelp.

"No way." She runs a hand through her lush black hair, which is tousled from sleep, and grins at me. I point to her seat belt, which she dutifully buckles.

"They were, too," I say. "No boys came over, did they?"

"Hundreds," she says, and closes her eyes and sighs.

I must like to torture myself. "Great."

"Did you have a good time last night?" she asks dreamily.

"Not as good as you," I tell her.

In the house before going to her room to take a nap, Sarah comes into the kitchen and asks, "Is Rainey coming over tonight?"

"No," I say. "You like her though, don't you?"

"You like her," Sarah says, yawning again, her eyes shut and her mouth wide open.

"She's okay." I smile. "You want a sandwich?"

"No, we just ate," she says, stretching. "I like her, too."

"Good," I say, looking away. "She likes you."

"What choice do they have, Dad?" Sarah teases. "You think they are going to tell you right off that your daughter sucks? They do that after they've got their hooks in you, and then you'll dump me, won't you?"

I look in the pantry for some soup. I'm sick of sandwiches. "That's me, kid," I banter. "I've been plotting to dump you in foster care for months." *Sucks!* How do girls talk when they're alone? I'm glad I don't know. I'd really worry then.

"I think she likes you, Dad." Sarah grins, her hand on the doorknob to her room. "She wouldn't tease you so much if she didn't."

Good, we all like each other. I feel suddenly irritated at Rainey. What is this not-going-to-bed business? The twentieth century ought to be good for something. I had invited her over tonight but she was driving to Memphis today with a girlfriend. She probably went with her old boyfriend and is horizontal in some motel room, laughing at me. "You know that jerk at the PD's office who's representing Sarver? He's horny as hell, but I wouldn't let him near me if we dated five years."

Sarah knocks on her door to get my attention. "You look out of it, Dad. Did you and Rainey have a fight?"

Ha! She won't let me get close enough to fight. "No, but I think she's planning to join a convent." Campbell's Chicken Noodle. How original of me. I take it, since it is all we have.

Sarah says, "What?"

"I'm kidding," I say. "Listen, I'm playing racquetball with Skip in a few minutes, okay?"

"Fine," she says, nearly asleep on her feet. "Maybe it will pep you up. I'll see you when you get back."

I am reluctant to let her go. "What movies did you see?"

"Debbie Does Dallas."

I look at her with horror. "Is that in video?"

She opens the door to her room. "Dad, let me go to bed! I don't know. 'Mr. Ed Goes to Washington.' I'm so sleepy. Good . . . afternoon."

I gulp down the soup and drive to the Y. Saturday afternoon is my regular racquetball match with my oldest and best friend, Skip Hudson. Rosa told me years ago she thought Skip was gay (he was married at the time) but it is something that has only begun to surface recently and now it seems to obsess him. I don't pretend to understand the gay world at all, and all I can do is listen and try to keep my mouth from dropping open at some of the things he tells me. Skip and I go all the way back to Subiaco Academy, a Catholic boarding school for boys in the middle of nowhere in western Arkansas that I was hustled off to after my father died. The Benedictine monks at the monastery there were hoping they had found a carbon copy of my mother's brother, who became a Catholic priest. Were they wrong! The monks could make the priesthood sound vaguely appealing until I learned priests were celibate. Now that I'm dating Rainey, I probably ought to look into it.

Since Skip has come halfway out of the closet, I have begun to feel a little self-conscious around him. Two middle-aged men going off to the Y saying they are going to play racquetball? Sure you are, Dad. I keep waiting for Sarah to ask me about Skip, and I have a speech all prepared: "So what?"

The downtown Y is one of the last bastions of democracy in Blackwell County. An old, dirty-looking building from the outside, it is ideally located, within easy walking distance of the law firms and federal and county courthouses. Within its doors during a normal weekday at noon you will find the most distinguished federal judge slipping into a cold jock strap alongside the lowliest law clerk.

Today at two o'clock I can find a meter near the entrance. Downtown on the weekends is like a Colombian whorehouse at eight in the morning. "This weather sucks," Skip says as I come into the locker room, which is practically empty. "I'm ready for spring."

Sucks, I think. Wonderful. He has already started. Come on, Skip, give me a break. I change the subject. "How's business?" I ask, and try to remember my combination. After a couple of false starts, the numbers pop into my head. Old age will be a real treat.

Skip is already dressed and sits down on the floor to wait for me. "Pretty good. I'm getting more work than a lot of people said I would."

"Great!" I say genuinely. Skip is a commercial artist who just recently left Meyers and Briggs, one of the biggest ad agencies in the state, to freelance. I admire his willingness to take the risk. He was comfortable there. I take a pair of athletic socks from my locker and look at them with distaste. If I don't take them home today, they will get up and walk off on their own. I begin to undress. "Want to come over and eat tonight with me and Sarah?"

"Thanks," he says, fingering his new racquet, "but I have a date."

Okay. Maybe if I don't respond he won't talk about it. I nod, keeping my head down, but that is all he needs.

"You know," he says, now tapping the racquet on the grass carpet, "the other night if I had died and gone to heaven right then I never would have felt any better. The sex was that good."

I look around to see if anyone has come into the room, but we are alone on our row of lockers. Skip stands and grabs a green headband from the top shelf of his locker. He is only five feet eight but works out on Nautilus equipment every other day and seems happy to show the results, disdaining a T-shirt despite the rules. My body is not bad, but I am no match for him in that department. I am careful to keep my eyes straight ahead. I don't want him getting the wrong idea. "Hmmm," I reply. If it starts sleeting, as the weather report predicts, we could get stranded at the Y all weekend. Maybe this wasn't such a good idea. I'm horny, but not this horny. This is ridiculous. I know he wouldn't make a move on me, but all this talk is making me nervous.

"I got a letter from Cleo," Skip says. He adjusts the strap on his goggles. I ought to wear them, but I can't see as well with them and don't. "She's getting married this spring."

We go upstairs to the courts. "That's really good," I say, relieved that I can make a comment that I'm comfortable with. Cleo is Skip's ex-wife. Even though I hadn't known for sure Skip was gay, I knew he had no business getting married. I thought Rosa was going to choke him when he told us. But we went through the whole bit. I was best man, his mother cried (probably for the bride, Rosa said), and they had a honeymoon. The marriage lasted two years. It is inconceivable to me that any man could love Skip as much as Cleo did, no matter what they do in bed together. Of course, the marriage was a disaster, but now Skip can say he tried, and if forced to, I think he would admit that is all he wanted to accomplish.

I flip on the lights and while we stretch on the cold wood floor, he talks about Cleo, his words echoing off the white concrete walls. He feels lucky to be forgiven for putting her through what he did. "I'm happy for her. I just hope she's not too old to have kids."

I feel my calf muscles protest as I extend my legs. I need to start jogging some, but I feel like a rat on a circular maze on the tiny, crowded indoor track here, and it is too dark when I arrive home.

I was a decent high-school jock once but it is beginning to seem like a long time ago since I set a state record for the 880-yard run. "What does her husband do?"

Skip pulls on the toes of his new Nikes. "He's an artist," he says, and, seeing the look on my face, adds, "Not all artists are queers."

I never understand why Skip talks this way. Like blacks saying "nigger." I try to reach my shoelaces, but a small sliver of fat around my middle just keeps me from them. At one-eighty I am okay, but ten years ago it was one-seventy.

We have a court reserved for an hour, which is all either of us needs, as hard as we go after each other. Why we are so competitive I can only begin to guess. During the first game, with the score tied nineteen to nineteen, Skip drives the ball into the floor and screams at himself, "You chickenshit fag!" Is it that I don't want to be beaten by a homosexual—a "chickenshit fag!"? What I lack in quickness, I make up in court savvy. Skip is content to drive the ball as hard as he can, and I catch him out of position on the last point and skim the ball past him down the right side of the court to win the first game. His face is gray with anger at himself, and the second game he slaughters me twenty-one to ten, blasting the ball by me on his serve time after time. Shades of Rainey creaming me in Ping-Pong. Even without goggles the ball is a blur.

We stop for a drink, but Skip is too intense to talk, and we play a third without a rest. He is suffering an inevitable letdown, his timing is a fraction off, and I get a big lead before he finds his rhythm and catches me at sixteen-all. Before then it was like Sherman marching through Georgia, but now I'm fighting to stay in the game. At eighteen to sixteen, overswinging, he finally mis-hits the ball, leaving me a kill shot that even I shouldn't blow. He guesses wrong, and as he goes left, I slice it down the right side of the court to regain the serve. Uncharacteristically, I serve like a professional, driving the ball down the left side of the wall with such precision he couldn't manage to scrape it out with a putty knife. The most he can do is tap it back weakly, setting me up to blast the ball in the right corner. Knowing he will be cheating on my last shot, I serve to the right, and he drives his shoulder into the wall, trying vainly to get to the ball. "Skip, are you all right?" I yell, as he caroms off the cement onto the floor.

"Shit!" he mutters, holding his arm. "You lucky bastard!" He is okay, but we take the opportunity to catch our breath on the floor since no one is waiting for the court.

I laugh, delighted to have played so well.

"You haven't served that well in all the games combined since we've been playing," he complains, rubbing his shoulder.

"You bring out the best in me," I say, splayed out on the court and still gulping air.

"Big deal," he says, wringing water from his shirt onto the floor, "beating an aging queer."

Since he won't leave the subject, this seems like as good a time as any to ask him to do me a favor. I gasp, "You been keeping up in the papers with the Hart Anderson murder?"

Skip lies spread-eagled on the hard wood, panting. "A little," he says. He takes off his headband to wring it out. "Yeah, oddly enough, I met the guy once. He was on some nonprofit board and got our agency to do some art work free. Why?"

I am embarrassed. I would like to find out if he had ever heard that Hart Anderson might be gay, but I don't know how to put it. I'm not sure how or if it would help me. Yet the more I know, the better off I am. "What did . . . you think about him?" I ask awkwardly.

Skip sits up and begins to stretch out. "You mean, did he ask me to draw a picture of a guy sucking on a big dick? No."

I should stretch, but I'm too exhausted. I turn over on my side and rest my head under my right elbow. His image is so ludicrous I laugh. I should have known I couldn't finesse this. "Not exactly."

"Was he a queer?" Skip asks, now interested.

It is hard to remember these days that Skip is a sensitive, intelligent man whose friendship I value highly. "I heard a rumor that he might have hung out at The Darkroom," I say and then explain, "I'm representing his killer."

Skip wipes sweat from his nose with his arm. "Which one?"

I blink. "The guy who pulled the trigger."

Skip wipes his arm on his shorts. "Shit, I should have figured. I don't remember seeing him in any of our bars, but that doesn't mean much. I haven't been out in public that long. But I could check around if you want."

"If you don't mind," I say, more going through the motions of stretching out than really pushing myself. Where does Skip get his energy? I was going to ask if he would check Anderson out, but I'm glad I don't have to.

Skip springs to his feet. "Sure," he says thoughtfully, "I'm curious myself."

Despite how he sounds, Skip is the kind of friend who would cut off his arm for you if you needed. Reminding me of Sarah learning to do splits when she was a child, he extends his legs and presses down hard. We talk about Anderson some, allowing him to speculate on the dead man's extramarital adventures. I will be glad when Skip calms down. He is like a teenager who has just discovered sex. Surely, he will pass through this macho stage where every conversation is confrontational. I feel he wants to shock me. What am I supposed to do? I will gladly admit that I do not know what he is going through, that gays encounter discrimination I can't begin to imagine, that I am unconsciously biased against them. All of this proves I want time to stand still. Actually, I would like it to back up about ten years. Somehow, I don't think it will.

8

Monday morning I go directly from home to the circuit clerk's office in the courthouse to pick up a copy of Berrenger's report. As I am reading it in the hall, Amy Gilchrist comes up and sees the file and tries to look over my shoulder. "Is this the only case you've got?" she says playfully.

I turn and smile at her. She has had her hair cut over the weekend. It is short, making her more of a pixie than ever. "I wish," I say loudly over the voices of lawyers and clients scurrying into courtrooms all around us. Over the weekend I realized how much work I am going to have to do on this case.

"If you've got time," Amy says, touching my arm, "let's go see Jamison's case coordinator and get us a trial date."

I look at my watch. I've got an hour before I am due out at the state hospital. We walk down the hall together, defense and prosecution, chummy as clams. I detest some of the prosecutors I go up against but not Amy. I say, "To answer your question, this is the only good case I've got. Even this new doc at the state hospital, Berrenger, admits Sarver's mentally ill," I add, tapping the report. "And he doesn't say he's faking."

Amy winks at a woman attorney from her office. "You and I both know," she says, as we turn left into Judge Jamison's offices, "that Kerner could have taught Perry Sarver to fake mental illness."

"A competent shrink ought to be able to tell whether Sarver's malingering," I say under my breath.

"Not necessarily," Amy replies, smiling at everyone she sees.

As usual, the rooms outside the judge's chambers are busy or at least crowded this time of day, as his court gets cranked up. Lawyers, deputies, defendants, and witnesses filter into the outer offices like ants, while the judge is probably inside his chambers reading the sports pages.

"Hey, Gideon, what have you been up to?" Dan Bailey, an attorney who has recently left our office for private practice, asks, a little wistfully, it seems to me.

We stand in front of the docket clerk's desk and shake hands formally, as if we were opposing counsel. "You rolling in it, yet?" I ask Dan. The firm he has joined has the reputation of representing anything that has a heartbeat, so, essentially, he hasn't improved his lot in life, since he doesn't get a regular paycheck. Such is the mystique of private practice. I can't afford to starve just yet.

Amy nudges Dan in the ribs. "Gideon's got Hart Anderson's wacko murderer, didn't you know?"

Dan pretends to wince and then grins. "That's a great one. Greta still setting you up, huh?"

I pretend he hasn't scored a direct hit. "Hey, it's a winner. I begged her for it. I paid Chick off to get it."

Dan snickers. "You paid him off or pried him off?"

Amy tilts her head back and rolls her eyes. "You guys. You're worse than prosecutors."

His hands flapping happily against his sides, Dan says, "Us, nothing. Hey, I'm outa there. I'm big time. I got an alleged prostitute this morning who's gonna pay me a hundred bucks—someday."

I forget how much I liked Dan. He always knew the score on everybody, including himself. "Better take it out in trade," I advise, "inflation being what it is."

Dan picks up his briefcase and bangs it against his knee. "Good point!" he says. "By the time I get my money, it won't even be worth a blow job."

Amy puts her hands over her ears. "Please. I feel like I'm in the eighth grade again."

"You love it, Gilchrist," I tease her. "You're just too good to admit it."

We decide we better ask for a two-day trial. Psychiatrists can't do much but talk, but they can do that.

June Keaton, Jamison's docket clerk, looks down at her calendar and says: "How about the first and second of March? We just had the Owens murder plead out, so I have an opening."

I feel my throat tighten. That is only slightly less than a month from now. "That's not enough time," I tell Amy. "I don't even have a shrink to examine Sarver yet."

Amy purrs, "Let's keep it, and if in two weeks you see you're not going to be ready, I'll tell Judge Jamison what happened and get us a continuance."

I check my calendar. That week is as good as any other as long as I can get the trial put off if I need to. It just means I'll have to get to work instead of fantasizing about the case. "What about Bracken?"

Amy is already looking through the Rolodex on June's desk. "I'll call him right now."

As Amy calls Chet Bracken, I try to figure out why Phil Harper would want such a quick trial. The only explanation I can come up with is that Phil is taking more heat for charging Jerry Kerner than he figured he would and wants this case to be behind him.

"It's fine with Chet," Amy says, handing the phone to June. "By the way, Phil told me that he wanted to talk with you after we set a trial date. Have you got a few minutes?"

The great man himself! "Sure," I say and follow Amy to the prosecutor's office, wondering if I'm going to get an even better deal than I've been offered. As she leads the way down the wide corridor in the inner sanctum of the maze that houses the prosecutors of Blackwell County, she is unusually quiet, as if Phil is on his own with whatever he is going to drop on me. At the end of the hall (the opposite end from her own office), Amy knocks, then pushes open the door and disappears. I wait outside, perusing the law books that line the shelves in the hall. How much of this case (if it goes off), will Phil let Amy try? Oddly enough, unlike most prosecutors in his position, as a trial attorney Phil is surprisingly awkward in court. Yet what saves him and makes him so effective is the sincerity he projects. He is like a shy and quiet preacher who conveys the feeling that the last place he wants to be is standing in front of his congregation to lecture it on its responsibilities. That kind of preacher tends to be believed.

Consistent with this image is the way he won his election, surprising everyone by sneaking into the Democratic Party runoff four years ago and then shocking them by actually winning it. Before that, he had been a mere assistant prosecutor whose record was much more impressive than those of the attorneys in the office who got more publicity. When his record became known, he won the general election going away. But no one seems to know him well. There are few stories about him, none juicy. Married with two kids, he keeps his mouth shut and lets his record speak for itself. A most uncommon achievement in a state whose politicians battle for headlines like pit bulls turned loose on old ladies. This is what is unnerving about Kerner's indictment. Phil isn't known to go out on a limb.

Amy opens the door and motions me in. Phil rises immediately and grips my hand with all the force of a three-year-old child.

"How are you, Gideon?" he mumbles, not quite looking me in the eye.

The longer he stays in office, the shier he seems to become. Every year he tries fewer cases himself and prefers to work with someone like Amy, who attracts all the jury's attention. Of average height, he manages to stoop slightly and has the look of someone who hasn't had a good shit in years. Despite his success, it is hard to take him seriously. "How are you, Phil?" I ask.

He nods uncomfortably and motions for me to sit down as he lowers himself into his chair. Back pain, I bet. He is holding himself like Ken Averitt in my own office. I look around the spacious room at the art work, hopefully done by his kids. On the wall behind him among the diplomas is a master of divinity degree from a seminary in Dallas. I had forgotten he actually was a preacher at one time. I look over at Amy, who has chosen a chair over in the corner as if she wants to distance herself from this conversation.

"Not so good," he says in a voice so low I have to lean forward to hear, "if you take Mr. Bracken's word that I've charged his client unfairly."

I finger a pen in my pocket, testing whether its cap is on. Yesterday in staff meeting Brent looked down to see his pen leaking between his legs, prompting Leona to observe that "crotch rot" had set in at an unusually young age. "Chet," I say, "makes a lot of noise and usually gets rewarded for it."

His hands behind his head like a prisoner of war, Phil turns his head toward Amy, who is uncharacteristically poker-faced. "Amy says that you seem to have the opinion so far that Mr. Kerner probably didn't have anything to do with Mr. Anderson's death."

"As I told Amy," I say, wishing she would show a few signs of life, "it's a little early to know."

"Gideon," Phil starts again, "I'd like to keep what I'm about to say completely confidential. It's not evidence or even close to it. Can you agree to that?"

I don't like the looks of this. Amy is looking down at her hands, a pose I've never seen her in. Yet, like every lawyer I know, I'm a sucker for gossip. "Even from Greta?" I ask. If she knew I was doing this, she'd grind her new two-hundred-dollar winter boots through the back of my neck.

"From everybody," Phil says, his long face and nose chopping the air.

I've kept a few secrets in my life. Not many, though. Hoping for a laugh to break the mounting tension, I say, "Cross my heart and hope to live."

Phil's thin, bloodless lips don't even quiver. "Have you ever heard any talk about things happening to people who beat Chet Bracken in court and who he considered used unfair tactics?"

I look quickly at Amy, who stares over the top of my head. "Those must have made the rounds before my time," I say, making sure to keep this conversation in the realm of speculation.

"I won a case against Chet a few years ago in which the key witness, an old con, put away one of Chet's drug dealers," Phil says slowly. "Convinced the state's witness had perjured himself, Chet, the story goes, had his knees broken. I can't prove it, of course, since broken knees have a way of affecting a victim's vocal cords when the PA's office comes around."

I give Amy a hopeless look. What has this got to do with my client? I know already I'm not supposed to trust Chet Bracken.

For the first time Amy speaks. "Gideon, do you know who the lawyer was who represented Jerry Kerner in his divorce case?"

Stupidly, I had forgotten. Chet Bracken, of course. "Yeah, I know," I manage. My mind takes the final leap. "You actually think Chet Bracken could have helped Kerner set this up because he was pissed about the way Hart Anderson blackmailed Kerner with pictures of him screwing his patients?" I say, my voice hitting another register.

Phil backs away immediately. "I don't think anything," he says, standing up. "I'm just telling you a story you promised not to repeat."

I nod, knowing he won't say more. I stand and ask him, "Is the ten years for Perry's testimony against Kerner solid?"

He takes my hand again and limply shakes it. "You have my word."

I nod dumbly and leave, pondering this new information. It is true that Chet Bracken doesn't like to lose under any circumstances. But killing a lawyer over it? Of course, Phil hasn't accused him. Yet, as he has intended, he has planted the idea in my head that Chet had told Jerry Kerner how he could pull it off. Chet knows as well as I do how little time someone who successfully pleads not guilty by reason of insanity can spend at the state hospital. I wouldn't be surprised if Chet had known Perry Sarver a long time, maybe even represented him at some point. I push the button for the elevator. If I were in a hurry, I'd take the stairs. Glaciers move faster. A Blackwell County deputy sheriff with two handcuffed prisoners in orange jumpsuits comes up to wait beside me. I nod at the man, who has a reputation for liking to use a nightstick—always in self-defense, of course—when things get out of hand at the county jail. I emerge from the east entrance to the courthouse and run into my boss, who, for a change, is without Chick. I had called the office before I left home to notify her I was missing the staff meeting, but I cannot escape a dirty look since, like every administrator, she considers her meetings sacrosanct. A raw north wind whips us both as we stand outside the glass doors. It must be twenty-five degrees. I struggle with an old pair of shrunken black gloves. "We've got a trial date in Sarver the first two days of March," I offer, hoping to mollify her with some news. I add, "I could use a little help, maybe from Brent."

With the collar to her white wool coat turned up in back, Greta looks like a haughty queen who is granting an unwanted audience to one of her least favorite subjects. "You didn't even give yourself a month to get ready!"

I explain that I can obtain a continuance if I can't get Sarver evaluated. "I'm going to need some help, though."

"When he's free," Greta says, drawing her coat around her like an ermine robe, "I'll let Brent come out to cover a few hearings for you in the afternoons."

I have no doubt Greta would like to see me blow this case. "How much can we spend for an expert?"

Her cheeks are red from the wind, or perhaps from anger. "If you would come to staff meetings like you're supposed to, we wouldn't have to talk about your cases outside," she says, glaring at me. "When I get the time, I'll check the litigation budget."

Driving to the state hospital in the Blazer, I think of the contrasts in our offices. The prosecutor is practically accusing the best criminal-defense attorney in the state of murder; the public defender doesn't even have time to discuss the case. Yet I wonder how eager I would be to take on this case if I were in Greta's shoes. It is a no-win situation for her. Hart Anderson was undoubtedly an acquaintance, if not a friend, of the U.S. District Attorney, Hal Carver, who would be Greta's boss if she gets up there. The damn state is too small. A politician can't turn around without bumping into somebody who can do her a favor. I wonder what Greta would say if I told her what I have just heard. Maybe she knows more than I think. I suspect I'm not the first person to whom Phil has told the knee-cracking story in confidence. Maybe everyone knows what is going on except me. I have never heard a word about Bracken's pulling a stunt like having someone hurt. From what I know of him, I wouldn't put it past him. He is a fanatic, and people like him have a hard time knowing when to stop. Yet where is the proof that Jerry Kerner hired my client? It's not there, unless Phil comes up with some harder evidence than he has so far. Or unless Perry implicates Kerner. I will talk to Perry this afternoon.

The Blazer bucks at every stoplight. Maybe I should ask Rainey to take a look. I had a tune-up just a month ago, but maybe I should have left it alone. It sounds as if it resented the intrusion. The old adage "If it ain't broke, don't fix it" probably applies to the legal profession as well. What do I do with this gossip? Nothing, probably, except stay suspicious as hell of my own client's story. Yet it is tempting not even to look for another expert witness. I've got the best expert witness I can have—Sarver's own doctor. I can always argue to the jury: "Who knows Perry better than his own psychiatrist? If she says he is not responsible for killing her husband, then if you are going to listen to psychiatric testimony, this is the person you have to admit is the most qualified to give it in this case. We haven't gone out shopping for a doctor who will give us a paid opinion that our client isn't responsible. How can you expect a psychiatrist to go back and give you a realistic assessment of a man's mental condition after the fact? Dr. Berrenger says he can do it, and we could have hired a psychiatrist who could say the same thing and come up with the opposite opinion. But you have heard from the one doctor who can say she isn't relying on the magic of hindsight, and her opinion is blah, blah, blah."

It sounds pretty good to me in the car, but whether a jury will be impressed is something else. How much will Phil and Amy be able to argue that Carolyn Anderson's guilty conscience has affected her judgment? Having interviewed her, I am afraid she is honest enough to admit that it could well be swaying her feelings. I can hear Amy singing to the jury: "Dr. Anderson is way too involved in this case to give an unbiased opinion about Perry Sarver's ability to appreciate his actions in this case. She has all but admitted that herself. . . ."

I'm convinced I have to get another opinion that Sarver was crazy, but whose? The ideal person is someone who hasn't testified for a criminal defendant before, but anyone with those credentials isn't going to want to get involved, not with the little money we can offer. I am so distracted that I miss the turnoff and have to get off past the state hospital. Before it is set for trial, a case seems academic. Now panic has set in, and I'm running around like a child looking for his mother. Fortunately, my first case is delayed because the witness hasn't shown up yet, and I sit in my office making a list of what I have got to do:

1. Talk to Sarver again and get some facts.
2. Line up witnesses who can give the jury a picture of Sarver before and during the time he went crazy.
3. Talk to Carolyn Anderson again.
4. Read up on the insanity plea and how to cross-examine a shrink.
5. Hire an expert witness.
6. Talk to Berrenger.

Writing all of this down has a calming effect. My big problem as a lawyer has always been organization. My theory, after endless testing, is that either you are born organized or you are born scattered. My resolutions to systematize my work have had a shelf life of about four days. After a week of semi-neatness my methodology reverts to what I call the vertical-stack-filing system. It's in there somewhere. My phone rings. Rainey, I hope, and it is.

"Hi!" she says, sounding fresh and happy, as if she has been in bed all weekend.

"Did you see any convents you liked?"

"Convents!" she exclaims. "What are you talking about?"

I doodle on my legal pad. "You want to go to lunch or not?"

"I brought enough from home for two," she says. "Come to my office, and I'll give you something a lot healthier than red meat."

"Okay," I say, feeling a little better. What do I need red meat for anymore? You don't need any strength to talk. I can forgo the roast-beef sandwich I brought. I wish I could run my conversation with Phil Harper by her, but instead ask, "How was Memphis?"

"Fun," she says brightly. "I'll see you about noon."

I put the phone down and smile. I got it bad. I have written her name and drawn a heart around it.

The rest of the morning is more comical than anything else. Hugh Bixby is mad because the principal witness is fifteen minutes late and nearly dismisses the petition until Danny Goetz begs him to wait a few more minutes. Hugh finally gives in, perhaps because he is late himself every other day. Thinking about Phil, I whisper to Danny that Hugh looks like he could benefit from a laxative and Hugh asks me what I have just said. I have to lie, and tell him I have an upset stomach, and Danny starts to laugh, making Hugh furious. When the individual who filed the petition to commit my client finally shows up (my client's mother) she probably thinks he is the one who is about to be committed because Hugh is so pissed. My client, a twenty-two-year-old kid by the name of Bobby Orsini, is suffering from bipolar disorder (manic-depressive).

Mrs. Lila Orsini, who looks as if she could use a good night's sleep, testifies that her son is in his manic phase and hasn't slept in a week. Plus the kid writes checks the way Michael Jordan signs autographs. There is no way he is "homicidal," "suicidal," or "gravely disabled," but Hugh can't get through the day without putting somebody away, and commits my client for observation and sets a hearing for next Monday. It was either a civil commitment or a "hot check" charge, so it is probably better this way, since Bobby will get some medication that will slow him down for a while. I make a note that this kid should be ready to get out of here by then.

At noon I walk over to Unit Two to have lunch with Rainey. The word must be getting out about us since the receptionist at the front desk gives me a simpering smile that says: forget it.

I can simper with the best of them and crinkle up my eyes just like hers. Rainey comes out as I am doing this and says hastily, "Come on back, Mr. Page."

Her office has a homey look but is not covered over with the signs that appeal to social-worker types: "Today is the first day of the rest of your life." When I worked for the Blackwell County Economic Opportunity Agency I used to have a sign that said: "If you've made it to this room, you've probably already lost two days' pay." On the wall over her desk Rainey has a series of prints that revolve around William Shakespeare's Stratford on Avon—the obligatory bust but, more interesting, the inside of Trinity Church, Anne Hathaway's cottage, and a grammar school and guild chapel. Despite all the books in her house and this shrine, she still doesn't seem the literary type. Though her office is painfully small, it is not cramped with thick textbooks reminding patients of their illnesses. She has only one chair for her visitors, but it is large and comfortable, probably brought from home or picked up at a garage sale. Her desk faces the wall (she has no windows), and she faces her guest with no barriers between them.

As I sit down, she says, "Would you like me to fix you up with my secretary? I think she's married, but she might play around."

Do I detect some extremely misguided jealousy? I doubt it. Her secretary weighs two hundred pounds and has a wad of gum in her cheek that weighs half of that. I hope it is gum. I want to ask: "Does she put out?" but restrain myself. "I think she's on to us," I say, running my hands on the imitation leather arms. "Actually, we were just commiserating with each other. We have to deal with the same female day after day."

"I see," Rainey says, handing me a napkin and what appears to be a tuna-fish sandwich on whole wheat. "Well, just don't start taking office hours to wring your hands over me."

I bite into moist tuna fish. "I promise."

Just looking at her makes me glad. She is saucy, vinegary even, but pleased, I think, that I am here. For the first time, she talks in detail about her daughter, who is having her fifth identity crisis in the past year. She wants to drop out of school and join a commune but is having difficulty finding one.

Rainey, her nicely shaped legs folded up in the chair beneath her, explains, "Get this. She says it's her way of coping with her own death. If she does something meaningful, maybe it won't be so bad."

Good God! Is this what I have to look forward to? I can't imagine something like that coming out of Sarah's mouth, but who knows? She isn't going to be Daddy's little girl forever. She already isn't, but doesn't want to stroke me out with the news. This child, however, sounds as if she is seventy-five years old and has been reading European philosophy from the 1930s.

"What about religion?" I ask gingerly. Your children are sacred. You can talk about them, but nobody else can. "Does she go to church?"

Rainey looks disapprovingly at the Diet Sprite I've brought and hands me a cup of tap water. "Too bourgeois." Rainey grins. "Preachers and priests are servants of capitalism in the United States. Or as Beth says, 'Mostly male prostitutes in the service of Mammon.' "

We both laugh out loud. I dare to ask, "Were you this . . . ?"

"Weird?" she finishes for me. She takes a bit of her identical sandwich and chews, a thoughtful look on her face. "Probably. But I wasn't as politically revolutionary. I was into feminism, ecology, protesting the war in Vietnam."

I have already scored all the points I can off my Peace Corps days. "Doesn't she know Gorby says capitalism is in?"

Rainey swallows and wipes her mouth before answering. "Traitor to the cause," she answers. "History is one betrayed ideal after another."

I hope I don't have to meet her any time soon. She will order me shot on sight. "Where did you say she's going to school?"

Rainey wipes her mouth. "Ole Miss."

I bet they love her down there. "Who was her father—Fidel Castro?"

Rainey giggles delightfully. "Hardly."

What is it about this woman that makes my blood race? She couldn't be less of a flirt. If, for example, Carolyn Anderson is a ten in the glamour department, it is reaching to say that Rainey is a five, and yet, I am finding I will stand on my head to make her smile. Oddly enough, I think it is her honesty that makes her appealing to me. In the brief relationships I've had since Rosa died, the women I've been out with and I have spent our time making ourselves palatable to each other so we would have an excuse to jump into bed. Rainey, I'm convinced, wants to see my warts first. Surely she has some of her own. I ask, "She's not perfect like her mother?"

Disdaining the obviousness of my ploy, Rainey wrinkles her nose, which is straight but a trifle short. "Will it make you feel better if I confess my sins to you?"

If honesty works for her, maybe it will work for me. I nod hopefully. "Why not just a couple?"

"Okay." She works on her apple and thinks. "I was three months pregnant with Beth when Randy and I got married. Let's see. Before that I hated my mother and worshiped my father, who ran around on her until she couldn't take it anymore and left him. I was sixteen. Like the idiot I was, I stayed with him while my younger sister, Liza, to her everlasting credit, reamed him out good and went with Mom. Why? Ask me in about twenty years. I'll have it all figured out then." She gives me a bitter smile. "Does this help you, knowing I'm not Wonder Woman after all?"

Somehow it does. I reach for the other apple in the white paper sack on her desk. One tuna-fish sandwich is not going get me past the middle of the afternoon, no matter how healthy it is. "It helps explain some things."

"Don't be too sure," Rainey says blandly, reducing her dwindling dessert to the shape of a barbell. "You lawyers like quick fixes, don't you?"

I polish the light green Granny Smith on my knee. "We're not visionaries—that's for sure." I think about what she has revealed to me. If these are her principal regrets in life, she is way ahead of everybody else I know. "What happened to your marriage?"

She buries the remains of her apple in the sack. "You want dirt, huh?" She is grinning now. "It didn't have a great start, but it bumped along okay until all my friends started getting divorced, and then I guess it didn't seem to make a lot of sense. Marriage was what one did, and then divorce was what one did. When you're young, you go along with the pack and just pretend you've got your own good reasons for doing things."

For an old woman, Granny Smith is wonderfully juicy. Goodbye potato chips, hello health food. Who am I kidding? It wouldn't last a week. Am I hearing cynicism or wisdom from my girlfriend? It occurs to me that occasionally they may be the same thing. Would Rosa and I have ended up getting divorced, too? I like to think not, but maybe she was just stubborn. Colombian women put up with a lot. I look at Rainey, now busy tidying up her desk, and try to figure her out. Today, she is dressed in a pink skirt and red blouse. Yet, the colors on her seem somehow subdued, not in the least flashy. Whatever statement she is making about herself, she isn't trying to attract attention. What does she want me to see—simply that she is older and wiser? "I take it you're not into repeating yourself."

Almost under her breath, she mutters mysteriously, "Everybody, I mean everybody, repeats themselves. We just think we don't." She takes my garbage and places it in her trash can, closing, for today, the subject of Rainey McCorkle. "So how is the insanity case of the century going?"

I guess I do take it a little seriously. But she would too if she were in my shoes. "We have a trial date the first of March, and now I'm looking for a psychiatrist. Do you know one who'll testify for practically nothing that my client ought to go free?"

She arranges herself back into her chair, visibly more relaxed now that we are off what appears a delicate subject. "Who have you thought about?"

I tell her that Carolyn Anderson has recommended a woman named Margaret Howard, but she doesn't have much experience.

From a desk drawer Rainey withdraws a telephone book and turns to the Yellow Pages. "I don't know her, but I suspect a woman would be more sympathetic."

The idea doesn't much appeal to me. Carolyn Anderson will already be testifying. A jury may wonder why there are two women. "I'll call her," I say, "but she won't be at the top of my list. I didn't think you were in favor of what I'm doing."

Rainey gives me a sly look, her eyes half shut. "If I have to go out with you, I don't want people saying you're a fool."

"Thanks," I say dryly. She may never admit it, but she likes me, I think.

Before the afternoon is out, I find time to make some calls. I'm told on the phone by secretaries and the doctors themselves not only no, but hell no. They don't do forensic examinations; they don't have the time; and there is not enough money in the universe to get them involved once I tell them the case.

Right before five I call Margaret Howard, who tells me that she can see me a week from Tuesday. Thinking there is no way for her to accept this case, I tell her the trial date, but she assures me that if we work out a satisfactory arrangement she will have time to examine Perry. Given the reception I've received thus far, Dr. Margaret Howard (whoever the hell she is) looks like my best hope.

My last call is to Carolyn Anderson's office to set up another interview. I hear a recorded message that Dr. Anderson is out of the office for a few days. Impulsively, I call her number at home but get no answer. Damn psychiatrists. All of a sudden I can't even get one to talk to me for longer than five minutes.

At least Perry Sarver hasn't gone anywhere, and I drive over to Rogers Hall to see him, realizing that I am now more curious than ever about what he will say.

Inside the first door, waiting for the receptionist to throw the switch that will snap back the lock to the second door with a crack that always startles me, I think of how truly hideous it is to be locked up in this place. Behind the receptionist's cubicle to my right is the cell block where thirty male criminal defendants wait for their evaluations. I was given a tour of the cell block when I first began representing clients at the state hospital, and I still remember the sick feeling I had as I passed by the cells and looked at the men caged inside. Some of the men (all of the women—there is only room for six—are kept together in a small room during the day on F Wing, whether they are undergoing observation or have been committed for treatment) were naked or almost naked, chattering like monkeys to no one in particular. Never in all my life have I seen such concentrated horror. The look in many of their eyes was one of utter wildness. Compared to some of those who were in restraints even in their cells, Perry Sarver looks like a choirboy. The psychiatrists were uncertain as to whether they could begin treatment on individuals sent to Rogers Hall for observation to determine if they were competent and legally responsible, so unless the men were uncontrollable they went untreated until the court issued an order on them. Granted, some of the creatures back on the cell block fake symptoms of mental illness, but what I have seen in their faces has convinced me that most of them are not.

As usual I jump when the bolt slams back inside the white metal door and I enter the tiny visiting area for all of Rogers Hall, which maybe has room for six or eight people at a time. Though visiting hours are over at four-thirty, I will visit with Perry in the staff break room down the hall where I can use a table. On the other side of the wall and farther down the corridor is another locked door which leads to A and B wings, where sixty men spend most of their day in two large rooms. Upstairs are the bedrooms. There is a game room, a gym, and a walled courtyard, and that is it—a prison environment called a hospital. If you aren't crazy when you come in, there is a good chance you will be by the time you get out. There is talk of doing some remodeling and rearranging inside Rogers Hall while Units Three and Four on the open units are being renovated to make the confinement of the criminally insane constitutional. Rogers Hall has been bad so long it is difficult to imagine any improvements.

As I wait for Perry, I realize how little information I have that will allow me to start investigating this case. Theory is all well and good, but a jury is going to want to see and hear some warm bodies who can tell them about Perry Sarver. I have asked that his records be brought up with him, so I can get some idea about his case.

As he comes in with the technician, a man my own age whose face has the permanently swollen look of a boxer who fought too often out of his weight division, Sarver, I notice right away, seems better. He is yawning as usual from the medication, but gone are the weird mannerisms he so vividly displayed the first day in court.

The tech gives me the records and leaves us alone. "How are you doing?" I ask. It is hard at this moment to imagine this man ever killing anyone, because without the bizarre behavior, he appears harmless. If he stays like this, it will be a plus. Some patients radiate hostility. One look at them would give a juror nightmares for a month. Sarver, however, right now, looks mild, even gentle.

"Sleepy," he says. His voice is still flat but whether from the medication or a symptom of the illness I don't know. He is dressed in sneakers, a blue work shirt, and white cotton pants. He sits down across the table from me.

"We have a trial date," I say. "March first and second. The state hospital thinks you are mentally ill but are responsible for killing Hart Anderson."

He stares at me. "Have you told Dr. Anderson?"

"I tried to call her but she's out of her office for a few days."

His face turns dark with alarm. "Do you know where she is?"

"No, but don't worry, I'll talk to her," I try to reassure him. "If I am going to help you, I need to get as much information about you and what happened as possible. Do you remember more about shooting Anderson?" I ask bluntly.

"Some," he says. "I think I shot him twice."

Good. This is correct, according to the autopsy report.

"How did it happen?" I ask.

He continues to yawn but gives me substantially the version that Carolyn Anderson gave the police.

"Why didn't you run after you shot Mr. Anderson?" I ask.

He shuts his eyes as if the question hurts. "Well . . . I don't know."

"What? Just say it."

He rubs his jaw and looks over my head as if he is embarrassed. "I thought we would get married or something. I know that probably sounds crazy to you." He laughs uncomfortably.

The crazier the better, but it has its own logic. With Anderson dead, the only obstacle to getting what he wanted had been removed. "Did you love her, or do you love her?"

He is sitting dead still. "Well, yeah, and she loves me, too," he says as if I am challenging him.

This statement, so direct and simple, is chilling. This guy is still sick, his delusional system intact. If I were Carolyn Anderson, I would not want this man out for a long time. I am surprised he didn't kill her, too.

"Do you really think she loves you, too?"

"Sure."

"Why?"

"I can tell by the way she looks at me," Sarver says evenly. "You know how women are."

"Sort of," I say, not wanting to anger him. I am not afraid of him, but I have an eerie feeling that he is stronger than he looks. "What did you talk about while you were waiting for the police?"

He screws up his face, trying to remember. "She was crying. I don't know. I was afraid she was really mad at me."

I have the feeling that if Carolyn had told him at that moment she hated him she would be dead today. Sarver doesn't seem the type to take rejection very well, and yet he doesn't look like the violent type either. "I've talked to Dr. Anderson. She says she thinks you used to have a girlfriend and you got real upset when she broke up with you."

Sarver, his face turning red, says urgently, "She didn't break up with me. I broke up with her. She was screwing other guys like crazy! Jesus Christ! She was an animal!"

I feel fear for the first time. Is it true that the mentally ill have on occasion superhuman strength? He is between me and the door. The room is furnished with a copying machine, a refrigerator, and a table and four chairs, the only objects I could throw at him if I had to. I find myself, probably like Carolyn Anderson, trying to pacify him. "That can make a guy feel pretty bad."

His face has started to twitch. "What a bitch! I nearly got fired because of her. I couldn't do my work or nothing because of her."

"What was her name?" I risk asking. I need to locate her. Even if she can't stand him, her testimony will help the jury to get a picture of his illness.

"Angela Satterfield."

He spits this out and glowers at me as if I were trying to defend her. I have never seen this much emotion in the four times I have been out here. "Where does she live?"

"Downtown," he snaps, "4207 Calvert."

That address doesn't sound right. Calvert doesn't go that high. I am making notes as fast as I can. "What's her phone number?"

"I don't remember."

I don't believe him. He has figured out that I want to talk to her, and it is putting some kind of pressure on him I don't understand. At least I got more out of him than Carolyn Anderson did, but she didn't need to know a name and I do.

"The prosecutor is willing to offer you a sentence of ten years," I say quickly, and watch for his reaction, "if you'll testify truthfully that Jerry Kerner hired you to kill Hart Anderson."

He looks at me as though he is hearing the name for the first time. "That's ridiculous," he says blandly. "I hardly remember him."

The tech raps on the door and hollers, "I got to take him back. You can read his records and leave them up front."

I put my pen down. It is just as well. I'm not going to get anything else out of him today. "I'll come back some other time," I tell him, but he doesn't speak. I watch the tech lead him away. Sarver walks stiffly. The medication will do that.

I look through his records, trying to find his social history. It is woefully skimpy. He has listed no living family members. There is an uncle in Rockford, Illinois, whose address I write down. After high school, he joined the Air Force. He had a job as a communications specialist, but it is not clear what he did. He was in for ten years, which makes me wonder why he didn't stay in for twenty to get some retirement. Never married. He ended up at Jacksonville Air Force Base, where he was honorably discharged last year. He got a job with At Your Service almost immediately and had been there until the murder. I write down his present address, which looks like an apartment building on Slater, one street east of Calvert. Maybe Angela Satterfield lives in the neighborhood. It will be something to check out. No previous history of mental illness, which is good for his prognosis.

I turn to the medical section and see Carolyn Anderson's name. Berrenger has been in contact with her. They agree on the diagnosis, but not about whether Sarver is culpable. Berrenger doesn't say why he thinks Sarver could appreciate the criminality of his conduct but only that in his opinion he does. The Progress Notes kept by the nurses and techs reveal little. Sarver has mostly slept, probably because of the medication. They have decreased it, and he is more alert though still sleeping a lot.

As I slide the records under the glass at the receptionist's window, I begin to have a growing doubt that Sarver is telling the truth about Jerry Kerner. He is not curious enough. He is much better and ought to be showing some interest in the charge against Kerner. He is staying much too far away from this subject to suit me.

9

"Go see Betty Logan," Amy Gilchrist says over the phone at eight o'clock on Tuesday morning, when I tell her that Perry Sarver is still claiming Jerry Kerner had nothing to do with his case. "Betty Logan," Amy says, "knows Jerry Kerner better than Jerry Kerner knows himself."

Though I do not tell Amy I have begun to suspect Perry Sarver is lying to me, I think she senses it. It was Betty Logan, Kerner's former secretary, who told an investigator from the Blackwell County Prosecutor's Office that Jerry Kerner had said to her that he would pay to see Hart Anderson dead. She also picked out a photo of Perry Sarver and told the investigator that she had seen him twice in Jerry Kerner's waiting room and that she remembered scheduling both appointments.

The difficulty in seeing Betty Logan is that she now lives twenty-five miles west of Memphis, a good two-hour drive on Interstate 40 from Blackwell County. In a voice as raspy as a carnival barker's, she tells me she has no plans to return to Blackwell County before the trial and prefers a face-to-face interview with anyone connected with it. If the prosecutor can send someone to see her, she has no doubt that the public defender's office can as well.

Yet getting my boss Greta to send Brent out to cover my afternoon hearings at the state hospital and agree to pay for my mileage is like negotiating with the Pope to allow abortion. Finally, just before noon, Greta calls me at the state hospital and says that Brent has pleaded out a robbery and will be out on the unit by one o'clock.

Frantically, I call Betty Logan back and ask for directions. She sounds grumpy but tells me to come ahead. I drive home at noon to leave a note for Sarah and by half-past one I am heading east on Interstate 40. If Greta would fill our investigator's slot, which has been vacant for a month, this trip would not be necessary. It is not as if we are looking for a Ph.D. in criminology from Harvard, but politics has to be served before anyone else is allowed to sit at the table in the PD's office. I should be the last to complain, of course.

The trip is like a homecoming of sorts. I will come within thirty miles of Bear Creek, where I grew up. Leesville, the small town Betty Logan now calls home, is about the same size. Immediately, the land is flat and stays that way on Interstate 40 except for the bump around Crowley's Ridge in St. Francis County, less than an hour's drive from Memphis.

When I was a child, cotton was king of the delta. Now soybeans have replaced cotton as the main crop. However, at this time of year the fields are bare and desolate. If I take a turn south I can be in Bear Creek in less than half an hour, but now that I'm here, I feel no urge to see the house where I grew up. Why do I not feel more for this region? Going to school before school integration (it was the late sixties before Bear Creek was forced to desegregate) and drugs had become a way of life, was a kind of white child's Garden of Eden, unconcerned as I was about our racist past. Yet, as I rumble past the intersection that would take me toward home, I realize I have a lingering resentment that thirty years haven't erased. My father, until he went crazy, was a respected pharmacist, a businessman—in short, an influential citizen in our small corner of the world. When he began to pace the streets and rant nonstop about the international Communist conspiracy, pressure was put on my mother to hide him somewhere far away. That done, without a man to protect her (there was no women's movement then), she felt she was forced to sell my father's pharmacy business for less than it was worth. Now I feel bitterness mixed with shame when I allow myself to think of my adolescent years when this occurred.

I get off Interstate 40 and follow the blacktop road into Leesville. Betty Logan's house is, as she has said, easy to find. It is one block south of the town square, where, mounted on a slab of concrete, sits Robert E. Lee astride Traveller. The town, with half its buildings boarded up, would break General Lee's heart. If this is not a third-world country, it is surely within hailing distance. What is it in our heritage that keeps us impoverished? Though it is after three, I see few children. At the corner of Maple and Hickory, I see on the left hand side of the street, as promised, the giant magnolia in Betty Logan's yard. As a child growing up in Bear Creek, I could not imagine living anywhere else. Now I cannot imagine returning there to live.

Betty Logan is more attractive-looking than her voice has hinted. A tall, thin woman with dark short hair who may be in her early thirties, she comes to the door in a snug pair of jeans and a red flannel shirt. "Mr. Page, obviously," she says and invites me in. She does not smile, and I don't have the impression I'm getting special treatment.

Her living room, with its high ceiling, seems larger than it actually is. The room smells of smoke and cold medicine. I hear someone cough in another room.

"My mother," Betty Logan explains, as she motions for me to sit on an old-fashioned love seat under a painting of a Confederate soldier, presumably an ancestor. "After Jerry fired me," she says, taking a cigarette from her shirt pocket, "I came home to take care of her. Free rent." She sits on a shiny silver metal folding chair by the door leading into the hall where the coughing sound has come from, as if at any moment she might need to get up and attend to her mother.

I unzip my briefcase and take out a yellow pad. I try to remember what Amy said when I first learned that Kerner had been charged—his secretary was mad because he wouldn't love her? I wish I had stopped at a service station to take a leak. My bladder already aches, but in this house I'm too embarrassed to ask to use the bathroom. Betty Logan and her mother would be listening for every sound.

I plunge into the interview and soon learn that Betty Logan is so honest she makes me uncomfortable. She begins, at my request, the story when she first went to work for Kerner five years ago, and I soon get a picture of a man who is obsessed with women. Betty Logan began to suspect almost immediately he was having sex with several of the women he was counseling. They would call him, and Kerner would instruct her to cancel his appointments and then would leave his office.

"It didn't surprise me at all when Hart Anderson blackmailed him with all those pictures," she says, stubbing out one cigarette and beginning another. "Jerry just hated him for that; he was paranoid his license would be revoked if it got out."

I make notes as fast as I can, afraid to slow her down. "Was he mad enough to have Anderson murdered?"

Betty Logan says patiently, as if she has covered this ground before, "Jerry was paranoid that Hart would use the pictures of him screwing his patients to have his license revoked. Neither he nor Chet Bracken believed they got all the pictures back."

I flip over the page, writing in a hasty scrawl I can barely read. This makes more sense: as long as Hart was alive, Jerry believed he was always in danger of losing his license. He wasn't motivated so much by revenge as by fear. In the next two hours, as my bladder stretches, we cover a lot of territory. Betty Logan tells me firsthand that Kerner had no compunction about adjusting his theories to any lawyer's requirements, especially Chet Bracken's.

"Jerry would have testified that little girl had been raped," she says, uncrossing her legs, "if the prosecutor had offered him more money, but the thing about Jerry is that he could set the Virgin Mary on fire and think he was doing her a favor—that's how good he was at rationalizing his behavior."

I can't stand it anymore. "Could I use your bathroom?"

For the first time she smiles. "I thought you were going to wet your pants the way you've been squirming." She points with her chin. "It's just around the corner to your right."

I grin weakly, waiting to hear if her mother is going to laugh. I go into the hall, fully expecting to see her mother's face staring at me from her bed, but I am almost disappointed that I can only see the end of her bed. I might as well not shut the door to the bathroom, it is so thin. I am surprised to find no pill bottles lying about and barely manage to resist the temptation to open the medicine cabinet for a clue as to her mother's disease. I lift the lid and aim successfully for the back of the commode. Still, it sounds like Niagara Falls. My knees almost buckle, it feels so good to piss, and out of long habit I time my urination to see if I have set a record. Seventy seconds for one continuous stream. Not bad, but still fifteen off my personal best.

Seated again on the love seat, I ask, "Do you know if Jerry Kerner uses cocaine?"

For the only time she falters, but just for an instant. "Yes," she says and cuts her eyes to the hall.

Her eyes grow big, and I know she is silently pleading with me not to ask her if she has used it with him. If I ask, she won't lie.

"Would you say," I ask delicately, "that he had a problem with it?"

"No," she answers firmly, "at least I didn't think he did when I was there."

I nod, believing her. Chet Bracken's story that Jerry Kerner is a cocaine addict seems even more of a lie now that I know he is a user. Lawyers learn their clients lie best when they can mix in the truth.

I ask about Perry Sarver, but she has only a hazy memory of him. There was nothing remarkable about him in comparison with others who came in for counseling. Sarver wasn't the only Air Force patient Kerner counseled. Why did he recruit Sarver, I wonder. Betty Logan has no idea.

I hate to ask her about her own relationship with Kerner with her mother in the next room, but I have no choice. I put down my pen and ask softly, "You know Chet Bracken will try to make you out to be an embittered liar. How can you answer that?"

Betty Logan makes a face, as if she couldn't care less. "I'm bitter because I'm such a fool. I still love the son of a bitch, and I have no idea why. Somehow, he believes everything that comes out of his own mouth, and he can make a woman believe it, too."

I feel myself growing impatient. She is too smart to be so stupid. "No matter what he says, huh?" I ask.

She nods as we hear her mother cough for the first time in over an hour. "You'd have to be a woman to understand how he can do it. Jerry honestly believes he loves every one of the women he seduces, and they believe it, too."

They or we, I wonder. "So why did he fire you?"

She stretches and gives me a wry smile. "I was getting a little bitchy, I suppose."

I wrap up a few loose ends and then stand up. "Has Chet Bracken contacted you yet?"

Her expression turns wintry as she escorts me to the door. "He'll be coming here next week."

Just keep your mother in the next room, I think. I thank her and leave, wondering what she thinks of me. Probably not much. A man too chickenshit to ask to use the bathroom, and under any circumstances no match for the king of women, Jerry Kerner.

On Interstate 40 the wind has kicked up as the darkness settles in. I am hungry but will wait till I get home to eat. If Sarah hasn't eaten, we will go to McDonald's probably. Two hours is a hell of a wait for a hamburger, but I'd rather do that than sit down to eat dinner in Leesville (not that I was invited) with Betty Logan and her mother. But maybe she feels she's lucky. Most of us are from small towns; maybe most of us would be better off if we had never left them. I wonder if Betty Logan ever slept with Kerner. Surely she did. It would have been so convenient. But then when he wanted to throw her away, he had to fire her.

As I pass by the turnoff for the town of Stuttgart, located on the rice-growing plain of the Grand Prairie, the alleged "Duck Capital of the World," I begin to wonder what I have really learned. No hard evidence, for sure. Betty Logan didn't hear any plot being hatched by Jerry Kerner and my client; she knew of no act of violence ever committed by Kerner. In fact, she said she had never heard the man raise his voice in over five years—until his divorce. Yet my feeling that Kerner hired my client to kill Anderson has been clearly reinforced by this woman, who admittedly suffers from unrequited love. Revenge, in my experience, is too fickle a motive. It must be acted on quickly, or it dissolves into mere harsh words; blackmail, on the other hand, is a festering invitation to murder. Anderson, if it is true that he kept some pictures or even left the impression that he might have, may have made a fatal mistake. While I have Betty Logan's impressions fresh in my mind, I should interview Jerry Kerner as soon as possible. I will call Chet Bracken tomorrow.

I arrive home at seven-thirty and find Sarah waiting anxiously. Often we pretend she is an adult but tonight there is such relief in her voice that she sounds as if she were entering adolescence rather than emerging from it. Later, over two bowls of canned soup (neither of us wants to go out in the cold again), I tell her about eastern Arkansas, and she listens politely but cannot keep from yawning. After all, the Civil War was light-years ago. Robert E. Lee was a boyhood hero of mine; to her, Marsh Robert seems like a poor, benighted soul if there ever was one. Sarah has difficulty understanding how anyone could possibly fight to defend slavery. I have no answers, but the older I become, the more I realize that I am no better or worse than the people around me.

"If I had owned some land back then," I tell her as I watch

noodles slip off my spoon into my soup like so many escaping worms, "I would probably have bought slaves, too."

Sarah shakes her head firmly. "No, you wouldn't have."

I wipe my lips, not willing to expend the energy to argue the point. Why should I discourage my own child from thinking I'm better than I am? So I change the subject, and we talk about her school. Let her learn the hard way that her old man is like everybody else.

"Oh, I forgot to tell you," Sarah says as she does the few dishes, "a man named Chet Bracken phoned about twenty minutes before you came in. He wants you to call him tonight. His number is by your chair in the living room."

I go into the living room and pick up the scrap of paper with Bracken's number written in Sarah's oval handwriting. The prefix tells me he is calling from his office. The man is obsessed. "How did he sound?" I ask.

"Irritated," she calls, "that you weren't here."

Bracken's eagerness can mean only one thing: he is afraid that Sarver will implicate Kerner and perhaps him as well. I wait until Sarah goes into her room to do her homework, and then I call Bracken. He answers on the first ring. "This is Gideon Page," I say, no longer comfortable using his first name. When I don't like someone, I try to avoid calling him anything.

"Now that Sarver's competent to stand trial," Bracken barks at me, "there's no reason for me not to see him tomorrow."

I lean against the kitchen wall and try to relax. My blood pressure went up twenty points as soon as I heard his voice. "First let me talk to Jerry Kerner."

Bracken doesn't miss a beat. "I'll have him in my office at noon. Then you and I go see Perry Sarver."

I explain that I can drive down and see Kerner at noon, but we'll have to wait to see Sarver until after five because of my hearings at the state hospital. That is fine with him, and I hang up, realizing I could have told Bracken to meet me at the state hospital at four in the morning and he would have obliged.

Exhausted, I go to bed wondering if Chet Bracken is worried or is simply doing his job. He has only one speed—full throttle. If I were in his shoes, I, too, would want to hear Perry Sarver say that Kerner had nothing to do with the murder of Hart Anderson. Maybe this intensity is what got Bracken his reputation for being the best in the state. But he is awfully eager.

At the state hospital the next morning I have the Hardin case again. My last hearing before we break for lunch is both abbreviated and distressing. Mrs. Hardin is back with her sister, who has filed a petition to commit her. The petition alleges that Mrs. Hardin is suicidal, and my client does not deny she has not only threatened to kill herself but was caught trying to swallow a handful of Valium. Last week Mrs. Hardin had, at least, looked presentable. Today she looks as if she hasn't slept since she moved in with her sister. Without makeup she looks sixty years old, and I wonder what the woman Mr. Hardin is getting looks like. Her sister testifies in a low voice about how guilty she feels for not having seen this coming. Her eyes brimming with tears as she talks about the last few days in her home, she looks as if she, too, could use some Valium. Feeling guilty myself (I could have suggested Mrs. Hardin sign herself in as a voluntary patient until she was stabilized on her medication), I cut short my cross-examination after a few perfunctory questions and let Hugh Bixby commit her for observation.

Heading downtown on the freeway to Bracken's office five minutes later, I wonder if I accomplish anything in this job. Mrs. Hardin's depression, is, I suspect, caused in part by the realization that her marriage is over. Due process of law doesn't have much to do with love.

Chet Bracken's office is a prisonlike structure near the courthouse. Feeding a meter across the street from his office, I notice the windows are barred. Is this to make his clients feel at home?

As I open the door, I think I see why. Law books cover the walls of his reception area. He has the largest collection of legal materials I've ever seen outside the county law library. I do not think of Bracken as a scholar, but since he's a man so consumed by his profession, maybe I shouldn't be surprised.

As he leads me into his office, I think of our pitiful library and comment, "You should take a tax write-off and donate some of this stuff to us."

He grunts unintelligibly, and I let it go at that. Bracken, dressed today in cowboy boots and a dark blue suit, doesn't seem like much of a philanthropist.

As I come through the door behind him, for the first time I see Jerry Kerner, who is seated at a small conference table in Bracken's spacious, book-lined office. Smiling, he stands and offers me his hand. It is soft as a woman's, and I realize I had forgotten how short this man is. He can't be more than five feet six, and once again I marvel at his appeal to women. Granted, his face is okay, but his body is scrawny, even wormy-looking. He is wearing gray slacks and a blue velour sweater open at the throat. I see no hair peeking through and wonder what he does that is so great.

I sit down and take out my yellow pad, and for once Bracken is silent and strangely passive, letting me ask any question I want. As the interview proceeds, I realize why: Jerry Kerner has a believable explanation for every question I put to him. He admits without prompting that he threatened to kill Hart Anderson but says it was in a moment of anger during his divorce settlement. I ask him why he was angry, and he tells me the same story I heard from Betty Logan.

He leans forward against the table that separates us. "Anderson had some pictures of me in bed with women I was counseling, and I had to buy them back." He looks at Bracken and then back at me.

I write this down as quickly as I can and ask him about Betty Logan's statement that he had said he would pay someone to have

Hart killed. He admits this, too. Same motive. On the subject of Betty Logan, he is amazingly charitable. "Betty fell in love with me. If she could have kept her mouth shut," he says, his voice wistful, "I would have kept her. She was a great secretary."

It is only on the subject of cocaine that Kerner, like Betty Logan, becomes embarrassed and reluctant to talk, but reassured by Bracken's promise that I have agreed to keep this confidential, he finally admits he is addicted and has no real memory of his counseling sessions with Perry Sarver. Perry was referred to him by the air base, and that's all he can tell me. Having said that, he launches into a diatribe against Phil Harper, who he says is trying to smear him because of his testimony in a rape case.

I look at my watch. I have heard all of this from his attorney. It is ten to one, and I have to get back out to the state hospital. The only significant information that Jerry Kerner omitted was his fear (if Betty Logan is correct) that Hart Anderson hadn't turned over to him all the pictures of him screwing his women patients. Otherwise, I have learned exactly nothing except that the only way Jerry Kerner will be convicted is if Perry Sarver testifies against him, and I knew that an hour after Kerner was charged. Kerner may be lying through his teeth, but unless some other evidence turns up, he will be a free man unless Sarver turns on him. I ask Bracken if I can use his phone to let Hugh Bixby know I'm going to be a minute or two late and am told that Hugh is sick and has canceled court for the rest of the afternoon. When I tell Bracken, he looks at his watch and says, "I'll meet you out at Rogers Hall in fifteen minutes."

I'd hate to be this guy's wife, I think. He is nothing if not persistent.

Exactly seventeen minutes later, Perry Sarver is brought to us in the break room at Rogers Hall. Instantly, he appears wary, and won't even look at Bracken as I introduce him. "This is the lawyer for Jerry Kerner," I say, surprised by Perry's reticence.

Perry has never been shy before. I shut the door and stand in front of it. Perry sits in a metal chair and Bracken stands beside me. "He wants to ask you a few questions about your relationship with his client, okay?"

Sarver continues to duck his head, and I say, "It's okay, Perry. Just tell him the truth."

Bracken looks at me suspiciously, but I don't know what to tell him. Bracken says, his voice firm but not overbearing, "When did you first meet Jerry Kerner, Mr. Sarver?"

Nothing. Perry doesn't even blink and continues to stare at the concrete in front of him.

"What's wrong, Perry?" I ask.

Perry has turned to stone.

Bracken sinks to his haunches and asks him in a low voice, "Did Jerry Kerner have anything to do with Anderson's murder?"

Perry, his eyes glued to the floor, stands up and walks around Bracken and me and goes out the door, careful to shut it behind him.

Bracken explodes, "What the fuck is going on?"

I look at Bracken and shake my head. "Maybe Perry's rethinking his deal with Kerner."

Bracken, his face now red, hisses at me, "Bullshit! Kerner's not in on this!"

I put my briefcase under my arm, convinced that Bracken isn't acting. "How do you know, Mr. Bracken?"

He gives me a look of pure hatred, knowing now that he might have been fooled by his client. "You talk to that son of a bitch, you hear me?" he yelps, and stomps out past me.

I wait for a moment and then go out into the hall to look for Perry. He is standing quietly by the iron gate that separates the administrative offices from the units. "Come back to the break room," I ask, "we've got to talk about this."

He shakes his head and looks down at the floor.

"They don't want you," I whisper urgently in his left ear, "they want Kerner. With good time you could be out in just over three years."

He won't even look at me. What is going through his head?

Fear, I guess. Prisoners have a way of dying. A guard from security comes to open the door for him. I can't make him talk to me. "I'll be back," I tell him.

From force of habit I get in the car to drive to Unit Four but remember I don't have a hearing. I sit in my car wondering what to do. It doesn't take me long to realize I don't have much choice. Unless or until Perry talks or I discover some evidence, I'm stuck with trying to show that Perry was legally crazy when he shot Hart Anderson. My stomach hurts and I feel a headache coming on. I wonder if I'm coming down with what Hugh has, until I remember I haven't eaten lunch. I may not know what in the hell this case is all about, but I've figured out I'm hungry. The plain fact is I don't know a thing about Perry Sarver, and I haven't left myself much time to learn. I look in my file and find the address at which Perry was living when he killed Anderson. It won't hurt to see if I can find where Angela Satterfield lives, though my impression is that the address Perry gave for her is wrong.

After two beef tacos and some cheese dip at the Taco Bell on Jefferson, I head back downtown for the third time today. Large houses on broad streets give the Slater Street area an innocent appearance, but closer inspection reveals that these old, once stately homes have been chopped up into virtual beehives. Many years ago this area was all white; now it is integrated by poverty. Drugs and crime are in abundance down here; it is not a place I would bring a date for an evening stroll.

After knocking on several doors I find Sarver's former landlord, a big, ugly guy who looks as though he moonlights as a bouncer at the Lovetrap, the neighborhood's local spot. He professes not to remember Sarver, which doesn't surprise me. Renting by the week, he says, he has too many tenants and makes it a point not to remember anyone unless they cause trouble.

Standing in front of his door, he crosses his arms, which are tattooed with the American eagle and the hammer and sickle, apparently a gesture of superpower solidarity. "You accept the premises as is, and if you don't pay your rent, you move within twenty-four hours," he lectures me, obviously thinking I'm here to rent despite my introduction that I'm an attorney from the public defender's office looking for a witness in the Hart Anderson murder case.

I show him a picture of Sarver from the paper and a dull light comes into his beady eyes. "Yeah," he says, "I rented to that guy. He paid okay until they put him in jail. That's all I know, though."

I ask him about Sarver's personal possessions. Without a trace of defensiveness in his voice, he tells me, "All possessions are put out on the curb as garbage once I have to evict you."

Realizing there is no way I'm going to convince him that I'm not dying to move in, I ask if I can knock on a few doors and talk to some of his tenants.

Magnanimously, he says, "Of course."

Nobody I find at home will admit to having heard of Perry Sarver or Angela Satterfield, and after canvassing a few doors on Calvert Street, I call it a day and head for the office, wondering why Perry lived down here and whether there really is an Angela Satterfield.

In my message box there is a slip that informs me Chet Bracken would like me to phone him.

"He's called twice," Laura, our receptionist, tells me.

I bet he has. In my office I call Bracken. "I don't know what's going on," I tell him. "He won't talk."

"You call me when he does," Bracken commands. "Jerry Kerner is a lot of things, but he's not a murderer."

How does he know? "I'll do that," I say and hang up.

Before I talk to Perry Sarver again, I want to find something out about him. And then I will call Chet Bracken.

Hugh Bixby squirms uncomfortably behind the table that serves as the bench in involuntary-commitment proceedings at the state hospital. "What I've been told is that Dr. Reardon has been diagnosed with pneumonia," he says. "He probably isn't going to be at work until this coming Friday."

My client, Bobby Orsini, whispers to me, "That's almost a whole week away. I want out of here today."

"Your Honor," I say, getting to my feet, "the statute says a person has to be released if their forty-five-day hearing is not held within the seven-day period."

Danny Goetz stands and strokes his beard. "Dr. Reardon was admitted to St. Thomas this morning, Your Honor. He obviously couldn't be here."

I glance to my right at my client's mother, who is sitting in a chair by the bailiff. She is biting her fingernails and gives me a look of undisguised contempt. "Dr. Reardon is not the only psychiatrist," I say, trying to keep the sarcasm out of my voice, "employed by the state hospital."

Danny says quickly, "As the court knows, and you, too, Mr. Page, the state hospital is extremely short-staffed at the moment."

"The state's problems," I argue, "can't affect my client's rights under the statute."

Hugh folds his hands in front of him. "I know how the statute reads, Mr. Page," he says, "but I can't help but think in this kind of situation the court has the inherent power to grant a continuance for good cause. If Dr. Reardon can't testify next Monday or the hospital doesn't have someone here who can, I'll release him then."

I try to contain my anger, but I can't. "You're violating his constitutional right to due process as well as violating the statute. Are you aware of that, Your Honor?"

Hugh, knowing Bobby Orsini will be eventually released before I can get an appeal to the Arkansas Supreme Court, says mildly, "I'll note your objection, Mr. Page. Let's go to lunch and start up again at half-past one."

Mrs. Orsini slumps in her chair with relief. I lean over and whisper to Bobby Orsini that I think we have a good chance to get him released next Monday. By then, his medication should have kicked in. I thought he would be better by today, but he seems shakier than when I saw him last week.

Danny claps me on the shoulder, laughing. "Get working on that appeal!"

"Kangaroo City," I mutter and go back into my office to wait for Brent Hoover, who is coming out to take my afternoon cases so I can begin to check out Perry Sarver. I am halfway through a ham sandwich and a bag of potato chips when Brent barrels through my door.

"You've probably saved the worst cases for the afternoon," Brent says glumly, looking at the files on my desk. He sits down in a metal folding chair and makes it shudder. It has been almost a week since Greta let him take my afternoon hearings so I could drive to Leesville to talk to Betty Logan. With only three weeks until the trial, Greta has relented and has promised to let Brent take more of my hearings so I will have time to prepare for the Sarver case.

"It doesn't make much difference today," I say, noticing that Brent has dressed almost decently. His gray wool trousers have a crease in the right place; his shirt is ironed and neatly tucked into his pants, but somehow the heels of his shoes, black, I think, are caked with mud. I start to jump him, but what the hell? It's not as if we're before the Supreme Court.

"Where're you going?" Brent asks, noticing my stare, and leans down to scrape off the big pieces.

"At Your Service," I say, handing the afternoon files to him. "It was Perry Sarver's employer."

"Bring back something to eat," Brent asks plaintively. "I ought to get something out of this."

"Virtue," I remind him, "is its own reward."

He grins, studying a wad of slime now on the floor. "Whatever PR person made that up must not have had much to work with."

I hand him a dirty tissue to pick up the mess. "I suspect it was a philosopher."

He wrinkles his pug nose and holds my tissue with his right thumb and forefinger. "Same difference."

Anxious to get away from the state hospital, I tell him, "I've made detailed notes for you on the cases. You won't do any worse than I've done."

As I am walking out the door, he calls me back. "When are you gonna let me go see Sarver with you?"

I haven't said I would. "There's no hurry." Perry is still keeping his mouth shut (at least he hasn't called me since our meeting with Bracken), and I am, too, for the time being. I want to find out something about him before I talk with him again. If he has any beans to spill on Kerner, he'll let me know.

I ask Brent the question that has been on my mind since I've seen him. "What girl dressed you today, Brent?"

He gives me a distracted smile and drops the tissue on top of the mess on the floor. "Bethany—she's new."

Girls can't resist taking care of Brent until they find out he really is eleven years old. I can't stand it any longer and reach down and pick up the mud and drop it into the wastepaper basket. "Better keep her for a while," I advise.

. . .

As I drive out to At Your Service, I mentally rehearse my upcoming appointments. In the next eight days I will interview three psychiatrists. Tomorrow afternoon (if Brent shows up, as Greta has promised) I will go talk to Margaret Howard, the psychiatrist referred by Carolyn Anderson. Wednesday afternoon at five I am to see Carolyn Anderson, who is finally back in her office (she has been ill), and Dr. Berrenger, the state psychiatrist who examined Sarver, has finally made time to see me next Tuesday.

Of the three shrinks, I am convinced that only Carolyn Anderson can really help me (Berrenger could burn me, of course). I think of the saying about virtue's being its own reward. Look what it got Carolyn Anderson: a dead husband and a guilty conscience. Rainey explains Carolyn's attraction to an asshole like Anderson as a matter of opposites attracting. Carolyn Anderson's halo glows brighter each time I hear something about her. Last night on the phone Rainey told me that Carolyn gives free psychiatric counseling to AIDS victims. She had received a memo on it as a referral source. I confess I have a horror of AIDS, so I find this commendable. Before Rainey I spent much of my time with women listening to their sexual histories. Oh no, I haven't had sex for years and the last man had just come out of a ten-year coma. Yeah, I went out with a man for a while but he didn't have a penis. But I guess some of my stories were just as pathetic. No, I won't submit to a lie-detector test. Is that really a polygraph machine on your bureau? Gee, I hoped you were into measuring earthquakes. Well, I've got to be going. I have already flunked Sexual History enough times not to take the test with a straight face. Only one partner in the last year? Sure, and the check is in the mail. But when Rainey tells me there has been only the psychologist in the last year, I have no doubt. Of course, at my rate of progress, the information is purely academic. Perhaps someday she will surprise me in the nursing home. The truth is, although she is driving me crazy, I respect her for holding to her guns. I tell Rainey she ought to cash in some of her stock while it is still high, but she tells me she wouldn't break even at this point. I am amazed I am still in the relationship. If I didn't see signs of a breakthrough I would be in total despair, but this past Saturday night we necked like old-fashioned teenagers, passionately gnawing on each other and then pulling back. Afterward, I told her this was cockteasing in its most virulent form, but it is clear I can take it or leave it. I also told her that she must have herpes, which brought a stare that removed the final coat of paint from the Blazer.

As I sit on the brakes for a long light at Darnell and Covington, I think how little information there is on Perry Sarver. The Air Force doesn't seem to give a damn whether Perry Sarver was hired to murder Hart Anderson. I must have talked by telephone to five people at the air base and got nowhere. The red tape is not to be believed. Mention the name Perry Sarver, and it's like asking about some prehistoric beast whose records may or may not exist in some underground site in the New Zealand outback. I am hoping his employer can enlighten me.

At Your Service is a brightly lit place that has food everywhere. Salads, meats, breads, cookies, and cakes scream to be eaten. I make a note to pick up some cookies for Brent before I leave. Behind the food case is the largest man I have seen in some time. The man, in his fifties, must be six feet eight and three hundred pounds. If this is the owner, he has beaten the IRS out of a substantial sum of money. Living well is the best revenge, and this guy has got it down to a science, because he doesn't look fat; he is simply enormous. His arms billow out from a red, short-sleeved shirt that hangs over shapeless blue slacks, but, despite his clothes, he does not have a sloppy look about him. I surmise it is because of his neatly trimmed salt-and-pepper beard that gives his massive head a symmetrical look.

Ron Hurt extends a hand the size of a first baseman's mitt and invites me into his office after hollering for someone named Bert to watch the front. Inside his office, which is covered with Razorback memorabilia, he introduces me to his wife, who is even smaller than Amy Gilchrist. I can't help but wonder what goes through the minds of couples who are this physically mismatched. Love surely conquers all. I think of a poodle mating with a Great Dane and try not to wince. Mrs. Hurt is wearing a navy-blue dress no bigger than size six that might have enough material to make a shirt for her husband. She is wearing blue flats as if to make the statement that an inch isn't going to make much of a difference here. If there is no point in being stylish, you might as well be comfortable.

The Hurts seem like my first real break. They are open, pleasant, and sympathetic. For the first time, Perry Sarver appears to be a human being, instead of a mysterious and bizarre maniac. Mr. Hurt had given him a job because he, too, had been stationed out at Jacksonville once and had received his discharge there and decided to stay in the area. He and his wife had built the business from scratch and felt a preference for veterans as employees.

"Perry seemed like a nice kid," Mr. Hurt says, kneading the strings on a red-and-white football he has picked up from his desk. "I needed a delivery man and he did a good job at first."

Mrs. Hurt, a bleached blonde with dark eyebrows, who apparently is the bookkeeper, nods sympathetically. "I know he was sick when he killed Senator Anderson. He wasn't like that at all when he started here. A nice boy."

I want to go over and hug them both. A nice boy but one who goes nuts through no fault of his own. A jury will love the Hurts despite Mrs. Hurt's eyebrows. If Mr. Hurt had just played for the Hogs and she had been a cheerleader, they would make the perfect witnesses.

"How long had he worked for you before he began having problems?" I ask, feeling comfortable enough with them to shed my coat and place it on the back of my chair. They face me across a desk cluttered with paper, a calculator, and Razorback coffee cups. The room is warm, but that may simply be Mr. Hurt giving off heat. It is like being in a room with one of those early-model computers that always seem to be on the verge of bursting into flames. Mr. Hurt looks like the sort of employer who has no trouble getting his help to follow instructions.

Mrs. Hurt's blue eyes squint at her husband. "Two months?"

He nods. "Yeah, he started muttering to himself a lot and making the customers nervous. He seemed upset but he never would say what it was about."

Two months seems a long time to fake mental illness, and this would have been only the beginning. I ask Mrs. Hurt, "Did he have a girlfriend?"

She looks at her husband and gives him an embarrassed grin. "Perry? I doubt it," she says delicately.

I ask her husband, "Why not?"

"Well," he says quietly, "we always figured he was probably gay."

Gay? What about Angela Satterfield? What about marrying Carolyn Anderson? There is no sense in my pretending I am not bowled over. "Are you serious?" I ask, knowing they are but unable to believe it.

Mr. Hurt puts down the football. "I can't swear to it; there were just a couple of guys that came in looking for him every once in a while. Now, I could swear to them."

Mrs. Hurt, twisting her hands in her lap, adds, "We didn't hold it against him. My nephew is that way, and he does fine. Perry didn't flaunt it either."

I ask, "Does the name Angela Satterfield mean anything to you?"

"I never heard him mention that name," Mr. Hurt says. His wife shakes her head.

I am confused, to put it mildly. Why would he make up something like that? I assume the story about having a girlfriend cheating on him is part of his illness. Not only did he fool me, but he has Carolyn Anderson fooled. But why not? All she can do is go by what he tells her. Sarver doesn't act feminine or swish in the slightest. "Did he ever say anything about being gay?"

"Not a word," Mrs. Hurt says, her eyes on her hands, which won't be still. "But it's not something most people broadcast around here."

Mr. Hurt exhales deeply, as if he were to blame. "I said something to him about the muttering, and he asked me if he could get off to go see a psychiatrist during the day, and since I liked him, I said it would be fine—that all I wanted was for him to get back to doing his regular good job. Then, just like that," he says, slapping the football with his right hand, "he was in the hospital a couple of weeks, and when he got out he seemed better, and then all of a sudden he was worse, and then I pick up the paper and saw he killed Senator Anderson. I couldn't believe it."

Apparently none of us can believe very much right now, for there is silence. Finally I ask them if they would be willing to testify and give them the trial date. They look at each other and nod simultaneously. We talk for a few more minutes and I go in the back with Mr. Hurt and learn that Perry was a loner who had almost no contact with the other employees. After thanking them, I tell them I will get back to them and start out the door. Mrs. Hurt hurries after me. I turn, expecting her to tell me she has changed her mind. "Yes, ma'am?"

She holds out a plastic bag. "We thought you'd like some chocolate chip cookies."

On the way home, I mull over the news that Perry is gay and wonder if it has any significance. It isn't until I park the car in the driveway that I remember the gossip about Hart Anderson's being bisexual. Could this somehow have been a lovers' quarrel? It seems so improbable that I can't take it seriously. Not that it isn't possible, but it doesn't fit in. If it had been a lovers' spat, Sarver wouldn't have gone to the front door and shot him and then just stood there while his wife called the police. Sarver is crazy. Not only does Carolyn Anderson believe that but also the state psychiatrist. That has to be the starting point. But maybe it is incidental to everything. I back up a step. Maybe Sarver isn't gay. Maybe, just like me, he has a gay friend or two. And maybe this is part of the cover Jerry Kerner and possibly Chet Bracken worked out for him: he gets out of the Air Force, gets a job, starts getting sick and goes to a woman psychiatrist, pretends to fall in love with her and kills her husband (my transference theory again) and pleads not guilty by reason of insanity with the help of a willing dupe at the PD's office. Who knows what the true story is? The way I jump to conclusions, it is a wonder I have ever won a case.

At home we have a major crisis. Chick's brother has popped the question: a real date. Not one of these group activities that are about the only things I approve of in her generation, but an honest-to-goodness come-to-the-door, drive-to-the-movie (I hope), and then God-knows-what-and-where date. Though I have been expecting this to happen and wondering why it hasn't, now that it has I don't like it. I have been counseled by Marty on this subject, but I have forgotten everything she told me.

"Come on, Dad, it's just a movie," Sarah says, standing in the kitchen, watching me open cans. "He hasn't asked me to move in with him."

Why don't they make more vegetables I like? It seems we eat the same ones over and over. I am sick of green beans, black-eyed peas, canned corn. Give me summer and fresh tomatoes and corn on the cob. "That's what you'll be wanting next," I say gloomily, taking a can of beets from the pantry. Give 'em an inch and they'll take a mile. I look at my daughter, who is uncharacteristically wearing a dress today. What is this all about? Does this guy go for the frilly, lacy type? Actually, Sarah's dress looks fairly plain, a high-necked purple job that doesn't hug her like sweaters and jeans.

"Right," she says sarcastically. "I'll move in with him and his parents. That sounds like fun."

I look around in the pantry for something else to have. Baked potatoes and sour cream with butter? Why don't I drill a tube into my heart and pour in cholesterol by the gallon? "Didn't we say something about you waiting until you were sixteen?" I ask.

"No!" she answers firmly. "We haven't said a word, and you know it. You've talked more to Woogie about this subject than to me."

At the mention of his name Woogie lifts his head. No more dates for him. I still feel a little bad about what we had done to him when I see him from behind. I don't think he has ever forgiven me. I get two potatoes. We'll use the sprinkle-on kind of butter and limit ourselves to just a little sour cream. Sure I will.

I take the potatoes to the sink to wash them off. I temporize. "What movie does he want to see?"

Sarah scrapes the kitchen floor with her shoe. "That's not the issue," she points out. "Can I go?"

"I don't know," I say irritably, the hot water burning my hand. "I have to think about it."

Sarah's face is full of frustration. She leans forward and roars, "Think about what? What do you think you can protect me from? I could be sneaking out now, and you'd never know it. Do you think other kids don't? I could be doing anything, and you wouldn't have a clue. I wish Mom was still alive!" With these words, she runs from the kitchen crying and goes into her room, slamming the door.

I throw a potato into the sink. Who in the hell does she think she is? If I had slammed the door when I was a kid, I would have gotten a whipping. She is too old to spank, but she is acting like a two-year-old. All I said was that I wanted to think about it. I go sit in the living room and try to think. The walls could stand a coat of paint. I ought to unload this dump while it is still standing. No, I think. There have been enough changes in the last couple of years. I'll wait until Sarah graduates. I get up and go over and straighten up a picture on the wall Rosa brought back with us from Colombia. It is a scene of the famous Caribe Hotel in Cartagena. I go sit down and study it, and my mood softens as I remember how Rosa used to grab my hand and make me dodge the waves lapping up on the beach behind the Caribe. Woogie hops on the couch beside me. "Am I Attila the Hun?" I ask him.

For an answer, he tries to lick me. I nod, feeling a wave of sadness wash up against me. I guess I am. Damn it, I wish Rosa were alive, too. I don't know how to raise a fifteen-year-old girl. I don't know what to say to her. I try to talk to her about her school work and it bores her to death. About the only thing we have in common is the stupid TV. But we don't even like the same programs. I realize I think of her more as a bad wife than a kid trying to grow up. I want her to be able to talk to me about sports, politics, and my job, and if she won't do that, at least to tell me about her friends and what she is thinking about. Usually, though, she looks at me as if I had holes in my head. I wonder if I'm jealous. What do I expect? Is she supposed to sit around the house with me the rest of my life? In some societies girls get married when they are twelve. But those are usually the places where they die when they're forty. But Chick's brother? Doesn't that indicate poor judgment?

I go into the kitchen and call Rainey. "Do you think I should let Sarah go out by herself on a date?" I ask when she answers.

"What is this all about?" she asks.

I can hear the humor in her voice, and I realize this might not be the most serious problem I'm going to face as a father. I tell her what's going on, and she listens patiently as I explain what has happened.

"I know what boys are like," I say, summarizing the situation.

"You know what *you* are like," Rainey says. "Do you think he's going to rape her as soon as he gets her out the front door?"

"Maybe," I say. I hadn't thought of that, but there are stories about date rape all the time.

Rainey's voice, a pleasant soprano, moves into another register. "Good God, Gideon, you've got one of the best kids I've ever been around. She's not weird, like my kid. Don't screw this up by smothering her to death."

"She's only fifteen." I can picture Rainey sitting all cozy on her couch, a box of health food in her lap.

Rainey yelps, "What century do you think we're living in?"

"I don't know," I say miserably.

"You're worried about sex," Rainey says, stating the obvious. "She probably knows a lot more than you think she does. Do you want me to talk to her?"

"Would you?"

She hesitates only a moment. "Sure. Want me to come over tonight?"

"Maybe I should leave," I whisper, looking around the corner to see if Sarah is coming out of her room. "She'll kill me when she realizes I asked you to talk to her."

"You could go get us some yogurt."

"It's a deal," I say, relieved. "Why don't you come about eight."

I go knock on Sarah's door and apologize. "You can go," I say, "but you have to be home by nine."

For an instant she believes me, then she smiles. "Thanks, Dad."

"But you have to be home by eleven." I should feel better but I don't. "How are you getting there?"

"He's got a license," Sarah says.

A license to rape and pillage. "Did he flunk a year or what?" Now that I've said okay, I suddenly feel depressed and old. Father and daughter dating. How ridiculous. Maybe we can double-date. Somehow I don't think so. Sarah follows me into the kitchen and I retrieve the potato from the sink and put it into the microwave with its twin.

Sarah smooths out her dress and sits at the kitchen table. "He just turned sixteen this month."

Maybe he is too young to have an erection. Fat chance. I had one twenty-four hours a day when I was sixteen. Who am I kidding? I can't remember what I even looked like at sixteen. I come around the table and sit directly across from my daughter. I feel as if I am sitting down to a negotiating session with an attorney who is holding all the cards.

I say in a small voice, "Rainey's coming over tonight for a little while."

"What for?" Sarah asks sarcastically. "To tell me about the birds and the bees?"

I am flabbergasted. I begin rubbing the table to feel its finish. It could stand a little oil on it. I get up to fetch the polish. "You don't want to listen to me."

I have horrified her. "Are you serious?" she asks.

"No," I lie. "You believe anything I say."

She smirks. "Most parents hope their children would do that."

I put on a long face. "What has happened to your sense of humor?" I say, coming back to the table, rag in hand.

She sticks her tongue out at me. "I lost it when you stopped being funny."

I begin to wipe the table when she says solemnly, "If you put any more oil on this table, I'm going to scream."

Around eight Rainey knocks on the door, and I let her in, feeling as though I have invited over a young Ann Landers. She is dressed in gray baggy sweats and a long-sleeved beige T-shirt. She is happy and talkative and greets Sarah pleasantly but doesn't overdo it. Wary at first, Sarah warms up quickly and soon the three of us are talking easily about nothing in particular in the kitchen while I heat up water for hot chocolate. "You should have tasted the potatoes Dad cooked tonight," Sarah teases me. "The skins were like eating bark, and the inside you couldn't have split apart with a stick of dynamite."

They weren't that bad, but I admit, "I tried to speed things up too much."

Rainey places her elbows on Rosa's table and, seemingly oblivious to my presence, tells Sarah, "I've noticed he does that."

Sarah giggles, a friendly smile spreading over her face. "And he likes to think he is so patient."

I might as well not be in the room. I am suddenly glad Rainey and I haven't been to bed. Nothing seems off-limits between these two. Like a third party wanting to add some complaints, my tea-kettle joins in with a tremulous but steady whistle, and I get up to empty the contents of individual packets of sugar-free Swiss Miss cocoa mix for hot chocolate. Woogie, lured by the smell of chocolate or perhaps the sound of laughter, pads into the kitchen, his nails clicking on the linoleum, and surveys us with a hopeful expression. "I'm glad Woogie can't talk. Now, he," I say, "has a legitimate beef."

Sarah grins, explaining to Rainey, "Dad had him fixed."

Rainey pats her leg and calls, "Come here, Woogie! What did this mean man do to you?"

Woogie promptly trots over to her, never one to miss his share of attention. Rainey scratches his back, and leans down to check the damage. "Ouch!" she exclaims. "Your master doesn't like competition, does he?"

I bring the cups of hot chocolate to the table. Woogie jumps up against her legs, and she brings her head down beside his muzzle. "No, he doesn't, does he?" she coos.

"All right! All right!" I laugh. "Since I'm such a monster, you might accidentally get this in your faces." Sarah distributes napkins to protect the table as I set down the steaming mugs.

Still ignoring me, Rainey asks Sarah, "Have you ever noticed how bullies have such a well-developed sense of self-pity?"

Sarah sips at her hot chocolate, her eyes on me. "They have to justify themselves, I guess."

I sigh but do not speak. A half hour later, I volunteer to go out for yogurt.

Sarah, her face suddenly red as if I had slapped her, gives me a stricken look that says: I can't believe you'd really do this to me. I feign an idiotic air of innocence and make my getaway.

When I return, they are laughing and joking around in a manner that suggests that a stand-up comedian has been telling the smuttiest jokes imaginable. Is it my imagination or are they both leering at me? The air seems positively blue in the house, and I spend an uncomfortable hour feeling somehow as if my sexual shortcomings have been dissected by a pair of old girlfriends instead of the two females who can claim complete innocence.

After Rainey leaves, I demand, "What on earth did she tell you?"

Sarah pretends to yawn, swelling her chest until I am forced to look at the floor. "None of your beeswax," she says.

My child now tells me she is going to bed, having been transformed into a hardened prostitute in the space of a few short minutes. What have I done? When I left, the house was a veritable Garden of Eden. Now it seems musty with ancient knowledge. When I call Rainey later, I get the same response.

"You're such an innocent," she says, hanging up, her voice full of affection.

I go to bed feeling out of sorts. Where before Rainey and Sarah had combined to present a friendly if bullying gang of two against me, tonight was a cabal. Sadly, I realize, the women in my life have more in common with each other than they do with me.

However competent Margaret Howard may be as a psychiatrist and as an expert witness, she is not a good-looking woman, which is sort of a relief. I had not wanted two fashion models as my principal witnesses, and now I don't have to worry about it. Actually, her only bad feature is a lantern jaw that any heavyweight contender would be proud to own. You won't see a stronger face on Mount Rushmore. I expect her to offer me her favorite steroid; instead, she gushes about Carolyn Anderson.

"I'm really flattered Dr. Anderson recommended me. She is just a superb therapist," Dr. Howard tells me. "Until this horrible thing happened, she was as busy as anybody I know."

I gather that Dr. Howard, who must be no more than twenty-seven, is not as busy as she would like to be. Her office is on the edge of a downtown area that the real estate market at one time had in mind for gentrification efforts, but from the looks of the neighborhood realtors gave up in midstream. For there is a checkerboard appearance to this area: one post–Civil War home may appear newly and often elegantly restored but is followed by another that looks as though it hasn't been touched since the turn of the century, which, even Southerners would agree, is getting to be quite a while ago. The good doctor's home is, alas, in the latter category.

"I take it you get other referrals from her?" I ask, looking out of barred windows in her small study, which has the look of a converted bedroom. My potential witness is dressed in black-and-white stripes, and I feel as if I am interviewing a prison matron in an old-time B-movie who has begun to dress like the inmates.

"Oh yes," says Dr. Rocky (as I have begun to dub her in my mind), "she's been very generous. I just finished my residency a little more than a year ago, so I'm grateful for all the patients I can get." She nervously taps a cheap blue Papermate pen on her desk as she speaks.

Such candor is refreshing in a doctor but won't play so well on the witness stand. Surely I can do better than this woman. Her desk, hardly bigger than an old typewriter stand, is cheap vinyl. In fact, if there were a fire, her office furniture, which consists primarily of two black plastic chairs and matching desk, would melt down into a chemical ash you could hold in your hand. She could take the insurance money and possibly get as far as Tulsa. "I didn't realize how recently," I say tactfully, "you had gotten out of school."

"I worked at Rogers Hall during part of my residency," she says eagerly. "I got excellent evaluations out there." Tap, tap, tap.

Round two for Dr. Rocky, assuming she isn't puffing. "How did you do in school?" I ask, shifting uneasily in the chair across from her desk. I can feel it straining to hold me. Any obese patients, for their safety, surely must be required to sit on the floor, which is carpeted with a material that feels as thin as an expensive condom. This is one rug you don't have to worry will clog up the vacuum cleaner.

"Number two in my class, and I wrote a paper that has been published about the inability of psychiatrists to predict dangerousness. You know a lot has been done in that area."

I can see the headline: DR. ROCKY FOR THE DEFENSE. "Not in the *New England Journal of Medicine,* by any chance?"

She laughs, displaying a set of canines a mother grizzly would be proud of. "I'm afraid not. I've got another article that's been accepted, though. Did you know the experience of a psychiatrist doesn't increase his or her ability to predict dangerousness in a patient?''

''No,'' I say, becoming more impressed by the moment, although I am a little disconcerted by her eagerness. ''Why would you be willing to testify? This isn't exactly most doctors' favorite part of the job.'' If we win, I may donate a chair for her office. I keep sliding out of this one.

Her voice loses its saleswoman's pushiness. ''I think there may be some truth in the old saying that I don't care what you say about me as long as you spell my name right. I do care, but as you may have guessed, I need the business. Five years from now when my waiting room is full—and not in this part of town, by the way—not one of my patients will know or care what I said in a murder trial.''

What the hell? I can get her cheap, and I'm pretty sure that her testimony will be supportive. She takes the price that Greta had ordained (two thousand dollars), and I tell her I will arrange a time for her to see Sarver. She stops the tapping long enough to take a few notes as I fill her in on the details. As I am leaving, she reminds me that I will need a consent from him for her to see the records that Carolyn Anderson has on him. Of course, she will want to talk to Dr. Anderson about him. Of course. Like a prisoner glad to get to the exercise yard, she accompanies me outside and lights up a filterless Camel, blowing smoke toward the deserted street. ''I really appreciate this,'' she says and pumps my hand. ''You won't be sorry.''

''I'm sure I won't,'' I tell her and walk to my car. Has she done everything except sign a pledge in her own blood that she will find Sarver as nutty as I want him, or does it just seem like that?

Rocky's lusterless brown hair blows in the northeast wind, and she massages her arms, now folded against the iron vault of her chest. ''Can I ask you a question?'' she says.

''Fire away,'' I say, suddenly pleased with my choice. It will be nice not to have to suck up to a doctor for a change.

"Do you think it's possible Jerry Kerner hired your client?" she asks, almost shouting the words because of the wind.

I look around and am grateful for the deserted street. Discretion is not Dr. Rocky's strong point, I see. I step closer to her, and as I anticipate, she holds her ground. We are almost touching. "It's possible," I say, "but I doubt it. Do you know him?"

She looks down, unexpectedly shy. "A little," she admits. "He's a first-class scuzzball."

For a fleeting second I think she has been out with him—but surely not. "How come you know him and what do you know?"

"Just conferences and stuff," she says, staring at me. "He's smart as hell, but he'll shave his data and say anything if you don't watch him."

I blink against the low sun. "The prosecutor would love to know about you, I'm sure. He testifies a lot." I see no point in filling her in on all the scut about him. She is supposed to be an unbiased scientist, not a reporter for *The National Enquirer*.

"That's what I hear," she says solemnly. Her voice sounds wistful.

As I drive off, she waves. I have to wonder about Dr. Rocky, but at least she thinks Kerner's a scuzzball.

In the office the next morning, my choice gets mixed reviews.

"You got a woman who's only been out a year?" Chick sneers while we are all in Greta's office. He is sitting on the edge of Greta's desk as if he owned it, while she leans back in her swivel chair watching him. "The jury will take one look at how young she is and dismiss her out of hand."

If I dug up Freud and brought him into court, Chick would have something negative to say. Besides, when the jury sees her jaw, they will be afraid to dismiss her. I tell our motley crew about her experience at Rogers Hall and find myself omitting all details about her grubby office. She may be a loser, but now she's my loser. I begin to tap my pen against the edge of my chair and catch myself.

"A jury might actually buy into a young shrink better than one who's been around awhile," Ken Averitt, whose losses in the area seem his only qualification, says quietly. "Most people have an idea that psychiatry rests on pretty shaky ground, since it is obvious psychiatrists don't cure anybody. A recent graduate with a fairly fresh publication might make a jury think she knows something new."

My friend Brent, trying for a change to get his tie to lie down flat under his collar, asks hopefully, "Is she a looker like Carolyn?"

I put my pen in my pocket to keep from tapping the chair with it, and wink at Brent. "She's a looker, all right."

"That's probably why you hired her," chips in Leona, whose black skin somehow exempts her from sexual teasing except from me in the office. The old are permitted everything.

I watch Brent give up on his collar. Too much trouble. I tell him, "I think she's single, Brent. I bet I could fix you up. I wouldn't mess with her, though. She looks like she can take care of herself."

Greta, who still hasn't taken her eyes off Chick, dismisses the topic, commenting, "The price is right, and that's a main consideration around here right now. The county is running a deficit, as everybody who can read knows. We can't afford to go out and hire Dr. Joyce Brothers, so let's move on, okay?"

As I go to my office to get my briefcase, Brent comes up to me. "You're kidding me, aren't you? She's a dog, isn't she?"

No, a horse. I put my arm on Brent's shoulder and look him in the eyes. "Pound for pound, and she doesn't weigh more than one-thirty, she's the toughest-looking woman I've met in years. Tell you what. The next time I interview her, you go with me, okay? If you don't agree, I'll buy you dinner. If I'm right, though, you buy me. Okay?"

Brent, like me, only bets when he thinks he's got a sure winner, claps me on the back. "That's a deal."

On my way out to the hospital, I stop at the law library and check out Ziskin's *Coping with Psychiatric and Psychological Testimony*. Ken has put me on to it. Despite his defeats, Ken is proving to have a wealth of information, and I suspect Greta realizes that Ken was due for a win, which is why she didn't give this case to him. She wasn't unhappy at all when I told her about Margaret Howard. Good ole Giddy. He's gonna screw this case up all by himself. She won't have to lean on me at all.

At five o'clock I am in Carolyn Anderson's office. She looks sleek, as usual, probably a little gaunt, but given the fact she has recently been sick, she looks damn good. She is wearing a tight black skirt and a white blouse so sheer it is almost see-through. I imagine she is wearing nothing underneath even as I see the outline of her bra. The contrast between her younger colleague and herself is so sharp as to be unsettling. Dr. Howard exudes as much sexuality as a pet rock; Carolyn Anderson, fully dressed, makes me think of a superficially tasteful lingerie ad: I really can't see anything but I keep going back to the same page in the paper just hoping something has fallen off.

"How are you feeling, Dr. Anderson?" I ask as she takes my hand. It is moist and soft as if she had rubbed lotion into her palms just for this meeting.

"Much better, thank you," she says, as we enter her consultation room. "Call me Carolyn, please."

We sit as before, not quite so close but close enough. "My first name is Gideon," I say awkwardly. She has a disarming way of creating intimacy. I decide I'm better off if I admit to myself that a sexual current has been buzzing in me ever since I met her. I wonder if Perry felt the same way I do. "My wife died, too," I confide, gripping the arms of the chair for support. "I didn't get sick, but I didn't exactly bounce back the first day after the funeral."

"I'm sorry," she says, crossing her legs, her voice not quite as low as I remembered it. Her black stockings make her legs look like a trip I wouldn't mind taking. "I'm sure interviewing me," she adds, "has stirred some things up for you. How long has she been dead?"

One thing is definitely being stirred. "A couple of years," I say, embarrassed. I am trying to give sympathy, not get it. "I'm doing fine now. I think it's helped having a fifteen-year-old daughter to raise. I haven't got the time to sit around and feel too awful about it."

"Good," she says firmly. "Many times men run out and get married immediately. They don't handle loss well."

I find myself nodding. At this rate, she will be justified in sending me a bill. "Since I last saw you, a lot has happened," I say and then begin to bring her up to date. I tell her about Berrenger's report, the trial date, my meeting with Margaret Howard, and finally what I've learned from my conversation with the Hurts about Perry Sarver. She takes some notes, and I continue. "Before we talk about whether Perry could possibly be gay," I say, "one thing is bothering me. Perry is now refusing to say that Jerry Kerner is not involved."

Carolyn narrows her eyes and purses her lips to indicate she is uncertain that she has heard me correctly. "What do you mean?"

I tell her about our meeting with Chet Bracken and Perry's refusal to talk with him. "With the trial coming up," I add, "I think Perry is starting to get nervous and is looking for a way out."

"I don't know what that's all about," she says rather grimly.

Perry, I think, is as big a mystery to her as he is to me. "Do you think," I ask, "that Perry's gay and was making all that stuff up about having a girlfriend?"

She has been listening carefully and now leans back in her chair to think. Finally she says, "It's possible. If he gave me any clues, I simply missed them, but he may have been fighting his homosexuality so hard his mind somehow began to believe that he had a relationship with a woman, and his way of resolving it was to imagine she was unfaithful. Would you give me a few moments to look at my notes on him?"

"Sure," I say and lean back in my chair. What I like most about this woman is her utter lack of defensiveness. As I watch her read, I think of the psychiatrists I have cross-examined in the last two years. Usually, not always, I have been met by an attitude of smug superiority. Doctors know best, even when it is apparent they don't know a damn thing and are guessing along with the rest of the human race. But I don't get any feeling of arrogance from this woman. Carolyn admitted immediately she could have missed something. Her candor is impressive. While I am waiting, I look around her office and realize she has changed the pictures on her walls. Instead of the neo-Cubist images that were so jarring, she has some Impressionist prints that create a warmer atmosphere. Flowers, boats, the sea, women—almost a hothouse effect. I take off the blue suit coat I've worn for this occasion and drape it behind my chair.

Finally she says with a rueful smile, "I think that may well be what happened. All through here," she says, tapping his file with a long, blood-red fingernail, "my notes are real vague. Do you have any hard proof we could pin down?"

"No," I admit. "It's obviously possible he had a couple of gay friends, but the address he gave me for Angela Satterfield doesn't exist." Now that she is thinner, her eyes seem even larger, and I catch myself staring at her and look down. "Could he still have a transference if he was gay?"

Carolyn pats a lock of blond hair on the back of her head, raising her breasts in the process. "There is the stereotype about gay men and their mothers. It obviously has some truth in it."

If I don't calm down, I am going to need one of those sleep masks to get through the interview. Confused, I ask, "So instead of thinking he was in love with you, he thought you were his mother?"

She laughs involuntarily and puts her hand to her mouth as if one of us had committed some indiscretion. "Not exactly. Transference would be for him a re-creation of the feelings he had for his mother as a child. We still call these feelings love as adults. I'm certain he never thought I was his mother. He attached those feelings for his mother that he had as a child to me. How that ties in with his mental illness and resulted in his killing Hart, I want to think about some more. I'm not certain that it changes much. If he is homosexual, in denying it he could have convinced himself that he was in love with me, so desperate might he have been to prove that he wasn't gay."

She stops and looks at me to see if I am following. "You've done a good job getting things out of him that I never did," she says, her lovely mouth widening in a smile.

I feel foolishly pleased, like a child who has given a right answer in school. "But we don't know for sure if he is," I say, wanting her to continue to praise me for not wanting to take more credit than I may deserve. I realize I have crept to the edge of my seat, and push myself back into the chair. Down, boy!

"That's true," Carolyn says, turning to her desk to get a book. "He'll have plenty of opportunities in Rogers Hall to show how hard he is fighting it."

She flips through the thick pages of *DSM III.* I watch her, fascinated by this woman. She is oblivious to the effect she is having on me. I'm sure not doing anything to her. It seems to me she should be repulsed by the very thought of Perry Sarver, but, incredibly, she is not. I don't know how she really sees him. Perhaps this is therapy somehow for her—a way of understanding how all of this could have happened. My instinct would be to repress it. A look of satisfaction crosses her face. "You may be aware," she says, looking at me, "that homosexuality is no longer considered a mental disorder since the advent of *DSM III,* but few people are aware that the desire not to be a homosexual is a mental disorder called ego-dystonic homosexuality. Listen to this," she says and begins to read. " 'This category is reserved for those homosexuals for whom changing sexual orientations is a persistent concern. . . . Typically there is a history of unsuccessful attempts at initiating or sustaining heterosexual relationships.' " She stops and excitedly taps the page with her forefinger. "You know what I think? I think there is a reasonable possibility his homosexual disorder has precipitated his schizophrenia. He's fought it so hard it has driven him mad. Of course, all of this is sheer speculation. I should examine him again."

I can't believe she would even want to go near him. I hold up my right hand as if I am directing traffic. "You can't do that, I'm afraid." She closes the book and looks at me with an air of surprise. I realize that she hasn't been thinking of him as her husband's killer. I add, "You probably wouldn't be allowed to anyway."

For the first time since I have been in her presence, she seems a little out of control. She asks, her voice almost shrill, "I will testify, won't I?"

I feel good that I can assert some authority. "Sure. I can't call you as my expert witness, but I can ask you on the witness stand about everything you did as his doctor. It'll be an ordeal, I'm afraid."

She gives me a determined look, her red lips a firm straight line. "It'll be a catharsis for me," she says softly.

I would never think of it this way, and I doubt many other people in her situation would either, but then, she is quite an extraordinary woman. I tell her that I have contacted Dr. Howard, and she seems pleased. She assures me that she will do well as a witness. "She has a real look of rock-solid integrity, doesn't she?"

I cannot suppress a grin, but I agree. I notice she looks tired, her eyes slightly red and strained. I apologize for having to contact her again. She protests, "No, I want you to. Believe me when I say it helps to talk about it."

I believe her. I stand and offer her my hand. She takes it and I feel more warmth than when I came in. As last time, the fragrance of her perfume fills the room. Her hand is spidery light, and I can feel tiny bones pushing against the skin. "You need to take it easy," I advise. "When my wife died, I ate the most horrible food. Are you getting enough rest?"

She smiles at me. "It's hard to sleep at night without taking something, and I don't want to stay groggy all day," she says. "My patients don't appreciate it when I fall asleep."

I find myself chuckling, though my intention was to be solicitous. Before I leave, I tell her I will be in contact with her again soon after I talk with Sarver's psychiatrist at Rogers Hall, Dr. Berrenger.

She surprises me by saying, "I've already called him."

I am amazed that she would initiate this contact. "Why?"

"I called him so he wouldn't be starting from scratch. It wouldn't be fair to Perry to let him suffer. I sent him a copy of his records and visited over the phone with him for a little while."

I don't like this, but there isn't anything I can do about it now. "What do you think of him?"

She gives me a puzzled look. "He didn't say much. Obviously, he doesn't agree Perry isn't responsible, but that is his privilege. I mainly called him to let him know what I had been giving him so he could get him stabilized as soon as possible."

"You're not going to talk to him again, are you?" I don't want Berrenger to be able to second-guess Carolyn any more than necessary.

She gives me a questioning look. "I don't think so."

I try to explain my fears, and she is receptive, since it won't affect his treatment before trial. I turn to go, and she says firmly, "He shouldn't be sent to prison. You know they would tear him to pieces, don't you?"

I nod, restraining myself from confiding in her about my father. I have to remember I am not the patient. "I agree completely, Carolyn." Should I tell her that under the Schock decision Perry could be out in months if he is found not guilty by reason of insanity? I do not, but somehow I don't think it would make a difference to this woman. I ask as I am leaving, "Do you know Rainey McCorkle? She speaks very highly of you."

She pauses for a moment, obviously trying to place her. "At the state hospital," she says, smiling. "Is she a friend of yours?"

I find myself blushing. "Yes."

A broad grin covers her face. "She seems like a good social worker."

I nod. "I think she is."

On my way back to the office, I think of the hold this woman has over me. Were I not dating Rainey, I would surely be having fantasies about her. I wonder if she is as attractive to others as she is to me. Perry Sarver, crazy or not, gay or not, must have thought so. I amaze myself. I realize I wanted her reaction when I told her about Rainey. Why? Did I want her to know someone found me worth going out with? Carolyn would have smiled if I'd told her that the most I have ever done with Rainey is give her a hickey on her neck. She was furious, of course.

Back in the office, I tell Ken and Brent about my conversation with Carolyn. As I talk, I note their interested expressions. For them, too, Carolyn Anderson is intriguing.

"You better watch out, Gideon," Brent says. "You'll be wanting to lie down on her couch."

Ken adds, "Wouldn't that be strange? Having a love affair with a witness, especially one like her?"

Brent loosens his tie and unbuttons his collar. If he could get away with it, he would come to work in his pajamas. "She should be getting horny by now."

I give Brent a hard stare, feeling a need to defend Carolyn. "Sex is probably the last thing that has crossed her mind."

Brent, embarrassed, inspects his tie, knowing that I have gone through the same thing. His unspoken question is: How long did you wait? The answer is, about two weeks. Women feel sorry for men, and it is hard not to take advantage of it. I went to bed with a friend of Rosa's at a motel about a mile from the house. She was married, and we had always had a little spark between us. Sex put it out. Probably it was the guilt and shame. It made me feel better for about two minutes, and then we both felt so bad we cried.

We talk for a few minutes about the case and then go home. On the freeway, I think about how well Carolyn handled the news that Perry might be gay. All shrinks must be used to surprises from their patients, but perhaps it never is a real surprise to them. They simply haven't found out yet. It seems to me that Sarver wouldn't have been able to cover up his homosexuality when he was the sickest. I would think it would come tumbling out somehow, but what I don't know about schizophrenia would fill up *DSM III.*

I feel I will have a slight edge on Dr. Berrenger now when I go to Rogers Hall next week to talk to him about his examination of Perry. He is not going to know that Perry may be gay, and I try to think how that can be used to hurt him at the trial. Probably he will shrug it off as easily as Carolyn. There is an imperturbability about the profession that is unnerving. Doctors work in the dark as much as lawyers, but they don't show their irritation. As Brent says about the psychiatrists at the state hospital, arrogance does wonders for their self-esteem.

12

At eight o'clock Monday morning Chet Bracken and I are ushered into the office of the prosecuting attorney of Blackwell County.

"Some evidence came into our hands this afternoon," Amy Gilchrist had told me last night, calling me just when I was almost asleep, "but we can't tell you until tomorrow what it is. I think you'll be real interested in it."

While Amy, like a child who is being punished, arranges herself in a corner chair, I look at Phil Harper, who appears even more preacherlike than usual this morning. He is frowning as if he is about to deliver a necessary but unpleasant sermon. Chet Bracken is furious that Amy wouldn't tell him over the telephone last night what this is about. He glares at Phil with such hatred that I feel uncomfortable. Bracken has a permit to carry a gun. He looks mad enough to use it.

"So, Mr. Prosecutor," Bracken says sarcastically, "what is this all about?"

Instead of delivering a sermon, Phil reaches into his desk drawer and pulls out a manila envelope that he hands to Bracken. I lean over to see what is inside. Bracken takes out several pictures, and I see at once they are of Jerry Kerner and a woman. Both are naked. Kerner cannot be identified in all of them, nor can the woman. But in sequence it is obvious they are all of Kerner. Now, I can see part of Kerner's attraction for women. He is hung like a donkey. Damn.

"A member of Hart's firm," Phil Harper says, his eyes downcast, "came to my home yesterday evening and turned these over to me. He said he found them in a file cabinet in Hart's office."

Bracken throws the pictures on the desk in front of him. "They don't prove shit!"

Phil looks at me and says softly, "The state will be introducing these as evidence of motive."

Bracken, who is wearing his cowboy boots again, kicks the bottom of Phil's desk. He turns to me and drawls, "Don't fall for this shit, Page!" With that, he gets up and strides out of the room, careful to slam the door.

There is silence for a moment while I retrieve the pictures and look at them again. Phil asks, "Has Perry Sarver said anything to you recently?"

The woman in the pictures is lovely. I wonder how much she charges for counseling. "I think," I answer, "Perry's thinking about what to say to me."

Phil stands and offers me his hand. "There's still time to make a deal on this." I place the pictures back in the envelope and shake his hand. Amy gives me a sweet smile as I leave the room. Phil may not have shit yet, but there is getting to be quite an odor. I wonder what Perry will have to say now.

I do not have time to go to Greta's staff meeting because of the Bobby Orsini hearing at the state hospital. When I arrive, we begin immediately, but it is obvious that there is not much fight in Dr. Reardon, who only returned to work on Friday. Though he maintains that my client is dangerous to himself, his testimony is vague and nonspecific. Reardon, usually insufferably dogmatic, obviously is still ill and simply wants to be done. I oblige him, realizing that for once he hasn't hurt me.

I move for a directed verdict and point out that, in addition to there being inconclusive medical evidence, my client has been detained illegally for one week. It is irrelevant, of course, but I want to work on Hugh's sense of guilt, if he has one. In fact, if I lose this one, I won't be too disappointed. Bobby Orsini, if anything, has deteriorated since his original admission. He was talking nonstop until I got him to shut up just before the hearing started.

While Danny Goetz responds rather perfunctorily that Dr. Reardon's testimony constituted sufficient evidence to withstand a directed verdict, I watch Bobby's mother's face. This is her third trip to the state hospital to see her son committed. She is a haggard-looking woman of about fifty, with permanent suitcases under her eyes, and her lips are moving, obviously in prayer.

"Mrs. Orsini," Hugh Bixby says after Danny sits down, "I know how disappointed you are going to be, but Mr. Page is entirely correct. The prosecutor hasn't shown that your son is homicidal, suicidal, or gravely disabled as defined by the Arkansas statutes relating to the involuntary commitment of mentally ill persons. I have no further basis to detain him."

Not only is Mrs. Orsini in shock, we are all in shock. Sometimes, weeks go by without Hugh's doing anything other than waving defendants on into the loving arms of the Division of Mental Health. He must have stayed up late watching a rerun of Perry Mason, because he has actually followed the law for a change. I can't see the difference between this man's case and those of a lot of the individuals I've represented in the past, but I'm not one to look a gift horse in the mouth.

After the decision I advise the kid to stay on his medication and to calm down and send him on his way before he can start talking again. I get up and hurry out of the courtroom before Hugh can change his mind, walking past Mrs. Orsini, whose face is drained of color.

"Mr. Page!"

Halfway down the hall, I turn and face an angry mother.

"Do you realize what you've just done?" she says, her face now flushing scarlet.

"Ma'am," I say, hiding behind the law, "I'm sorry, but I was appointed to represent your son. The law says he has to have an attorney."

Her hands shaking with rage as she reaches for a cigarette from a bulging black pocketbook, she ignores what to her is clearly a worthless technicality. "Until these past two weeks, no one in my house has slept for a month because of Bobby," she says, shouting so everyone on Unit Four can hear. "My husband works two jobs. He is practically sick he is so tired, and instead of helping your client, you prevented him from getting help. Is that what you lawyers are supposed to do?"

"He is free to get help if he chooses to," I say, feeling sweat run down my sides. My blue pinstripe fifty percent wool suit hasn't seemed too warm until this moment. It isn't any consolation, but I don't know what to suggest in these situations.

Her green eyes narrow into slits, and her voice takes on a loud, sarcastic whine. "Oh sure, he is completely free. You know what he's like."

I am becoming embarrassed, because it is almost noon and there are several patients and aides in the halls at this time of day. "He wanted me to keep him from being committed," I say, feeling more guilty by the second. Actually, I have done very little. "He didn't meet the legal criteria for commitment," I tell her. "Even if he hadn't had a lawyer, the judge wouldn't have committed him." As soon as I say this, I do not believe it.

"He is sick!" Mrs. Orsini screams at me. "Goddamn you! You knew that and helped him anyway."

She bursts into tears, and I feel sick myself. It will do no good to tell this woman it is wrong to lock up her son. As she says, I have not had to live with him.

"I'm sorry," I say quietly, "it's my job."

Her voice shaking, she sobs, "What do we do now? He can't work, he can't take care of himself, he won't take his medication, what do we do now?"

At this moment the door opens and her son, who has his mother's pouty-shaped mouth, comes out behind her. "I'm all right, Mom," he says shakily. "I'm all right."

He is not all right and never will be. Her son is as thin and wasted as a spent candle. I know I will see him again. In my two years I have represented many, many individuals who have had multiple admissions. Hugh could have committed him to outpatient treatment. I suppose he is sensitive to my criticism that he never turns anyone loose and wants to prove he can.

Mrs. Orsini glares at me as if I had tried to rape her. "Why don't *you* take him home? Would you like to do that?"

I want to go up and pat her on the shoulder, but I don't dare. "I'm sorry," I say. "I really am."

"No you're not," she sneers. "You won. That's what being a lawyer is all about, isn't it? Isn't it?"

I do not want to lose my temper with this sad, worn-out parent, so I turn and practically sprint out of the building over to Rainey's unit. I barge past the secretary and go on back to her office, even though I am supposed to have checked in at the desk. She answers my impatient knock in a more friendly tone than I would ever manage, given the probable identity of her visitor—either a shrink or a client. "Come in."

I open the door, ready to beg for sanctuary, and find a good-looking man who must be six feet four sitting in my spot. Something is real familiar about this guy.

"Hi," I say to Rainey, "are you free for lunch?"

"No," she says, her voice uncharacteristically flustered. "Gideon, do you know Norris Kelsey?"

As soon as I extend my hand, I realize who is in her office with the door closed. "How do you do?" I say, straining my neck looking up at this bohunky freak of nature. Where does he think he is? He is dressed like, as a child, I always imagined Paul Bunyan: red checkered shirt, suspenders, boots, work pants. To say this man has hair doesn't do him justice. It is everywhere—on his head, on his face, peeking out beneath his shirt on his chest, on the knuckles of the hand that swallows mine. I feel my bald spot expanding exponentially by the second. No wonder no one seemed to know about their relationship. This guy is the Missing Link.

"Hello," he says, his voice a rich baritone.

Good. An ape who can sing. I tell Rainey, "I'll catch you later."

"Okay,"she says, having the grace to appear uncomfortable. Her right hand flies to an earring and begins to tug at it, a sign she is feeling frustration. Her mouth opens and closes and opens again. "Okay," she repeats.

I trudge past the receptionist with my head down, feeling as unwanted as a case of bad breath. I look nervously around for Mrs. Orsini. She is probably planting a bomb under my car about now. This past weekend I noticed Rainey was slightly cool toward me, and now I know the reason: it was because Mr. Prehistoric had been receiving reports that she was about to reach the point of no return and decided to put an end to all this nonsense. Like an idiot, I attributed Rainey's lack of ardor this weekend to a heightened resolve not to go to bed with me until she was ready, but now I realize she may have been too worn out. Surely she hadn't been going to bed with him. But why not? She is a normal human being. But so am I, and I feel right now that I am being jerked around pretty good. I retrace my steps and go into my office and open the little cooler I keep in the corner behind my desk and extract a Diet Sprite and a puny bologna sandwich that makes me sick just to look at it.

Danny comes in and grins. "You're supposed to be out celebrating." He laughs. "What do you suppose got into Hugh? He must be having his period."

I put my feet up on my desk and try to smile at this feeble attempt to explain the inexplicable. "You look like you got run over by a truck," Danny says. "I heard poor Mrs. Orsini screaming at you."

I like Danny okay, but we aren't close friends. I can't tell him I'm getting the shaft from Rainey. He'll find out soon enough. Gossip travels out here like a staph infection. I reply, "What am

I supposed to do? Stand up and argue with Hugh that he's made a mistake? That's your job."

Danny's gray eyes narrow under my attack. He likes to get along with everybody. Fondling my doorknob, Danny agrees, "I know. You heard what I said. I'll ask Hugh in a couple of days why he wouldn't keep him. It wasn't like you did anything brilliant."

Danny is a pro at making a person feel better. "Thanks."

"You know what I mean," he blusters. He wants to say the right thing, but he just doesn't know how. "Hugh probably had his mind made up before we walked in there."

Danny leaves, and I get up and shut my door. What in the hell is going on? The look on Rainey's face was classic: How do I deal with this crap? The least she could have done was to tell me what was coming down instead of letting me walk in on her and Monkey Man. I thought she was classier than that. I realize I am furious, and force myself to stop thinking about it. Finally, I have the Berrenger interview this afternoon.

We are down to two weeks before trial, but that will be more than sufficient time to work on cross-examination. I go over the questions that I have written out for him, but it is no use. I am devastated. In the last week I had begun to think that someday Rainey and I might get married. How is it possible to completely misread another human being? Yet people do it all the time. Why should I be different? Actually, I'm a novice when it comes to women. Rosa spoiled me. Looking back at my relationship with Rainey, I realize I have taken things far too seriously, reading into it signs and portents that were never there. She didn't go to bed with me because she didn't want to. Now she's horny, so she is letting the Mountain Goat back into her life to do the job.

I throw my stinky excuse for a sandwich into the trash and sip at the Sprite as though I were nursing a bourbon and Coke. I wish I could go home and have one. If they awarded degrees for jumping to conclusions, I would have graduated Phi Beta Kappa. If Rainey liked anybody, it was Sarah, not me. They were getting to be real buddies. Sarah will be upset. Somehow I've got to learn to protect her better. I'm not doing her any favors by letting her get close to women she'll never see again. Maybe it's not such a bad idea. That is how life really works. I shouldn't have expected perpetual luck, but you get spoiled. Rosa was my lucky streak. Welcome to the real world. When I think about the last month, I wonder if I should have seen this coming and tried to avoid it. Perhaps. I'm not ready to feel this bad. But maybe it's a sign I'm getting over Rosa's death. Right before we are to get started again on the afternoon hearings, the phone rings.

"Gideon," Rainey says, her voice warm with emotion, "I'm sorry that was so awkward."

I bite my tongue, determined not to lose my cool. "I should have called, not barged in like that."

"We need to talk," she says—the inevitable words. "Can you come over for a few minutes tonight?"

A few minutes? "What's the point?"

"Please. About eight?"

I might as well go through the motions. "Okay." I hang up, feeling I'm going to cry. Mr. Dumpo. Well, it's about time. All the women I have screwed in the last year and then never called again—at least I am getting the courtesy of a formal dump. If it had been me, I probably would have done it over the phone if I could have gotten away with it.

The rest of the afternoon drags on until Brent shows up at three. I am glad to see him. Somehow the knot on his tie has worked under his right collar. He looks ridiculous and I point to his neck, giving him a sickly grin. He makes a stab at straightening his tie and says, "You're really up for this interview with Berrenger, aren't you?"

I moan, "It's not official yet, but the handwriting is on all the walls out here. I'm getting my walking papers from Rainey tonight."

Brent's face glows with sympathy. He is genuinely dismayed for me. "No kidding? I thought this was the real thing."

I stare at the floor. "So did I."

Brent begins to pace up and down in front of my desk. "What happened?"

"I don't know," I say morosely. "The bull ram started missing her, I guess."

"Maybe you could fight him for her," Brent suggests, stopping to finger his fly. For the last two days when he has come to work it has been at half-mast.

"That'd be a lot of fun." I grimace, picturing myself trying to penetrate all that hair. "He looks like he got cut from the Dallas Cowboys for being too slow, but not too big."

"What a bummer," Brent says sympathetically. "Well, go over and give Berrenger hell."

I feel I'm in hell, but I no longer feel like giving it. Maybe Berrenger will give me a shot of Thorazine and we can call it a day.

Berrenger is an oddly shaped man. It is as if he had a physical deformity, but I don't know what to call it. He has rooster-thin legs, a sizable paunch, and is as tall as his interviewer. It is his head that is weird. His features are grotesquely large; his milky blue eyes are cow size. Long, greasy black hair makes him seem probably younger than I am, but not by much. I can't place his accent, but if he is from the South, it is a part we don't claim.

"I appreciate you working me in," I say, not too dryly.

"The law must be served, mustn't it?" he says, his expression mild and calm. He sits behind his desk and rests his hands on his stomach as if he is the Pope and I'm in to beg for his blessing.

Since he gets paid by the state of Arkansas to perform forensic evaluations, I can't disagree with him. I look at my questions. "Dr. Anderson tells me she has contacted you."

"Yes," he says pleasantly. "I was quite pleased by that. She didn't have to be cooperative at all. It's nice how psychiatrists work together down here. In New York, we are a bit fractious sometimes."

Good. A Yankee. "Is that where you're from?"

"California. But there are too many nuts over there. New York is a lot more civilized."

And what must he think of us culturally deprived savages? I feel a little fractious myself. I begin making notes. "You practiced psychiatry in New York City?"

He is wearing a blue three-piece suit and begins to toy with the buttons on the vest that is straining his pot. "Ten years in the Brownsville section of Brooklyn."

Paradise on earth, I want to exclaim, but restrain myself. "I take it you came down here," I say, with a straight face, "because the opportunities were better?"

"Not exactly," he answers uncomfortably. "I'm a recovering alcoholic. I lost my license and only recently got it back. I have a relative in Fort Smith who saw an ad and contacted me. I needed a fresh start."

Despite my hostility at being put off and my general bad mood, I feel some admiration for the guy. I doubt that I would have found out the problem about the alcohol. I'll try to use it, but it is arguably irrelevant and may draw some sympathy. There are a lot of recovering alcoholics in the general population. I'll check to see if he has been charged with DWI since he has been down here. "I take it you disagree with Dr. Anderson."

He looks down at the records on his desk for a moment. His office is as small as mine. In some ways we are professionally equivalent in status, given that most criminal defendants who plead insanity are poor. "My only real disagreement is in my assessment of Mr. Sarver's responsibility."

There is no sense in irritating this man unnecessarily, and I try to inject some friendliness into my voice. "Why don't you think he's not responsible, Doctor?"

Berrenger slowly blinks as if mentally composing himself, and now I know why he looks so strange. His eyelids are the size of garage doors. He could get the Lord's Prayer on them easily. He says, "Because I can't see the cause and effect here. As I understand the law, you have to prove that Mr. Sarver could not appreciate the criminality of his conduct by a preponderance of the evidence. I can't find the evidence."

He talks as if I should be looking for a lost bullet or semen stain. "I guess we are ultimately talking about your professional medical opinion. Is that right?"

"No, Mr. Page," he says earnestly, "I'm not. What I'm talking about, or at least what I want to talk about, is science. Though research on the brain is coming along all the time, we're still in the Dark Ages compared to research on the rest of the body. Psychiatry, as it is practiced today, is pretty much a hit-or-miss proposition so far as forensic work goes. I'd be lying if I told you I could state to a reasonable degree of medical certainty that Mr. Sarver didn't know the difference between right and wrong or couldn't control himself when he shot Mr. Anderson."

Busy writing, I manage, "Are you saying that nobody can, or that you can't?"

He blinks again and says carefully, "I don't know of anybody who can. Let me put it this way: I haven't seen the research if someone is claiming to be able to give us that information."

I hate to admit it, but I like this man. He isn't baiting me or playing games with me as I feared he would. I wish he were on my side. "If you don't feel comfortable giving an opinion, I hope you will state this to the jury."

His eyelids at half-mast, he moves his lips to give me a smile. "Oh, I didn't say I wouldn't give an opinion. That's what they pay me for. But all I can say is that there is no scientific evidence that allows us to be certain of our opinions."

I feel my stomach tightening up. I can't resist arguing with him. "Then they shouldn't let psychiatrists testify at all if they don't have the expertise."

He licks his lips. "I quite agree."

I lay my pen on his desk. "But you have to put food on the table."

He pats his stomach. "I could go without food for a while, but unfortunately our society creates other demands."

He is smiling, so I guess this is his idea of a little joke. He adds, "Mr. Page, I know you consider that in light of the fact that I will be testifying, in effect, for the prosecution in this case, my comments might be considered somewhat disingenuous, so to speak, but this isn't my intent at all."

I sense genuine discomfort in this man. "You're going to have to spell it out for me, Doctor. I don't follow you."

He unbuttons and then rebuttons the bottom of his vest. "My background isn't forensics at all," he says nervously. "When I came down here I assumed that I would be working under someone board-certified in this area, and it is my understanding that there isn't even a board-certified forensic psychologist in the entire state. Even if there were, the field of psychiatry is not capable of really answering my understanding of what the law asks. For example, as you know, we are often asked to predict dangerousness. It's been demonstrated over and over in the literature we can't do that. In the criminal area, we are asked to go back and reconstruct the mental state of a person we have never seen as if we had mystical powers to see into the past. Unless the situation is extremely obvious, we may as well flip coins on this issue, too."

Dr. Berrenger's speech has left him warm, and he pulls out a dirty handkerchief and wipes some of the grease that is congealing on his forehead. This guy has to be an original. I have never heard a state psychiatrist come close to making such admissions. Ziskin's entire book, both volumes, argued the points that this man has summarized in thirty seconds, but getting a shrink to say it is amazing. The problem is that he is perfect for the prosecution because the burden is on the defendant to prove insanity and lack of responsibility. His argument will be that medical testimony is little, if any, help in deciding these issues.

I look down at the questions that I have so laboriously constructed about the psychological tests supposedly used to aid a psychiatrist in determining guilt. I know what his answer will be, but I throw one out anyway. "Did you use the Rorschach test, Dr. Berrenger?"

He tugs at the piece of filthy linen in his hand as if it were a security blanket. "All of the normal paper-and-pen tests, the projective tests the psychologists use, were given here, but their reliability and validity leave a great deal to be desired, and I can't say they really played any part in my opinion."

So much for my plan to destroy him on cross-examination in this area. "What do you normally rely on, Dr. Berrenger?"

He gives me an ironic smile. "What we say we all rely on in these inquisitions—our clinical judgment, which is invalid as well."

I look down at my pad and then back to his strange face. "Why don't you think he's malingering, Doctor?" I ask. "As you know, that is the theory of the prosecution's case—that my client was hired to kill Anderson. You'll say he could be, won't you?"

Berrenger empties his left nostril on the dirty rag in his hand without a trace of self-consciousness. "Sure, he could be," he says casually, "but I haven't seen any evidence of malingering while he's been out here, nor did Dr. Anderson, for that matter."

I follow up with the obvious. "Couldn't a trained psychologist have taught him?"

He smiles, showing a mouthful of large, crooked teeth. "Probably."

I wonder if he knows how brilliant his entire position is in a legal sense. If he can get away with it, he will totally destroy the opinion of any psychiatrist or psychologist who testifies against him simply by saying forensic psychiatry is garbage. At the trial I will have to find some way to discredit him. He is too honest. I pick up my pen and ask: "Do you sometimes feel like a hypocrite in this job, Dr. Berrenger?"

A look of misery steals across his face, replacing his smile. "We become doctors to help people get well. In psychiatry that rarely happens, especially with the chronics we get out here. Then we are asked to do things in the legal field we know we can't do. Yes, I do feel occasionally fraudulent."

I feel I have become his confessor—a lawyer who understands him. He must feel as if he has been sent to purgatory or to work off a penance for his alcoholism. "You must hate it down here."

"The South?" he asks, shaking his head and brightening for the first time. "No, on the contrary, I love it. There is much less arrogance down here. I sometimes think the South is behind the rest of the nation because its people intuitively have a distrust of what on the coasts passes for progress. It costs you, technologically speaking, but I think, for whatever reason, you are pessimists by nature and don't think you will be saved by science—that is, unless your politicians shame you into thinking you have to ape the rest of the nation."

Goodness! He is a political and social philosopher as well. I can't quite see him on TV talk shows, however. He is too ugly, too negative, too wrong. Our historical inferiority complex makes us create our own demagogues. They pander to us, but do not mislead us.

Now that we have established the absurdity of mixing apples and oranges, we talk more comfortably. Antipsychotic drugs (God only knows how they really work, Berrenger readily admits) have considerably improved Perry's ability to think and remember. Berrenger waxes at length about how impressed he is with the concern shown by Carolyn Anderson for Perry Sarver. It would have been entirely normal for her to hope he would commit suicide. I think this is a little melodramatic but don't disabuse him. Nor do I throw into the hopper the possibility that Perry is gay. I have seen nothing in Sarver's records to indicate he has picked up on this, and I might want to spring it on him at trial. I ask Berrenger if he thinks that Carolyn Anderson might have screwed up Sarver's medication and been responsible for him losing it. Typically, he won't go that far.

"Medicating the patient is a crap game," he says, burping gently into a fist. "You can figure it out pretty well if you have them in the hospital in a controlled environment, but when they get out, you don't know what they are drinking, injecting, eating. She shouldn't blame herself in the slightest. Who knows what set him off? Psychiatrists are given too much credit and consequently too much blame."

Dr. Know Nothing, I resolve to call him at trial. Ladies and gentlemen, what this man doesn't claim to know would fill a book. I will have to think about this approach, but I can't imagine what to do with him unless it is to ridicule him. We talk for a few more minutes until he begins looking at his watch. It is closing time.

I ask him, "Do you think you will ever go back home?"

He arches his eyebrows in surprise, and says fervently, "This is home. If I'm able to save some money, I'll try private practice again. If not, I'll try to persuade the powers that be to let me do community mental health work after I've stayed here a decent interval and if I can continue to stay off the bottle."

With this he stands and offers me his hand. I wish him good luck and leave, wanting to digest what he has told me instead of visiting my client while I'm here. A thoroughly decent human being, whom, because of the way our system works, I will be obligated to try to make look like a fool or some cunning outsider who pretends ignorance is bliss. We know when somebody is trying to put us on. Yankees can make fun of us on the Johnny Carson show, but, by God, don't come down here and tell us to our face that medical science is a lot of bunk. We watch TV. We know better. If they can transplant a human heart, they can tell us what those little neurons inside somebody's head are saying. What Dr. Anderson is saying, ladies and gentlemen, is that those little neurons caused Perry Sarver to go kill her husband, and he couldn't control what he was doing any more than could a chicken with its head cut off.

Will that garbage fly? I doubt it, but at least it has kept me from thinking about Rainey for a couple of hours.

As I wait for the receptionist to throw the switch that will release me from Rogers Hall, I am tempted to turn around and go talk to Perry. But I want him to call me. I do not want to be accused of talking him into implicating Jerry Kerner. As the prosecutor has said, there is plenty of time left for him to make a deal. I wonder what Chet Bracken is doing now. I haven't heard from him. Maybe he is trying to make a deal of his own. I wouldn't be surprised.

13

Rainey lets me in with a sad smile that lets me know I am doomed even before I sit down. I am not offered the couch. I perch across from her in a new cherry-wood rocker that creaks each time I shift in it. She is dressed in unseasonable white jeans that look great on her and a T-shirt that says, "Don't blame me—I voted for Gorbachev." To get the ball rolling, I ask, "Do you wear that much outside?"

She gives me the slightest of grins. "Only when I'm feeling extremely masochistic."

I try to sit perfectly still to stop my creaking. "Is that what this is all about?"

"I've been getting cold feet," she says, "and then I let Norris give me a call, and now I'm all confused. I need to take some time off and regroup."

Regroup? She sounds like a settler who has narrowly beaten back an attack by wild Indians. I know she wants to keep the door open a crack so if she changes her mind, she can. I tell her this wouldn't play too well if the situation were reversed. "You wouldn't like it a minute if I said an old girlfriend had given me a call."

For the first time since I've known her, Rainey is abashed. "I suspect Norris is an excuse, Gideon," she says sadly. "I don't think I want him. I'm afraid right now I don't want anybody."

I feel as if my face had been scorched by a blowtorch, and I stand up. "I'm not the type," I say sarcastically, "to sit by the phone waiting for you to have a change of heart."

Tears glisten on her cheeks. She is in the exact spot on the couch where we necked just a week ago. "I know that," she says, her voice gentle. "I feel awful. Women complain about men being jerks, and I finally have one who is willing to take a cold shower for me until I tell him to stop, and I don't have the sense to jump on his bones. What do you think is wrong with me?"

"Probably nothing," I say, sitting back in the chair and feeling its spindles chew into my back. I study Rainey's face, which radiates dejection. She doesn't like this any more than I do. What's wrong with you, I think, is that you have an excess of integrity. With no social restraints we jump into bed with each other after we have known each other at most a few days. Rainey is feeling pressure to do this and can't think of any way to resist it except break up because we are headed for the bedroom very soon one of these nights. I know that and so does she. The problem is that I can't take us back to the nineteenth century. Forty-year-old women are expected to come across pretty quickly or they are out of luck. In Rainey's mind, sex is a shortcut to intimacy. Maybe it is; maybe it isn't. As a man, I don't necessarily worry about it. My mind hasn't been programmed to deal with metaphysical questions on this issue. At any rate, I can't tell her how she feels. All I know is that I can't stand the way she is looking at me, and I ask, "What do you think is wrong?"

Her mouth twists unpleasantly as she struggles to respond. "I guess I'm a coward."

I have to smile at these words. Surely, most cowards aren't quite so honest as Rainey McCorkle. "If you're a coward, I'd hate to meet someone in a dark alley you consider courageous."

She digs her nails into the couch like a cat. "I wish," she says irritably, "I had met you when I was eighteen. I didn't have a history then."

I want to correct her. I wish she wouldn't worry about it. "You put a lot of pressure on yourself, you know," I tell her.

She says nothing. There is no sense in prolonging this misery. She is beginning to look as bad as I feel, so I get up again and go out the door into the frigid night air and head for home.

In the car I feel like I have a tree trunk resting between my skin and lungs. I haven't felt this kind of sadness since Rosa died. I figure I may be getting too old for this love business.

At home I make myself a stiff drink. Sarah comes into the kitchen where I am sitting and drinking an ounce and a half of Old Crow mixed with Coke. She is wearing sweat pants and a Milwaukee Bucks sweatshirt that she has worn periodically ever since the former Razorback star Sidney Moncrief gave her an autograph after a Bucks-Lakers exhibition game three years ago.

"What's wrong, Dad?" Sarah asks, sitting down across from me. "You've been quiet the whole night, and since you've been back from Rainey's you haven't said a word. Did you have a fight?"

She has been so full of herself since her romance with Chick's brother began that I am surprised she has noticed. It has been good for her. She has been more excited and happy than I can remember seeing her since before her mother got sick. I tell her the bad news. "Rainey's dumping me. Her old boyfriend's back in the picture, and she's bailing out."

Sarah's face falls like one of our cakes. "Oh, Dad, I'm sorry."

She gets up and comes around and hugs me, tapping my shoulder repeatedly, a gesture that reminds me of her mother.

"It's not the end of the world," I say lightly. I don't want her to start mothering me or acting like a wife. She needs to be a kid, period.

Suddenly, though, her bottom lip trembles, and I see she is near tears. "I liked her so much."

Damn it! I want to call Rainey up and tell her to go to hell. "We'll get over it."

The telephone rings and, like an idiot, I hope it is Rainey, but, of course, it is not. While Sarah talks on the phone, I go into my bedroom to try to figure out what went wrong. If I stay in the kitchen, Sarah will worry. I go over to a picture I have of Rosa on my dresser and pick it up. She is wearing her nurse's uniform but has her swimsuit in a bag slung over her shoulder and is standing in front of the La Playa hotel in Cartagena. I realize I no longer feel guilty for loving someone else. Unfortunately, that someone doesn't love me. The problem is that nothing went wrong. I turn off the light and lie on the bed and let the hurt feelings come. Why should I be immune to this kind of pain? I had forgotten how much it hurts, but it is nothing compared to what I felt when I knew Rosa was going to die. And yet, this is a kind of death, too. Maybe I should feel good that I can feel this bad. I wipe my eyes. Crying over a woman that I've been going out with for less than a month! I didn't cry over Rosa until a month after she died. I was going through some letters that her friends wrote from Colombia. She really loved me, they said. I knew that, of course. Maybe, I am crying for her now.

At ten Sarah calls through the door, "Good night, Dad. I love you."

I get up and go hug her. "I love you, Sarah. We'll be fine."

She smiles, knowing I want her to fake it. "I know."

We pat each other on the back in sympathy. She says, "Maybe she's going through something and when she gets over it she'll call."

I've wished that a thousand times already. When reality turns shitty, you get through life by wishing. Not much of a compensation but all that we get. In the South, God forbid, we still sing under our breath, "I wish I was in the land of cotton . . . " Tomorrow Rainey will call me up and say, "Boy, was I having a bad day. Come here, my little balding lawyer man. I don't want that big hairy ape. . . ." But, in my heart, I know it is not to be. I think she has been scared for years, and that was what the no-sex stuff was about. I imagine Prehistoric Man has been told more than a time or two, "Let's wait until I'm really sure." If you wait until you're really sure, you will go into the nursing home and be told: "Mr. Page, this is your penis. Remember that?"

I go back into my room, take off my pants and shirt, and go into the bathroom to brush my teeth, hoping I can get to sleep. My usual pattern will be to get into another relationship, no matter how shallow, as soon as I can. As horny as I am, I will try to resist doing this. Brent read me an article last week at work that since AIDS, singles have made masturbation an art form. This past couple of months I think I have perfected it.

At almost midnight the phone rings, and I get up to answer it, thinking again that it is Rainey.

"Is this Mr. Page the lawyer?" asks a female voice hoarse with emotion.

"Yes it is," I say, disappointed and alarmed at the same time. I do not recognize who it is, but at this hour of the night it can't be good news.

"This is Lila Orsini," the female voice says, crying. "My son committed suicide tonight, and I just wanted you to know that I hold you responsible!"

The telephone is slammed down in my ear, and I feel my heart pounding rapidly. I know she was telling the truth. Sarah comes into the kitchen and sees my face.

"What's wrong, Dad?"

"A woman just called whose son," I barely get out, "I represented today, committed suicide."

"Oh, Dad, no!"

"The judge dismissed the commitment petition and let him go. She was furious at me."

Sarah is crying for me. "But it wasn't your fault."

Was it? Of course it was. Poor Hugh Bixby, who heard this case. He is going to hate himself. For Sarah's sake, I say, "Not really."

She stands there, dressed for bed, in a yellow T-shirt that comes to her knees, a look of horror on her face. "You were just doing your job."

I know. That is what I am telling myself. I think an odd thing. I think about interviewing Berrenger and how during the interview I thought about ways to discredit him. Just doing my job. Maybe another job is what I need. It is cold in the kitchen. I turn out the light. "Let's go to bed."

No sleep tonight, I realize, but I am too numb to read. I lie in bed replaying the hearing this morning. If I had kept my mouth shut, this kid would still be alive. He was so young, not much more than Sarah's age. He was a little loose, but he was insistent he didn't want to be committed. Where will you go? Lots of places. Why don't you take your medication? I do take it. Okay. What is his mother going to do the rest of her life? I will bury this somehow, maybe not completely, but part of her life is over. How could it not be?

"Dad?"

Sarah's voice is muffled. I can barely hear her through the door. "What, babe?"

"Can I sleep with you the rest of the night?"

"Sure." I don't care what Ann Landers says.

Sarah comes in, and plops down heavily in the bed with a sigh. "How awful!"

Awful isn't the word for tonight, but it is the best we have. "I know," I say. We hear the sound of nails scratching on the floor and then the bed sags further. "Hi, Woogs," I say. He has been sleeping with Sarah and is not going to accept an empty bed gracefully.

"Can he stay?" Sarah asks.

"Sure." No sense in his feeling bad, too.

"Poor Daddy," Sarah says. "How mean can a person be?" she says, her voice full of anger now.

I tell her about the hearing and how the woman hadn't had any sleep. "She sounded hysterical. I can understand that. What if I had just lost you?"

She pats my shoulder in the dark. "You won't ever lose me."

If only someone could guarantee me that.

I get up at three in the morning, my stomach queasy, but I do not throw up. Thoughts of that boy's death, Rainey's rejection, and Rosa in her final months fumble around the edges of my mind as confused as the Doctrine of the Trinity. I am not a religious person, but I find myself offering a prayer in my mind to Whoever or Whatever blessed me with Sarah. My life seems ridiculously bizarre right now, and I am grateful for my child's impossible promise. She would protect me. For some reason, I begin to think about Perry Sarver, too. He seems an integral part of this madness I am living through.

My feet freezing on the tile, I finally manage to concentrate enough to relieve my aching bladder. I climb back into bed and listen to the sound of my daughter's breathing. I do not want to be responsible for another person's death again. If the jury doesn't buy the insanity plea for Sarver, I can see a jury coming in with the death penalty. I can hear Phil Harper telling the jury: Okay, even if Sarver is mentally ill, his illness has nothing to do with his ability to tell right from wrong and keep his behavior under control. It is time to send a message to all these so-called crazies roaming the streets!

Sarah rolls against me, and it is nice to feel the warmth of someone else and not just a dog. As if in protest, Woogie groans in the darkness. How nice Rainey would have felt in this bed. I had begun to fantasize almost daily about her. It is pathetic what the mind will and won't tell itself. In the last day or so I knew something was wrong but I offered up every rationalization for her behavior I could think of. If I had forced myself to think about it, I would have confronted her. It wasn't Rosa who couldn't accept her death but me. Long after she had accepted the fact that she wouldn't live, I was still pretending that she was actually getting better! She hated that in me, I think. Finally, there came the night in this bed when she dug her fingernails into my wrist and said: "I'm dying. Will you shut up and face that?" The panic that set in at that moment was not to be believed. I thought I was going to have a heart attack. I couldn't breathe, and she held me in her arms the entire night like I was a baby. After a week, when I had finally calmed down, I watched her tell Sarah, and then like tonight we all came in and got into bed and cried and held each other. That night was the beginning of my acceptance, I think.

In the dark Sarah asks, "Are you awake?"

"Yeah," I admit. "Can't you sleep?"

"I was," she says. "Are you okay?"

I say, "I'll be okay. We've lived through worse things."

There is a silence while she remembers. "Yeah, we have." she clears her throat and asks: "Do you still think about Mom much?"

"Sure," I say. "Don't you?"

Sarah says honestly, "I miss her sometimes real bad, but I don't think about her a lot. Do you think that's bad?"

I say quickly, "Not at all. It's normal for you not to. I'm glad you don't. This is a time when you're supposed to be growing up and thinking about boys, school, your friends. Don't worry about that," I plead. God, she worries about enough.

"I won't," she says. "You're a good man, you know that?"

"Thanks," I say. "Let's try to go to sleep, okay?"

"Okay. Is Woogie still here?"

I can feel his back against my shoulder. If he farts, I'm a dead man. I think about what Sarah has said. A good man? I don't feel good; I feel weak. I spend my life trying to protect myself and her. I wanted to protect her mother, but she couldn't afford to be protected and demanded that I stop it. Was it better? I guess, but I can't stand pain, and I got a full dose of that. How ludicrous it was for me to pretend! She was beginning to hurt, and I said to myself she was getting better! My capacity for self-delusion knows no bounds. I wonder how different Perry Sarver is. If he really is mentally ill, I suppose the difference is that I can control my capacity for self-deception and he can't. But how does anyone ever really know what we can control and what we can't?

The only thing I really know is that while I am standing by Perry Sarver's side I do not want a jury to come in and pronounce his death sentence. Six months ago I had that happen, and though I have replayed that trial a hundred times, I will always believe I could have said something to the jury that would have persuaded them not to demand that my client be executed. If anyone deserves to die, maybe Harry Potter does. So what if he was abused, lived in four different foster homes, is functionally illiterate? The system fails people every day, but they don't go out and kill two clerks in a convenience store because they are afraid they will testify against them.

I worked on that trial for weeks; today I paid no more attention to that boy than to a stray dog, and now he is gone. Harry Potter is still on death row and will be for years, appealing his case until every last tree in Arkansas has been cut to keep him in paper. Yet it really hasn't hit me yet how casually we all treated Bobby Orsini. We were playing legal games, and he was thinking about suicide. But isn't that what I am supposed to do? I don't know anymore. I do know, but cases like these and Sarver's case upset the apple-cart. What I haven't admitted to myself is that Sarver's case, even if you throw out Jerry Kerner, smells wrong. I have tried too hard to make it fit a scenario that is too pat. The truth is, a lot of what I know about Perry Sarver is straight out of Carolyn Anderson's mouth. Is Perry Sarver crazy because he is crazy or because she says he is? In looking back on the last few weeks, I realize that I can make a good case for the proposition that she has controlled the whole show. She called up Berrenger; she suggested that I contact Margaret Howard. She even wanted to go examine her husband's killer and is willing to testify he isn't responsible. The next thing she'll want to do is serve on the jury. Is any of this normal, or is it all normal? Maybe all of this comes from a legit-imate sense of guilt. God knows I feel guilty enough right now myself.

At least the cat is out of the bag, and I can no longer pretend anything about this case makes sense. It takes a kid to die to make me realize that, given the slightest opportunity, I'll revert to type. A good man? If I'm good, don't let me meet a bad one.

Sarah, obedient as usual, is sleeping again, and I have got to sleep so I can start to think again. What motive would Carolyn Anderson have for setting this up? I don't see one. Maybe I will tomorrow if I don't sleep through it.

Sarah cries out in her sleep suddenly, but I can't quite catch what she said. I am reminded of Perry Sarver's incoherent ranting in the courtroom and when I visited the first time. He was totally out of control. Unless he has been faking all this time.

The chasm between happiness and sorrow, sanity and insanity, life and death, seems hideously narrow right now. If I didn't feel so goddamned helpless, I think I could stand it better. The only lesson I ever seem to learn, and in the past month or so I have been learning it over and over, is how breakable life is.

An hour's sleep does not help my mood or my appearance. As I stand in front of the bathroom mirror, I am consoled only by the fact that I am scheduled to have my picture taken for the Blackwell County Bar Association address book tomorrow and not today. No wonder poor Mrs. Orsini looked so bad. My eyes, the color of month-old grapes, look as if they have been stolen from a not-so-fresh stiff. As I think back through the hearing yesterday, I reach for a toothbrush, feeling with my tongue the inside of my mouth, which tastes as if it had been used to test a formula for dog food. Yet no matter how bad I feel, I am alive and that boy is dead.

The telephone rings. I am scared to answer it. I cannot listen to a tirade from that boy's mother. It isn't fair to make Sarah pick up the phone. Resigned, I go into the kitchen. "Hello," I say gruffly.

"Is this Mr. Page?"

God knows who this is, I think, but at least it's not Mrs. Orsini. Sounds like an old black woman. "Yeah."

"This is Effie Williams, you remember me?"

I rack my exhausted brain and get nothing. "I'm sorry," I say lamely. "I have a lot of clients."

"You kept me out of the state hospital jes' a few weeks ago. I'm jes' callin' to say thank you. I'm doin' real good."

Now I remember. A neat, white-haired old lady whose daughter-in-law didn't want her. Suddenly, I am crying. "I'm real glad to hear that, Mrs. Williams. You don't know how glad."

"I'm in Maris Towers downtown," she says. "You come see me sometime. You know where that is?"

I clear my throat. A high-rise for the elderly off Southern Avenue. "Yes, ma'am."

"I'll fix you some turnip greens and black-eyed peas."

"I'll call you," I promise. "Thank you, ma'am."

"Who was that, Dad?" Sarah calls from her bedroom.

I put the phone down, thinking that after this Sarver mess is over, I'll call Mrs. Williams and see if Sarah can come, too. "Just a client," I say. I'll tell her when I'm not so emotional. As she bustles about, getting ready for school, Sarah drives me crazy with her solicitousness until I yell at her, "I'm fine, okay? All I need is about twenty hours sleep."

"I was just worried," she says crossly. She hasn't slept so well herself. She is wearing 501 jeans, a green-and-white-striped shirt, and her denim jacket. For once, at least, we will not have to argue about whether she is warm enough.

As she backs out of the driveway, I tell her, "I'm supposed to be the worrier, not you." Now that she is behind the wheel, I have something to worry about. Here we go again. I close my eyes.

We bump into the street. "Maybe you can take a nap at work," she yawns at me.

I yawn back, too tired to complain. "Judges really appreciate the lawyers dozing off."

She grins and unintentionally pops the clutch. A little harder and I would have whiplash. "You know, Dad, you've given new meaning to the term 'having a bad day.' " We roar around the corner onto Stimson Street, which is clogged with traffic.

I realize this is the Sarah I like. A smarty-pants. Sympathy is too easy to wallow in. "That's for sure," I say, feeling my muscles assume their usual locked position. If we go on a trip this summer, I will have to be carried in and out of motels. We creep up behind a Toyota Celica presumably so we can inspect its license expiration date. In a former life Sarah must have been a tow-truck operator. Normalcy. There is something to be said for it.

At the state hospital, I feel obligated to tell Hugh Bixby about my telephone call last night from the dead boy's mother. I have halfway expected that he received one, too. Hugh's normally bland face becomes ashen, and I realize he doesn't know.

"Could it have been a joke?" he asks, his normal alto voice dropping to a whisper. We are back in his office—chambers would be stretching it a little.

Danny Goetz, whose face is also sleepy and puffy, probably from a night of drinking and chasing women, grabs the *Gazette* from Hugh's desk and begins to go through it.

I slump down in the chair across from Danny. "He may have done it just before she called. I doubt if it'll be in the paper."

Hugh says, his voice now shaky as the truth sinks in, "I knew thirty seconds after the hearing that I shouldn't have let him go." He lowers his head and lets out a long sigh.

I want to scream at him, Why didn't you change your mind, then? But it would have been too undignified, too unjudicial. Why am I blaming Hugh? He only did what I asked him to do.

Danny and I barely go through the motions the rest of the morning. Hugh would have committed the governor if Danny had asked him.

It is noon before I begin to think about what to do in the Sarver case. I stay in my office, making sure I avoid running into Rainey. It would be my luck to see her, but I do not. Part of me wants to, of course, hoping for a miracle. The other part wants to drive a stake through her heart.

After throwing away another uneatable bologna sandwich, I lean back in my chair and try to remember how Perry Sarver has acted since the first moment I saw him. In five minutes I am asleep.

At ten after one Danny wakes me up with a knock on the door. "Hugh's gonna hold you in contempt if you're not there in thirty seconds."

I wake up out of the soundest sleep I've had in months. Maybe

I ought to stay up all night more often. If looks could kill, I'd be drawn and quartered, but Hugh, taking uncharacteristic pity on a fellow lawyer, holds his tongue and merely glares at me as I come running into the courtroom.

It is not until three, when Brent arrives to take my last hearing of the afternoon, that I have another opportunity to think about Carolyn Anderson. I drive back to the office and look for Ken Averitt.

He is in his office working, and I stroll in and tell him that this case doesn't add up. But as I take him through Carolyn Anderson's actions I realize that if somehow she, and not Jerry Kerner, had somehow set this up, the prosecutor's action in charging Kerner had given her and Sarver the perfect alibi, which only Sarver seems to be considering. All they had to do was take the deal offered by Phil Harper, which may get sweeter as we get closer to trial. Yet, from the beginning, Carolyn has maintained Kerner had nothing to do with the murder. How easy it would have been for Carolyn and Perry to go along with the prosecutor's story that Jerry Kerner had promised Perry money to kill Hart Anderson by pretending to be crazy and becoming his wife's patient.

Ken, whose back has been acting up lately, stands ramrod-straight behind his military-neat desk as we talk, listening carefully. But I can see him growing impatient as I talk about the control Carolyn Anderson has maintained in this case.

Finally, he says, "You're turning into a shrink yourself, and they admit they don't know what the hell they're talking about. So what if she's trying to manipulate everybody in this case. Is that anything new?" He lowers his voice. "Look at Greta. She drives herself crazy trying to control us. You are forgetting what happened to Carolyn Anderson. In one split second her world is blown to hell. So how does she cope? The same way she always has—by trying to fix things, make them come out right. She'd probably have a nervous breakdown if she tried to keep her hands off this case. She's got to rationalize this. It's therapy for her. Some people would want to take time off, but doctors are the most compulsive people on earth. You're the one who told me she's working herself sick. She probably can't help herself any more than Greta can. A conspiracy theory is always appealing to us because it's the most rational. But in my experience, people aren't rational."

Ken reaches around and rubs his spine. I realize I have rarely seen him without a coat. The pain is making him irritable, and I go to my office, wondering how to get some perspective on this case. Ken makes sense, but he hasn't talked to Carolyn Anderson. Maybe I'm overreacting because she is so involved. She cares about what happens in this case, and it is showing. Raymond Berrenger comes off cool and logical because he doesn't give a damn. Forensic psychiatry is a big joke to him, so he sits back and laughs at it. I realize I never asked Carolyn Anderson about how much she believes in what she does, but the answer ought to be obvious. She has a successful practice, and Berrenger is a lush. So she is trying too hard. Since when is that a crime? Whether it is the exhaustion or the case that is making me paranoid, for some reason I feel I must check in with her, and I call her number but am told she has a patient until six. I ask that she call me at home and decide to leave for the day. I am not going to get anything else done here.

As I meander around in the kitchen at home, the lack of sleep hits me full force, and after I have scrounged around unsuccessfully for something new to fix, it takes little effort on my part to convince Sarah that we should go out to eat. Despite the traffic we are at the order window in ten minutes. A McDLT is just what I need, and we almost scrape the building, so close does Sarah come to the window where we pick up our food.

"We can practically grill our own from the car," I say, putting the best face on Sarah's driving.

"It's better this way," giggles Sarah, who is happy because we aren't eating our own cooking. "We can't lose our change."

I could open a small savings and loan from the money lost in the exchange between my hand and the hands of McDonald's employees in this parking lot over the years. The first thing they probably do in the morning is drag the lot for coins. I am glad of my daughter's company, no matter how mundane our conversation is. I have blocked Rainey from my mind as much as I can, but now that I am not working, I am fighting a losing battle.

I hear the phone ringing from the porch and rush in to get it, hoping that it is Rainey. Instead, as I should have realized, it is Carolyn Anderson. I try to sound as laid-back as possible, but I realize I am coming across a little antsy, because she asks me if something is wrong. I tell her no and try to arrange a time to see her, but she is going out of town for a few days. She asks me if I would like to come over to her house to talk tonight. I am dead on my feet and should tell her that we will have time before the trial, but I feel an urgency to confront her that drives me to tell her I will be over about eight. I hang up, wondering how I am going to stay awake.

"What are you going for, Dad?" Sarah asks uneasily. "Can't you just talk on the phone?"

"You can't ask somebody questions over the phone like you can in person," I tell her, my mouth full of bread, lettuce, and out-of-season tomato. "She's going out of town."

Sarah looks perplexed, and I realize that she is superstitious about my going over there. In little over an hour I will be standing in the precise spot where Carolyn's husband was killed. I wonder if it is somehow possible she killed Hart. It isn't likely. The lab report found only Sarver's prints.

"I'll be back in an hour," I tell Sarah. "I'm too tired to stay any longer."

"I think it's stupid for you to go at all," Sarah says, pouting like a child.

I have to reassure myself that I'm not being taken for a ride. "You worry too much," I tell Sarah, already wondering what to say to Carolyn Anderson. Sarah begins to say something, then thinks better of it. We eat in silence, and she goes into her room to do her homework. She is mad, but I will be back soon.

Twenty minutes later I have found Carolyn's house, which is

downtown, off Romaine, only a few blocks from Margaret Howard's modest dwelling. Yet, there is all the difference in the world. Here most of the houses are two stories, done in the Colonial Revival style with a hipped roof and wide eaves. Carolyn's home has four squat columns, a tile roof, and a Dutch gable dormer. Perry lived only about six blocks east of here, I realize.

I ring the bell, which plays chimes, and wonder how often she replays her husband's murder when she hears that sound. I feel self-conscious at this time of night, wondering if her neighbors are peering out their windows. One strange car has done enough damage at this address. For what seems the longest time she does not come to the door, and I wonder what in the hell has got into me. Do I expect her to confess to some diabolical scheme? She knows I am not her lawyer, so she would be incriminating herself if she even hinted she was involved. So why am I here? At this moment I no longer know. The temperature is dropping rapidly, and it was already cold enough. My head is beginning to ache from the cold or lack of sleep. I should have worn my London Fog, but I changed from a coat and tie to jeans and an old leather jacket. Somehow an overcoat doesn't go with Nikes. As I wait, stamping my feet in the cold, I feel tension beginning to form in my chest. Maybe I am having a heart attack. That is all Carolyn would need.

She comes to the door looking comfortable in worn-looking jeans and a sweater. Though I have decided she doesn't look as good as when I first met her (her experience seems to have visibly ravaged her), she is still far more attractive than most of the women I know.

"How are you?" she says formally as she takes my jacket and leads me into what is a combination living room and library with a fireplace. The floors are hardwood with rugs, not carpet, covering them. The fire is gas, but it is inviting nonetheless, and she sits me across from her in a chair Hart must have sat in every night. I decline, then accept a beer, though I know, as tired as I am, it is absolutely the last thing I need. Yet, I want to appear relaxed and would very much like to unwind so I will be coherent.

As I wait for my beer, I look around the room and see traces of Hart Anderson everywhere. He may be dead and gone, but he is very much alive in this room. On the wall above the fireplace is an almost mural-size painting of his father who was a lawyer and who, before his own death, was appointed to finish out a term on the Arkansas Supreme Court. The painting, an oil, illustrates the superiority of the medium over photography, because somehow the picture brings out the similarity between father and son, an identity I hadn't noticed in life but one that existed, if only in retrospect now. Both were tall, good-looking men with full, strong faces that drew your attention regardless of your sex. The younger Anderson reminds me of Dan Quayle. He had the sort of face that reporters have taken to describing as "seamless," which, I assume, means no jutting jaw or excessive angularity. A beefy, marbled Robert Redford.

On the wall next to my chair there must be a half-dozen plaques and awards that were given to Hart. It has always seemed odd to me how the biggest bastards are usually the most lauded. A "Man of the Year" award from two different civic groups, the Blackwell County Bar Association Award for outstanding community service, a citation from a child-advocacy group, etc. I remind myself that he was being recognized for his power. These groups that had honored him wanted him to continue working on their behalf. On the table is a small picture of him and Carolyn obviously made on a trip, perhaps their honeymoon. They look happy enough, but his expression is more one of pride and ownership. Look what I got me. Carolyn, I notice, was a fuller-bodied woman in those days, not fat, but voluptuous. Maybe I am just horny and tired, but it is apparent that living with Hart took its toll.

She comes up behind me with my beer, and when I turn around I glimpse a pained expression on her face and realize she was looking at that picture, too. A happier time, the picture says.

15

Carolyn and I sit before the fire like a pair of overworked yuppies too exhausted at the end of the day to enjoy their riches.

"You seem really troubled," Carolyn says, her words professional and cool. Even seated, she has lovely posture, a virtue that accentuates her lithe body. She is wearing a baby-blue cashmere sweater that matches her eyes perfectly. She crosses her legs and holds the stem of her wine goblet in her lap with her left hand while her right strokes the arm of her chair.

"There is some thinking in my office," I not quite lie, "'that you are somehow involved more deeply in your husband's murder than has been revealed." I had not intended to accuse her, but now that I have, I feel somehow relieved to have it in the open between us.

She looks into the fire a long time before she speaks. "Is this confidential?" she asks finally, her voice high and wispy, as if she is about to cry.

For the first time since I have known her, Carolyn is totally and completely vulnerable. Startled, I stare at her now flushed face, which is turned directly toward me. I am in a difficult position. I do not have a relationship with this woman that can be protected; further, I'm an officer of the court and, most important, have an obligation to represent my own client. If she tells me she has had her husband murdered, I can't pretend I didn't hear her right. Yet I am about to burst. Shit, I think. I don't have a choice. "No," I say, "whatever you tell me I can't promise to keep between us. I will if I can."

She stares at me for such a long time I am forced to look away and into the fire. Finally she says, "I'm going to tell you anyway. You'll just have to decide what to do with it."

I nod, and find myself leaning forward, my exhaustion forgotten. "Okay," I say. "Shoot."

She gives an ironic nod at my choice of words and takes a swallow from her glass of white wine before saying, "You can't imagine how many times I wished Hart dead. I hated him and was working up the nerve to divorce him when, incredibly, Perry showed up that night and shot him. I've thought over and over whether there was anything I ever said to Perry that encouraged him in the slightest, but I swear I didn't! Ask him! He knows I didn't!" She runs her right hand through her hair. "But I feel horribly guilty about it. Unconsciously, I must have done something that gave him permission." Tears come to her eyes and she begins to cry.

I reach into my pocket, but all I have is my typically dirty tissue. I can't give that to her and, embarrassed, I stuff it back inside my pocket. I was all set for a murder confession and all I have is wishful thinking. Doubtless, she isn't the only person in the world who has ever wished for someone's death, but she may be closest to looking the most woebegone. Her mascara and eyeshadow are running down her beautiful face, and I feel uncomfortable watching. I get up and turn my back, hoping she will go to the bathroom and try to repair the damage. She does, and I am left to contemplate what I have learned. Did she cause Perry to kill her husband? God only knows. I don't. In some ways, this all seems ridiculous. Her unconscious can't be put on trial. Probably she didn't do anything except wish his death, and her wish came true. I sip at the beer I had forgotten about. Despite myself, I find that I am feeling sorry for her. The sleepless nights she must be having! When Rosa died, all I felt was grief mixed with relief that it was finally over. I felt enough guilt about that, and finally I went to a therapist who got me to see how normal my feelings were. Here she is, a psychiatrist, and she has no more control over herself than the rest of us.

When she comes back into the room, I see she has done a masterful restoration job. Except for a slightly red nose, she looks fine.

"I'm sorry," she says. In her hand is another can of Miller Lite and a full glass of white wine for her.

"Don't apologize," I tell her, taking the beer and opening it. "It helps explain some things." What does it explain? That she is a skilled actress who can cry on cue? Any woman can cry, I tell myself. I sit back in the chair and sip the beer. It tastes delicious. Outside, I can hear the wind picking up, and I scoot my chair closer to the fire. We make a cozy couple, I realize. Were someone who didn't know us to come in now, it would appear we were a married couple, making up after a tiff.

"Ever since Perry pulled the trigger," she says, her voice tremulous and small, "I've been obsessed with thinking I am responsible. Do you think I am?" She is staring at me as if I am to decide whether she lives or dies.

I put the can of beer on the round table beside my chair. For the first time I notice how soft the lights are in this room. Though there is overhead lighting, the room is lit by only two dim lamps and the fire. "Not if what you are telling me is the truth."

Her voice takes on an urgent, higher-pitched tone as she nods. "I know logically that I'm not, but you see why it's so important to me that Perry be found not guilty by reason of insanity. When he first came to see me, I wished he or somebody like him would kill Hart!"

There is a long silence, and to fill it I pick up the can and take a long swallow. For the first time, I begin to see how eerie she must feel. If I were she, I would want to move out of this house. She can't come in the front door without thinking about her wish. "Was Hart as bad as I imagine?" I ask sympathetically.

Her pink bottom lip, which matches her nails, begins to wobble. "He was horrible! Psychiatrists are supposed to have these things figured out, but like a fool, I married my father. After six months, he was the coldest man I've ever known. You've heard he was going to run for governor? I was to be his campaign ornament. I think he picked me out because I photograph well, or I used to before all this happened."

This bit of vanity is endearing. I smile, but, her eyes flashing, she says fiercely, "When he knew he wasn't going out again, he used to drink until he couldn't answer the telephone, and at least twice in the last year while he was drinking he hit me so hard in this very room I couldn't go in to work for days!"

She has begun to breathe heavily, but she manages not to cry. The physical abuse shocks me. My own pulse has quickened. Hart seemed too refined to be a wife beater. It is not one of the stories I have heard. "I didn't realize that."

She makes a valiant effort to remain composed. "No one did," she says, her voice straining to keep control. "Mostly it was verbal abuse, but underneath this makeup," she says, pointing to her right cheek, "there is a scar where his ring cut me. And we hadn't been married a year when he came home drunk, with lipstick smeared from ear to ear. This didn't happen just once, either."

I realize I am gripping the arms of my chair and relax now that she is apparently finished. While she was speaking, her face had become rigid with anger, and for the first time I have seen the bitterness that had to be lurking beneath her normally controlled exterior. What surprises me is that her anger is not more apparent. Yet I cannot still my curiosity about how this could happen to such an attractive woman. "How could a woman like you let yourself be abused?" I marvel.

This brings fresh tears, but fortunately she is now armed with her own tissues. "It's a lot easier than you think," she answers, a jangling note of irony in her voice as she dabs at her face. "My mother could have left, and she didn't either. When I left home, I swore I wouldn't marry a man like my father, and in some ways you couldn't tell them apart. I used to wish he would die, too. Some days I feel like a case study in Freudian psychology. I think we have almost no control over what we do. We repeat ourselves endlessly."

Hadn't Rainey just said this? Given my own behavior with women, I tend to agree with both of them. She tells me something about her childhood, and I can see Hart Anderson waiting to take center stage. From my days as a social worker investigating abuse and neglect cases, I heard stories like Carolyn Anderson's once a week. It is a familiar one, though I can't help but be fascinated. Her father, a doctor in northeastern Arkansas, had a serious drinking problem and physically abused her mother and herself. What makes it unique in my experience is the economic difference. Growing up, Carolyn was, if not rich, well off. The cases I saw in juvenile court involved poor people almost exclusively. The rich can avoid court by promises (which may or may not be kept) of private hospital admissions and private counseling. When her father got too badly out of control, it would be arranged for him to dry out in Memphis.

Now holding tissues in both fists, Carolyn pleads with me, "I know I've interfered in this case, but you would have, too, if you had been me. You've got to get Perry off. He really is crazy, but it's not his fault that he killed Hart; it's somehow mine."

The idea that Perry was hired by anyone is now far away. I am deeply moved by what I have heard. Each of us has our own secrets. Certainly I have my own. Yet, at the risk of implicating herself, she has insisted on explaining why she has acted in the manner she has and makes no apologies. I feel I understand her now. What had eluded me was her motive. The natural reaction would have been for her to get as far away from Perry Sarver as possible. Instead, her guilt moves her toward him like a magnet, and I realize now that she will not rest until he is free. While, like a voyeur, I watch her cry, it occurs to me that I have a most powerful and remarkable ally in my case. Each of us has our reasons for wanting to help Perry, but I suspect her reasons are even stronger.

Before I can speak, she continues, her words coming in a long, fast burst. "Ever since he was killed, I've lived in fear that Hart might have told someone how much I hated him. I was sure I would be a suspect, because it's been obvious that Perry is sick and so easily manipulated. You can't imagine my shock when I heard someone else was charged. I was upstairs in my room when I heard on the radio they had charged a doctor. I thought it was me. I knew someone would think it was my fault."

Watching her weep is making me intensely uncomfortable. I get up and touch her shoulder, which prompts more crying. "It's not your fault," I say. "It's not yours at all."

She begins to sob against my shoulder, and I smell that wonderful fragrance I first encountered in her office. She draws back and wipes her eyes before they run. I find that I am aroused and begin to feel heat coming off my face.

She mumbles so low I can barely hear her, "Would you just hold me for a moment, please?"

I am glad for an excuse to hide my erection and step against her, feeling an indelible warmth from her body. She lifts her mouth toward mine and kisses me. Her lips open and I feel her tongue in my mouth. Never in my life have I felt such tenderness. Even while her mouth is searching mine, I can feel her hands gently massaging the small of my back. We are hip to groin, and there is no longer any question of hiding my excitement. My heart is pounding wildly, and without a word she leads me upstairs. I follow behind her, my shoes squeaking on the bare wood in the hall that I can see leads to her bedroom. I do not allow myself to think whether I should be doing this—all I think of is how much I want her.

In her bedroom there is no trace of Hart. Downstairs must be for appearances. The room is surprisingly intimate. Reading my mind she turns and explains, "This is the guest room—I can't sleep in my bed any longer."

I nod. I did not come up here to make small talk.

Like an obedient child waiting to be undressed for bed, she gives me an expectant look. Her fragrance, sweet as honeysuckle, suffuses the room. As I lift her sweater over her head I feel as though I am about to explode. I barely remember the packet of rubbers I keep in my wallet.

Afterward, as we lie panting side by side, I take time to note that though she is almost touchingly thin, she is lovely naked. I touch her right side with my knuckles and am able to count her ribs. In my deprived state, of course, I would think Margaret Thatcher looked good. In my need, I fear, I have almost raped her.

"Are you all right?" I ask, removing the rubber, which is embarrassingly full, and dropping it into the bamboo wastepaper basket on my side of the bed.

"I'm fine," she whispers, patting my thigh. These are the first words either of us has spoken in thirty minutes. I turn on my side and smooth down a lock of her hair, which is damp.

"You're quite something," she says, and I can make out a smile in the gloom.

"So are you," I say, reaching for the sheet and the blankets, which have fallen completely off the bed. I realize now for the first time it is cold in this room. I pull the covers up to our chins. How could Hart Anderson have been so stupid as to play around on this woman? Whatever he found, it couldn't have been this good. I look over at Carolyn and for the first time notice the digital clock on her nightstand. It reads 10:30. I told Sarah I wouldn't be more than an hour. "I'm sorry," I say sincerely, "I told my daughter I'd be home an hour ago."

"Please stay," she asks, her voice low and rich.

I told myself I wouldn't do this to Sarah again. It isn't the first time. "I have to," I say regretfully and slide out of bed to dress.

Self-consciously, she gets out of bed and goes to her closet for a robe. In the soft light of the lamp by her bed she looks about twenty. Her face clouded with doubt, she says, "There won't be any need to reveal what I've told you about Hart, will there?"

I want to reassure this woman. "I don't think so," I say glibly. "If wishing were a crime, most of the population of this country would be behind bars."

This brings a bitter smile to her face. She follows me down the stairs. From a hall closet she hands me my jacket. I am standing in probably the exact spot where Hart was standing when he was shot. This is the awkward part. What do I say—"Had a nice time"? I say the obvious: "Have a nice trip. When do you get back?"

"In a few days," she says almost shyly, looking small and swallowed up by her robe. Quickly, she steps forward and lightly embraces me. My chin, which is now stubble, brushes against her hair. Breathing her scent, I crush her to me, and wonder if I ever will be this close to her again.

I am not even at the car when I begin to acknowledge to myself what I have done. I feel like one of those lawyers who chase their clients around the office and take their fee on the couch. Rumor has it that Kenny Hinson, a municipal judge now dead, had sex with a female defendant on the desk in his office. If Carolyn ever breathes a word about this, I could be fired. I can see Greta shaking her head at me in mock sorrow and Chick coming by my office to say how much he has enjoyed working with me. What the hell got into me? I went there ostensibly to talk to a witness to a murder and ended up screwing her! I can feel my face glowing in the darkness as I drive out of her rich, imposing neighborhood.

Supposedly there are no accidents. Did I go there hoping to take advantage of this woman because I knew she was vulnerable? As I found out when Rosa died, the old saying is true: nature abhors a vacuum. While it may not be an established scientific principle in Sociology of Sex 101, what I have done is common enough. There are no decent intervals in life anymore. Gratification is my name, fucking is my game. I feel self-disgust running into my brain like a remorseless tide. I feel myself welcoming the pain. It is too bad I can't take it. I get rejected and, bingo! I'll get even. I'll make myself feel better. I don't care who it is, what the situation is, whom it hurts. . . . As the realization of what I have done begins to sink in, my body begins to acknowledge its own complaints. Suddenly I feel sixty years old. Yet, as old as I feel, I wonder when I am going to start to grow up. It would be nice. With my right fist I pound the steering wheel in anger at my stupidity, but, like sex, it provides only temporary relief.

At home, Sarah comes to the door when she hears my key, like a wife who is mad but relieved her drunk of a husband has made it home another night. "You've been drinking," she says primly, but her face is tense, betraying her anxiety. She is fully dressed, jeans and sweatshirt and Reeboks, apparently ready to go to the hospital at a moment's notice and identify my body. Yep, that's my old man—the one with a hard-on.

"She offered me a beer," I say defensively, taking off my jacket and hanging it up in the closet by the front door. I wonder if I have the smell of sex on me, too. "It's not exactly office hours," I add, checking my watch to make sure I made it home by eleven. I have, but not by much.

"I thought you went there because of the case," she says, following me into the kitchen while I get a drink of water. The last few hours have made me thirsty.

"You don't get information by acting like you're the Gestapo," I point out, downing tap water from the blue plastic glass as if I were chugging beer at a University of Arkansas fraternity party. "Let's go to bed."

Her voice trembling, Sarah points with her chin like her mother used to do. "You've got makeup on your shirt."

"I know," I lie glibly, wiping my mouth with the back of my sleeve. "She started crying, and I put my arm around her to comfort her."

Sarah rocks back on her heels. "Dad!"

"It's true!" I yell, bringing Woogie into the kitchen. "You don't understand. I need this woman on my side. It's not going to help

Perry Sarver if I treat her like she's some kind of freak in a carnival. She's a human being, too."

With her hands on her hips, Sarah looks at me with undisguised contempt. "You didn't have to seduce her!"

"I think you're getting way out of line, young lady!" I hiss, sounding to myself like my mother yelling at my sister Marty thirty years ago for some real or imagined insolence. "You'd better go to bed before you get in big trouble."

Because I am talking to her as if she were about nine, she is on the verge of crying. "I'm sorry."

What a shit I am! I'm the kind of bully that makes women and children detest men. I go to her and put my arms around her. "I'm sorry, too, babe. I'm just tired." Woogie, who has been watching this little drama, jumps up against my legs, obviously glad the shouting is over, too. If I can't be honest, as least I can be loving to my own flesh and blood.

In bed, under the covers, listening to the house tick as it cools down, I am too exhausted to sleep. I wonder if Sarah noticed I didn't deny her accusation. For some reason it reminds me of the White House during the Watergate investigation years ago. Allegations were confirmed when they weren't denied. It makes me want to get out of bed and go lie some more. Yet it slowly dawns on me that maybe I didn't seduce anybody. Have I been set up? I retrace the night's events in my mind. I could have talked to Carolyn over the phone just as easily. I wanted to see her in person, but why? Was it really to go to bed with her? Even allowing for mass doses of hypocrisy on my part, I doubt it. I went there suspicious as hell and I have come away surely as she intended, thinking she is guilty only of bad thoughts. To throw dust in my eyes, she goes to bed with me, which is obviously the oldest and most effective scam in the world, given the fact that men are such fools. I feel lost in a maze. Have I hopelessly compromised myself from understanding what the hell is going on? I should be consoled that the prosecution is as much in the dark as I am. Amy would give her eyeteeth to know that Carolyn Anderson hated her husband, but would it do Perry Sarver any good if I told her? I don't think so. Amy would simply be more convinced that this case is rotten. And it may not be at all. What did Carolyn really have to gain by admitting she couldn't stand her husband? She relieved her own guilt, which is exactly what she needed to do. What is wrong with that? The simple truth is she trusts me or is acting as if she does. And the last thing I want to do is to be part of a process that causes another innocent person to be thrown into a legal snake pit. I have had enough of that in the last forty-eight hours. Has it only been two days since all this started? It seems like two years. As I toss around, I realize that the key to this is Sarver. I cannot wait any longer for him to call me. Carolyn Anderson is too slick for me. Unless something unforeseen happens in the next two weeks, I am never going to find out anything from her except what she wants me to know. Sarver knows. But how to get it out of him? I have no idea. Woogie jumps up on my bed, startling me. Lately he has been sleeping with Sarah. She probably sent him in as a peace offering. There is a chance she sent him in hopes that I will be content to sleep with my own dog instead of reverting to my old habits. I reach over and pet Woogie as he falls heavily against my side. "Don't you fart!" I warn him.

Woogie licks my hand. I feel I am doomed to be mean to the ones who love me best.

16

The next afternoon at four I wait for Perry to be brought in to see me in Raymond Berrenger's overheated office. If he has been lying to protect Jerry Kerner or Carolyn Anderson, now is the time to find out about it. Yet even Raymond Berrenger, who is theoretically unbiased, thinks Perry is telling the truth. Ray and Perry. We are one big, happy family now.

"We might as well go by first names," Berrenger has just told me after inviting me to use his office to interview Sarver. He is at a meeting of the Rogers Hall Utilization Review Committee, which is supposed to decide every sixty days whether a patient should be transferred to the much less restrictive environment of the open units.

Berrenger is fast becoming an adopted son of the South. He has begun to sound and look like Jimmy Carter, flashing a hundred teeth at me and drawling as though he has never been north of Plains. What have we done to this man? I look around his office for clues. He has remodeled since the last time I was here. Incredibly he has even taped to his desk one of those black-faced signs sold in service stations: "Save Your Confederate Money, Boys, the South Is Gonna Rise Again!" What could be worse? The next time I come in here I expect to see the flag of the Confederacy covering an entire wall. On his desk there is a tiny tin Confederate soldier decked out in knapsack, gray uniform, and rifle with a fixed rubber bayonet.

Berrenger does not seem like a racist any more than Perry seems like a killer. But no native professional that I know would be caught dead with this crap in his office. Someday during an interview, one of his black patients is going to take his little soldier and shove it down his throat. Does he actually think we would like to secede? Perhaps Berrenger is a chameleon and reflects whatever his surroundings happen to be. He has no qualms about saying forensic psychiatry is fraudulent, so maybe this is his way of telling us that our hard-earned civility in race relations in the South is so much thin ice, but despite voodoo psychiatry and racism he is happy to be here. For all I know, Berrenger may see us as such blatant racists that he doesn't understand the offensiveness of this good-ole-boy bonhomie. He could be mocking us and we are too unsophisticated to catch on, but probably he is not. When in Rome, hold your nose and do as the Romans do. . . .

The rest of his office has a more conventional but homey touch. He has obviously brought in his own furniture, because no state psychiatrist I know has been issued a genuine leather couch. Berrenger does not look like the type to seduce nurses or his patients, God forbid, though at any one time there are about five women kept in Rogers Hall, so I'm told. There would be more if there were more space. On the wall behind his desk, there is, in Old English script, complete with whorls, the Serenity Prayer.

I get up and go behind his chair to read it. I, too, wish for acceptance of those things I cannot change. If I could bring my father and Rosa back to life, if I could bring that boy who committed suicide back to life, if Rainey hadn't dumped me, if I hadn't slept with Carolyn Anderson . . . I have a laundry list of "ifs," and right now I am finding it hard to accept any one of them.

I find myself wanting to shock Berrenger with the news that Sarver may be a homosexual. Of course, I will not tell him, but, as with Carolyn, I'm sure the news wouldn't faze him. Perhaps psychiatrists are so used to being wrong, nothing they screw up is worth raising an eyebrow over. He thinks Sarver may still be dangerous. Why? Just a hunch. He grins. Certainly, no evidence. Perry has been a model patient.

A young, attractive Filipino RN brings Perry to see me and hands me his records in a plastic blue book. Perry looks at me as mildly as anyone can who has been locked up with about sixty other crazy people, some of whom are as psychopathic as any crazies in the country. For years before he died, Rogers Hall was home to a man who had allegedly killed his mother and then eaten one of her eyes. I think it would be beyond the ethical pale to lie to Perry, but it won't hurt to give him a dose of reality therapy.

I invite Perry to sit on Berrenger's couch. He might as well be comfortable, because I am going to be here awhile. I lean back in Berrenger's chair and study him. He has on a blue-and-yellow striped T-shirt that is tucked neatly into a pair of Lee jeans and tennis shoes. His face, more rounded than when he came in, is more clean-shaven than my own. His short, sandy hair is neatly combed, with a part that is straight as the second hand on the clock above his head. He looks like either an all-American boy or an all-American psychopath.

"If Jerry Kerner was involved," I say, "you better tell me now. We're running out of time."

A sullen look on his face, Perry says, "Kerner didn't have anything to do with it."

"Why didn't you tell Kerner's lawyer," I ask angrily, "when he was out here?"

Perry mumbles, "I was afraid of him."

I pause for a moment and say evenly, "The jury could believe that Dr. Anderson got you to kill her husband. I hear they didn't get along."

Perry begins to squirm a bit on the couch, shifting his weight forward as if he is about to rise. Finally he says, "They'll believe Dr. Anderson."

I lean on Berrenger's desk. "Not necessarily. They could as easily believe Dr. Berrenger, who thinks you were completely responsible."

Surprisingly, Perry relaxes and leans back against the reddish-brown leather. "Even if the jury doesn't find I'm not guilty by reason of insanity," he argues, "they'll take into account I've been diagnosed a mental patient." Who has been talking to him? Carolyn? Berrenger? Other patients?

"Not if they think you're faking," I say abruptly, keeping up the pressure. "They'll put you to death."

His turquoise-blue eyes far back in his head, he squints at me as if to make sure I'm on the level. Stubbornly he shakes his head. "They won't do that."

I stand up and sit on the edge of Berrenger's desk, not more than a foot from him, and get right down in his face. This guy has way too much confidence. "Why did you kill him, Perry?"

He looks over the top of my head as if there is a script for him to read. "I did it so me and Carolyn could get married."

I say quickly, "Did she tell you if her husband died that maybe you and she might get married?"

He picks at a piece of lint on his pants, obviously thinking. "She didn't say that, but she told me . . ." He stops, turning coy and staring down at his crotch.

"Told you what?" I demand, so close to him I can smell the staleness of his breath.

A shy but proud smile comes to his face as he lifts his head. "She told me that sometimes she thought she understood me better than anybody in the whole world."

What in the hell is this all about? Ever since I got up this morning, I have begun to wonder if Carolyn has set him up and is still working on him. At least some of his phone calls are referred to in the Progress Notes in his records, but the hospital apparently does not listen in on them, and I have no way of knowing what she has said to him. "What do you think she meant by that?" I ask. In the past there has been no mention in his records of her calling him.

"Just that we're kind of alike," Perry says, his voice smug, as he rearranges his genitals in his pants.

I get off the desk and go back around and sit again in Berrenger's chair. If he walks back in while Perry is fingering himself and I'm hovering over him, God only knows what he would testify to. "Do you talk to anyone on the phone about your case?"

He responds in a matter-of-fact tone. "I call Carolyn."

"What does she say?"

The corners of his mouth turn up in a smile. "That we'll be married after my trial."

My blood runs cold. I know he is delusional, but what if she has told him this? Most likely he is repeating what I have just suggested to him. Yet, he seems as confident as any future bridegroom I've known. I ask, "Can you hear her voice in your head?"

He snickers, "You think I'm hearing voices, huh?"

I make sure I do not lead him. "When did she tell you this?"

He thinks. "About a month ago."

I doubt it. A month ago he was just short of bouncing off the walls. The woman I slept with couldn't be that diabolical. She is working too hard on his behalf to have deliberately tricked him into killing her husband. Yet it is easy to want to trick a person who is crazy. Am I not out here trying to do that to my own client? I don't feel like a lawyer at all. My job, which I have forgotten, is to fight for Sarver, not outguess him. If he is lying, then so be it. Criminal defendants lie every day to us. The rules are that a lawyer can't permit a client to lie when he knows he is not telling the truth. But there is no way an attorney can practice law if he doesn't give his own client the benefit of the doubt.

I stand up and go over and look out Berrenger's one window, which, of course, is barred. How does anyone live a day being locked up? "Do you want to testify?" I ask.

"Sure," he says, his hands folded in his lap now that I have moved away from him. How could I think otherwise, his expression says.

"Fine," I tell him. "You have that right."

Where it gets sticky is when the attorney knows his client intends to lie. The lawyer can ask to be relieved as counsel if he is in private practice; public defenders don't have that luxury. In law school they teach that if the attorney knows his client is lying on the witness stand, he is supposed to ask for a recess and talk to his client, but if he continues to lie, he is supposed to tell the judge. Sure, as Perry would say. But I don't even have to worry about it, because I am as much in the dark as I was when I first read in the newspaper that Hart Anderson had been killed.

Outside, the sun is trying to peek through dark clouds. "How are you going to explain to the jury why you killed Mr. Anderson?"

He gives me a pained expression, as if to say he may be crazy but he isn't stupid. "I couldn't marry Carolyn if he was still alive."

I rest my head on the window ledge. Most people see divorce as a less drastic alternative. I stand up straight and nod. "Just tell that to the jury." His logic is impeccable. No bigamy for my man. But not for the first time today, it occurs to me that all of this could be an act. If he is sane, he knows how crazy it sounds.

"Perry," I say, still looking out the window into the feeble rays of late-afternoon sunshine, "you won't get mad, then, when I argue to the jury you were mentally ill when you shot Carolyn's husband, will you?"

"I know that," he says, hunching his shoulders. "You think I'm crazy now, don't you?"

That is a good question. I think he probably is, but the longer this case goes on the more doubts I have. "It doesn't matter what I think," I lie. Of course it matters what I think. The best trial lawyers I've seen are the ones who can convince themselves of the justice of their clients' cases. They can turn a simple slip-and-fall case in a supermarket into a conspiracy by corporate giants to squeeze the last cent of profit out of the consumer by neglecting to set up a "Wet Floor" sign.

As badly as I want to believe that my only job is to give Perry the best defense money can't buy, I find I want to know the truth. I've spent almost the last two years giving lip service to the idea that truth isn't the defense counsel's job—it is the jury's—but at this moment I don't buy it. And this is an unforgivable point of view for me to take ethically, for if my skepticism isn't kept in check, the jury will surely pick up on it. And I could well be responsible for an innocent man's death or imprisonment because I was too superior to play by the rules of the game. I go back to the corner of the desk and hope he doesn't unzip his pants and wave his dick at me. I watch while Perry feels his fat with a thumb and a forefinger. Rogers Hall does not have much in the way of athletic facilities. Women from the air base come out every few weeks and put on a dance for the patients in the gym. Every girl's dream—a ratio of ten to one. "What are you going to do if Dr. Anderson remarries before you get out?"

Perry looks at me sternly, as if I have committed a serious breach of etiquette. "She won't do that," he says flatly.

For the first time I consider the distinct possibility that Sarver may be a stone-cold killer, a sociopath who isn't bothered by questions of right and wrong. He may have gone to the Andersons' house to rape Carolyn that night and changed his mind after he killed Anderson because he knew he wasn't going to get away with it. Perry isn't stupid. He could have set this up all by himself.

"The prosecuting attorney may try to get you mad," I tell him. I realize there is a certain irony in our situation. I have achieved what Perry presumably killed for. I wonder what he would do if I began describing what Carolyn looked like without her clothes on. Impulsively, I ask, "Why didn't you have sex with Dr. Anderson after you killed her husband if you loved her so much?"

Perry answers laconically, "She was crying too hard."

"Why didn't you run when you saw she was upset?"

He shifts restlessly on the couch. My questions are boring him. "She kept talking to me."

Behind Berrenger's desk I scribble down what he tells me. How could anyone have the presence of mind to sit down with the murderer of her spouse and talk to him? The normal reaction would surely be hysteria. Can anyone really be that cool—even a physician? Wouldn't the most normal reaction be to scream or to run? Even as manipulative as Carolyn is, wouldn't a violent act like this cause her to lose control? Perhaps not, if as she told me, she saw that in one horrible but timely moment, Perry had done as exactly as she wished. It may well be that Carolyn feels uneasy about her own reaction. I wonder if Carolyn were on trial instead of Perry and I were the prosecutor whether I would argue to the jury that her behavior was just a little too heroic to be believable.

I finish with Perry in another fifteen minutes. I don't know what questions he will be asked, but I cover as many as I've been able to think of. I will try to get out as much of the story on direct as I can, but there are huge gaps I can't do anything about. Is Angela Satterfield real, and if she is, where is she? Perry is no help. I have to remind myself that it doesn't matter—in fact, it is to his advantage if she does not exist. What look like discrepancies you could drive a truck through are really signposts of his madness, I will argue.

I open Berrenger's door and ask a secretary in the main administrative office to call someone to take Perry back. Perry comes out and tries unsuccessfully to bum a cigarette. He has learned I can't help him there. I have always found bizarre the normality of much of the behavior of the mentally ill. Even my strangest-acting clients can usually pull themselves together to light a cigarette. Perry has had so great a remission that the secretaries and social workers now treat him as if he were here for a routine checkup. So long as you stay off the subject of Carolyn Anderson, he is fine. Edna Beavers, a social worker who is a friend of Rainey's, says to him, "Perry, if you gain any more weight, we're going to have to put you on a diet."

Perry pats his stomach jovially and says to Edna and Linda Merida, a secretary who is retiring this month after thirty years with the Division of Mental Health, "As my sergeant used to tell me: 'Perry, three squares and a place to flop—you never had it so good!' "

We all laugh obligingly, and Edna gives me a wan smile. Gossip comes to Rogers Hall as fast as any place else in the hospital. What would Rainey say if she ever found out I slept with Carolyn? It pains me to think about it. Willie Spain, a black technician twice the size of the little nurse who brought Perry in, walks into the room, and I watch Perry's eyes cut to Willie's muscular body. His eyes show genuine animation, and I make a mental note to review the Progress Notes before I leave for any signs of homosexual behavior. "I'll be back before the trial," I tell Perry, who is now more interested in watching Willie than listening to me.

Edna, Perry's social worker, nods at Perry's back as he disappears around the corner with Willie. "He's a real mystery man. We tried to get in contact with his one relative in Illinois, but the letter came back marked no such address."

"How's he doing?" I ask casually, leaning against an employee bulletin board. Rainey and I went to a party at Edna's three weeks ago. Divorced herself, she had been nice to me, as though Rainey had made me out to be something special.

Edna, who isn't bad-looking, gives me a look that says I might want to try her next. "While he's on his medication, other than his one delusion, he's as normal as you or I," she answers, giggling, narrowing her brown eyes at me.

How do you know, I think. Nobody saw Perry professionally except Carolyn, but they sound as if they have known Perry all his life even as they admit they don't know a thing about his past.

Sorry, Edna, I'm too busy screwing witnesses in this case. I smile at her and return to Berrenger's office and go through the most recent records. The Progress Notes section is usually the most revealing because it contains direct observation of the patients by nurses and techs. I look at yesterday's entry: "7:00 A.M. to 3:00 P.M. Pt. complained of mild headache. Refused aspirin. In dayroom helped break up fight between Dowd and Stackhouse during pool game. Said he didn't know who started it. Ate good lunch. Received call from Dr. Anderson. Pt. called her back on pt. phone. Talked for ten minutes. Cooperative and quiet as usual. Dwight Dorsey, Tech."

There it is. Carolyn called Perry and told him not to implicate Jerry Kerner. If she did it, why did she do it? Is there a conspiracy between Carolyn and Kerner? I don't know.

I look again at the entry. Sarver is a perfect patient and human being here. Reports fights but won't snitch. A boy scout of a patient. His other reports are unremarkable. They show an individual who is well-adjusted and even pleasant in trying circumstances, a feat most of the outside world couldn't manage. This is no sociopath stirring up a pot of trouble. If he is homosexual, there is no hint of it. However, in contrast to his model behavior are the weekly interviews he has with his treatment team, composed of Berrenger, Edna, a psychologist, and a psychiatric registered nurse. There is reference after reference testifying to the belief that his delusion persists. At the latest meeting only three days prior, a note signed by Berrenger states that Sarver "still maintains victim's wife is in love with him. When asked how he knows, when this is denied by Dr. Anderson, pt. stares angrily at questioner but won't answer. Admits he continues to call victim's wife occasionally. Checked with Dr. Anderson. She requests that his calls not be prohibited and may be helpful to pt."

I put down the records and rub my eyes. Men and women have been obsessed with each other since Adam and Eve. What, if anything, will make a jury think Perry Sarver should be treated any differently than anybody else? I, too, am becoming obsessed with Carolyn Anderson. I haven't killed her yet, but if she doesn't quit fucking with this case, I am going to consider it.

As I am finishing up, Berrenger returns to his office, happily whistling "On the Road Again" by Willie Nelson. We are just two good ole boys together.

"Well, Gideon, how do you think Perry is doing?" he says, motioning me to keep seated behind his desk as he sits heavily on his couch. It is as if we have switched places and I am the doctor and he is the lawyer.

I resist the urge to put my feet up on his desk and instead fold my hands on my stomach, not so subtly mocking him. "He still seems to have the delusion about Carolyn Anderson, doesn't he?"

He cannot resist, his hands coming together over his pot as if they could go nowhere else. "Who wouldn't?" he jokes breezily. "Perry may be crazy but he's not stupid. You've seen her, haven't you?"

I nod, hoping I will not blush. Would he be envious of me if he knew what I had done, or would he think I was a damned fool, or both?

A big smile on his satisfied mug, Raymond says, "She's a hell of a good-looking woman. I've had a few fantasies about her myself."

Like a zoo animal, I ape his smile. But I can't imagine this man having sex with a woman like Carolyn. I laugh obligingly. Good ole boys too civilized to start talking about "poontang" or whatever we called sex when I was a teenager, but we know what we mean. I ask him, "Why do you let Perry call her?"

He notices that one of his shirt buttons has come undone and attends to it. "She thinks, and I agree, it'll help him hear from her that she doesn't love him. She's an amazing woman, all right."

Amazing, that much is certain. My back is still sore. I pick up his Confederate soldier and balance him on my palm. "Do you really want the South to rise again?"

He gives me a sheepish smile. "We all have delusions or illusions of one sort or another, don't we? Actually, I got that sign for myself. When I look at it, I substitute my own name for the South. I guess I identify with it. Alcoholism has kicked me around pretty good for a long time. Since I've been down here, I've begun to feel like I can lick it. I get out of bed now thinking I'm going to rise again myself. It may be pure bullshit just like this sign, but we all need a little hope, don't we?"

I nod, abashed. This guy does open-heart surgery on himself every time I see him. As much as I would like to think of him as the enemy, I can't dislike him.

"Raymond," I say, using his first name for the first time, "I hope you beat it, too."

On the freeway on my way home, a lime-green Datsun dies six cars in front of me. I do not think this signals something portentous like the beginning of the decline of the Japanese Century, but as traffic whizzes past, I do have time to reflect on the future of my representation of Perry Sarver. I need to get my head on straight. Whatever is coming, and I have no idea what it will be, does not look like a happy ending. There is too much I don't know about this case to feel good about it any longer. The other lane, as I crack my neck trying to see, looks awfully fast.

17

My daughter is in love. I have been too preoccupied to notice before, but all the signs are there. Eric Brady's name has begun to appear on pieces of paper all over the house: on the cover of the telephone book, the calendar on the pantry door, the chalk board on the refrigerator. His name is worked into every conversation, no matter what the subject. This morning while I was eating breakfast, I was informed that Eric, like myself, has a bowl of Cheerios every day. And, not the least, Eric's thoughts have become so ubiquitous and commonplace around our house that one day I will begin quoting him myself.

And at this very moment, Eric the Great, looking very ordinary in frayed but clean jeans, hightop tennis shoes, and a K Mart work shirt, is sitting across from me with my daughter on my sofa in my living room, drinking my Coke and eating my popcorn, pretending he is not in love. He and I are holding forth on the subject of the Dallas Cowboys, who were acquired by an Arkansan, Jerry Jones, a former Razorback who has made a fortune in oil and gas. Eric doesn't see why this is such a big deal, and I am having trouble describing the delight Arkansans of my generation feel about the transaction. I know the reason: we are small and poor; our neighbor Texas is big and rich. When we play the University of Texas each year in football, the Longhorns usually find a way to win or we find a way to lose. I uncross my ankles on the footrest of the recliner. "We hate them because they don't take us seriously," I explain. "There is nothing worse than being ignored."

Sarah, who lately has begun to dress equally badly (presumably to keep in style with her beloved), watches Eric as if he were a magician who has promised to do his tricks this one time only and then never again. Eric the Great envious of anyone? Never! Eric is smart enough to call me Mr. Page, but he can't understand why I am all worked up over this. After all, he is young, strong, and he has Sarah. He asks dubiously, "You think people really care about that?"

I sip discreetly at a Coke laced with a shot of bourbon. He is right, of course. How embarrassing to give a damn over something so trivial. I resist saying that it must be nice to be so young and virtuous. What is wrong with me? This poor kid is doing the best he can to entertain his girl's old man, but it is uphill all the way. "I'm not saying it is our finest hour," I reply sourly, despite my good intentions.

Eric scratches his head as if we were discussing how the universe came into being, wondering how to respond. Get up and get out of here, you old killjoy, I think to myself, but I won't just yet. I search through the nearly empty bowl in my lap looking for corn that is neither burned nor unpopped. Eric is not a bad-looking kid, I have to admit. Six feet, not an ounce of fat on him, and a nice Roman nose, as my mother used to say. Better-looking than his skinny brother. Actually, what I like is his short, neat haircut. If he looked like Rainey's Mountain Goat, I wouldn't be having this conversation. I know Sarah wants me to go to bed, and I will in a moment, but by God, it's my house and I can sit in the living room for a few minutes if I want to. They are sitting on opposite ends of the couch, and I know the moment my door closes the space between them will be filled like electricity jumping across the gap on a spark plug.

I change the subject to baseball, and we talk more easily for a few minutes. I am reminded of the evenings when my sister Marty would wait impatiently for me to leave the screened-in porch and go in to bed so she could entertain her dates in a friendlier fashion. Get up and go to bed so they can get down to business. I do, and it is all Sarah can do to keep her sense of relief in check. At least she isn't in a parked car somewhere with some drunked-up kid slobbering all over her.

Turning over to get comfortable on the king-sized mattress I no longer need, I try not to think about what my daughter is doing on the couch. He has to go home by eleven, so it will be only thirty minutes before I can completely relax. Is this what I have to look forward to for the next two years? Woogie scratches at the door, and I get up and let him in. "Come on in, Woogs," I say. "This is the reject room, so get on up here." He does, and I pat his smelly head, offered in gratitude. At least my dog still likes me.

Through the door I can hear Sarah titter. So long as I don't hear any moans, I guess I should be happy. Why is it that sex is so important? Aren't I a little old to be this miserable? It is warm inside, and I get up and open the window. The air feels wonderful tonight—it's about sixty degrees out. There is that warm, lush sense of spring that makes the middle South a pleasant place to live until the humidity requires air-conditioning to cope with the summers. Everybody in the state of Arkansas is doing something tonight except me and Woogie. Rainey and the Missing Link especially.

I have seen her from a distance, but I have made it a point not to bump into her. After the trial I need to get back into circulation. Yet the prospect isn't particularly appealing. Rainey has spoiled me for a decent woman, and, given what happens when I start to think about her, Carolyn Anderson has spoiled me for something else. Is she a murderer or a saint? Since my brains have moved to a new location, it doesn't look as though I'm going to find out any time soon. I whisper to Woogie who is huddled up against my side: "Let's face it—humans are a weird species." He shoves his cold muzzle into my hand as if to say, "What else is new?"

At eleven the front door slams, and Sarah comes and knocks softly on my door. "Dad, are you asleep?"

"Come on in, babe." Has he proposed? Is she going to tell me she is pregnant?

She sits on the bed in the dark and pets Woogie, making his collar jingle. "Eric asked me to go to church Sunday with him and his family and have lunch afterward."

Church! I was afraid he was going to ask if he could borrow my rubbers. I pet Woogie in gratitude. I hope Eric is a fundamentalist who believes that even heavy breathing before marriage is a sin.

"Sure, go ahead," I say in my old man's voice. "I'll be okay. Woogie and I'll just open a couple of cans. We'll be fine. Don't worry about us."

She laughs, making the bed bounce. "I love you, Dad."

"What church?" I ask, shifting the pillows to get comfortable if we are going to talk. I haven't done too well in the religion department, having let my subscription run out after Rosa died.

"Baptist," she says, her voice almost in another key with excitement at the thought of a few unexpected hours with Eric the Great.

"Good," I mutter. "They'll keep you awake." But if there is a heaven, Rosa is right now asking for a bus ticket home with a box of matches in her purse. After setting me on fire, she'll head straight for Billy Graham. There have been times when there was some doubt if the Pope was Catholic, but there never has been about Colombia.

"Good night, Dad," Sarah says, hugging the top of my head in the dark.

"Good night, babe," I say. "Do you want Woogie?"

"You keep him," she says, getting up.

Unspoken is her thought that I need him more than she does. She has Eric to dream about; I have a middle-aged dog to cuddle up with. What will I do when she goes off to college? Get a dog for each room of the house? I feel a mixture of sadness and pride.

Someday, and it isn't far away, some guy will take her to church to get married. I know I feel sad for no good reason. She has to grow up and get out of here before I drive her nuts. If I had my way, I'd chain her to the house. I hear Sarah humming in the bathroom. Her life probably seems as complicated as mine, but it can't touch it in that department. I drift off to sleep, knowing I will probably never discover the truth about this case.

Saturday morning I work down at the office on my opening statement. I sit at my desk and try to concentrate on what I'm going to say. No one else comes in, and I begin to sink my teeth into it. I spend a large part of my time setting the stage for Carolyn's testimony. If I can hit the right tone, the jury will accept the implication that Perry shouldn't be held accountable for murdering Hart. I want to draw as vivid a contrast as I possibly can between Carolyn and the state's expert, Dr. Berrenger. Carolyn is warm and caring yet fallible; Berrenger is an intellectual who looks into a mirror and still doubts his own existence. But this is argument, and I am not allowed to argue the case until my closing statement. The trick is to tell the jury what they will be hearing in such a way that by the time those twelve men and women have finished listening to me speak, they will be predisposed to trust Carolyn and be skeptical of Berrenger. I fill up the wastepaper can in my office with three drafts before I feel I am getting close.

At half-past twelve I eat a sandwich brought from home and then drive to the Y to meet Skip to play racquetball. We have only played a couple of times since I asked him to check on Anderson for me—he has had to work or has been out of town hustling new art advertising business, so I am glad for the exercise.

Skip is waiting for me in the locker room in his usual racquetball outfit—shirtless with skimpy shorts—and he watches me dress. "You still want to find out about Anderson?" he asks. Like Eric, he doesn't have an ounce of fat on him.

Though I know I have no reason to, I feel increasingly uncomfortable changing clothes and showering with Skip and nearly trip myself putting on my jockstrap. "Yeah," I say, but at this late date there doesn't seem much I can do with it.

"A guy I know is willing to talk to you after we finish," he says, evening up his racket strings with his fingers.

"So what does he know?" I ask, zipping my shorts.

"Sorry, partner," he says, embarrassed, "he's got a lock on it."

I slip on a ragged gray T-shirt that advertises a 10K race I was lucky to finish. What the hell, I think. It can't hurt to talk.

Upstairs, Skip, quiet for once, concentrates on his game and whips me badly the first game twenty-one to thirteen. He plays even more aggessively as we begin the second, and I find myself behind six to zip when I look up above and see a man about our age watching us. Skip is showing off for this guy, I see now. Something about this irks me, and I decide to bear down. Skip, I realize, has been intimidating me, bringing his racquet back in a wide arc, and I have been letting myself be forced out of position, afraid I will get hit by his racquet. To hell with this, I think, and begin moving in front of him to cut off the ball and drive it past him as I should have been doing all along. This works wonders until, with me leading fifteen to fourteen, he drills me in the back of the neck with the ball. I feel I've been jabbed with a frog gig, but I am damned if I am going to admit it. Skip, rattled by my show of toughness and afraid he will hit me again, folds quietly, and I run out the game twenty-one to fourteen.

"I guess that's enough," he says as we go out the door to get a drink. "Darron's waiting on us."

I follow Skip up another flight of steps and he introduces me to a man about my height who is dressed in a plaid shirt, jeans, and cowboy boots. There is nothing about this guy that is even remotely stereotypical of someone gay, and his right hand springs down on mine like a small game trap. "Darron Walker," he says quietly. "Don't flinch much, do you?"

I smile and say dryly, "Sometimes you got to stand up to Skip—he'll take advantage of you if you let him."

Skip is all smiles, too, now that the game is over and he greets Darron warmly. "Glad you could make it," he says.

Leaning against the opposite wall, I towel off and try to size this guy up as he and Skip make small talk. He has a mustache, salt-and-pepper hair, and is as wiry and brown as a Colombian stevedore. If he is gay, I'd never spot him. After a moment of silence that isn't long enough to become awkward, he turns to me and says casually, "Hear you got a trial coming up soon."

I nod and hang the towel over the wall leading down to the court. Who is this guy? For all I know he could be an undercover cop, looking for gays to bash.

Skip foolishly straddles the ledge, showing off again, and interjects, "I've told him what you're looking for."

I feel compelled to explain. "I guess you know I represent the guy who killed Anderson."

Without warning, he says, "I saw him—Sarver—and Anderson coming out of a bathroom in Baxter Park about eleven at night around nine months ago."

I prop one foot under me against the wall and digest what I have just heard. Baxter Park, right on the southern boundary of Blackwell County, is a notorious hangout for gays. I have represented a couple who got busted. "No shit, huh?" I manage.

Expressionless until now, Walker gives me a look that says there is no turning back. "No shit."

What is Carolyn Anderson going to say to this, I wonder. Perry and Hart. I never would have believed it. God knows what this will do to my case. I can't begin to imagine. I have no choice but to ask: "I take it you're gay?"

He looks at Skip as if to say: your friend's a real genius. "Yeah, I'm gay," he drawls.

The viewing area above a racquetball court is a weird place to prepare for trial, but at this stage I'm not choosy. I ask, "You'd be willing to testify and have that come out?"

Again, he looks at Skip, and this time gives him a grin. "Hart Anderson wasn't exactly on my top forty."

Though "Tex," as I've already come to think of him, doesn't know it, his stock starts down. "What'd he do?"

"His law firm cheated my sister out of some land last year," he says, hooking his thumbs in his pants. "The bastard didn't even have the decency to return a phone call."

It is my turn to look at Skip. I've showed my ass literally in this case, but I'm not a complete idiot. "Surely," I say bluntly, "you've got more at stake than this. Once the prosecutor finds out, and I have to tell him my witnesses, it could get real ugly for you."

Tex shrugs. I haven't impressed him.

Like a kid who is stalling for time before a fight, I ask, "You got any witnesses?"

Skip climbs down off the ledge and says pointedly, "It's not something you invite your neighbors to come watch."

Improbably, Tex rescues me. "I was supposed to meet a guy."

I am beginning to feel a little strange up here discussing this in short pants. "Did he show?"

Tex scratches his face. "About ten minutes later."

Looking at Mr. Walker, I tell Skip, "It'd be nice if we had someone to back this up."

"The guy who showed up isn't what you'd call a real publicity hound," Tex advises us. "I don't think he's around here anymore."

We hear a door open below, and a man and woman appear on the court and turn to look at us. It is time to move these discussions to a more private venue.

In my office fifteen minutes later, however, I still am not learning much more than I already knew about why this guy is willing to stand up in court and admit he is gay. Arkansas isn't exactly San Francisco. If he is telling me the truth, by testifying he stands to lose his nonunion job as a loader for a warehouse off Carver Avenue. My private guess is that Hart rejected this man, and he is willing to get even. What bothers me is that this is information you usually get by pulling teeth. I ask him point-blank: "Did you ever have sex with Hart Anderson?"

Slouched down in a metal folding chair and looking far more comfortable than I would in his situation, he says, "No, sir."

I look over at Skip, who is studying a spot on the floor, and give Tex my perjury speech, my credibility speech, and my truth-and-the-American-way speech all rolled into one, but he doesn't budge. Thirty minutes later, after getting his home address and telephone number, I thank him, let him out of the office, and go looking for Skip, who is browsing through Ziskin's book on how to screw psychiatrists in the courtroom. "Is this guy for real?" I say, standing in the door.

Skip puts down the book and laughs. "How the hell do I know? I've known him twenty-four hours longer than you have. The gossip I heard is that he was telling the story around that after he and Hart screwed, Hart made fun of the size of his dick. He swore to me, though, he saw your client and Hart at Baxter Park."

I go sit down in my chair and prop my aching feet up on my desk. "So he's not getting mad, he's getting even."

"Could be," Skip says, looking at his watch. "I got a meeting with a prospective client in fifteen minutes so I'm out of here."

I walk him to the front door. "I don't know whether to thank you or cuss the day we met," I say truthfully. "What a can of worms!"

He gives me a broad wink. "What are friends for?"

I let him out after telling him to let me know if he hears anything else and go back to our machine to get a Coke. I sit at the back of our offices in our small law library trying to figure out what I have. Even as slowly as I think, it doesn't take long for me to figure out that unless I am misreading this entirely, I may have Phil Harper by the throat. If Walker's testimony is admissible (and it should fit right in with the diagnosis that Perry is denying his homosexuality), the pressure on Phil to keep Hart's homosexuality out of the papers will be intense. As soon as the evidence comes in, it's fair game for the media. Now it is just gossip, and the papers won't touch it for fear of libel suits. I can see Phil sweat as the calls from Hart's most powerful friends pour in, suggesting that he make a deal on this case to keep the evidence that Hart was gay out of the papers. If Phil is unethical enough to charge Jerry Kerner for the purpose of smearing him, he won't have any scruples about caving in to the pressure that will be brought on him.

I knock back half my Coke in one long gulp, still dehydrated from the game, wondering how could Hart Anderson have been such a fool as to risk getting caught in a public bathroom. I remind myself that it happens all the time. If U.S. congressmen don't have any better sense, why should a state senator from Arkansas? For a change I smile at our bare-bones library, which consists of two sets of the Arkansas statutes (we each have our own separate volume of the criminal code), the *Arkansas Digest*s, and a few reference books on criminal law and evidence. A good witness is worth a thousand books.

I put my Coke can down and head for my car. It is dawning on me that, assuming Tex is telling the truth, Perry has been lying to me all this time. Now is the time to find out. As I get on the freeway and head for Rogers Hall, I begin to think about the risk in calling Tex as a witness. I will be handing Phil the motive he needs to convict Perry—a homosexual affair that went bad somehow—it won't matter how, as long as the jury hears the word "homosexual" first. I am going to have to think some more about the pressure that will be brought to bear on him to knock down the charges to something reasonable. My gut reaction is that Phil will do most anything to keep this from going to trial now, but my gut has made too many decisions already in this case. I will need some advice.

I park in Dr. Berrenger's space at Rogers Hall—God knows what he does on a Saturday afternoon to keep from drinking—and wonder again how Carolyn is going to handle the news that not only was her husband gay but he was also his murderer's lover. Not well, I suspect, but the bigger question is how she will handle its going public if Phil calls my bluff and takes this case to trial. I doubt there are too many widows out there who would like it if one morning they picked up the paper and read their husbands had been getting it up in a public park with a boyfriend. Screw her. She isn't my client, I remind myself. Somehow, I keep forgetting that.

I wait for Perry in the break room and try to think how to deal with this. It is way past time to cut the crap out in this case. I don't feel like being cute and trying to trick him.

He comes in, and I can see the surprise on his face that I am out here on a Saturday. A licensed practical nurse near retirement age, whose name tag ironically identifies her as Mrs. Perry, stares at me, her white eyebrows raised in a question. "You didn't want his records?"

"Not today," I say briskly, glancing at Perry, who is dressed in faded jeans with a hole at the knee and a short-sleeved green T-shirt. She leaves, and I close the door behind her.

"What's wrong?" Perry asks. He seems a little nervous.

"Sit down," I direct, coming around to the side of the table that faces the door, "and I'll tell you."

For the first time since I have been coming out to see him, I think I can detect a glimmer of fear in his eyes. He sits down on the edge of a folding chair and waits for me to speak.

"What's wrong," I say loudly, "is that an eyewitness has identified you as coming out of a bathroom in Baxter Park with Hart Anderson last year."

He looks down at the table that separates us and says, in a choked voice, "That's not true."

I do not believe him for a moment. When he raises his head, he has a wild, trapped look in his eyes and begins to rock slightly back and forth. There is no point lecturing him at this point on the fact he hasn't told me the truth. "Do you know a man named Darron Walker?"

He says he does not, and I tell him who he is. "The prosecuting attorney is going to try to make the jury believe you killed Hart Anderson for some reason connected to the fact that you and he had a homosexual relationship. Do you understand?"

He shakes his head. "I'm not gay!" he practically shrieks.

"You have to stop lying to me, Perry," I tell him as calmly as I can. "Not a single person on that jury is going to believe you if you say that."

"I'm not!" he insists hoarsely.

He has begun to sweat. It is so obvious he is lying that I want to slap him. "When did you first meet Anderson?"

Perry shakes his head. "I've never met him."

I come around the table and get in his face. "What were you doing in that bathroom with him?"

He has begun to shake. "I don't know what you're talking about."

"Bullshit!" I hiss, trying to intimidate him. "We are going to look like the biggest idiots who ever graced a courtroom." I try to think of a way to bring this home to him. "Did you kill him because you were mad at him?"

He wags his head again. "I told you already. So me and Carolyn could get married."

I slap the table in mock frustration. "You're lying."

He gets a mean look on his face, but I am too mad to be afraid of him. We glare at each other for a few seconds, and it occurs to me that although it is obvious he is not telling the truth, his actions are consistent with what Carolyn has said. He is denying his homosexuality just as he had concealed it from her while he was in treatment. I wonder now if it was an accident that he went to her in the first place. Obviously not. It is pointless to pursue this with him. I realize I could sit here all day and not get a thing out of him. I nod and try to relax in order to get us both calmed down. If this goes to trial and he takes the stand, will a jury be able to understand the psychological mechanism of denial, or will they just think he is lying for the hell of it? I could explain in my opening statement that Perry is going to deny what is obvious to everyone, and why he does it, and tell them Carolyn and Margaret Howard will explain to them that a part of Perry's illness is an inability to admit what is obvious to everybody. These thoughts are too fresh for me to know whether they are the last gasps of a defense that is rapidly going down the drain or have some kind of plausibility. I tell Perry the truth—that I need to talk to Carolyn and to Margaret Howard. His sense of relief is visible, as if Carolyn is truly the only person who does understand him. I tell him I will be back to see him in the next couple of days. I open the door and find nurse Perry dozing at one of the secretarial desks outside Berrenger's office.

"Ma'am," I say loudly, "he's ready to go back."

The old lady's head snaps from her starched white chest, and we give each other an understanding grin. As she takes Perry away, I realize the first thing he will do is call Carolyn Anderson.

For once I do not call Carolyn Anderson. From the kitchen in my house I telephone my own expert witness, Margaret Howard, who, instead of sounding irritated at having her Saturday afternoon interrupted, seems glad to hear from me. She may not be by the time I get through, and sitting down at the kitchen table, I tell her exactly what I've learned. When I'm finished, I ask: "Does his behavior sound consistent with someone who has"—I search for the words—"an ego-dystonic dysfunction?"

There is a lengthy pause at the other end. I listen for Sarah coming in. She has gone riding with Eric, getting her innings in, since I won't let her go out with him two nights in one weekend. This has caused major unhappiness, but I have stuck to my guns. The house is deathly quiet. This is how it will be on a daily basis, when she goes off to college. Woogie comes into the kitchen and goes behind the table to drink noisily from his water dish, and I am glad of his company. I stand and watch him empty the bowl. It is as if he has been a worried parent, unable to drink or eat until his child has arrived safely home. He gives me a disgusted look: If you want me to live, I need more water than this. I mouth the words "Okay, okay." Sarah has been after me to get a portable phone, but they seem like such an extravagance. Your basic black with an extended cord does nicely. Sarah has begun to dare to say aloud to my face what I've known for years: basically, I'm tight as a tick. Her mother, who knew what things cost, thought it was a virtue.

Finally, Dr. Howard gives a long sigh and says, "I think so, but I'd really like to talk to Dr. Anderson before I'd be willing to give you an opinion."

As I talk, I fill the water dish and then return to the kitchen sink and bend down to the cabinet to get a rag and the furniture polish. The kitchen table, wiped free of crumbs this morning, looks terrible. "I'd like to wait on talking to Dr. Anderson if you don't mind," I say. "A jury might be more impressed if you settled on that conclusion yourself before talking to her." I pour the liquid onto the rag and begun to rub, thinking my table has more give in it than my expert's jaw.

Rocky, to my surprised delight, answers briskly, "That's fine with me. Let me do some reading, and I'll call you Tuesday."

There is a slight pause, and I can hear the frustration in her voice as she adds, "The truth is I feel somewhat manipulated by Dr. Anderson on this case."

Welcome to the club. My sentiments exactly, except in my case I would remove the word "somewhat." I make a stab at diplomacy. "We have to remember she feels responsible for Hart's death."

I hang up realizing I have hurt Perry by relying on Carolyn so heavily. Even if she is telling the truth, Carolyn will be vulnerable because of the argument that in testifying for Perry she is motivated by guilt. As I rub the table, I think of calling my sister Marty. I am in desperate need of the perspective of a woman I can trust. Though we are not close and have not talked in a month, I know I can count on her to tell me exactly what she thinks. I call and invite her to dinner. My sister, who is divorced and has two kids in college, declines my invitation but tells me to pick up three sirloin steaks and bring them over about six.

"You and Sarah aren't exactly James Beard and Julia Child, you know?" she says, her voice sounding much more Southern than my own. "A bottle of wine would be nice, too."

Why aren't we closer? I like her, and she's crazy about Sarah, but the truth is I have never felt entirely comfortable with Marty. I never have pinned it down. She has always judged me too much, I think. Well, I need some judging now. As I hang up, Sarah walks in the door, still irritated with my decision. I can tell by the way she walks straight to her room. I go knock on her door and tell her we are going to eat a steak at her aunt's, and this peps her up. "Can we stop and get a movie?" she asks. "She's got a VCR."

I had counted on her watching TV while I talked to Marty, so I can pretend to be the indulgent parent. "If you want."

Sitting on her bed, wearing her worst pair of jeans and a faded Hendrix College sweatshirt, she says, "Gee, Dad, I'm thinking of nominating you parent of the year."

She can't be too mad if she's talking to me like this. "Would you like to slip into something a little more attractive?" I ask, but do not wait for her retort. "Come on. Let's go to the store."

To further effect our reconciliation, I let Sarah drive, and as soon as we hit the first stoplight on our way to Kroger's, she announces, "Eric has invited me to a dance at school Saturday."

"Are you asking me or telling me?" I ask as we creep up on a mauve Mercedes in front of us.

"Can't I go?" she wails, hitting the brakes finally. They squeal as if they have been stabbed.

I nod. If we live, I think. "Please don't hit that man, Sarah. He may have to operate on me sometime." Driving with my daughter is good isometric exercise.

"Why are you being so hateful?" Sarah demands. She is on the verge of tears. Her eyes are moist, and her jaw is set as if it had been wired shut.

Impressive. Woogie isn't in the car for me to kick, so I abuse my child instead. "I'm just getting uptight because of the Sarver case," I tell her and turn toward her to show I am smiling. "I'm sorry."

It takes a moment or two, but Sarah sniffs, "It's okay." An apology gets her every time.

By the time we stop at Kroger's for the meat, Al's liquor store for wine, and Lynn's Video for *My Stepmother Is an Alien,* it is six, and I insist on driving so that I can speed and not worry about it. Marty lives on the western edge of Blackwell County, and it is a good fifteen minutes to her house. While Sarah listens to KKKY and daydreams about Eric, I try to sort through why I am seeking Marty out. Her life has been, not to put too fine a point on it, a little ragged. With three ex-husbands, she seemed destined to find a fourth, until about a year ago she gained nearly fifty pounds, which delayed the trip to the altar. Then, six months ago, she lost her third job in the last three years as a real-estate agent through, as she cheerfully admits, her own laziness. Yet despite, or perhaps because of her own untidy life, she has always been adept at helping me find the log in my eye. Most recently, she has pointed out if my taste in women didn't improve (she never met Rainey), she was going to have me declared legally blind. "For God's sake, Gideon, are you finding your dates in a whorehouse now?" she later asked on the phone after dropping in on me unexpectedly during the Christmas holidays. After our father died, she told our mother that I was turning into a little punk and persuaded her to ship me off to Subiaco to be straightened out by some men who wouldn't take any crap from me. The Sarver case ought to be a piece of cake for her. It does not take a great deal of insight at this point for me to realize that the pieces are not all neatly laid before me like a ship I am going to squeeze into a glass bottle.

At one point it seemed logical enough, but to make everything fit, I am doing far more pushing and shoving than I like. Today's news that my client may have had sex with the man he murdered seems the final straw, but maybe I am overreacting. Marty will tell me.

Hutto is a town of about seven thousand just inside the county line. We pass Marty's shop, The Wigwam, on the corner of the town square. Next to it is a hardware store. Marty now sells used clothing on consignment. "You wouldn't believe the people who come in," she told me at Christmas. When I asked if she meant they were poor, she explained, "Rich. Very rich." I find her house and turn into the driveway. Small businesswoman that she is, it is a small red brick duplex whose upper story she rents out.

At the door she coolly appraises her younger brother even as she hugs Sarah. "You've lost hair since Christmas," she quietly observes to me.

Same old delightful Marty. She is dressed in what appears to be a red maternity top and the bottom of a blue warmup suit. I hand her the bottle of Chablis. "I didn't mean for you to dress up," I say, trading insults in our familiar fashion. We go in and are greeted by Olaf, a full-blooded tan-and-white boxer, who is as jowly and big-chested as some of the women I've dated, according to Marty.

"How's your love life, Sarah?" she teases her niece as Olaf comes over and pretends to bite my hand, a trick I hope he remembers from Christmas. My hand emerges from his jaws intact, nicely topped off with a couple of ounces of slobber. What a cute couple. I look around her small living room. She has it lined with plants and ferns hanging from the ceiling, probably to hide the fact that she has so little furniture. The room is bare, except for a green-corduroy-covered couch, a battered coffee table, a tan throw rug, and a couple of cheap lamps on small tables next to two chairs, one a La-Z-Boy recliner, perhaps the first one ever made. Even with the plants, the room looks cheap, and I wonder how she is making a living.

Sarah blushes and reaches down to Olaf so he can give a repeat performance. One trick seems his limit.

I answer for her, "She's the only one of us who has one." I go into her kitchen and set down the sack on the kitchen table that used to belong to our parents. Because of the familiar table, I find I want to stay in here. Marty follows me and inspects the meat. "Not bad, better than the wine," she mutters and turns to Sarah. "How old is he?"

Sarah, embarrassed, shrugs, and whispers more to Olaf than to anyone else, "Sixteen."

Getting a pair of wineglasses, Marty says, "Should of brought him. Maybe he likes older women."

I check Sarah to see how she is taking this. She is at least trying to smile, so I go out back and start the fire. When I get back in, she and Marty are making a salad and laughing. I quit worrying about Sarah and sit at the oval brown table sipping my wine. The table, made from an oak tree on my grandfather's farm, is in good shape. There are a couple of stains and scratches but it looks remarkably handsome. Keeping kitchen tables up to snuff may be the only thing Marty and I really have in common anymore, so why am I here? I listen to Marty quiz Sarah about Eric, school, and her friends. She misses her own kids, I suppose.

We get through dinner mostly using Sarah as a message board. Through their conversation I learn that my sister has had viral pneumonia, was arrested for passing a hundred-dollar hot check (dismissed after immediate payment), and had spent a week in Ontario, Canada, with a man she knew for all of a week and hasn't heard from since. Marty learns that I have been rejected by Rainey and have a big case that I am reluctant to talk about in front of my daughter.

"Your dad's a real barrel of laughs tonight," Marty says, working a piece of meat that has surely yielded its flavor by now. She is not wearing a maternity smock for nothing. "Is he this lively all the time?"

Sarah, forced to defend her old man, says, "He's got the biggest case of his life coming up."

A child shall lead us. Moments later, Sarah excuses herself to go watch her movie, and side by side, my sister and I wash the dishes, the way we did thirty years ago (me washing and she drying), in a less complicated period of our lives. For the next hour in a low voice over the dishwater and then across the table, I talk almost nonstop, using few names but virtually telling her everything except that I have slept with Carolyn. When I finish, I ask, "What do you think? Do you think I'm being used?"

Her gray eyes appraise me over reading glasses that rest on the end of her nose. She is knitting what I take to be a red sweater. "Has this woman come on to you?"

I feel my heart speed up. "Sort of," I admit, my face turning red.

She looks down at her needles, expressionless. "You've screwed her, or come close, right?"

I lean forward in my chair and whisper, "Yes."

She shakes her head. "Gideon, have you lost your mind?"

I did not come out here to beat myself. "You had to be there," I say softly.

She puts down her handiwork and says in an outraged voice, "She killed her husband or had him killed!"

I motion for her to lower her voice. "There's no proof of that."

She leans toward me and chuckles maliciously. "I sure wouldn't let any women on that jury if I were you." She picks up a needle and examines it. "For all I know, she's telling the truth, but she's admitted she hated the son of a bitch for some very excellent reasons. And, she's done everything except hook you up to a cart and let you pull her around town."

I ignore her last remark and address the first. "Lots of women hate their husbands, but they don't have them killed."

She takes the two yellow needles and lays them down side by side on the table. "That's true."

"Do you think," I ask, "that Jerry Kerner and possibly Chet Bracken are in on this?"

"Why not?" she says. "They both had every reason to hate Anderson."

I stand up and go over to the sink for a glass of water. The meat and alcohol have made me thirsty. I have gotten what I came for. Now I have to decide what to do about it. "How're you doing?" I ask to change the subject.

She gets up and comes over to the refrigerator and opens the freezer. "Do you realize that's the first real question you've asked me in years?"

I hand her my glass for some ice cubes. "It's none of my business, really. I know you've had problems."

She puts ice in my water. "You're my goddamned brother, for God's sake."

I take the glass back and study the ice cubes. I do not know what to say. "I'm sorry," I mutter.

She takes a half gallon of Borden's chocolate ice cream from the freezer and holds it out to me. I shake my head. From the cabinet to her right she takes a saucer and spoon for herself. "You've never gotten over thinking I'm your big sister who was supposed to have it together, you know that?"

"You did when we were growing up," I remind her. I sip water while she spoons out a pint of ice cream.

"You always thought I was so wonderful because I went to see Daddy in the nuthouse before he died and you didn't go. I went because I could stand it, and you couldn't. It tore you up too much. If I had loved him as much as you did, I wouldn't have been able to go with Mom either. Jesus Christ, Gideon! I never had it together for a minute."

Thirty years fall away and I remember seeing them drive away that unbearable July morning. "Eat the sandwich I fixed you," Mom said as they drove away. I lay on my bed for eight straight hours until they got back. Mom came to my room and said he was doing okay. He had asked all about me. I got up and went downstairs but I still couldn't eat.

I pour the water out in the sink. "I'm really sorry." I am sorry, but I still don't know what to say to Marty.

"I'm not asking to move in with you," she says, gulping the ice cream in fist-size bites. It is gone in thirty seconds. "Just a phone call from my own brother every now and then."

"Want some more?" I ask, as if getting her ice cream could make up for the bitterness in her voice. I reach for her bowl.

She covers it with her own hand, anger in her voice. "I think I'll stuff myself in private."

I look down at the floor so I don't have to look at her tears.

"I've always thought you were pretty good at landing on your feet."

She wipes her eyes with her knuckles. "I've had enough practice, haven't I?" she manages to laugh.

"I'll do better," I promise. "You know you could call me."

She leans toward me with the saucer and spoon, making the chair creak as it is released from her weight. "When I call you, all we talk about is whether Sarah needs a lecture on sex or what case you're winning or losing or how hard it is for you to find a decent woman."

I take the dishes and rinse them off. What can I say? She is right. I nod. "Do you need any money?" I ask, wondering how I could borrow some. Maybe I could co-sign for her.

"No," she says wearily. "Look, I'm too depressed tonight to talk. Why don't you give me a call after the trial, okay?"

"Sure," I say, enormously relieved.

I let Sarah drive home, since we are no longer pressed for time. At night she is more cautious, and I find myself relaxing. She asks over sounds of the radio, "Did you and Aunt Marty have a fight? She looked kind of sad when we left."

"She's just lonely," I say. "I need to call her more."

"We didn't have to leave," Sarah says defensively, slowing down as we see the red light of a patrol car coming from the opposite direction.

"It's okay." It stuns me to realize that I have been the strong one in the family. That is not to say I've been a battleship, the way I've run after women since Rosa died. But I've had more going for me than Marty, except I haven't ever thought of it that way. It's taken only thirty years to figure that out.

When we arrive home, Sarah goes into her room, and I head for the kitchen table with a yellow pad to figure out what I'm going to do with the Sarver case. I don't have thirty years to get this right. Woogie comes into the kitchen and looks at me. Just the necessities is all I ask, his brown eyes beg. I get up and get a scoop of Purina Fit and Trim for his bowl. Lite dog food. I can't believe I've bought it. "Don't look at me like that," I tell him. "Anybody can make a mistake." His look says that I'm living proof of that.

Okay, so I've made some mistakes in the Sarver case. Have I lost my mind, as my sister has suggested? No. Have I acted like a fool? Yes. I make a list of the possibilities:

1. Sarver was crazy when he killed Hart and should be excused.
2. Sarver was crazy when he killed Hart but should not be excused.
3. Sarver was not crazy when he killed Hart.
4. Carolyn somehow killed Hart and is trying to frame Sarver.
5. Sarver, Carolyn, Bracken, and Kerner are in this together.
6. A combination of the above, or none of the above.

Just because maybe all four of them have been plinking me like a cheap banjo, should any of this matter to me? My professional duty is to represent Perry Sarver zealously and to the best of my ability. I did something like that just recently, and a boy died from it. Maybe if I do it again, I will keep a guilty man out of jail. Nice system we have.

Woogie eats as fast as my sister. He looks at me until I get up and pour him some water from the teakettle. "It's too late to trade me in," I tell him. I sit back down and try to concentrate. It occurs to me that if I take this case in front of a jury, it may well backfire on Carolyn and Perry. If it is this obvious to Marty, the average juror is going to dig his heels in, too, and come to the conclusion that this beautiful, distraught woman is trying way too hard. Why not give Carolyn and Perry what they want? Give it my best shot and let the jury decide?

Finally satisfied, Woogie walks out of the kitchen as though he has been dealing with a nitwit. I call after him, "Well, nobody said I was a genius. And you're not so smart yourself."

Yet I have to decide what to do with the information I got this afternoon, because my friend Skip kept his promise to nose around. Again, I can imagine the look on Phil Harper's face when I tell him I'm going to put on proof that Hart was gay. I will have to check this out, but my guess is that he will come back and offer Perry a better deal than ten years. The question, of course, is whether I can persuade Perry to take it.

Sarah comes into the kitchen and says crossly, "I'll be glad when this case is over."

I lean back and yawn. "I will, too, babe, I will, too."

It is too hot in my boss's office, or it may simply be that my rumpled friend and colleague Brent didn't quite get around to taking a shower this Monday morning. He, Greta, and I are waiting for the rest of the attorneys to drift in for the staff meeting at which I plan to spring on them Saturday afternoon's revelations that Perry and Hart were seen leaving a public bathroom in Baxter Park. Sunday I had considered calling each of them at home, but I want each one's advice on the record. If this blows up in my face, I don't want their memories to go bad.

Greta closes a new Neiman Marcus catalogue and asks me to open the window as Chick the Prick and Ken Averitt wander in. Greta, who is wearing an expensive-looking blue wool suit over a red pleated blouse, wrinkles her nose at Brent, who, typically, looks like a bomb-blast victim, so poorly did he shave this morning.

"I've got a stick of deodorant in my office if you promise to use it," I whisper. Chick has pointed out that it is increasingly easy to forget that Brent made the top score on the bar exam. When he starts smelling worse than our clients, I'll begin to complain.

Brent can't resist a quick whiff of his right armpit. "I'm okay," he assures me earnestly.

Before I can say anything, Leona, her black face beaming, comes in bearing a box of blueberry doughnuts and announces she is getting married. Her boyfriend is a CPA and is five years younger than she is.

Chick raises his coffee cup. "To Leona! Hear! Hear!"

We all coo our congratulations and toast Leona. Brent sloshes coffee on his wrinkled khaki pants, and Chick laughs. After two years, Chick doesn't even know the names of Leona's kids, much less her boyfriend's, but he is smiling as if he were announcing his own wedding. I give them a minute to bullshit and then say loudly, "I also have an announcement."

Everyone becomes quiet and looks expectantly at me. As they sit slack-jawed with amazement (it's not every day you catch a state senator coming out of a bathroom with his killer), for the next five minutes I summarize the events of Saturday afternoon and throw out the question, "What do I do with this?"

Brent wipes his greasy hands on his khakis, saying, "You go lock up your eyewitness in a closet and call the prosecuting attorney and say, 'Gotcha!' Phil Harper will offer you a deal so quick you won't believe it."

Ken, flicking doughnut crumbs off his suit (undertaker black, Chick has dubbed it), points out the down side that bothers me the most. "Assuming they don't have any more on Jerry Kerner than what you've told us, you hand them a believable motive. I'd say thanks but no thanks."

Leona, lost in reverie, is looking out the window, and Chick is looking at Greta, naturally. Greta, who has refused a doughnut (her lipstick is in place and must not be disturbed until noon), stares at me and says sourly, "It sounds to me like you're trying to blackmail Phil."

Chick nods, his marching orders in place. "It smells pretty bad to me. It's awfully late in the game to be coming forward with a surprise witness who's going to dump all over a dead man who can't defend himself."

Sometimes, and this is one of them, I wonder if Phil signs their checks. I look at Chick and say as snidely as I can, "A dead man as prominent as Hart Anderson, you mean."

Greta, smarter than Chick, won't allow herself to be trapped publicly. She opens a desk drawer and slips the catalogue inside and closes it. "All Chick means is that this could backfire on Sarver. Ken's right. Based on what you've told us, Phil isn't going to be able to prove anything except your client knew Jerry Kerner and went to therapy. But once your eyewitness testifies he saw Perry and Hart coming out of the bathroom together, Phil will wave this at the jury until they can't think about anything else except that Sarver probably shot Hart during some homosexual quarrel."

If this were coming from Ken, I could tolerate it better. Greta doesn't give a rat's ass about Sarver. All she is concerned about is our budget and whether it is going to affect her chances of getting out of here. I glare at her. "There is absolutely no evidence of any quarrel."

She smiles as if she is trying to reason with a five-year-old. "You know that won't matter."

I explode, as much at her facade of reasonableness as at what she is saying. "Then it's okay for the prosecuting attorney of Blackwell County to become a demagogue and turn this case into an antigay campaign!"

Looking ready to come out of his chair at me, Chick snarls, "She didn't say that, Gideon, but that's the way it is."

He doesn't have the guts. You weak piece of shit, I think but don't say.

Ken clears his throat and says, "On the other hand, I have to agree with Brent that I think there's a good chance Phil will get some pressure to deal this down to something Sarver could live with. Don't you, Greta?"

Brent nods eagerly, but nobody pays attention. Bless Ken's undertaker heart. If only because of his longevity and usual unwillingness to rock the boat, Ken has put Greta on the spot.

Greta nervously twists a lock of hair into place. The expression on her face is not a pleasant one. Ken will pay for this. "This Darron Walker—you don't know a thing about him."

As public defenders, we don't have the luxury of ordering our witnesses from Neiman Marcus and Greta knows it. "I don't know much," I admit, "but yesterday I did some checking. Except for being gay, Walker is apparently as normal as any of us. I even found out where he goes to church, in case you're interested."

Greta waves her hand contemptuously. "He could have a rap sheet a mile long."

I try to keep my voice even. "I just got here, too, Greta. I'll start checking him out as soon as I can."

Greta pushes her chair back as if to distance herself from me. "I've never heard of a story that stinks worse. Of course, this Darron Walker has no witnesses to this fortuitous event, does he?"

"No," I say, beginning to feel sweat creeping down my sides. "But it's not something you sell tickets to." Better than any of us, Greta knows the pressure that will come down on Phil if I tell him I'm going to call Darron Walker as a witness. "If he's even halfway clean," I say, looking directly at her, "I'm going to tell Phil I'll call Walker to testify. The way this case is looking right now, the only real chance Sarver has is to plea-bargain. If this goes to trial, on cross-examination Phil will eat both Carolyn Anderson and her buddy Margaret Howard alive." Saying these words aloud makes me realize for the first time that our defense is weaker than I've been admitting to myself. The jury will conclude that Carolyn feels too much guilt to give an objective opinion, and, like an idiot, I let her recommend Margaret Howard. That will be the first question to Dr. Howard out of Phil's mouth.

Greta sits up straight at her desk, almost arching her spine. Her voice is cold. "Gideon, whether you call him as a witness is my decision, and I don't want you calling him."

My heart is pounding. Who has ultimate authority to decide what happens in a case has never been clear in our office. If I screw up in a case that I'm handling for the office, I'm the one who risks contempt of court, not Greta. I look across Brent at Greta and challenge her. "I'm the person Judge Jamison appointed to represent Sarver. He didn't mention your name."

I am walking a thin line, and Greta knows it. She tells Brent, who is still new, what to do in cases all the time. Greta leans forward and rests her chin on her hands. Her lips draw back in a grimace that is supposed to be a smile. "He doesn't have to, Gideon. It's understood," she says softly. "It's also understood that I'm the boss of this office."

I scan the room quickly to see how this remark is playing. Chick, seated across from me, gives me his usual sneer. Leona and Ken have suddenly found something interesting in their laps. Only Brent, and he doesn't count in this situation, looks sympathetic. I say more loudly than I should, "If I'm handling a case and show up an hour late, it's my ass that goes to jail for contempt of court, not yours."

Greta frowns, her mouth turning down in a deep scowl. She likes to be one of the boys occasionally, but we don't usually mention her ass. "There is no way in hell I'm going to authorize you to call Darron Walker to testify."

I try to figure out her meaning. Is she backing off a bit? She may not "authorize" me, but she isn't stopping me. I lower my voice. "I'm not expecting you to say you agree with me. But what if Darron Walker went to the press and told them he came forward with the information that he had seen Hart Anderson coming out of a public bathroom at night with his killer and that we didn't do anything about it?"

Chick, his face now as dark and twisted as Greta's, says, "Now it sounds like you're trying to blackmail your supervisor."

That is exactly what I'm trying to do, but I can't even come close to admitting it. "That's bullshit, Chick," I say. "I'm trying to keep a man from going to the electric chair, or have you forgotten that?"

Chick flushes, but all he does is look at Greta. It was his case originally.

Greta looks at me for what seems an eternity. Finally, she says, her voice a whisper, "You just better hope your client gets a good deal from Phil, Gideon."

I have just won, but I have also been threatened, and everyone in the room is aware of it. The effect of what Greta has said immediately changes my relationship with the other attorneys. I am a marked man, and each person in the office will be watched to see how they respond to me. Greta stands up, a signal we are done. I look at Leona, whose happy news has been all but forgotten. As we walk out, I tell her, "I hope he's a real nice guy after the wedding as well."

Leona, subdued by what she's just witnessed, says simply, "I do, too. God, I do, too."

I do not have to be out at the hospital for a hearing until nine-thirty and go by Ken's office to thank him. He is putting on his coat. "Appreciate your support," I murmur.

Ken straightens the knot in his tie in a mirror he has on the back of his door. "I hope for your sake you know what you're doing," he says briskly. "Do you know for sure that Sarver will even take a deal?"

The truth is I don't. With his dark blue tie and black shoes, Ken looks as if he is on his way to a casket-sellers' convention. "I don't see he's in much of a position to refuse given the statistics on these kinds of cases."

He fusses with the Windsor knot in his tie. "Gideon, I wouldn't call what I said in Greta's office support if I were you."

Okay. But thanks anyway. Ken would dearly like to have his words back. He likes the county pension plan. "I understand."

Ken pulls out a comb and passes it through his thick brown hair. "If I were you, I'd go apologize to Greta before she leaves the office this morning. You can't show her up that way," he warns, "and get away with it."

Despite himself, I think Ken would like to see me protected. He wants me to have my words back, too. "You're right," I concede and go on to my office and call around to see what the state of Arkansas has on Darron Walker. While I am on hold (the computers at the Blackwell County Sheriff's Department are notoriously slow), I have time to think about whether I am cutting my own throat. I could put the telephone down right now and march into Greta's office and tell her I'll apologize publicly at the next staff meeting if that is what she wants. How can I do that, though? She is looking at this whole mess as a political decision and nothing more. It's Cover Your Ass 101. And yet, if I go through with this idea, isn't it a political decision? Instead of letting the case be tried, am I not trying to blackmail everyone into letting a possible first-degree murderer out of a long prison sentence?

I hang up the telephone. I need to think about this. Maybe I've lost my perspective on this case. I may not be acting any differently than Greta or Phil Harper, assuming Phil does what I want him to do if I call him. I lean back in my chair and shut my eyes. What the hell is my job, after all? Under the canon of ethics I am to be a zealous advocate for my client. But does this entail trying to apply political pressure to avoid a trial? My responsibility is to make sure the state follows the law and gives my client a fair trial and to advocate every possible defense I can on his behalf. Is threatening to expose the sex life of a state senator, which may in turn expose the sex secrets of other individuals, ethical? I doubt it.

Yet I am not so naive that I don't know political pressure is exerted on the system all the time. The real power brokers don't hesitate to use their leverage. Hart Anderson never gave it a thought. Whatever he is, Perry Sarver doesn't have that kind of influence, and neither do I. So if I am serious about truly representing him, shouldn't I use what little power this kind of information represents? I won't be violating a single rule. Phil has the discretion to decide what to do with this information. I don't. He could say that he will allow the chips to fall where they may. And if he cares about an abstract concept of justice, that is exactly what he will do. Phil's witch-hunt against Kerner has convinced me that justice is the least of his worries. If I care about fighting for Perry Sarver, I should take advantage of what I know about Phil's character. I scratch my head. Maybe they covered this in my ethics class and I missed it.

I pick up the phone again and dial the sheriff's office and lie glibly, "I'm afraid I got cut off." I'm told Walker has no record, not even a skipped parking ticket. I hang up, knowing my job is to get Sarver the best deal I can, not just go through the motions and tell myself I did all I could do.

There is a knock on the door and Brent walks in. "Thanks," I say. "You could have kept your mouth shut."

Brent shuts the door behind him. "Why doesn't Chick just get a spoon and go to work on her in front of the entire office?"

I smile. Brent's shirttail is already half out of his pants. If he knew the basic elements of grooming, he could get on with any firm he wanted. The sad part is he loves it here. "Greta'll burn your ass if this doesn't have a happy ending," he says, following my gaze and stuffing his shirt into his pants. "She'll probably burn it anyway. You've still got time to change your mind."

I write down Walker's address and phone number on a slip of paper. "Get me a subpoena on Walker, okay?"

He takes the paper as I pick up the phone. "Sure."

"Thanks, Brent."

He takes a halfhearted swipe at the coffee stain on his pants as he goes out the door. "Any time," he says.

I ask for Amy. If I got Phil, he might say something he'd not want to back down from later.

"Gideon, what's up?" Amy's voice is fresh, ready for a new week.

"You're not going to believe this," I begin and then tell her basically the same story I told our staff a few minutes earlier about Darron Walker.

"You're shitting me, aren't you?" Amy demands, her voice shrill. But by the time Amy gets off the phone and walks down the hall to Phil's office I am counting on her to have figured out both the good and bad sides to my story.

I give her Walker's number and address. "I'm getting a subpoena out on him right now."

Amy lets out a low whistle. "You know how to make things interesting, I'll say that for you."

I know she is dying to get off the phone. "I got to get out to the state hospital. Check you later."

"Sure," she says and hangs up.

As soon as I hang up, there is a buzz on the intercom. I pick it up. "There's a Carolyn Anderson waiting to see you," says Laura, our receptionist.

"I'll be right out," I tell her. Too late, Carolyn, I think. Just a little too late.

Carolyn Anderson is undoubtedly the best-looking woman ever to sit in our waiting room, which is practically bare, since all the attorneys except me have left for court. A middle-aged black woman, probably the mother of a defendant in jail, is waiting at the reception desk. Dressed in a shapeless gray smock that hangs out over her jeans, she looks exhausted, probably having worked through the night cleaning a building downtown and having stopped in to drop off some information. Carolyn is wearing a green, full-skirted dress with a black belt and black heels. Her face is tense, but she manages a smile. "Surprise."

"Come on back to my office," I say, wondering how to handle her. It is coming home to me how little independent action I've taken in this case. "Would you like some coffee?"

She shakes her head, and I take her red wool coat and hang it up on the back of my door. "Have a seat," I say and go around my desk and sit down.

"What is going on?" she says, her voice even. "I was out of town this weekend, and this morning when I drove in, I had a message from Perry on my machine saying that a witness was going to testify that he had seen Perry and Hart coming out of a bathroom in Baxter Park."

It is strange having this woman in my office, but for the first time I feel in control of the case. Carolyn is trying hard to appear relaxed, but she is on my turf now. I sip at the coffee I have brought in from the staff meeting. "That's essentially correct," I say and then repeat for the third time this morning what occurred Saturday afternoon.

Her eyes redden as I tell her this and she bows her head, and for a moment she looks as haggard as the woman standing at the reception desk. Why in the hell shouldn't she be? It is a tough way to start Monday morning. I remind myself that this may all be an act, but, in truth, I can't bring myself to believe it. She looks too . . . there is no other word that comes to mind, forlorn. "Do you realize I may have AIDS, then?" she says, tears now streaking her makeup. Her eyes seem enormous.

I have not thought of that. How could I not? But the only thoughts that have crossed my mind since Saturday have been about the case. I come around my desk and give her a hug. I have never felt as sorry for anyone in my life. She leans against me and sobs like I have never seen her do before. I pull myself away and hand her the box of tissues from my desk. Usually, they are used by mothers of sons I cannot save from prison. I look at my watch. I am due at the state hospital in twenty minutes and will have to leave. "Carolyn, I'm going to have to go in a minute, so listen to me," I say sternly. "I think the prosecutor will offer Perry a reduced sentence to keep this from coming out. There are some important people who are going to want this buried." I realize I should assume she is one of the persons I'm talking about, though, of course, for different reasons. Being married to a homosexual is as big a scandal as having an affair with one.

Wiping her eyes, she practically shouts, "Perry isn't guilty! You've got to take this to trial and get him found not guilty by reason of insanity!"

I am stunned by her vehemence. Why shouldn't she want this kept quiet? It will be much easier on her without a trial. I explain, "I can't risk Perry getting thirty or forty years," I tell her. "His chances aren't that good."

She steps forward toward me, waving her finger in my face. "I'm still going to testify for him. Can't you understand that?"

I find myself practically shouting, too. "I've told you it doesn't matter! They don't have to believe a damn thing you say!"

She runs her hands frantically through her hair. "It's up to Perry," she says urgently. "If he demands a trial, you've got to give it to him."

This makes no sense, but I can't stand here and argue with her. I have to go. I get our coats from the back of the door. As I put mine on, I say firmly, "Carolyn, don't tell me you're going to prevent Perry from accepting a decent offer. You've done enough damage."

My arms are caught in my sleeves, and since I am against the wall, I can't even step back as she slaps me hard across the right cheek. The sound rings in the room. "Gideon," she says softly, "you will take him to trial if you want your job. I'll tell your boss exactly what you've done and when and how you did it. Do you understand me?"

Is this happening or am I imagining it? "Yes."

"By the way," she says, slinging her coat over her arm and throwing open the door, "I'd get tested for AIDS if I were you."

With that, she slams the door, leaving me touching my face.

My face burns all the way out to the state hospital. What kind of obsession is this? I risk a ticket and get up to seventy-five on the freeway. All I can figure is that she has made Perry a promise she cannot keep. I have never seen a woman so consumed by guilt. She is being devoured right in front of us, and there seems to be absolutely nothing I can do about it. If she has her way, Perry will insist on a trial, and we will all go down in flames.

The rest of the day drags, giving me more time than I need to realize that if I take this case to trial and call Darron Walker as a witness, I have guaranteed Sarver a long sentence. Between hearings I sit in my office with the door shut and try to figure out what to do. I suspect it is not too late to tell Phil Harper I have changed my mind and won't be calling Walker. Why not forget Walker and try the case and do the best job I can? I realize I am getting a taste of my own medicine—blackmail. At one point, and not so many hours ago, I was willing to be noble and take on Greta for the sake of a client, but now I am not so sure. Why am I changing my mind? It would be the humiliation of being found out. Not only would I be fired, but I would be let go under the most embarrassing of circumstances. Having it made known that I was being canned for screwing the widow of the man who was murdered by my client would be appalling in and of itself, but doubtless Chick will tell his brother, and there is no way it won't get out at Sarah's school. Hi, Sarah. I heard what your old man did. Do you like to fuck as much as he does? My face turns crimson as I think of her reaction. Sarah already suspects I slept with Carolyn, but she doesn't know. Don't I owe my own kid a little dignity? The hypocrisy of what I've threatened to do by calling Darron Walker as a witness comes home to me. Don't those people who want Hart Anderson's sexuality kept quiet deserve some dignity, too? The issue, however, is not whether I'm a hypocrite (I can live with that) but what quality of representation I give a man who is charged with murder.

At noon I sit in the sun eating my BLT and watch a patient-staff volleyball game played to the accompaniment of ghetto blasters. No one is Olympic material—instead of steroids, most of the players are on Thorazine, and a more laid-back game there couldn't be. A female tech serves, and the ball flies lazily toward the center of the court as two male patients stagger together in a vain effort to return it. The other patients laugh, delighted with the collision that has hurt no one. In my mind, I go back and forth on what to do. How could Carolyn lose it like this? Threatening me, slapping me? If I thought there was a prayer of keeping her away from Perry, I'd be on the phone to the state hospital right now, but then Carolyn would raise a stink that would reach downtown. She will undoubtedly see him today and give him a blood oath that if he goes to trial he's a cinch to be found not guilty by reason of insanity. I am damned if I do, and damned if I don't. Two women have me by the balls like no man ever has. Hooray for women's lib! I tell myself to take a good look around—I may not be out here much longer.

I am about to go back to my office to get ready for the afternoon when a familiar voice says, "Won't they let you play, lawyer man?"

I turn around and squint into the sun at Rainey. She grins and sits down beside me on the steps in front of Unit Three. Damn, she looks good. She is wearing a black knit dress and black stockings and has her familiar mischievous grin in place. God, I have missed her. How do I open this conversation? Hi, I probably have AIDS and am about to get fired. How are you? "Hi," I say. "These guys are pros; I'm just an amateur."

She says softly, watching the game, "I've missed you."

Out the side of my mouth, I say, "Welcome to the lonely-hearts club."

She bumps against me and then moves away. "How's your case going?"

I clap as Virgil, a skinny white tech, manages a vertical leap of two inches and spikes the ball into the net. "You really don't want to know. At the rate I'm going, Perry and I both will die by firing squad."

She grins. "That good, huh? I knew the moment I laid eyes on you that you were a hotshot."

I turn and give Rainey a good looking over. Most women I've dated recently wouldn't allow themselves to be buried in knit, much less wear it in public. She doesn't blink. "You look like you're still going to Jazzercize," I concede.

Mockingly, she gives me the same treatment, her eyes roving up and down my body. "You never know when the right guy's gonna come along."

Self-consciously, I plunge my hands into my pants pockets. "Where's the Link these days?"

"Who?"

"Lucy," I say and stand up. "Hell, Boris. I don't remember his name."

Her frizzy red hair blowing in the wind, she says, "I don't either. Why don't you call me when your trial's over?"

I look over her head at the game. "I'm afraid I've sworn off masochism."

She stands up and places her hand on my sleeve. "I'll do better this time. I promise."

What should I say? Just let me get my AIDS test out of the way and I'll be right over? I don't want to get hurt again. And I don't want to hurt her. My life is too much of a mess right now to throw this in the hopper, too. I look at my watch. "Let me think about it a little while, okay?"

She gives me her determined look that says, You stupid son of a bitch, I mean business. "Gonna make me beg, huh?"

I won't kid with her. "No."

She nods. "I'd forgotten how serious you can be."

I can't make myself smile. "This case has got me down."

Her eyes are warm with sympathy. "I wouldn't have your job for a minute. I know you'll give it all you've got. You're all Sarver has."

All he has. This is literally true. I look at Rainey and nod. Whatever promises Carolyn has made to him, she can't fulfill them. The way the system works I am responsible for Perry, and if I don't have enough guts to fight for him, the system fails. Not that the system is so great, but for the first time in a while, I accept the fact that I have the responsibility to be an advocate, whatever the cost.

Solemnly, I tell Rainey, "I'll call you this weekend." I sling my jacket over my shoulder and head on back to my office at the state hospital, leaving her watching the game. If she finds out what I have been doing, I suspect she will tell me to forget it. And yet, maybe not. By her willingness to try to get back together, she may be telling me (and herself) that she is willing to risk the pain that is a part of every honest relationship. On the other hand, it may be she is lonely. If I decide to get back in it, time will surely tell. At the moment I can't allow myself to get sidetracked about Rainey until this case is finished. I can't worry that I might have AIDS. I did use a rubber, didn't I? But how old was it? At least a couple of months. I should be tested when this is all over. What is this called? Denial? My therapist after Rosa's death said it was okay for a while. How the hell else is a person going to get through the day? Walking back to my office, I begin to daydream about Rainey. What is this called—wishful thinking?

• • •

Hugh Bixby looks at me as if to say, He's your client—so interview him. Danny Goetz is pretending to study his file but in fact is shaking with laughter. It's not funny, damn it. My client has gotten out of his chair and is lying on the floor. William Patterson, a twenty-three-year-old unemployed carpenter, is obviously suffering from mental illness.

His father, obese and completely gray (I can understand why) gets up from the witness chair and squats down by his son, who is a nice-looking kid. "Be a man, Billy," he pleads with him. Until this happened, I actually had thought there was a chance Hugh would throw this one out. Living at home, this guy had almost stopped eating and rarely came out of his old room. But I thought all he needed was a good kick in the ass until, during his father's testimony, he got out of his chair and carefully lay down in front of Hugh's desk, putting his arms under his head and closing his eyes.

"William," I say, feeling ridiculous, "are you all right?"

His father, a construction worker whose jeans and T-shirt are stained with grease, has testified that his wife left him earlier in the year because of Billy. He turns and looks at Hugh, who looks at me as if I'm to blame for my client's behavior.

"Can I," I ask, "have a recess, Your Honor?"

Mercifully, Hugh says, "I'm finding probable cause." He motions for the techs to pick Billy up and carry him back to the units. I look up and see Brent, who has come to take over the rest of the day so I can worry about Perry Sarver. Out in the hall, Brent shakes his head. "Jesus, they can fool you, can't they?"

I hand Brent my files, thinking that I can't even tell who is sick and who is not. For all I know, Perry Sarver, a hundred yards away in Rogers Hall, has never been mentally ill a day in his life. "Yeah," I say, "they can fool you."

Back downtown, there are no messages from the prosecutor's office. What if this case doesn't settle and Perry gets forty years? Whatever else happens, I will never forgive myself.

. . .

I sit in my office and loosen my tie as I try for the hundredth time to figure out what kind of jury I want. The defense gets to strike a dozen prospective jurors for any reason. My initial thoughts have been to strike as many women as possible. If my sister Marty can be this suspicious of Carolyn Anderson, will the average female juror be any different? Yet won't men feel they have to protect the sanctity of the home by convicting a man who dared invade it? Women, it seems to me, would be more naturally sympathetic if Carolyn weren't so damn good-looking.

I look up from my yellow legal pad and see Greta standing in the doorway. The scowl on her face tells me this is not a social occasion. She wastes no time in getting to the point. "Carolyn Anderson just called," she practically bellows, so Chick and Ken can hear in their offices across from me, "and said after the case was over she wanted to come in and discuss your conduct of the Sarver case."

Carolyn, I am learning fast, is not shy about turning the screws. "She thinks we should go to trial," I say, relieved I can say something honest. "I haven't heard anything from Phil or Amy, so she may get her wish."

Greta leans against the doorjamb, her arms folded under her breasts. "I had the feeling it was more than that," she says darkly. She is staring at me as if the answer were printed on my forehead.

It won't do Carolyn any good to have played her cards yet. I pretend to be unconcerned and put my feet up on my desk. "What'd she say?" I ask.

"Gideon," Greta says, "if you get my office in trouble over this case, you're gone. You hear me?"

"My" office? I wonder what she paid for it. "Yes, ma'am," I say and whip off a mock salute to her. With a look of unconcealed disgust on her face, she turns and marches down the hall.

I lean back in my chair, but I can't relax. If I can begin to feel screws turning against my own flesh, I can at least imagine the pressure Phil Harper is feeling at this moment because of my threat to disclose in open court that Hart Anderson was gay. Right now, I would like to be a fly on the wall in his office as he debates what to do. No wonder men die sooner than women.

At five o'clock I cram my briefcase full and head for home. I've had a bellyful of Greta's office today.

20

Spring is here, if not in reality then in spirit. How do I know? Out my back window old Mr. Cutter, my neighbor, is hard at work at seven-thirty in the morning digging just inside his side of the fence. Steadily bobbing with his yellow-handled hoe, he reminds me of an old black crow pecking for food. With more cold weather on the way, it is too early to begin a garden, but Mr. Cutter, by the way he is working, suggests to me that he cannot wait. I am beginning to know the feeling. Last night I slept all of five minutes, it seemed, worrying about whether I would get a phone call from the prosecutor's office this morning.

I check my briefcase and watch Sarah finish trying to sew the number 47 on a plain white T-shirt. "It looks horrible, Dad!" she wails, holding it up for me to see.

The lettering is crooked, uneven. The four is bigger and higher than the seven. We need a wife. "The judges won't even notice," I console her. "You're trying out for cheerleader, not school seamstress."

"They will, too," my daughter says angrily, accidentally jabbing her finger with the needle. "Damn!"

Her grandmother in Barranquilla sews professionally. How she makes enough to live on, I do not know. We took Sarah to see her after we knew Rosa was going to die. She told Sarah she would teach her to sew, but, of course, that was the last thing Sarah wanted to do. She wanted to go to Cartagena and see where her parents met, and since Rosa and I wanted to go, too, that is what we did. If I were a saint, I would offer to bring her grandmother to the States to live with us. I tell myself and firmly believe that she would be miserable.

I get up and begin making my lunch. "Guess who came up to me yesterday and wanted to get back together?"

For the first time this morning Sarah smiles. I assume she isn't trying out in jeans. I don't see how she can walk in the ones she has on. Her red sweatshirt is bulky. Maybe too many boys were going blind. "I knew she would."

"Sure." Hindsight. I'll take it over 20/20 any day. We are out of everything—bread, meat, even mayonnaise. "I told her I'd think about it."

Sarah breaks off the thread. "About two minutes," she says. "The rest of the time will be to see how long you can wait."

I close the refrigerator. I'm sick of eating healthy. I'll go over to McDonald's and get a chocolate shake. "You'd like me to call her, huh?"

She studies her handiwork. "Come on, Dad, admit it. You're nuts about her."

That's why I'm afraid to call her. I've been manipulated enough by women lately. The telephone rings, and I pick it up. "Hello."

It is the prosecuting attorney of Blackwell County. "Gideon," Phil Harper says abruptly, but trying to keep the anger out of his voice, "I'm willing to make one offer and one offer only. Your guy pleads guilty to manslaughter. We recommend four years. What do you say?"

With credit for good time Perry would be out in sixteen months. This is one offer I won't have to think about for two minutes. I try not to sound too relieved though my knees are about to buckle. "I take it you'll be dismissing charges against Jerry Kerner if Perry accepts?" I ask.

"Yes."

"Sounds good to me, Phil," I say, smiling at Sarah. "Let me go talk to him, and I'll call you as soon as I can."

Sarah looks disappointed. "I thought it might be Rainey."

I collect my briefcase. "You've got Rainey on the brain. I've got to get to work. Let's go."

Despite my impatience, I hand Sarah the keys, and I have not been in the car with her two minutes when I realize that something magical has happened: she has learned to drive. No grinding of gears, no bucking, no following too closely. She glides to an even stop at the last stoplight before she accelerates. "You're driving better," I say, trying to keep the amazement out of my voice as we pull away from the light.

"Eric's been helping me," she says, cutting her eyes nervously at me as she shifts smoothly into second.

There is no stopping time. Whatever happens in the Sarver case, Sarah is going to leave me someday. You have to make the most of the time you have. "Well, good," I say. "He's doing a good job."

"Thanks, Dad," she says, flashing me a dazzling smile. Score one for me.

As I drive away, I turn and watch her walk up the steps of her school. I hope I am always as graceful in letting her go.

At Rogers Hall I look for a space to interview Perry and am told that I can use the cafeteria. From one of the cooks, I get a cup of coffee and go sit at one of the tables nearest the door and wait for Perry to be brought in. I wonder who put the pressure on Phil. I will probably never know, but if statistics mean anything, there are over one hundred thousand homosexuals in the state, and not all of them are tucked away in some large closet. Hart Anderson had many important friends. Phil, who is no white knight, given his willingness to charge Jerry Kerner without more evidence than he had, is nothing if not educable, and the lesson for the week is that discretion is the better part of valor. As I look around at the freshly wiped tables, it is a lesson I hope to teach my client as well.

A nurse brings Perry to me, and, unsmiling, he sits down across the table from me. For the first time since he started responding to the medication, he looks sloppy. He has not shaved as closely as he usually does, and he looks tired. It should not surprise me that he is beginning to feel some pressure, with the trial so close. Doubtless Carolyn has already talked to him, and this is as good a place to start as any.

"Have you talked to Carolyn in the last twenty-four hours?" I ask.

He glares at me angrily. "I have a right to talk to who I want."

This is not the time to talk tough to him. "I know," I say. "Want some coffee?"

Get on with it, his stare says. I do. "The prosecuting attorney called and says that if you'll plead guilty to manslaughter, he'll recommend a sentence of four years, which means with good time you'll be out in sixteen months."

As I have feared, he isn't even listening. "I want a trial," he says, staring past me. "If I'm found not guilty by reason of insanity, I could be out in a few months, and you know it."

At this moment I feel close to despair. Carolyn, I see, has a bond with him that I can't cut. Perry is like a small child without his mother. I wish she were here—she would be easier to fight. I could at least point my finger or wave my arms at the source of his stubbornness. So much is at stake—for both of us. A long prison term is a nightmare for the mentally ill, who are often at the mercy of the regular inmate population. At the state hospital, at least, they are isolated from the everyday cruelty of the sociopaths who inhabit the prison world. A prisoner on a major tranquilizer cannot protect himself from the institutionalized violence in a penitentiary. Perhaps he could make it a year and a few months, but any longer he would slip unnoticed into the routine horror that is the existence of the helpless, long-term inmate.

But it is myself that I am worried about the most right now. I can see everything I have worked for in the last five years slipping away. As I stare at Perry, suddenly I can see Rosa's face, wondering what happened to me. Why couldn't I have coped better? The choices I have made since her death seem all wrong. And now because of the decisions I've made in this case I stand on the verge of losing my job and being humiliated in front of not only my colleagues but my daughter as well. And what will this do to my relationship with Rainey? I think she would understand, but how many women really want a man who has just been fired because he slept with a witness in a case that was the biggest and most important in his career? What disturbs me the most is what this will do to Sarah. She is at such a critical age in her life and needs all the positive reinforcement she can get. Now is not the time for her old man to botch up his life in front of her. Is this what happened to me? Have I been paralyzed since my father's death? I was a little younger than Sarah when he died, but not by much. I feel myself about to panic and I fight to keep myself under control. "Perry, Carolyn is making promises to you she can't guarantee," I say quietly. "She's biased in your favor, and the jury will have their noses rubbed in it."

He slaps the green wooden table with his right palm. "What psychiatrist knows me better than her?" he argues. "You tell me that."

I keep my voice low. "That's precisely why they won't believe you. She knows you too well."

He shrugs, but I can see the beginnings of doubt creep into his face. "People hate gays in this state, Perry. They won't give a damn what Carolyn says. You should know that."

"I can't wait a whole year!" he yells. "You tell the prosecutor we're going to trial, goddamn you!"

One of the cooks pokes his head out of the kitchen and calls, "Want some more coffee? We're pouring out the pot."

My mug is untouched. "We're fine," I call. By the agonized look on his face, I judge Perry is near the breaking point, but if he doesn't change his mind, it won't matter. "Perry," I whisper, "let me tell you a little story. My dad was a schizophrenic. When I was about fourteen, he was committed indefinitely to the state hospital, which they could get away with then. After a year he committed suicide, I think because he felt he never was going to get out. I think you could stand knowing you have sixteen months, but if you're convicted, it could be a lot, lot longer. Ever since I've been a lawyer, either rightly or wrongly, I've tried my damnedest to keep people from getting locked up because I think it kills something in them."

My little speech leaves me strangely nervous. I take a sip of coffee for something to do. I can count on one hand the number of people I have told that story. For the first time since I've been coming out to see him, Perry looks at me as if I am a human being. He rubs his eyes, which are bloodshot. "Carolyn swore I'd never get convicted," he mutters.

I reach across the table and put my hand on his arm. "If I could make that kind of guarantee," I say, my voice raspy with emotion, "I'd do it."

For what seems like a full sixty seconds he looks at me. I meet his gaze. I know he is deciding whether he can trust me. Ideally, trust is based on knowledge, but if Perry knew that I had slept with the woman he loves, he wouldn't be in the same room with me now. Once again, I have a sense of my own hypocrisy. I can't even be honest with a client who is utterly powerless. Yet, under the circumstances, I can't be honest and influence him to do what I know to be in his best interest. I move my hand back and sip at my coffee. If he decides to go to trial, at least I will have given it my best shot.

Finally he nods. "Shit. I let her talk me into it. Okay, I'll take the sixteen months."

I let her talk me into it. These words can have only one meaning. I should have known. What an utter fool I've been. Carolyn is in on this. I feel I'm going to throw up. I lean across the table and mouth my words as softly as he has. "What I don't understand is why she hired you, Perry."

He turns and looks behind him to make sure none of the kitchen help has come out to the dining area. He puts both hands to the sides of his face and says, his voice barely audible, "The son of a bitch gave us both AIDS. I'm positive, and she's dying."

I feel all the air in the room being sucked out. *By the way, I'd get tested if I were you.* Of course, you idiot. She has been dying in front of you. "Carolyn can be pretty persuasive, can't she?"

Perry nods. He looks relieved. He clears his throat and says, "Yeah, but so was her goddamned husband."

I look at Perry and marvel that he could have pulled this off. Yet this nondescript delivery boy, thanks to his psychiatrist, has fooled lots of people—not just me, I realize. Like a good magician, Carolyn has kept the attention on herself. Not many people have that kind of ability. I am too blown away to think about how I feel about all of this. If she follows through on her threat, I will have plenty of time later.

Perry looks strangely forlorn now that he has confessed to me. Gone is the posturing banty-rooster hardness from his face. His eyelids droop, and he ducks his head. "I'm sorry I've had to lie to you."

My God, he wants my forgiveness! I ought to be able to work up some righteous indignation, but I can't. The sense of my own duplicity and conniving is too strong. "You're not the first client to lie to me," I mutter. What in hell do I do now? The son of a bitch deserves a long prison term. I rub my eyes, marveling at the planning he and Carolyn put into this. They must have spent hours together figuring out everything from how Perry would come to the house to kill Hart to how he would act in court. If any lawyer has been a bigger fool, I have yet to meet him. Every meeting with Carolyn Anderson, every tear, every word, was an act. She didn't have to try too hard. I was ready to pull my pants down around my knees five minutes after I met her. Damn her! Damn me!

Perry looks at me as if he thinks he's blown it. "You're going to take their offer," he says nervously.

For a moment I just look at him. If there was ever a premeditated murder, this is it. I would love nothing better than to say to him: Perry, you and Carolyn want a trial and, by God, you're going to get it. Why the hell not? What do I owe this man now? He and

Carolyn have manipulated the system in the most cynical manner imaginable. The criminal justice system depends on at least a modicum of honesty and truth telling, and there hasn't been a moment of it since Perry met Carolyn. I get up and take my mug back into the kitchen. How many others fake mental illness to commit a crime? Few get away with it, because they don't know how. Perry had an expert. A cook's helper, a man Perry's age, takes my cup with a smile. He probably doesn't bring home much more than a hundred dollars a week. Yet, damn it, nothing has changed. Rainey's words come back to me: *You're all he has.* My job is to give Perry the best representation money can't buy, and I can do that by pleading his case out. If Phil changed his mind and demanded to go to trial, I would be off the hook, but I can't see I really have any choice. I come back to the table where Perry is waiting. "Yeah, I'm going to take it."

I call Phil and the office from the open units, since I do not have time now to get downtown and back out to the state hospital for my first hearing. Phil sounds relieved and says he will go see Jamison immediately and find out if we can get him to accept a plea tomorrow. Next, I call Chet Bracken. I tell him that Perry Sarver will be pleading to a reduced charge of manslaughter. He will tell the court that he acted by himself. Bracken slams down the phone in my ear after telling me again that his client should never have been charged. I put the phone down, knowing Phil had him worried.

As I wait for my first client of the day, I sit at my desk with my fourth cup of coffee of the morning and allow myself to realize again how thoroughly fooled I have been. Perry has been magnificently rehearsed, and yet under the rules of the game I am going to be the only person to know that this all has been a performance. My anger at Carolyn builds. I have pulled her chestnuts out of the fire. What made her think she could get away with this? She will, of course. Perry is my client, and I can't turn in Carolyn without implicating him. Do I really want to?

What a nice system we have.

EPILOGUE

An inch of snow has fallen during the night, but the *Gazette* is dry and snug inside its plastic bag. There is nothing like a little competition to get your attention. Too bad it is to the death. I bring the paper in and sit at the kitchen table and thumb through it while I sip my coffee. I look up and see old Mr. Cutter standing on his back steps in a tattered purple bathrobe, putting out some birdseed. It will be a while before he can even begin to think about his garden.

Flipping through the paper my eyes are drawn to a name in the obituary section.

CAROLYN ANDERSON, PSYCHIATRIST

> Dr. Carolyn Anderson, age 36, a psychiatrist in private practice, died last night at her home. Dr. Anderson was the founder of the Blackwell County AIDS Support Center, which she began in 1986. She was also a member of the American Medical Association. Dr. Anderson was the widow of Hartley Anderson, Blackwell County state senator for eight years, who was murdered last year at his home by a former mental patient, Perry Sarver. A spokesman for the Department of Corrections

said last night that Sarver is due to be released this fall. In lieu of flowers contributions may be made to the Blackwell County AIDS Support Center. Services will be at 10 A.M. tomorrow at the First Baptist Church. Dr. Anderson is survived by a sister, Helen Doud, of Gainesville, Florida.

I put down the paper and look again out the window. The Blackwell County AIDS Support Center. So that is where Carolyn and Perry met. Perry has never said another word about his relationship with Carolyn, and she refused to return my calls after Perry pled guilty to manslaughter. I left a message on her answering machine that I had given my notice at the PD's office. She never called Greta, leaving me to wonder if she was bluffing. As with a lot of my cases, I have my share of unanswered questions about the Sarver case. Did Phil Harper make up the story about Chet Bracken having someone's knees broken? I've hinted around for an answer, but no one has ever mentioned he has come close. I've heard rumors that Chet Bracken is going to run a candidate against Phil Harper in the next election, but so far it's only been talk. The question that nags at me the worst is, why was Carolyn Anderson sure she could get Sarver found not guilty by reason of insanity and out of the state hospital so quickly? A lawyer convinced her of that, but who? It had to be somebody who didn't know much about the insanity defense but must have known her well. Knew her arrogance. You'd have to be arrogant to think you could train somebody to fake mental illness and convince him that he could get away with murder. Yet I wasn't the only person fooled.

Woogie walks stiffly into the kitchen and stares at me. "You won't like this snow one bit," I tell him as I get up to let him out. You do what you got to do, his expression says as he sniffs at the cold white powder and then makes his way gingerly into the front yard. The snow sparkles in the morning sun. It is not more than an inch, but a little goes a long way here.

When I come back into the kitchen, my daughter is looking out the window. "It snowed!" she says. "How neat!" We hear Woogie barking from outside, and Sarah lets him in.

I put my arm around her. "You and Mr. Cutter have matching bathrobes," I tell her.

"Poor Mr. Cutter," Sarah says, touching the frigid glass with her palm as if to wave to him. "He misses Mom."

I squeeze her shoulder. She means all three of us.

Sarah looks up at me. "Dad, you look so sad. What are you feeling right now?"

"I'm okay," I mumble and look up at the clock over the sink. It is seven-thirty. "You've got to hurry or you'll be late."

With a mock sigh of horror, she hurries to her room, Woogie at her heels.

I sit back down at the table and stare at the obituary. What am I feeling? Ambivalence, I guess. A murderer who used me will be free in the fall. But it is hard to get worked up about Perry. After all, he wasn't the brains behind the operation. What do I feel about Carolyn? I find it difficult to say. I put too much energy into believing her to feel comfortable with the thought I shouldn't take what she did to heart. It would be as if a man who had been a priest found out his faith was a cosmic joke but was told not to take it personally. Would she have refrained from intercourse had I not produced a rubber? Did she even care? I don't know. Carolyn did convince Perry (assuming he was wavering when he refused to talk to Chet Bracken) to resist the temptation to try to pin the rap on Jerry Kerner in exchange for a lighter sentence, so I suppose there were limits to what she would do. But why? Did she think it would backfire, or was she determined that her only victim would be a man who had given her a death sentence? It is not so much the powerless and the dying that I worry about late at night when I can't sleep and get up to sit in the kitchen with a drink and polish the table. I worry about former seminary students and prosecutors who will go to whatever lengths necessary to ruin the reputation of a bad man; I worry about the psychologists and psychiatrists who will testify to anything for money; I even worry about lawyers who blackmail the system by taking advantage of human weakness.

I shove the paper aside and pick up the postcard I received yesterday from Rainey. The front of it is glossy white sand and blue ocean. Rainey goes to Florida every year with a group of women. The card doesn't say much, but it is comforting to hear from her.

Rainey, for good reason, is now taking our relationship slow and easy. She didn't exactly jump with joy when I told her the truth about Carolyn. Though I have been tested and retested for AIDS, she is in no hurry to become intimate. I know I have scared her off for the time being, but perhaps it is better that we learn how to be friends before we become lovers. There is time. Meanwhile, I busy myself with Sarah and work. Six months ago, I became an associate at the firm of Mays and Burton, who do a pretty good job of chasing ambulances without managing to look like it.

Again, I look out the window at Mr. Cutter, who seems to be staring forlornly at the winter sky hoping for an early spring. I know the feeling. Rainey has ended her card: "The water looks great but it is still a little too cold for me. One of the Florida girls, Rainey."

ABOUT THE AUTHOR

Grif Stockley grew up in Marianna, Arkansas, and graduated from Rhodes College in Memphis. For the past eighteen years, he has been an attorney for Central Arkansas Legal Services, which is funded by the federal government to provide representation to indigents in civil cases. He is also an adjunct professor at the University of Arkansas at Little Rock Law School. He and his wife, Susan, have three children, Erin, Adam, and Carrie.